KING OF
RAVENS

KING OF
RAVENS

CLARE SAGER

TRANSWORLD PUBLISHERS

UK | USA | Canada | Ireland | Australia
India | New Zealand | South Africa

Transworld is part of the Penguin Random House group of companies whose addresses can be found
at global.penguinrandomhouse.com.

Penguin Random House UK, One Embassy Gardens, 8 Viaduct Gardens, London SW11 7BW

penguin.co.uk

Penguin
Random House
UK

First published in Great Britain in 2026 by Wayward TxF
an imprint of Transworld Publishers

001

Typeset in 12.5/16pt Granjon LT Std by Six Red Marbles UK, Thetford, Norfolk
Printed and bound in Great Britain by Clays Ltd, Elcograf S.p.A.

The authorized representative in the EEA is Penguin Random House Ireland,
Morrison Chambers, 32 Nassau Street, Dublin D02 YH68.

A CIP catalogue record for this book is available from the British Library.

ISBNs
9781911751250 hb
9781911751267 tpb

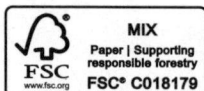

Content Warnings

This book contains themes and scenes that some readers may find distressing, including:

- Death, violence, blood and murder.
- Prejudice and discrimination.
- Trauma related to medical experiences, including fear of death, medication side effects, medication shortage, and harmful behaviour from loved ones.
- Ableism.
- A morally complex, villainous love interest.
- Explicit sexual content.

For the ones who smile even when they're hurting

I

SUNSHINE. SEA AIR. The fresh scent of peppermint as I harvest its leaves from within the safety of our garden walls. Life is good.

Except, that is, for the part where I'm slowly but surely dying.

No pity, please.

It's just a fact of nature, like the tides or the start of spring, which is happening all around me, clear in the nodding hellebore blooms and the buds stuffed full of furled petals on the cusp of bursting open.

Besides, it's not as though I'll die today or tomorrow. This creeping sickness has been my companion for a long time, and deep in my aching bones, I know it's winning. I hold on from a sort of cheerful stubbornness, but it would take a miracle for me to get well.

In fact, tomorrow marks what I call the tipping point. The moment when I go from having been healthy for more years of my life than I've been ill to . . . well, the opposite.

Happy thirty-third birthday, Rhiannon.

I dislodge a weed and throw it over the wall that surrounds my family's cottage. The sun warms my skin, white winter honey-suckle scents the air with lemony sweetness, and these small pleasures are reason enough to smile. With a little luck, we'll have a good crop of peas in the summer, with a surplus for drying, and tonight we'll eat leafy chard alongside the catch my father will bring home.

With a nod, I throw another spindly weed into the wind.

Beyond the wall, the sea roars against the cliffs encircling our home. Every so often a great wave hits, and I swear I feel it vibrating through the ground I'm sitting on. I once read a book that said the sea eroded headlands over time, forming natural archways like the one leading to our cottage on its rock. The sea just might be more determined than I am.

I drag myself to my feet, using the drystone wall for support, careful not to dislodge any of the rocks, even though my head spins. The sea stretches before me, wide, endless, churning blue-grey and capped with white waves. Down in the bay, a small boat approaches the village docks. A quick squint confirms it – yes, my father's.

But my head doesn't stop spinning. Long seconds open up between heartbeats, feeling like eons.

'Oh, shit.' Another episode.

I clutch the trug of mint and set my gaze on the glinting hatchet Pa uses to cut firewood, sitting on a log by the oak door of our little stone cottage. Eyes fixed, I focus the rest of my being on placing one foot in front of the other in front of the other. I need to get inside. Walking should be a simple thing, but I weave and stumble.

Still, as I make it inside, I spread a smile on my face for my mother – my annem – even though my vision narrows to the kettle that's already on the stove.

'You look pale, sweetheart.' Her voice cuts through the fogginess following me. 'Did you take your pills this morning?' The bottle of red tablets rattles – I guess she's shaking it, but I'm too focused on the kettle to turn and look.

The pills leave a bitter taste in my mouth, but the medicine keeps me alive, so each morning, I swallow it down gratefully.

Nodding, I grope for a cup. 'Tea.' It clatters on the side as the world dims, forcing me to catch the counter top.

'Oh, Annon!' Annem rushes in and takes over, ushering me to a chair at the worn old table before pouring me a tea. 'You should've said you weren't feeling well. I could've done that.'

'I'm fine.' I smile up at her as I fish for the deep blue bottle I keep in my pocket and unscrew the lid, revealing a tiny scoop. 'You already do enough.'

When I first started taking it, I'd told her it was just a mixture of herbs to give me energy. Technically, that is true. But the main ingredient in the powder I carefully measure out and stir into my tea is belladonna leaves. Grown in the garden and dried in the rafters of my attic bedroom, then crushed and sifted.

The tea scalds my mouth, but I gulp it down, and soon the belladonna numbs my tongue.

Poisonous – deadly, if you take too much – but just the right dose . . .

Ba-dum. Ba-dum. Ba-dum.

My heart surges; no more long gaps between each beat. A fresh wave of dizziness washes over me, but this is more akin to giddy excitement than my body slowly shutting down. It warms me, spreading, thrilling, and I feel like laughing for no reason at all.

The world opens back up, with bright sunlight spilling through the kitchen windows and the door I've left open. Gulls wheel outside, their cries jarring but lively.

Annem bumps the back door shut with the basket of washing on her hip, giving me a worried look as she rubs her head. 'Are you sure——?'

'You've got a headache?' After another beat of my body and

brain catching up, I'm on my feet, dizziness fading as I grab the jar of willow bark from the shelf. I harvested it earlier in the month from the stalks we keep coppiced in one corner of the garden. Along with our apple tree, they're the only things that grow straight around here – all the shrubs and trees clinging to this rock and the rest of the coast are stunted and bent, whipped into sub-mission by the sea wind and salty air.

'Don't you worry about me.' She shakes her head with a faint laugh, though this light shows new lines in her deep olive-brown skin and she wrings her hands before easing me back into my seat. 'That's my job, especially when you work too hard in that garden.'

She fusses around me until it's clear I'm not about to collapse and comments that I'm looking a healthier colour – thank you, belladonna – before finally taking the basket of washing outside.

Only once I'm alone do I let myself slump over the table. When I read about belladonna years ago, I'd noted that it could increase the heart rate and thought it could be a solution for my fainting spells. I'd written down all the information I could find about it and started an experiment to find an effective dose – cautiously, of course, since its other name, deadly nightshade, is no exaggeration.

I was careful, so I hadn't been too concerned. But that was when I'd only taken it once every couple of weeks.

Now I need it every other day. And despite my search, none of the books have told me anything about the long-term effects or whether it can accumulate in the system, a slow creeping death.

Just as I tuck away the blue bottle, the door flies open and in sweeps my brother. Tall and dark-haired, he takes after Annem, while my hair is blond like Pa's. He pants, beaming at me as though he's run all the way across the stone arch, between the spiky gorse bushes that line the path and through the garden gate.

'I've got something for you,' he huffs like he can't wait to get the words out.

I sit up. He promised to bring me another book borrowed from his employer's library, so I can add to my notes.

If anyone asks, my notebook is a collection of information on medicinal herbs, but there's another section at the back, compiled from Lowen smuggling me books on anatomy and disease.

Annem and Pa told me there was no cure for my illness, but in all my years of research I still haven't found a name for it. I've written to professors at universities and visited a doctor in the village. Herbalists have examined my tongue and prodded my cheeks. Once I even threw logic to the wind and went to a travelling fortune teller passing through the area. He'd turned over a strange card that showed a woman bound, blindfolded and hemmed in by swords. From that one image, he'd spoken for a long while but explained nothing of my illness. As I tried to leave, wearing a polite smile despite my frustration, he'd grabbed my hand, pointed at a line across my palm and declared I would never find love in this world. Superstition and nonsense – nothing of use.

No one has been able to give me a proper diagnosis. And in that unknown, I guard a tiny flicker of hope.

So I trawl through the medical books Lowen borrows for me, searching for a diagnosis . . . and a cure.

Everything I discover goes in that notebook, carefully copied out in sharp pencil. It hasn't saved me yet, and time is running out, but as long as I breathe, there's a chance.

When Lowen's caught his breath, he goes on, 'I know it isn't your birthday quite yet, but no harm, right?' His cheeks are flushed, his eyes bright.

Not the book, then. But either the belladonna is still buzzing through my system or his feverish excitement is infectious. Probably both. I can't help laughing as he checks the door is shut and hurries to the table, carrying something under his jacket.

Gifts could definitely soften the blow of this tipping-point birthday. 'Do I get to guess what it is that has you so excited?' I crane to look at him as he circles behind me.

"Fraid not. I haven't had a chance to wrap it, so . . .' With one hand, he covers my eyes, and something clunks on to the table, a finality to the sound. 'Ready?'

The bright world cuts back in, revealing a round mirror. Birds and moths cover its gilded frame, their wings layering over each other and punctuated by pointed spears. The birds have fierce, thick beaks, ruffed throats, and wing feathers like the slash of a blade. Ravens.

It's one of the most beautiful things I've ever seen. Certainly more beautiful than anything I've ever owned . . . or that he can afford.

'Lowen. No.' I shake my head, burning eyes stuck on the mirror even though I want to look up at him. 'This is too much. You can't afford something like—'

'Well . . .' There's a rueful tone to his voice as he takes the seat next to mine, still half bent over the table like he's also fascinated by the mirror. 'I didn't actually buy it.' He raises his hands as soon as I suck in a breath. 'And no, I didn't "acquire" it, either! I found it. I had this urge to go for a walk on the beach. It's such a nice day – feels like it hasn't been sunny for months.'

A spike of envy pierces me. I used to love walking along the shore. I'd pull off my shoes and socks and enjoy the crumbly feel of the dry sand beneath my feet, observing how it became more claggy and solid as I approached the lapping waves, until at last it squelched between my toes and the sea came washing in. It's years since I've had the strength to tackle the steep path down to the beach and the village.

But my envy isn't fair on Lowen. My illness isn't his fault. And here he is giving me a gift for my birthday.

That's when it hits me – a pang in my chest that's nothing to do with my heart rate.

Our brothers had all married by the time they were his age. Yet here he is, twenty-five years old, helping Annem and Pa care for me, where once, as the eldest child, I'd been the one to look after him and the others.

Oh, I've been a fool to not see it before. The link. The horrible, inextricable link.

I've been blaming other things for years. Our mother's clinginess. That he hasn't found someone yet – he's special, sensitive, artistic, and this town is too small to provide him with the right person.

But really . . . he stays for me.

The thought steals my breath.

My brother has put his life on hold, refused to live it because of me.

I should be waxing lyrical about this gift. Yet I can't get a word out through this terrible tightness.

Instead, I fold down my guilt like a neat handkerchief I can hide away and spread my cheerful smile wider.

He seems lost in the mirror, though, and as I tilt my head, I notice how its reflection seems . . . off.

The mirror is whole and smooth, but it fractures the room around us. It doesn't show me the ceiling, like it should from this angle, instead I see shards of the kitchen, and in one section, I'm sure I catch a glimpse of an ornate bed made of dark reddish wood and covered in heavy velvet drapes. But when I blink, it's gone, replaced by the stove.

'And . . . you found this on the beach?'

'What? Hmm? Oh, yes! I had to dig through some seaweed and shells to get to it. It must've washed up this morning. I can't believe it isn't broken – what luck is that? As soon as I saw it, I just felt that you needed to have it, so I raced back here.'

Part of me understands that I should be concerned by this. Shouldn't he be at work? But the mirror is here and its wholeness is a little miracle. There isn't so much as a dent in its frame.

There has to be something special about it. And if that's possible, then maybe anything is. Maybe even the thing I've been working on all these years.

I expect to feel something when I pick the mirror up. A zap, a tingle, a sign that it's magical or supposed to be mine – that the gods have sent it to give me hope.

But there's nothing.

I bite back my disappointment, fully aware of how silly it is, and instead I tilt the mirror, searching for my reflection.

I find it. And instantly regret it.

A few years ago, all the mirrors in the house slowly . . . disappeared. It was so gradual, I didn't notice until I fainted and knocked my head. When I went to check if I had a cut or bruise, I couldn't find a single mirror. Annem found me searching, and hustled me into a chair by the window so she could examine me. She'd put witch hazel on the bruise, and that had been that.

Once, I'd been proud of my thick, shiny hair – a little vain about it, to be honest. My skin had been a slightly lighter version of mother's olive brown, which contrasted with my golden-blond hair and brown eyes. Some said I was beautiful, others that I was exotic, which always made me roll my eyes.

But the woman whose fractured reflection looks back at me is none of those things.

Flat, dull hair has been tied into a neat braid, fastened with a bow, but the braid is much thinner than it once was. Purplish hollows beneath her eyes contrast with the pale, sallow skin clinging to her gaunt cheeks. The only colour is the lurid pink flush from the belladonna, but even that looks unnatural, like I'm a child who's found her mother's rouge.

I almost don't believe it's me, but when I swallow, her throat bobs.

No wonder Annem hid all the mirrors.

I've felt the changes. The eroding of my body. The coarseness of my hair. The sharpness of my cheekbones. But seeing it spelled out in a looking glass is a different matter entirely.

But if this one survived the sea, perhaps there is some magic to it. Fae are no mere legends – they are real and negotiated with our queen not so long ago. I've heard of magic mirrors and some say they're not just stories, but ways to speak to ancient fae in distant realms. What kind of wisdom might such a creature have? What knowledge of the world – of medicine? What cures might they possess?

Then I could walk down to the beach and the village. I could meet the friends Lowen tells me about. I could be the woman I once was.

I could have a life.

It's tissue-paper-thin hope. But that's better than none at all.

The woman in the mirror smiles.

I touch the hopeful line of her lips, then hug the mirror to my chest, ignoring the way the spears prick through my dress. 'Thank you, Lowen. This is . . . it's truly special.'

He blinks up, brow creasing as he looks at me, then at the mirror in my arms. 'Oh. Right. Yes. Your gift.' He shakes his head as though shaking off a rogue thought and kisses my temple. 'Nothing's too special for my big sister.'

'You need to put that sweet-talking to use.' I ruffle his hair, this close to reminding him that he should be married and in a home of his own by now – living his life rather than stuck here with me.

'Though . . .' Leaving the mirror on the table, I rise and start towards the cabinet of medicinal herbs I keep separate from the cooking ones. 'I wouldn't mind if you did me a favour and took these to Mrs Davy down in the village. Annem mentioned her new baby was colicky and that she was still sore after the birth.' I pluck out two small jars and press them into Lowen's hands. 'Lemon balm, vervain, and chamomile tincture for the baby – one drop under the tongue before he feeds. Chamomile and daisy tea for mother. Oh, and putting a rolled blanket under the baby's feet when he's sleeping will help. At least that's what I read somewhere.'

His eyes twinkle with amusement as he looks up from the jars. 'Of course you did. But you're in luck. I'm actually going back down to the pub tonight.' The corner of his mouth quirks as he looks away. 'I can drop these off on my way.'

That secret smile. Maybe there is hope for him. 'You know . . .' I nudge my hip into his. 'If you wanted to take some flowers with you, I'm more than happy to make a bouquet from the garden.'

His head snaps around. 'Flowers? Why would I want to take flowers to Mrs Davy? Her husband would clobber me.'

'Not for *her*. For whoever it is that makes you smile like that.'

He pales, sucking in a quick breath as his gaze skims away again.

So he does have a sweetheart but is shy about it still. 'I won't pry. But whenever you're ready to talk about this mystery person, I'll be right here. It's not like I go anywhere else.' I grin as I lift my shoulders.

Pulling a face as though it pains him, he half laughs. 'This isn't for ever, Annon.'

I pat his jaw, which has turned stiff with this suddenly grave expression that doesn't suit him at all. 'I know.'

He means I'll get better. I mean I won't be here for ever thanks to the whole business of dying. But my gaze slides over to the mirror sitting on the table.

The mirror that shouldn't exist. That shouldn't be whole. But that maybe, just maybe heralds something more.

2

I DON'T KNOW where I am. In these dreams the location is always different and never somewhere I know from real life.

There's a lake, flat and black. The air is too misty for any reflection. I can barely see the trees stretching upward, black and leafless in the depths of winter. The caw of crows cuts through the thick silence, the sound passing overhead, but they're shrouded in mist.

One thing that remains the same each time is here, though.

A dark figure lurks at the lake's edge.

Every hair on my body strains to attention. I know who he is, though he's never spoken, never mind told me his name.

It's the kind of thing you just know in your bones, and his name is an aching voice in mine.

Death.

I've dreamt about him for years. He started off far, far away, but over time he's come closer.

Normally he's little more than a shadow, but now he seems solid and is perhaps twenty feet from where I stand.

The closest he's ever been.

Cold closes around me. I want to turn and run.

But there's something else in me, too. A warring want that draws me to him.

I never move in these dreams, but maybe one day I will run towards him.

Maybe now.

Just as I gather myself, there's a whispered voice in my ear.

'The hour is near.'

Gasping, I wake to firelight and a warm touch on my brow.

'Oh dear,' Pa chuckles, pulling back from kissing my forehead. 'Didn't mean to wake you.' He crouches and tucks the blanket around my lap.

I rub my face, trying to clear the cold fog from my dream and the scattered lines of an old nursery rhyme from my head.

Death upon the water . . .

The fire helps, as does Pa's familiar scent. He smells of the sea, salty and fresh, mixed with the soap he always uses before coming home so he doesn't bring the stink of fish guts into the house. 'You're back. How long have I been asleep?'

'Not sure how long, but aye, I'm home, safe and sound,' he says with a reassuring smile.

That isn't a given in his line of work. Annem had begun to tell me that once, before I was born, his boat had almost gone down in a storm, but Pa had arrived home, cutting her story short. 'Speaking of it tempts *her* back,' he'd said in the sternest voice I've ever heard him use, and I heard nothing more about the storm that had nearly taken him away.

He never admitted it, but I know he was afraid of *her* – not Annem, another storm. He even went to the trouble of moving us to the other side of the country, which I suspected was to escape the memories.

I shove down the worries and give him a bright smile. 'Good catch?'

'Fish caught, gutted and sold. I'll help your ma with a few jobs, then you can tell me about your day.'

'I can't wait to tell you about the dragon I battled,' I call as he turns away.

He pauses there, back to me, the stillness strange in a man who is always busy, always working on the boat or around our home. Then he heads to Annem in their bedroom at the back of the house.

As the grogginess of sleep fades, my fingers close around a clothbound cover. Lowen had indeed brought me the book he'd promised, and I'd fallen asleep going over it and adding to my notes.

I smooth my hand over the cover of *Causes of Diseases Investigated by Anatomy* and peer next to the armchair. I must've knocked my notebook to the floor as I slept. But there's no sign of it. I feel down the side of the cushions – perhaps Pa tucked it down there with the blanket. Nothing.

Stiff, I heave to my feet, pull the cushions off the chair, and search all around it. In case it's been tidied away, I check Pa's basket of nets that need repairing – the work we'll do by the fire this evening. Frowning, I spread my search further, circling the living space, glancing through the kitchen door, in case Annem picked it up and left it on the table. Through the window, Lowen stands at the garden wall working on something.

I call towards the back room, asking if Annem has seen it.

As I wait for a reply, my stomach knots at the thought of her flicking through the pages. I keep quiet about how much I long for the days before I was ill – I don't want my parents to feel bad for my sake. She worries about me, and he . . . sometimes I get the impression he feels *guilty* like it's all his fault. I don't want them to know about the pain I'm in most days or quite how often I have the dizzy spells. I don't want them to think I suffer. And I really don't want them to know it's so bad that even after all these years, I still search for a cure.

Only Lowen understands.

No reply from Annem, but as I continue my search, footsteps approach from their room.

'I can't find it anywhere,' I call, returning to the armchair. I must've missed it. Maybe it fell underneath and—

I stop in my tracks. I blink, swaying.

There's something in the fireplace. Not a log. A flat oblong shape. Blackened. Flames leaping around it.

I lean on the mantelpiece, eyes burning as I stare and hope, hope, hope that I'm wrong. With the poker, I try to hook the object out of the fire, but the blackened shape flakes into ash. I drop to my knees, joints crying out.

One fragment comes out whole, landing on the sandstone hearth with its edges still glowing orange.

The spine of a book bound in green leather. An inch wide. No title or author name, just a single hellebore flower embossed and painted black.

My notebook.

A small sound escapes me. Not quite 'No.'

All that work. All these years. All those books borrowed from locals, from market towns inland when I was well enough to travel, from folk passing through the village. Observations from my own experiments with belladonna and foxgloves, willow and witch hazel. Speculation about how my illness is like one aspect of this disease but shares symptoms with this other, unrelated one.

All of it.

Ashes.

I stare. I blink. I wish it into something else – anything else. I need this not to be real.

Brown leather boots edge into view. 'Oh, sweetheart,' Pa sighs.

He isn't surprised. He did it or he knew about it and did nothing.

I choke on the shock. The betrayal. The crushing pain at the thought he could do this to *me*. His own daughter.

'You know there's no cure.' There's this gruff edge to his voice that scrapes my skin, my insides, leaving me raw. 'You're only torturing yourself.'

My heart tightens like a fist. Isn't it my business if I want to torture myself?

I'd take torture by hope over torture by despair any day. My hand shakes, fingers straining around the poker's handle.

For a moment, it's as though *I'm* the fire. And the heat of it terrifies me.

I want to explode. That dreadful potential quivers inside me, battling the stillness I try to cling on to.

I'm dimly aware of Annem's soft footsteps approaching. 'Your father's right.'

They did this. Together. Planned it, perhaps.

They looked through the pages I'd written. Understood my hopes. Saw what I'd been working for all this time.

I can't speak. There are too many things that are too big trying to get out through my throat.

All I can do is stare.

The fragmented pages twitch, settling and merging with the logs and kindling as the fire consumes them. It leaps as the back door opens, but my chest remains a clenched, hard thing, unable to unlock itself.

'What's going—?' Lowen gasps as his steps get closer. 'What happened?' I think he sees my frozen face, the tears gathering in my eyes and there's a shuffle as he turns to our father. 'Pa? Did you do this?' A harsh note of accusation cuts through his usually warm tone.

It cuts through *me*.

'Watch how you talk to your pa, lad,' our father says.

I kept the book's contents secret to protect my family from my pain. I don't want them arguing over it or me.

They're my whole world, and I know my illness binds them all to this house – someone always has to be here to keep an eye on me. But I can't be a raincloud making them miserable, too.

As the fire consumes the last of my notebook, I stamp down the fire licking through me.

I will not be a source of strife. *Stamp.*

I can't be angry at them. *Stamp.*

I can't bear to see them angry at each other. Not when I owe them everything. *Stamp, stamp.*

Soon all that's left is the burning in my eyes as I drag in a breath.

'Or was it you?' Lowen goes on, turning to our mother. 'Why would you—?'

'It's fine.' I tear myself away from the fire and force a smile in place.

His eyes go round as he stares at me for a beat. 'But don't you want to know who—?'

'No. I don't.'

Desperately, I do.

But I shrug, and it's the hardest thing I've ever done. 'It's *fine*. Like Pa said, there is no cure. It was silly of me to waste paper writing all those notes.'

Pa's brow lowers and his mouth flattens, like all the doors in him have shut. When I turn to Annem, she looks away, wringing her hands.

But it's the stricken look on Lowen's face that makes my eyes burn harder. He gapes as though I've slapped him.

I push myself to my feet, leaning on the poker like a walking stick. 'I think I'm going to go to bed now.' The poker clangs as I return it to the stand, and I can't help thinking of it like a bell tolling for the end of all my work.

So much destroyed in so little time. I try not to curl in on myself.

I want to fling myself into the chair and scream that it isn't fair. The notebook. My illness. Everything.

But it won't achieve anything besides letting misery win.

Instead, I take a breath, smile and remind myself how lucky I am.

I have a family who love and protect me. With them, I'll always be cared for. And with them, I have no reason to fear the figure of Death, because he will not find me alone.

3

GRIPPING THE BANISTER, I take the first step, hips and knees groaning. I worked too hard in the garden this morning.

Before I can take the next one, Lowen rushes in to help, slipping an arm around my waist and half carrying me up the stairs. Up here are my bedroom and the room he used to share with the rest of our brothers but now has to himself. Halfway up, he murmurs, 'Are you all right?'

I try to answer, but between focusing on the staircase and wrestling my emotions, I can't form words.

Below, there's the sound of Annem and Pa having a low conversation, then the back door opening and closing.

Lowen helps me to bed and pulls up the blankets, frowning. 'Why didn't you want to know which one of them did it?'

I shake my head, swallow down the residue of my hurt and anger that are still trying to burst from me like smoke caught in a blocked chimney. 'Because it doesn't matter. Whichever one it was, they were protecting me from false hope. I can't be angry with them for it.'

Can't.

Shouldn't.

I shrug and try a half smile that I hope reassures him. 'And even if I was, it's not like I'm going to . . . I don't know . . . punish them? It's like Annem says – blood is thicker than water. Or, in this case, *ink*.'

That pained look covers his face again, though his shoulders ease a little lower. 'Is it, though?'

'Well, it's keeping you here . . .' The guilt twists inside me, rawness upon rawness. I want to tell him to leave – to live. But those words are impossible. Not yet, at least. 'When you should be heading to the pub, I mean.' There, that's easier. And, even better, I seize on a change of subject: 'Oh, do you have those herbs I gave you?'

He grumbles, patting his pocket as he stands. 'I do. Just . . . maybe look after yourself as well as everyone else, eh?'

'Look, see? Medicine.' I shake the little brown bottle I keep on the bedside table and drop the straw-coloured tincture under my tongue. Willow bark, valerian and evening primrose. Bitter. Foul-tasting, to be honest. But I give him a grimacing smile as I return the bottle to its home and lie back. 'I *am* looking after myself.'

I wave off his worries and ask him to put the window on the latch, so it's not quite shut. The fresh air feels good, quenching the hot rush that swept through me earlier.

'Love you, Lowen,' I call as he reaches the door.

He pauses, turns, gaze on the floor. 'I know why you always say that when you say goodbye.'

'Oh?' I say it lightly, but it is heavy.

'In case it's your last chance. You want that to be the final thing you say to me.'

I swallow as the weight grows.

'But I've told you before . . .' His dark eyes snap up to meet mine, and the corner of his mouth twitches. 'If Death comes for you, he'd better run, because I'm coming after you.'

I laugh and wave him off. 'Poor Death doesn't stand a chance. Now get to the pub or your friends will be worried about you.'

He grins and shuts the door after him, calling through it, 'Love you too, Annon.'

That's when the tincture catches up with me, making my weary body sink into the mattress as I take deep breaths of the green, floral scent of herbs drying in the rafters. The dimming light cradles me as I drift deeper and deeper inside, somewhere between sleep and the waking world.

'. . . there are better ways than that.' Annem's voice floats along the same currents I drift through.

My body feels far away, but maybe I frown.

'Do you want her to find out? It will ruin everything.' That stern voice from my Pa again. Strange to hear him like that when he's usually so softly spoken.

'It's her *gift*. I'm not so sure—'

'You agreed to this,' he cuts her off.

My birthday gift. What have they bought me? Has Annem changed her mind, worried it cost too much? I can sell more of my tinctures and teas. It will be all right, I want to tell her.

'It's too late to change things,' he goes on, sounding more and more distant with each word. 'It's too late, no matter what we might . . .'

The thread of the conversation unravels as I spill over into a deep, dark sleep.

I'm in my room. I never normally dream of places I know in real life, but here we are.

Through the window, I see the garden, but it's etched in scratchy lines of grey and black, like the images in my borrowed books, but the lines flicker and twitch, unreal. At the wall stands a familiar figure.

I can't move. My heart clamours in my chest. There is no space for breath. Cold closes in.

The moonlight hits his back, making him a darker silhouette in the dark landscape. A slate-coloured sea twitches behind him, the waves moving in unnatural rhythms.

Slowly, slowly, like ice carving a mountain, he lifts his head. In the shadows of his face, his eyes glow with preternatural light.

Just as that unnerving gaze meets mine, there's a shriek, and a pale shape crashes into the window. A dark voice speaks right in my ear.

'Wake up.'

I jolt awake, clutching my chest where my heart pounds like I've just taken belladonna. A scraping sound at the window has me turning, expecting to find an owl scratching at the glass.

But there's nothing, just my window swinging, blown off the latch.

I catch my breath, blinking in the dim light that creeps in from outside.

An owl's screeches must've woken me.

But when my breaths die down, I can hear something in the garden. Movement. Scrabbling.

I pad out of bed, joints looser thanks to the tincture I've taken, and go to the window. Dawn threatens in the east, giving me a little light to see by.

A dark shape bends over the wall.

Death. The sight grips me, so I can only stare at the form inside the garden facing out to sea. The figure straightens and I recognize the set of his shoulders. Lowen.

'Bloody hells,' I sigh, shaking my head. What the fuck is he doing? I peer through the open window, a chill wind nipping at my cheeks. He bends over the wall again. Must be throwing up.

'How much have you drunk?' I mutter as I shut the window. He's going to wake Annem and Pa at this rate. I grab my dressing gown and slide on my slippers, then as I turn to the door, movement snags on the edge of my vision. A fluttering darkness.

For half a second, I think an owl has actually flown into my room. But, propped up on the side, the mirror looks back at me, empty. Its scattered reflections take a moment to still. As I turned, I must've seen my own reflection, rendered strange by its odd surface.

Shaking my head, I hurry downstairs as quickly as I can. I consider grabbing something to help settle Lowen's stomach, but I need to get him inside first, then I can assess just how bad he is and the best course of treatment.

The chill wind nearly tears the back door from my grasp as I make my way outside. It bites through my nightclothes and slippers, making me grit my teeth.

'Lowen Archer, you nearly gave me a bloody heart attack.'

It sounds like he's stopped vomiting, at least. He bends over the wall, arms and shoulders moving like he's doing . . . *something*.

As I draw closer, I catch him muttering but the words are lost on the wind.

'Come on, let's get you inside.'

He turns, and I hold out my arms ready to help, but instead of coming towards me, he tosses something on the ground. *Thud.*

In the darkness, I have to squint at the thing that lands alongside still more dark shapes.

Ignoring me, Lowen turns his back and bends over the wall again. This time he tosses two objects to the side, which clack into the pile he's created.

Stones. From the wall.

'Lowen? What're you doing?' I come up beside him.

'Pull it apart,' he mutters without looking at me, fingers scrabbling into the wall. 'Let me in.'

As he turns and tosses the stone to one side, I catch sight of the gouge he's torn through the wall. Swearing softly, I realize he must've been here a while – he's pulled a section down to knee height.

'Lowen. Hey.' I touch his shoulder, but it makes no difference. 'You're sleepwalking. Come on. Let's go inside, eh?' At least I hope that's all this is. What if he has a fever or some other delirium? My illness isn't contagious, but if he has the same thing and it's just taken longer to show in him . . .

No. Logic. This behaviour isn't one of my symptoms. He's gone out drinking, then he's come home, gone to sleep, and drink has taken him from bed to do whatever this is. We can fix the wall in the morning.

'Come on, little brother. Time to rest. Let's—'

He whips around, eyes blank as he pushes his face into mine. 'Wake up.'

I stumble back, cold gnawing on my bones at hearing the words from my dream.

He bends down and grabs at something in the wall. The scant light catches on metal. Long and thin – a wire that disappears beneath the stones. He strains, pulling on it, letting it bite into his fingers without even a whimper.

'No, don't do—'

'Pull it apart.' His shoulders strain as he puts his body weight into it. Blood glistens, welling up around the cruel wire.

'Lowen.' I tug on his arm, but he's immovable. There are tendons in his fingers – if he severs them . . . 'Please! Stop!'

He doesn't.

I search for something that can stop him hurting himself more. Pa's hatchet glints on top of its log. I grab it, the weight unfamiliar, and wedge myself in next to my brother.

If I miss the wire and hit him . . .

I grit my teeth. Please, gods. Make my aim true. I raise the hatchet.

Damn it. His fingers are in the way.

'Come on, Lowen. Move over.' I nudge him, nodding like this is the greatest idea he's ever had and I'm ever so keen to join in.

He doesn't even look up.

'I'm helping.' Desperation roughens my voice. 'Move over so I can help you cut the wire.'

He stills. His fingers unfurl, dark blood dripping on to grey stone.

I heave. The hatchet's blade sparks on the stone. Two ends of wire ping back.

A peal of thunder shakes the air, the ground, my bones.

Lightning shatters the sky.

Thunder *then* lightning? No. That's not possible.

I'm the daughter of a fisherman. I've grown up by the sea all my life. I know weather. Lightning *then* thunder. Always.

'Annon?' Hunched over the wall, Lowen blinks up at me, cradling his hands to his chest.

'You're awake.' Huffing out my relief, I pat his cheek. 'Let's get inside and take a look at you, eh?' I smile in reassurance and nod, but the aftermath of that impossible thunder still rumbles along my nerves.

As he straightens, he frowns into the distance. 'What's that?'

On the horizon, I can barely make out a dark shape. It could be a cloud – it follows the cold wind battering the shore, except . . .

It moves faster than every other cloud in the sky.

And it's coming straight towards us.

4

'WHAT HAPPENED?' PA comes rushing from the house, pale in the gloom, Annem not far behind. A harsh sound escapes him as he sees Lowen's hands, but when he sees the wall, his whole body lurches.

'No,' he says softly, like his voice is broken. '*No*. What have you done?' A great breath racks his body, and another. 'Get them inside,' he growls.

Annem fusses over Lowen and I stand there, watching Pa pick through the remains of the wall.

'He was trying to—'

'Get inside!' he roars, almost as loud as the thunder.

I go still. I tried to stop Lowen destroying his hands. Yet somehow that has upset my father . . . disappointed him . . . angered him.

The beat of my heart suddenly feels hollow.

I hover there, wanting to crouch and help, afraid I'll only make things worse.

Caws pierce the night air – not the usual shriek of gulls.

The dark shape is no longer a smear but a flock of birds – crows or ravens – their flight as swift and true as any arrow aimed at our home.

Annem's hand closes around my wrist as Pa leaps up, swearing. They bundle me into the house, but I can't help glancing back.

The ravens – they're too big to be mere crows – gather into a seething mass, almost at the tufty grass that stands between the garden wall and the cliff edge.

Dozens of black eyes glint between the ferocious flap of wings and snap of thick beaks, then the door slams shut.

While Annem and Pa clatter through cupboards and drawers searching for I don't know what, I tear a clean cloth in two and wrap it around Lowen's hands. I find myself peering out the window as I tie the knot.

As one, the ravens swirl and lengthen into a tall form, and from those feathers and shadows steps a man.

My fingers fall still.

A pale face, set hard. Gold eyes fix upon the door to our home. A man – no, not a man, too beautiful, too untouchable, with ears too pointed.

A fae.

He strides forward, long black hair unruffled as the last of the ravens' wings seem to fold in on themselves, disappearing into the darkness of his tailored coat.

A sound comes from me. Shock. Fear. Denial. It isn't a word, but it conveys all those things together with the breaking of my understanding of the world and how it works.

My mind stumbles in its attempt to form questions. It certainly finds no answers.

With a calm economy of movement, the fae steps through the gap Lowen made in the wall and approaches the house.

'There's a man,' Lowen blurts. 'He's coming. Fae – he's fae!'

Pa strides past us, brow set in a low line. With shaking hands, he slips something over the door handle and stands back, eyes wide as he waits.

From a ribbon hangs the shape of an eye made of dark, silvery metal, and he holds several more.

My own eyes widen. 'Is that iron?' Can't be – that stuff's illegal. Only smithies are allowed it and that's kept under lock and key, then prayed over as it's worked into steel.

There's a bang at the door. Once. Twice. Three times. It shakes with the force but remains shut.

'Fisherman,' the fae calls, voice cold and clipped. 'I have come for the bargain that was made.'

Satisfied the door will hold, Pa turns to me and ducks his chin. 'Aye. It's iron. It'll keep the bastard out.'

'Will it?' the fae calls with a mocking lilt. 'Do you dare defy The Morrigan?'

Lowen and I stiffen as one, and I give Pa a questioning look.

Jaw set, he ignores us and joins Annem, circling the ground floor, hanging the charms at each window.

The Morrigan. The goddess who rules fate, war, death. Tales say she takes insult if anyone writes her name without a capital *T*, and even in my thoughts I give weight to the word *The* when it comes to her.

I'm not about to add an insulted deity to my troubles.

'Pa?' I follow him into the living room. More charms, including one at the front door. Annem has lit the lamps, casting a cheerful golden light around the room that's at odds with the chill clinging to my skin. 'A bargain? What's he talking about?'

He shares a glance with Annem and comes to me, taking my hands between his calloused ones. 'We only wanted to protect you. You need to remember that.' His mouth curves slowly, like it hurts to even try to smile.

The way he looks at me, the talk of protection – it makes dread unfurl in my chest, a cold counterpart to the spring flowers outside.

'How touching.' The fae stands at the window. 'But you cannot protect her from your own promise. Tell her the truth, human.'

Eyebrows drawn together, Pa bows his head. I glance at Lowen in silent question. He shakes his head, face ashen.

This has to be some fae trick. They can't lie, but they can manipulate humans, cast glamours, wear shapes that aren't their own, hunt us through the forest and commit a hundred other cruelties. They aren't beyond casting doubts among a family, trying to crack us apart.

I square my shoulders and glower out the window at him.

'Sweetheart.' Pa squeezes my hands, hunching over.

A gnawing silence stretches on until Annem speaks. 'You remember I told you about the storm? Not long after we married, it tried to take your father and his boat. He was out of sight of land and would have surely drowned if she'd gone down. He didn't want to leave me alone in the world, so he begged the sea for help and then the land. And when they didn't answer, he called for the Lady of Fate herself.'

'A hand reached out from the dark and thunder,' he says softly, face hidden in the shadows, clinging to my hands like I'm the one who saved him. 'She pulled me from the waves and stilled my boat, but she said she would cast me back to my doom if I refused to pay the price.'

'What price did she name?' Lowen growls the question, a bristling tightness at my side.

'My firstborn daughter.'

Lowen hisses out a breath.

I can't react.

'I refused to leave your ma alone, so I agreed and the Lady steered my boat back to shore, though it should've sunk to the bottom of the ocean. She told me her son would return one day to claim on our bargain, then she was gone. When I got home, your ma told me she was pregnant and in the spring we had you.' At last he looks up, eyes gleaming. 'We hoped for a boy. I only have brothers, and your ma's the only girl in her family. We thought we'd escape the bargain. That it wouldn't matter. But . . .'

I stare at him. I turn over his words, trying to make sense of the impossible. But the shapes of my life slot together, leaving space for this thing he's just told me, making it suddenly seem not just possible but . . . the only piece that could fit.

He moved across the country, not to escape the memories of almost drowning, but because he hoped The Morrigan wouldn't be able to find him and his firstborn daughter.

He chose this remote cottage even though village life would be easier for us all, because he thought it would keep us – *me* – safe.

The wire in the wall – iron. It stopped the fae entering, and when I cut through it with the hatchet, I made it so the one outside could cross.

Her son. That means . . .

I've read that The Morrigan's sons are the Kings of Death. Unseelie fae who rule the Underworld as demi-gods, each with their own cruel domain. And one of them stands at our door.

'I had to promise you to her before I even knew you existed. My little girl.' He shakes his head, brow creasing. 'My Annon.'

I've always thought laughter a happy sound, warm and lively. But the laugh coming from outside is cruel and mocking without the slightest trace of anything so warm as *happiness*.

'Annon. *Annon.*' Another harsh laugh. 'You called her "Anonymous" because you thought it would stop us finding her.'

'No,' I find myself blurting. 'It's Rhiannon . . .' I search Annem and Pa's gazes. 'I'm Rhiannon, not . . .'

But their gazes slide to the floor.

No name.

The realization is a sudden pain deep in my gut. My chest squeezes, heart on the edge of betraying me.

I have no name. Does that mean I'm even . . . real? A person? Or just a thing?

Part of me understands the logic. They did it deliberately, like the old superstition that says parents shouldn't name babies until they're six months old – too big to be carried away by the fair folk and replaced with a changeling.

But I'm not a baby. I'm thirty-three years old and fucking nameless. 'Rhiannon' is a lie.

'Oh, that is precious,' the fae goes on. 'The foolishness of humans will never cease to astonish me.'

I whirl, something hot and ugly searing my skin. 'Shut up.'

'Why?' Lowen bites out to Pa. 'She made you bargain Annon away – what does a goddess want with her?'

'Oh yes.' Outside, the fae smirks, golden eyes locked on my father. 'Do tell her the full nature of your bargain, fisherman. Tell her what you agreed.'

'I agreed . . .' Pa takes a shuddering breath. 'To give you to her son, as his bride.'

5

'BRIDE?' I DON'T mean to say it out loud, but good fucking gods. I'm supposed to marry that man? Not just given to the fae as a servant or pet but *in marriage*? 'Absolutely not.'

'It's all right.' Annem squeezes my shoulder. 'He can't come in. The charms will protect us.'

The fae straightens, the mocking amusement on his face fading as he reaches his full and considerable height. 'Does this mean you're reneging on your bargain?'

There's a long silence.

'I'd caution you against insulting a goddess.'

Annem and Pa exchange looks. She dips her chin, and Pa lifts his, sliding an arm around me. 'You cannot have our daughter.'

'Very well.' The fae lifts one shoulder and adjusts his cuffs. 'Don't say I didn't warn you.' He steps out of sight.

Surely he hasn't given up so easily. Or is he simply retreating for now to let his mother come and deal with us at her leisure?

Huddled together, we wait. And wait.

Slowly, we creep to the nearest window. No sign of the fae. We pull apart, each checking a different window. I don't see anything, but beneath my feet there's a soft trembling, so slight I almost don't notice it. Then, in the garden, right where I sowed peas yesterday morning, the soil shifts.

Is he going to destroy my garden? I grit my teeth. Plants grow back. I can sow more seeds.

As I scowl, a hand reaches over the wall. Pale, but not the fae's – it's grubby and spindly and—

And followed by a fucking skull.

I stumble back from the window, staring as the bloated remains of a fisherman, oilskin coat dripping, shambles over the wall. Seaweed draped over his shoulder glistens in the emerging dawn. A moment later, the bed of peas bursts upward, revealing a hand groping for purchase.

The world slows down as a skeleton crawls from the earth and starts this way.

My heart. I clutch my chest. It isn't the world slowing, but my heart choosing the worst possible moment to stretch out the beats and make the kitchen spin.

From the other end of the house, Annem shrieks.

I need to go and help her. How, I'm not sure, but . . .

I fumble with my bottle of belladonna. No time to boil water. Instead, I press my little finger to the tiny measuring scoop, capturing a little of the powder on my skin.

Consuming it directly will make it more potent than steeping it in water, but . . .

I lick the bitter powder from my finger and swallow.

The bottle is sealed and back in my pocket by the time I reach the living room just as something slams into the front door. With her back braced against it, Annem screams again. Lowen and Pa throw themselves at it.

Heart leaping, cheeks feverish, I hurry to the front window, letting the giddy world spin around me.

I can't see the gorse bushes or the stone arch that leads to the mainland. The dead block my view in all directions, some nothing more than bone and rags, some almost whole, clothing only a little tattered and muddy. One wears the kind of steel armour I've only seen in books, half a spear still lodged in its armpit.

They groan and rasp. The sounds of creatures who've forgotten how to speak but long to remember.

Meanwhile, the fae leans against the garden wall, one ankle crossed over the other as he inspects his fingernails.

Bastard.

More of the dead pour over the bridge and into our garden. They throw themselves at the house, bones scraping over the walls and the oak doors, skittering against the windows. They trample the garden and tumble more stones off the wall.

Each stone that falls tolls in my heart. Each thud on the door is an ache in my chest. Each time my mother whimpers, part of me cracks.

My home. My family. He is willing to destroy them all just to claim me as his bride.

Pa has one arm around Annem, even as they push their backs against the door.

But it bucks in the frame with each assault. They can only hold back the tide for so long.

Thuds come from above and tiles crash to the ground. They're on the roof. They'll climb down the chimney next.

I lean against the window frame and meet the fae's gaze. My fingers twitch around the frame. I wish it was his damn throat. Through the glass, I call, 'What if I come willingly?'

He cants his head, one eyebrow rising. 'I'll call off my army.'

'And my family will be safe?'

'They'll have nothing to fear from me. *If* you come willingly, like a good girl.'

'Annon, no,' Lowen whispers. 'What are you doing?' He grunts as the dead pound once more.

'This is my fault. I cut through the wire. It was meant to protect me, wasn't it?' I raise my eyebrows at my parents.

'It kept you hidden,' Pa confirms between gritted teeth.

'It wasn't you,' Lowen hisses, hands curling into fists around his bloodied bandages. 'His voice – I heard it in the mirror. He whispered to me that I should give it to you. He told me to take down the wall. At the time, I couldn't remember where the ideas came from, but now I've heard him . . . I know. I brought the mirror into the house. I let him influence me.'

'Maybe. But *I* can stop it.'

Glass smashes. Somewhere in the kitchen. They've broken through. They'll be in here in moments.

'This home. This family.' My voice cracks on that last word. 'You're all I have. And he'll kill you to take me. I can't let that happen.' I shout, 'Stop them, and I'll come with you.'

Silence. The crashing and thuds, the groaning rasps, the scratching and skittering. It all stops. There's only the sea, a distant sigh in comparison to the chaos of their assault.

The fae lifts his chin, but otherwise doesn't move. 'If you don't step out of that door in ten seconds, I'll tear out your father's tongue.'

No time to pack. I spin on my heel and run to the kitchen, grabbing my medicine. The dead stand at the broken window pane, staring at me with empty eye sockets.

I shudder. His bride – his *queen*. Are these the creatures I'll rule over?

'Tick-tock,' he calls. 'Five seconds left.'

I burst into the living room. Annem and Pa step away from the door, faces creasing as they let me pass.

'Four.'

Lowen stands fast. 'Let them come.'

'Three.'

'Lowen. *Move.*' I've never sounded so firm. 'I'll find a way back.'

'Two.'

His jaw tightens and this horrible brightness pools in his eyes, making mine burn.

'Please.'

'One.'

Shoulders sinking, he shifts to one side and opens the door in one movement.

I step outside as the fae says, 'Zero.'

The dead don't move, and I let out a long breath.

With fearful glances at the creatures surrounding us, Annem and Pa come forward in turn and wrap me in tight hugs.

'We never meant . . .' Annem begins.

'We thought it would never happen. If we could just protect you enough.' Pa pulls back, frowning as a tear snakes down his lined cheek. He's aged a decade since yesterday. 'You understand, don't you?'

I don't trust myself to speak. He made that deal. One that bargained me away. That's a tight ball of hurt at the centre of my chest.

But he'd been soaked through, freezing, clinging to a little fishing boat in the middle of a huge storm, at the sea's mercy.

At The Morrigan's mercy.

Facing death alone.

Isn't that a fear I understand all too well?

I manage a small smile of reassurance as I nod.

Chin trembling, Lowen takes their place at my side as they back away to the safety of the house. 'You don't have to—'

'I do. To keep you safe – *alive*. I do. Now stop being a pain in the backside and give me a hug, little brother.'

He huffs and throws his arms around me, squeezing so tight I'm afraid my bones will break. When he finally pulls back, he presses a package into my hands, holding my gaze intently. 'Remember what I promised.'

It takes me a moment. He can't mean his joke from last night – about coming after me.

Before I can question him, the fae's voice cuts through the air, as cold as the wind.

'Are you coming, or do I need to remind my army of the feel of living flesh?' He still perches on the wall, one eyebrow raised.

Oh, he's going to be a fucking delight of a husband.

I give my family one last, reassuring nod. 'I'll see you soon.' Then I turn to the fae and spread my arms, presenting myself. 'Here I am, willing, just like I promised. You said you'd leave my family unharmed.'

He makes a soft sound in his throat and straightens from the wall. Stalking closer, he takes me in. His expression reveals nothing other than that he has this perpetual look of mingled contempt and irritation, lips pursed, eyes half-shut. His pale skin is stark against his deepest black hair, and the fierce line of his eyebrows reminds me of those slashing raven feathers I observed on the mirror's frame.

The pre-dawn light doesn't cast any warmth on his face, only deep shadows below the sharp lines of his cheekbones and jaw and around the faint golden glow of his eyes.

He puts me in mind of a cold winter's night where ice grips the land and makes the way treacherous even as it paints everything with its frosty, shimmering beauty.

As he comes closer, I realize quite how tall he is, how broad his shoulders are, how easily he could've broken the door down on his own. And I understand why he summoned the dead.

Because he can.

And that means he's the figure from my dream. Undoubtedly.

I had expected Death, not a King of Death.

'Come, then.' He holds out his hand, small black feathers edging the cuffs of his coat.

I look back.

My parents huddle together, watching with tear-stained cheeks. Lowen stands to one side, frowning like that can prevent him from falling.

I give them a single nod then take the fae's hand.

Slowly, his lips curve, like I've stepped into a trap.

Before I can change my mind, he pulls me against his chest and the world folds into feathers and darkness.

6

IN PIECES, I am nothing. Fractured. Falling. Caught between feathers and buffeted by great wings.

I have no body, but my soul panics.

The scattered pieces of me can't possibly come back together.

This is death. Oblivion. And I'm alone.

I reach, but I have nothing to reach with.

There is only darkness. Chaos. The glinting eyes of ravens. I am them. I'm between them. I don't know, and that's the most frightening part of all.

Please. Someone. Something. Save me from this, because I can do nothing.

Then, like a giant's breath, the air shifts, expands, there's light between the wings and I can suck in cool, fresh air. I gasp at it, drag it down, half-sobbing as I realize I'm whole.

It takes a while with my eyes screwed shut to understand I'm clinging to something. And it takes a while longer to register it's cloth with warm flesh beneath.

The fae.

I'm clinging *to him*.

With a sound of disgust, I push, but it does nothing – his arm holds fast around me. When I look up, I find him watching me with an icy smirk like this is all *terribly* amusing.

I have never in my life been violent, but if I don't slap that look off his face one day, it will be a fucking miracle.

As my steaming breaths return to something like normal and the cold snaps at my toes, I take in my surroundings – anything's better than looking at his horrible, beautiful face.

Snow carpets the ground. There are no footprints leading to us, though my feet sink inches into the crisp white. We must have . . . *landed* here, just as I'd seen him land at our garden wall. It was no illusion, then.

Snow even clings to the walls that surround us, piling high on the roof, looking like it could slump to the ground at any moment with an exhausted sigh. No cosy lighting shines through the narrow windows overlooking this courtyard. Icicles cling to the eaves, as sharp and glittering as spears.

Black branches stretch overhead, cutting the grey sky into shards as jagged as the pieces of me as we travelled here.

Two ravens perch among them, and I swear they're watching us with interest. Then again, after everything that's happened in the past hour, I shouldn't really dismiss the possibility that they are. The gleam of blue-black on their feathers is the only colour.

Even the tree's bark is grey, its branches utterly bare, making me think it's dead and not simply waiting out the winter.

But as I frown at its bleakness, I note the strangest thing of all.

The sun is black.

I swallow, throat tight. This is not home. Not Albion. Not even earth.

I'm truly in the Underworld.

The fae jerks his chin up. 'Can you walk?' His lip curls as he speaks, as though he doubts I'm capable of anything.

I clench and unclench my fingers, trying to reconnect with my body after it was ripped apart. Trembling, only slightly. Cold. As always, it sends my heart racing – worse thanks to the hurried dose of belladonna. My toes are growing numb. But I appear to be whole and my legs seem steady enough.

Nodding, I press again on his chest and he lets me go.

'Good.' He turns on his heel and strides through the snow, opening a door with a gesture.

Before I follow, I squeeze the pocket of my dressing robe. The two bottles are a reassuring weight – my medicine and the powdered belladonna. I slide Lowen's parcel in the other pocket and hurry after the king, trying to keep to his footprints to save myself wading through the thick snow.

But his steps are too long for me, and by the time I get inside, I'm soaked from the hips down. My sodden nightclothes cling to me, and I fold my arms to try and ward off the inevitable goosebumps.

At the edge of my vision, I glimpse a shape at one end of the corridor, but when I turn, there's nothing. Once I'm sure no one's lurking, I follow the fae.

The two ravens swoop past me, one landing on his shoulder, the other continuing ahead, landing on the orbed light of the wall sconces. They're joined by a third – a smaller, white raven, which perches on a windowsill. Light catches on its feathers with a violet sheen.

They definitely watch me pass. The white one blinks its pale-lilac eyes slowly, and I find myself pulling my dressing gown tighter and hurrying to catch up to the fae.

'So good of you to join me,' he says without sparing me so much as an instant of his brooding look.

'Your legs are a touch longer than mine.'

He barely slows. 'I expect my future wife to be able to keep up with me. Though, perhaps that's an unrealistic expectation when my mother has chosen a *human* to tether me to.'

So that's why he's such an insufferable prick – he hates me because I'm human. Well, that isn't about to change.

'You could always take me home and then choose someone else to marry.' There's a bright note in my voice, but deep down I know it's hopeless. Whether you're a fisherman or a demi-god King of Death, you don't deny The Morrigan.

Even if my parents' attempts to keep us safe from this fae had worked, it would only have been a matter of time before she had come to see the bargain fulfilled.

Though at some point, it has to 'count', right? There will be some moment we can say the bargain is technically complete and if I leave then, they have to allow it, because we've carried out the agreement to the letter if not the spirit. I need to know more about the bargain.

This place gives nothing away. The walls are a polished grey stone that gleams coolly in the unnatural light coming from the orbs. The floor is bare, and my slippered feet pad across it, but his booted steps are silent. We pass ebony doors with black handles.

The white raven flies over my head and circles repeatedly as though fascinated.

Much as this place and these birds are strange, their master is familiar. 'You're the one from my dreams, aren't you?'

'Dreaming of me already? So declining to marry me was just playing hard to get.' He speaks with a detached amusement, like nothing is serious or important. It raises my hackles – no doubt exacerbated by events of the past hour and the dull exhaustion setting in.

'*You* came into *my* dreams. And they certainly weren't pleasant ones. More like nightmares.'

'Whatever you need to tell yourself. I know your kind can lie and do so readily.'

'Lying would be me saying you are a delightful prospective husband and I can't wait to be married to you. The truth is that you came into my dreams. It's really quite creepy when you think about it. Why? Spying or just trying to get me to come to you willingly?'

He huffs a sigh like *I'm* the infuriating one. 'Don't flatter yourself, Nameless. Just as you didn't choose to dream of me, I didn't choose to appear in your dreams. Thanks to the bargain our parents made, our fates are tied. We're Fatebound. Not even iron can block such threads.'

'Then you didn't influence my brother to break down the wall around our home?'

'Oh, no. *That* I did. The mirror let me bypass your primitive iron boundary.' His gaze grows distant for a moment as he shakes his head. 'They truly thought they were safe.'

'Until you raised a damn army, yes, we were safe. And happy.' But questions nip at the edges of my irritation, chasing it along. 'So . . . do you rule over the dead, like the ones you set on us?' I glance at a window, expecting to find more of those hollow eye sockets watching.

'Not quite.' He says it in this way that makes me feel like the most ignorant creature that ever lived. 'The kingdom of Mordren is home to unseelie fae. Perhaps your backwards kind have stories of how we were banished from the surface many ages ago.'

My smile is gritted and accompanied by a sarcastic toss of my head. 'We have an alphabet and everything.'

'Only thanks to us.' Before I can ask what he means, he goes on. 'You will find the Underworld different to the surface. It is not a soft place, and I have no doubt you will consider our ways equally harsh. But as my future bride and this land's future queen, you are expected to follow our rules. The first of those is that my word is law.'

I expect another smirk or for him to preen that he holds such power, but his expression doesn't falter, not even as the third raven flies past, disturbing the smooth lengths of his hair.

'Here, names hold power. Asking for a name is seen as rude

at best, an act of aggression at worst. You must offer yours freely and wait for one to be offered in return.' His gold eyes slide to me. 'Since I already know you are Nameless, nothing, I offer mine. Drystan. Though you will refer to me as "Your Majesty".'

'Will I, now?' I mutter under my breath.

His lip curls, though I hesitate to call it a smile – it's much crueller than that. 'Just like you will mind your manners while you are in my court. These rules are vital, Nameless One. Mock them, break them and be prepared to live – or die – with the consequences.'

The raven on his shoulder caws and peers past him to give me an accusatory glare.

The cold already biting into me deepens, like my body understands the warning. The sun isn't the only thing about this place that's different.

Still, I can't help pursing my lips as I meet the fae's – *Drystan's* – strange, glowing gaze. 'You want me to be a good girl, is that it?'

That one, simple question is what makes it all hit me. I'm in the Underworld, under his rule. Alone. Stuck. Bargained away. My eyes burn and my vision blurs. To think I was upset about a notebook being burned, and now . . .

'Your emotions are a weakness, and here weakness is deadly.'

I swallow and quickly look away. Not only because of my threatening tears, but because my illness must be considered a weakness, surely? I may be dying anyway, but I have no intention of being killed here, alone, a world away from my family.

If I must go, I will do it on my terms.

I'll have to hide my frailty. Somehow.

As for my feelings . . . Well, haven't I been hiding those for years?

With a deep breath, I will the tears down and straighten my back. The tincture's effects are still with me, so I can at least move easily, though that will stop if I stay in these cold clothes much longer. I wish I'd grabbed the tincture bottle before I left, but there wasn't time.

Lifting my chin, I hold his unnerving gaze. 'What else?'

His eyes narrow for the barest instant and he makes this soft sound that *might* be something like approval. 'Generosity is never as it seems. Accept no gifts and give no insult.' We turn down another corridor with large double doors at the end. 'Beware any debt.'

I want to ask questions, but the need to mentally note every rule wins out. I will not die here. I will see my family again, even if it's the last thing I do.

'Fatework is the consort's gift and duty. You are expected to apply yourself and learn the skill.' There's a slight aquiline curve to his nose, refined and haughty, and he looks down it at me. 'Especially since as a human you lack any natural talent for it. My *dear mother* is clearly punishing me.'

I can practically hear him holding back a sigh. He hates this arrangement almost as much as I do. Perhaps I can use that.

'Here.' He spreads his arms and the double doors sweep open revealing a bedroom decorated in shades of grey and white. 'There are more rules for you to learn, but it's late. You will sleep until sunset when Min will come to prepare you.'

The raven on his shoulder takes flight and circles. Its sharp *caw* sounds right behind me, making me gasp and lurch across the threshold.

The room is the biggest I've ever been in, with a seating area around a fireplace, a dining table to one side and a large bed at the centre surrounded by dark drapes.

The biggest room, but probably also the bleakest.

Joy.

I turn, ready to ask who Min is and what I'm to be prepared for, but he's already gone.

7

IN THE SUDDEN silence, I circle the room. The rich, dark furniture is unlike anything I've ever seen, exquisitely carved with twisting forms, occasionally broken up by jagged points as though daggers fight to break through the organic shapes. Beady eyes peek out, and on the doors of the armoire, I find little pointed faces peering from between the vine-like tendrils, their expressions twisted with cruel intent. The full-length mirror next to it looks normal enough, but I turn it around, unable to stand looking at the skinny drowned rat before me.

There's a spacious bathroom with a large bath at its centre made of black, smooth rock – perhaps onyx or obsidian. My muscles ache at the sight. I will escape this place, but it wouldn't hurt to have a hot bath or two first. For now, I strip off my wet clothes, empty my pockets on to the bed and wrap myself in a silky robe that's warmer than it looks.

Restless, I peer out one of the narrow windows. Snow piles upon snow, it glitters in the strange cool light from this place's black sun. Drystan . . .

I refuse to think of him as my future husband. I'm getting out of this mess before that happens.

He said it was late, but the sun is high – mid- to late-morning, by my guess.

So the unseelie are nocturnal. I've always assumed the stories have them appearing at night because the new moon is what allows them to travel across the veil between our worlds. Plus, isn't that creepier? A creature that only comes to inflict its cruelty at the time when we humans are at our most vulnerable, with eyes too weak to be of use in the dark. Seems I was wrong.

I lean against the window frame, head bowing.

Seems I've been wrong about a lot of things.

Rhiannon is a lie.

My fate has been bound to this place since before I was born.

My parents have been carrying a dark secret all these years.

If they'd told me, I might've been able to help. I could've turned my research to ways to escape fae bargains or thwart goddesses or . . .

But one thing burns through all the others with cold fire.

I am a lie.

All of these things I've been wrong about drag on me – or maybe it's just that the tincture is wearing off. Wrists and knees aching, I trudge over to the bed and flop down. The velvet covers are soft and lulling, but they don't smell of home. Sweet and woody. Not Albionic, warmer, like the carved wooden box Annem brought from her homeland and keeps jewellery in. And there's something else. Something that lulls me further but I can't place it. Familiar and yet strange, like a dream.

As I shift to try and get comfortable, the items I emptied from my pockets dig into my hips. I retrieve the bottle of tablets and the smaller one of belladonna, then the parcel Lowen pressed into my hands as he said goodbye, and place them in a row before me. All I have of home.

I expect to cry. I *should* cry. But I'm all wrung out.

Tearing back the brown paper of Lowen's parcel, I uncover oxblood-red leather, and maybe I'm not entirely wrung out, because my vision blurs when I realize what he's given me.

Another notebook.

This one has entwined thorns embossed on the spine and a slender pencil tucked inside, ready for work. I press my hand to my mouth, holding in a sob.

It only gets worse when, slipped into the front, I find one of Lowen's sketches. This one is unfinished, the bottom right corner disappearing into rough outlines where the rest is a perfect rendition in light and shadow of the beach by the village and the sea beyond.

He knew I missed seeing it. He did this for me.

And I couldn't even bring myself to tell him to go and live his life.

Now I might never get the chance. I need to get home. If nothing else, to tell him. I owe him that much.

Head and heart heavy, I tuck the sketch back in the notebook and pick up the bottle of tablets.

My medicine.

I didn't take one this morning – what with being dragged away to the Underworld and all. I tip out the blood-red tablets. It feels like the only spot of colour I've seen since coming here. Everything is grey, black, or white – except for Drystan's eyes.

There are ten left. *Ten.*

The travelling apothecary is due to come to the village next week – we would've restocked then. But now . . .

Perhaps I can stretch them out, cut them in half. Will half be enough?

It has to be.

My nail bends as I try to snap a tablet in two, so I end up using the edge of the hairbrush on the bedside table to break it. It's messy, crumbling the centre, but it kind of works.

Even halved, the tablet is a little too wide to swallow comfortably with a cupped palmful of water from the sink, but I've grown used to relaxing my throat and lifting my chin and enduring the sensation of that hard knot slowly working its way down.

Before I drop back into bed with the new notebook hugged to my chest, I gulp down more water in an attempt to wash away the bitter taste. As always, it's a losing battle.

'My lady?' A singsong voice summons me from a suffocating sleep.

I sit up, clutching the robe to my naked chest. The dream flees as I catch my breath, but whatever it was, there was something chasing me. Something with sharp teeth and even sharper eyes. A half-remembered rhyme drifts away.

Death upon the water.

Death upon the land . . .

I blink into the darkness surrounding me. The black drapes. The velvet pillow at my back. The monster was a dream, but this . . . I have truly been bargained away to the Underworld.

'It's evening, my lady. Time to get up.' I barely have the presence of mind to shove the bottles and notebook under the pillow before the drapes open, and I wince at the sudden light, which silhouettes a slender woman. 'Oh. *Oh.*'

Once my eyes adjust, I squint up at her.

Pale skin contrasts with black hair, though she isn't nearly as pale as Drystan or sickly like me. Pointed ears peek out from between her thick hair – another fae, then. Dark eyes narrow as she surveys me and her small mouth purses gently. 'Well,' she says on a breath. 'I was not expecting *that.*' A glint enters her eyes. 'And I'm sure no one else is.'

She wears a simple knee-length tunic that skims her figure, with wide trousers beneath. Their simplicity only accentuates the flowing silk, which shimmers from silver to pale gold to whispering aqua, depending on how the light hits it.

I'm no longer wearing my worn linen nightclothes, yet I still feel like a piece of broken driftwood among grand, lacquered sculptures.

Despite my discomfort, I clear my throat of its sleep roughness. 'Good morning?' Does that count as minding my manners?

Her straight eyebrows shoot up. 'And a human who's more polite than I am, no less.' She bows her head, though I catch the edge of a grin before she does so. 'Forgive me, my lady. I'm Min. The royal sartor.'

I'm not sure what a sartor is, but she works for Drystan and she's fae – each of those on their own is enough to make me wary. Thank the gods I hid my medicine.

The confusion must show on my face, because she adds, 'I advise on clothing, hair, accessories – anything relating to appearance. Or, at least, I'm supposed to. But now you're here . . . His Majesty has tasked me with preparing you for the night.' Her gaze passes over me quickly and her expression remains neutral, but I know what she sees and what she must think.

She has her work cut out for her.

Still, she offers a hand to help me out of bed. Holding the robe around myself, I just about manage to take it and hop out of the too-high bed without falling. And hopefully without the stiff agony of my joints showing.

This close, I can see a pinkish crescent scar sits below her left eye, dimpling the otherwise smooth skin of her cheek.

'Thank you.' I squeeze her hand, remembering Drystan's rule about manners.

Though maybe I'm making an etiquette misstep, because her expression . . . Well, it doesn't so much change as go suddenly still.

Of course. I haven't introduced myself. 'My name's Annon.' It may be a lie, but it *feels* true.

Her head cocks, making her shiny hair catch on her shoulder. 'An unusual name,' she says at last. She nods as she leads me into the bathroom, where the air is thick with steam and the scent of jasmine and honeysuckle. Foam overflows from the bath.

'Oh, Min, you are a star.'

The corner of her mouth flickers as though she's resisting a smile. 'And *you* are clearly in need of a little looking after. Come on.' She gestures at the bath with one hand and holds out the other, giving the robe an expectant look.

Not-so-subtle jab aside, I suppose this is the life of rich folk . . . of future queens. Last summer my illness got worse after we changed my medicine because of a supply issue. I was so weak, Annem had to help me bathe. Is this so different? Besides, Min seems considerably more approachable than Drystan. Even if I don't trust her, I can ask her questions and get to know a bit about this predicament I need to get myself out of.

I relinquish the robe.

I know I'm too skinny. No matter what I eat, I can't seem to put on weight, like my illness takes all the sustenance out of food and leaves nothing for my body.

But Min merely makes the robe disappear with a gesture and again offers her hand to help me into the bath, gaze averted all the while.

The intense wave of gratitude that breaks over me is warm and for a moment scours my throat. Annem always tries to make me eat more. She doesn't say anything about my weight, but every time I bathed last summer, she would stare at my jutting hips and the deep hollows above my collarbones. I know she worries, but could she do it more quietly?

I sigh as I sink into the hot water and the bubbles pop against my skin. For a while I sit there and Min busies herself gathering objects from the cabinet into a basket. My muscles loosen and melt away – it feels like they come clean off the bone like slow-cooked meat. Even my heart beats at a calm, steady rate.

By the time she comes over, I'm so relaxed, I don't mind her dipping the sponge in the water and washing my back. Once more, I find myself grateful – this time for her gentleness.

Now my body is quiet, my mind pipes up with one question. Preparing me for what?

'What happens after this?' I ask so softly, it's barely audible over the quiet slosh of Min's work.

She pauses. 'He hasn't told you anything, has he?'

'Only some rules and that you'd come at nightfall.'

'Hmph.' She lifts my hair and circles the sponge over my neck. 'You're to be presented to His Majesty's court. They will be . . . intrigued to meet you. That's the courtly way of saying they'll be very surprised.'

'His whole court?' Despite my best efforts, there's a squeak of panic in my voice. I'm a fisherman's daughter. I've never been any-where fancier than a bakery that sells lemon puffs.

She leaves the sponge to float in the water and eases me back against the bath. Her hands dart into sight, taking a bottle from the basket that's now sitting on a little stand. She pours oil into her palm and smooths it between her hands before they disappear from sight again. 'I take it that isn't familiar for you?' She smooths my hair and combs her fingers through it.

I'm not sure how to answer. He warned me against revealing any weaknesses. My inexperience in this area is one.

With a firm touch, she massages the oil into my scalp and a nutty scent drifts through the sweetness of the bath foam.

'Well,' she says at last when it's clear I'm not going to answer, 'I dare say even familiarity with human courts won't help you here. It would be useful for you to understand a bit about our ways – just in case they're different from what you're used to.'

Pretending I have any idea about human courts when it must be abundantly clear I'm – well, frankly, a pauper – seems ridiculous. The fae are not known for their kindness. Illusion. Deception. Treacherous bargains. Yes, all of those.

This must be some ploy, perhaps to get me to loosen up and spill more information than I should. I don't doubt anything I tell her will be fed back to His Royal Prickishness.

'Our rules tend not to be written down or spoken aloud,' she explains as she works on combing more oil through my dry hair. 'But we know them as though they were etched into our bones. I'll try to keep to those that will be most useful to you – otherwise we might be here for nights.' Her soft laugh ruffles my hair. 'I'm afraid you've already broken one. No thank-yous and no apologies.'

'Wait, but aren't they just polite?'

'Perhaps it's as simple as that for humans. But here, they imply a debt. You thank someone, you owe them. You apologize, you owe them.'

I take a long breath, rubbing my forehead. The sun is different here, but so is the very fabric of society.

'It'll probably help you to speak only when spoken to. Those in court enjoy having an audience. Let them talk and they'll love you.'

'That sounds easy enough.'

Another soft laugh. 'You'd be surprised. When someone does address you directly and asks a question, it's best to answer it with another question or a metaphor. Direct answers are considered gauche and utterly dull. If you can, use clever wordplay or reply with a riddle or something veiled. You'll seem interesting without revealing too much.'

I lower my chin, letting her reach the nape of my neck. 'Is that so?'

'You're a quick study, I see. Hmm, what else? Obviously, don't make any bargains or promises. And beware generosity.'

'His Divine Eminence did mention that one.'

She makes a soft sound and I'm dying to know if she's fighting a laugh or if my sarcasm is a mortal offence in the Underworld.

I wince and try an awkward laugh that sounds more like a

cough. 'He also said something about good manners? Is that just to avoid pissing him off or . . .?'

'It's a matter of . . . armour. No matter who you're facing, if you can maintain a facade of politeness, it will help. My people appreciate good manners, even from their victims.'

'*Their*. Not *our*?'

She pauses, silent, still. With a huff, she continues brushing my hair. 'Well, aren't you observant? My status and temperament mean I can't play the games of court life, and I don't indulge in the cruelties some of my kin enjoy. Even if they try to inflict those cruelties upon you, rudeness will only make matters worse. Trust me on that, Annon.'

I shiver at the fact she says my name – or what I have left of it. It carries power, impressing on me how serious this is. Weakness means death.

She continues working on me, applying oils, thick creams and even a gritty powder that buffs away the roughness on my elbows and hands, until I no longer feel like myself, but some creature that has shed its skin.

And her attentions continue after we leave the bathroom. I'm dried, moisturized, the dead ends of my hair are snipped off and my body hair removed using a shimmering oil. Is this what fine ladies back home go through or is this an unseelie thing? There's also food – bread and fruit, cheese and meat, together with water and wine, all served on iridescent glass tableware.

Kneeling, Min straightens from applying the last of the hair removal oil to my toes. She glances towards the door before leaning in and murmuring, 'You didn't bring any of the dark metal here, did you?'

I blink at her for a moment before realizing. 'You mean iron?'

She rocks back like I've hit her, eyes wide.

Shit. What have I done now?

It takes a long moment before she masters herself, throat

bobbing. 'It is forbidden to bring that stuff into the Underworld. Even the word is taboo.'

'Oh, sorry. I didn't know.' I clasp my hands together. Great work, Annon. The first chance you get to speak to anyone other than the king and you've already offended her.

And now I've apologized. I wince.

'Just avoid speaking of it. I thought I could smell the stuff: that's the only reason I even raised the subject.'

'My parents had charms around the house to ward off fae. They were made of . . . the dark metal.'

'That must be it. Well.' She slaps her thighs as she rises, and for a horrifying moment I think she's about to say that I, sitting here naked, am ready. Do unseelie nobility wear clothes? Thankfully, she goes on, 'That's your body ready – now for what we're going to put on it.'

Remembering Drystan's warning about emotions, I barely swallow back a sigh of relief. It's one thing letting Min see me naked, but the thought of a whole court full of fae? No, thank you.

Oblivious to my suffering, Min carries on as she crosses the room, 'I had some outfits brought in so we have plenty to choose from.' With a gesture, she throws open the two matching armoires.

The contents glisten and sparkle, twinkling like distant stars, making a soft breath fall from my lips. White, silver, steel, charcoal and black – there are outfits in every shade of grey. There's colour too, though it's mostly cool tones like the icy world outside. Pale, whispering blue and a clear, soft aqua like Min's outfit. Deep midnight and blackened purple. Blood red that feels dangerous.

I usually wear brown, with off-white shifts underneath. Once I had a woad blue dress. A gift for my eighteenth birthday. I wore it all that day and to the pub that night and it came off when I went down to the beach and lost my virginity at midnight. It grew too big a long time ago, and I gave it away. That's the last time I wore colour. I make do with my flowers, instead.

Perhaps unsure what my look of shock means, Min pulls garments out one by one and holds them out for me to examine. Gems nestle among careful pleats and embroidery. Strings of pearls weave between sheer fabric that's somehow been manipulated into the pattern of scales or perhaps rippling water. Every piece is exquisite.

These armoires are like treasure troves.

Then Min opens an actual treasure trove. The dressing-table drawers house necklaces, bracelets, rings and even tiaras and circlets, some solid metal, others made of glittering chain and strings of jewels.

All I can do is gape and murmur how incredible each item is as Min lifts her chin in pride and picks out pieces for me to wear. A backless gown of shimmering turquoise, aquamarine earrings and a matching set of chains.

I can't wear these. But I also can't summon my voice to say that.

Min hums as she works, helping me step into the gown, closing it with clever hidden fastenings. She clips half the chains at my shoulders, hanging down my back. They serve to keep the shoulder straps in place as well as adorning my bare skin. Then she sets to work on my hair, braiding and coiling the wild waves it's drying into, clipping sections in place, leaving others to hang loose, all while I silently panic.

I can't walk into a whole room of fae. I've seen the same three people for the past three years. I don't know how to behave. I don't know what to say.

But Min continues preparing me, binding more of the chains into my hair and smoothing the loose sections with more jasmine oil. She moisturizes my lips before applying rouge and dusts iridescent powders over my skin.

At last, she steps back and admires her work – admires *me*.

She lifts her chin again, something preening in the gesture. I suppose the way I look must make her feel better about her own appearance.

I exhale my relief when she pulls out flat shoes, embroidered to match my outfit. I've read about aristocratic ladies wearing heeled shoes and the idea fills me with dread. Without a doubt, I would topple over.

But these are soft and comfortable, and once they're on, Min helps me to my feet and leads me to the full-length mirror I've been avoiding since I arrived.

'Ready?'

I almost say no, but she looks so pleased with herself, I don't have the heart to, so I nod and brace myself for the woman I saw in the mirror yesterday.

But that's not who stands before me. This woman doesn't look half dead. Granted, her cheeks are still too hollow and her arms too spindly, but she looks much better.

The gown skims over my frame, disguising how much weight I've lost over the years. My hair isn't as glossy as it once was, but there's a sheen to it. My rouged lips aren't chapped, and the turquoise silk makes my skin look less of a sickly tone. The iridescent powder dusted on my cheekbones shifts from turquoise to gold as I move, distracting from the shadows that gather beneath them.

I look like a woman. Not a girl or someone who's dying.

I only realize I've stepped forward when my fingertips brush the mirror's cool surface.

'Is this magic?' I ask softly, voice close to cracking. Is the mirror just showing me a lie? Is it under the king's control, and when I walk out into court, they'll all laugh at me for thinking I look . . . pretty?

'No.' She catches my hand and lowers it. 'No illusions. No tricks. This is real. The only magic here is care . . . and some of the best cosmetics in the Underworld.' The corner of her mouth twitches, and I can't help chuckling.

'Thank you, Min.' It isn't enough, so I squeeze her hand and say it again. Still not enough to convey how it feels to almost look like the woman I used to be.

'You shouldn't—'

'I know. But I mean it. And I *am* indebted to you for this.'

Her eyes widen for a moment before she dips her chin. 'Come on. Let's get you to the king.'

8

I HEAR THE gathering before I see it. The halls are empty, but the sound of a haunting, twisting tune dances through them, making the shadows gathered in the corners seem thicker. It feels like someone trails us, but when I turn, there's no one there. I edge closer to Min.

She doesn't respond until we reach a large set of doors that hum. 'Just remember what I told you.' Briefly, she fusses with my hair, then she nods and the doors swing wide.

The noise hits me first. A hundred conversations. Raucous laughter. Wild music I can't make sense of. It all whips together like a physical force – a breeze that winds around us and tugs us inside.

As if trying to keep up with the odd rhythm of the music, my heart pounds. I press my palm to the belladonna bottle I've tucked into my underwear. Still there.

Near the door, someone's laughing so hard they start coughing, and against the wall, a couple are lost in each other's arms . . . though I swear I count six hands sliding under velvet clothing.

I've never seen so much velvet, in fact, nor so much satin and chiffon, all made of lustrous silk. Dark jewels glisten and glitter on hems and at throats. Shells gleam with iridescence, presented on bracelets and in hairpieces with as much pride as the gemstones. Pearls and, I realize with a sudden flush of cold, the ivory tone of bones and teeth adorn ears and collars alongside leaves that shimmer with unnatural light.

It takes a moment to register the strangeness of that light in this huge hall. Scintillating from gold to pink to violet to turquoise, the colours merge together and change from one corner of the room to another. They catch in the rafters that arch overhead, leaving shadows that twist and creep.

I'm blinking from them to the kaleidoscope of people before me when the crowd begins to turn. Eyes fix on me. Sharp. Small. Bright. Large. Pale and dark. So many, so different from one another. They prick my skin like the needles some old fraud of a doctor used to let my blood.

One woman with her hair in fine braids and shimmering scales across her cheek and collarbones leans towards her neighbour. 'A human? Perhaps His Majesty has reconsidered his position on having them fight to the death.'

The man at her side eyes me, his slitted pupils almost making me stop in my tracks. He scoffs a brief, dismissive laugh. 'Well, I won't be placing any bets on *that* one.'

Ouch. I bite my lip against the urge to wince. They must know they're close enough that I can hear. Yet they don't care. Still, this seems to confirm it's Min being a bit too nice rather than the king being unusually dickish for the unseelie.

I push a polite smile on my mouth and continue into the crowd of fae.

They undulate around me, never quite touching, but never opening a clear path, either. I can only ever see a few feet ahead as the fae move like shifting sands. At one point, I stop mid-step, as before me is a huge, craggy face, its chin at the floor, its hairline somewhere above my head. My mouth drops open, the careful smile falling away. How big is this being if that's just its head?

But as I stare, it moves, expands – the creases around the mouth open up, the heavy brow lifts and the whole thing unfolds, until I'm left blinking at the back of a tall fae who wears a suede cape the same light beige as what I thought was a face.

Was that a trick of the light or true magic? I've read hundreds of stories of fae magic and glamour, their illusion and tricks.

Now I walk among them. And my only weapon is a vial of powdered belladonna that I need to keep myself conscious most days.

The king's diatribe of warnings suddenly makes a lot more sense.

I turn to my side, expecting to find Min, but she's gone. I wish *I* could just disappear. The back of my neck prickles, and I remember my false smile.

With that in place, I continue on, my neck twisting this way and that, attention caught by something I've never seen before with every turn.

Acrobats balance, barely. Laughing, they tumble and teeter on each other's shoulders and heads, carrying towers of glasses filled to the brim.

When word of my presence spreads and the audience turns to me rather than the entertainment, they screech with frustration.

Drinks splash. Glasses shatter. No one seems to care.

I push on, not wanting to get into trouble, and find myself near a wall where shadow puppets act out a story. Except, there's no sign of a sheet or puppeteer – or any puppets. The audience is enthralled as a shadow dragon spreads its wings and breathes shadow flame, destroying a town. Meanwhile, more shadows creep across the stone floor, formless as they feel their way around the audience's ankles.

As I back away, I meet the gaze of a woman who's so exquisitely beautiful, I stop in my tracks. She's the definition of arresting. Full, red lips. Crystal-blue eyes. Black hair as rich and shiny as a crow's wing. Her pale complexion almost seems to glow with radiance. Slowly, she smiles, and before I see her canines, the predatory patience of her expression reminds me of just how dangerous she and every other fae in this room is.

I swallow, avert my gaze and press into the crowd. This is meant to be my presentation. I suppose I'm meant to find the king, but how the hells am I meant to find anything in this chaos?

Blood-red hair catches my eye. A group of fae stand together, all tall and perhaps the most beautiful of those gathered, which is saying something.

I once read a story that claimed red hair was rare among the fae, so it's considered appealing to them. Perhaps the author was mistaken. I count thirteen with that same colour – in a room of a few hundred people that doesn't seem so unusual.

Around them, smaller groups of fae knot together and they're the few who don't look in my direction – their gazes keep flitting to the red-haired beauties with distinct looks of admiration. So at least that part must be true.

Taking mental note, I turn in the opposite direction. And that's when I spot him.

Eyes half-closed, gaze off to one side, ankle resting on his knee, the king looks bored. With a casual flick of his wrist, he swirls the deep berry-red drink so it almost reaches the top of the glass.

I feel it when his attention snaps to me. A subtle shifting of the air, like the press on your ears when you plunge underwater. My pulse speeds – it understands the truth of the fae king. For all he's pretty to look at, he is just as dangerous as the others.

He takes his time looking me up and down, then flows to his feet. Gods, I envy the ease of his every move. The casual grace as he steps down from the dais. The assurance with which he enters the crowd and knows – just *knows* it's going to part for him. He doesn't slow for even a second, he simply trusts they will move. And they do.

And they . . . change.

As he comes closer, eyes never leaving me, the fae's wild energy calms. Their laughter softens. Their frenetic, undulating dances shift to something more courtly, with hands pressed together and steps carefully measured as the music finds a steadier beat. They bend their heads together and murmur, glancing from me to him and back again as if wondering what their king will do when he finds a human in their midst.

My feet have fallen still, I finally realize, and I'm holding my breath. The air prickles with anticipation.

With arms raised, dancers cross the path between us and I lose sight of the king. Just for an instant, but that's all it takes – once they're gone, so is he.

The held breath huffs from me, and I search the crowd, but there's no sign of Drystan. He's toying with me. He could be an illusion, for all I know.

'Not bad.' A voice in my ear, low and familiar, warm breath tickling.

A gasp tears through me as I spin around and find myself toe-to-toe with the king. 'How did you . . .?'

Slowly, one side of his mouth curls. 'Remind me to give Min a raise. She's outdone herself.'

Despite hating him, I find myself briefly, foolishly soaring. It's been a long time since anyone complimented my appearance, and although it's backhanded at best, part of me still enjoys it.

But I can't help noticing how perfect everyone here is – him included. My hair is shinier than it was, but it's still dull compared to theirs. Only his is a flat black, like it sucks all light from existence. Even the pallor of his complexion is unearthly and beautiful, like he's carved from marble rather than made from anything so mundane as flesh and blood.

And yet when he steps into place at my side and slides a hand under the chains to the small of my back, it's warm and not nearly as hard as stone. 'Come.'

My breath catches at the unexpected touch, but I let him lead me through the room as fae melt from our path. Whispers carry on the air, though I can't see anyone's lips moving. Their voices layer, so I only catch the odd word or phrase. *Unusual. Human . . . she's here for . . . Odd little thing.*

'You don't want me to touch you,' Drystan states softly enough that it's for my ears only.

Is that true? I don't like him, no, but like the compliment, it's been a long while since I've been treated as anything more than a daughter, a sister, a patient. And in this room full of fae all looking at me with varying degrees of curiosity, surprise and spite, a warm hand on my bare skin is not the worst thing.

'I wasn't expecting it.'

He makes a low, thoughtful sound as we reach the centre of the room and he draws us to a halt. 'Friends and fiends.' His voice rises above the music and hubbub, and the hall falls quiet. 'Meet my future bride and your future queen.'

Where the room was quiet a moment ago, now it's so absolutely silent it's deafening.

The exquisitely beautiful woman from earlier is near by. Her crystal-blue eyes go wide as her red lips part. In an instant, her expression snaps back, composed and coolly detached, but her gaze still flicks between me and Drystan as though trying to make sense of such a pairing.

Frankly, I can't blame her. I stand out here, and not only because I'm human.

As if picking up on my thoughts, someone mutters, 'A *human*?'

That soft question breaks the silence and dozens of whispered conversations break out across the room. The scrutiny on me is a physical force, and my knees wobble under its weight.

'Well,' the blue-eyed woman says on a breath as she steps forward. 'Your Majesty certainly knows how to keep us on our toes. Such an *interesting* idea to marry a human. May we know what we're to call our future . . .' She swallows and licks her lips. '. . . *queen*?'

She isn't asking *me*, so perhaps that doesn't break the rule about names.

The king shoots me a quick, unreadable look and I think he's going to tell them all I'm nameless, but inclining his head, he answers, 'Rhiannon.'

'Hmm.' Her black hair gleams as she tosses her head. 'Like the stories of old. How . . . *interesting*. And isn't she pretty? Do we really believe that pretty little neck can carry the seal?'

'*Phaedra*.' His voice carries a note of warning that I don't understand.

She gives a tight little smile, then steps forward. 'Allow me to be the first to offer congratulations to Your Majesty and . . . *Rhiannon*.' Even though her mouth is still curved in a smile, the look she gives me is sharp enough to gut herring at a hundred paces. It's a wonder I'm still standing.

All I can do is smile right back, bright and sweet. I've had practice at smiling through pain – this is nothing.

Drystan's thumb slides up my spine, making my body stiffen. He doesn't so much as glance at me as he inclines his head to her. 'You speak most generously, Phaedra.'

After she bows and slips into the crowd, more fae come forward, congratulating us on our impending nuptials. I need to escape before that comes to pass, but a royal wedding must take a while to arrange, even for fae. I hope.

When a black-haired man approaches and the king stiffens, it catches my attention. The sharp lines of his cheekbones remind me of Drystan's. But as he bows over my hand, he smiles charmingly, like the king never could. 'Effan,' he says simply before flashing me a roguish wink and disappearing into the crowd.

Next, a couple steps forward, reminding me of Min, who there's still no sign of. A woman with the same pointed chin and small, pert mouth, together with her husband whose eyes are the perfect match for Min's. They're introduced as Lord and Lady Song.

Yet even as I smile at them more widely than I've smiled at the others, they only return cool, polite nods. I'm foolish for thinking they reminded me of her at all – they have none of her sparking warmth.

I lose count of how many more folk we receive, how many pretty speeches they make, as my head starts spinning.

Before the next one steps forward, the king bends closer. 'Haven't you eaten? I told Min to ensure you had breakfast.'

I blink up at him. Shit. The last thing I want to do is get Min in trouble – she's the only person here who's been friendly. 'I ate.'

'You're swaying.'

That would be weakness. And weakness means death. I try to hold myself still, strong, upright. 'It was a little while ago.'

'What do you want?' At my blank look, he huffs. 'To eat. Anything you desire.'

Anything?

Not an option I've been given before. Every day of my life I've existed on some combination of vegetables and fish, sometimes with bread, and at festivals and birthdays with rich, buttery pastry.

But I'd feel silly digging into a full meal in front of all these fae, whose stares are intensifying as this hushed conversation between us continues. I'm not sure why, but it would feel weak to eat a meal while they all stand there – an admission of my human frailty and all the silly, mortal needs that go along with that.

I need something I can nibble on. Something quick and easy.

The king's lips purse with building impatience.

'Biscuits,' I blurt.

When I was little, Annem and I would bake them, with her in charge of the huge rolling pin and me responsible for cutting out the little discs. She'd always let me eat one while they were fresh out of the oven, still piping hot. Later, when they'd cooled, they'd be crunchier, the lightly spiced flavour more pronounced and I'd get a whole new experience. Perhaps part of me is seeking something familiar.

We haven't had those in a long time.

I nod and say it again, more sombrely. The sugar will give me a temporary energy boost.

'Biscuits?' He says that one word flatly, and when I don't respond, he shakes his head, eyelids fluttering like he's trying not to roll his eyes. 'Very well.' He holds out his hand and a delicate glass plate appears covered in thin, round biscuits.

I open my mouth to thank him, then remember myself and snap it shut. Annem and Pa hammered good manners into me too thoroughly. Instead I incline my head and take one. It snaps between my teeth, perfectly crisp, and the sweet spice of brown sugar and ginger fills my mouth. A small sound escapes my throat. I can't help it. It might be the best thing I've ever eaten. Another small pleasure to squirrel away.

When I open my eyes – though I don't remember closing them – I find the king watching me, his eyebrows raised, lips barely parted.

How can he be so irritable when he lives in a world with food like this?

'They're incredible.' I grab another as he just watches, and that makes me wonder— 'Wait, have you even tried them?'

His mouth flattening is all the answer I need.

That is a tragedy. It sweeps me up in a sudden need to share something simple, something *human* with this imposing, *in*human King of Death and I find myself offering him the biscuit. 'You're missing out. This is the best thing I've ever put in my mouth.'

His lips twitch. '*Is* it, now? I can't decide if that's a sad reflection on your life or if the biscuits are just that good.'

My face grows hot, but I cock my head like I'm not embarrassed by the way he's twisted my words. 'Trust me. It's the biscuits.'

He holds my gaze a long while and suddenly I feel foolish. He's not just a king – he's the son of The Morrigan, a demi-god in his own right. He isn't about to start eating sweet treats in front of his subjects. There's probably some rule against it.

I pull my hand away – or at least I go to, but he captures my fingers. There's this faint shake of his head, gently admonishing me for withdrawing, then he takes the offered biscuit. 'They *do* seem to have pleased you.'

There's something surreal about watching him bow his crowned head and lift something so simple and unadorned to his lips. I can't look away as I take another biscuit for myself. His gaze has slipped to one side, but somehow he perfectly times his bite with mine.

The crunch is like an explosion in my mouth – in his, too, given away by his eyes widening. Next comes the buttery melt, spreading the ginger's heat, just this side of fiery. A soft breath leaves his nose as though he's melting, too.

Then comes my favourite part – the flood of heady pleasure from the sweetness. Slowly, slowly, his eyebrows lift, and when his eyes turn to mine, the pupils are wide.

He may not be human, but he is still a person, beguiled by baked goods just like the rest of us.

'Hmm?' I cock my head.

Taking a deep breath, he inclines his. '*Hmm.*'

How he's lived in the same world as these without ever eating one before is beyond me.

As he swallows, throat knotting, his attention on me is focused and hot, like the glowing point of a poker just pulled from the coals. I hold still, worried I've displeased him by breaking some rule I don't understand.

'You have . . .' With a crooked finger, he lifts my chin. It's surprisingly gentle, and yet my heart leaps knowing his hand is so close to my throat. I'm suddenly vulnerable, suddenly too close and at the same time there's this intimacy to his gaze on my mouth that's so unexpected, it stills me.

Softly, his thumb grazes my lower lip and lingers. The pad is soft, warm. A flush of pleasure runs through my nerves, chasing the earlier sugar rush. I wonder how it would feel if he pressed harder, if his fingers bit into my chin, clamped me in place, if he bent down and—

I suck in a breath, blinking away the thought. The wild, foolish thought.

But we're still held in this quiet moment, and maybe that's because I swear there's this slight softening of his gaze that says he feels this too. That right now, for however many seconds we linger here, we are merely people, not an unseelie king and the human who's been bargained away to him.

'*There*.' His tone is less sharp than usual, a caress that slides through my flesh as his physical touch retreats. 'Are you ready to continue?'

The fae. The whole room of them, here to congratulate us on our betrothal. Right. Yes.

And also, *no*. Not ready at all.

My eyelids flutter as I remember myself. My foolish, foolish self.

I may be stuck here for now, and they might have incredible biscuits and gorgeous people here, but I'm not staying. I'll enjoy whatever small pleasures I can find, but the first chance I get, I'm gone.

I nibble on the biscuits as we receive yet more of his subjects. My back and hips grow sore, so I have to shift my weight and try to subtly move and stretch without tipping over the little glass plate. Just as I'm wondering if I can ask for a seat without seeming weak, the thirteen red-haired fae who caught my eye earlier approach and bow.

'My royal guard, the Twylth,' Drystan offers by way of explanation. He's taken no more biscuits and stands with his back straight. 'This is the Baloran – their leader.'

The tallest somehow dwarfs Drystan and is twice as broad, at least. Face set in a stern look, he steps forward and thumps a fist to his chest. 'Threnn.' He doesn't so much as spare a glance for me.

One of the women comes forward and bows her head, right fist over her heart. 'And we are my lady's guard now, too.' Her eyebrows are lighter, the colour of driftwood, but her full lips have been daubed with the same crimson as her long hair, which is worn in a thick braid, with one side of her head shorn. 'I am Astrid, second in the Twylth, and I pledge to serve my future queen.'

Drystan nods approval as the others introduce themselves and mirror her gesture. It's only when she straightens her right arm that I realize the other ends just below the elbow.

I take a step forward before she backs off. 'May I ask . . .' I lick my lips, conscious of the need for manners while also consumed by the needs of my own curiosity. 'Your hair – the colour.' I glance at her companions, who, now I'm closer, look nothing like her beyond the hair. One has a long, narrow face. Another has broad cheekbones and a pointed chin. Astrid's complexion is amber brown, where the others range from as pale as my Pa to the same rich brown as the burnt umber paint in my brother's watercolour palette. 'I was going to ask if you're all related, but . . .'

She shares a look with Threnn. They laugh, and inwardly, I cringe at the group's mocking tone. Have I made a foolish mistake in the world of fae etiquette?

Drystan's expression betrays no reaction – not even amusement – and a moment later Astrid's laughter subsides to a warm grin, and she shakes her head. 'I can understand my lady's question. Tales of us maybe haven't made their way to the surface world. We are redcaps, His Majesty's warriors, and our hair is the same colour because we bathe it in the blood of our enemies.'

For a second, I think it's a joke. A way to shock and terrorize the human.

But only for a second.

Because no one is laughing.

Because that is exactly the kind of thing fae do in the stories.

And most of all, because that colour . . . it is the exact shade of freshly spilled blood – kept that way by some kind of fae magic. I have no doubt their corded arms and broad shoulders are for more than just show. They are beautiful lethality personified.

At my side, Drystan is still, his chin in the air, like a statue carved from ice.

'Well.' I nod like Astrid has just told me a fascinating story. How much blood is required to allow someone to wash their hair in it? That times thirteen fae. A tremor runs through me, and I try not to let the remaining biscuits rattle on the plate. 'That's . . . You're right, tales of your . . . *prowess* have not reached us.'

Drystan turns to me slowly, a sculpture waking, but his gaze remains flinty. 'Pray for your people they never experience it first-hand.' There's none of the earlier tease in his voice.

Our moment of warmth and intimacy from earlier is entirely gone. Instead, beside me stands the King of Death, cold and hard, a threat in his words.

This is the natural order of things, his tone says. A mouse quakes in the hawk's shadow. It knows its tiny, too-fast heart is made to be nothing more than a tasty morsel.

I should've known that even something as seemingly innocuous as a pretty colour would come with a deadly origin story. I may have shared a human moment with Drystan, but he and his people are *not* human. They have two eyes, a nose and mouth like us, their bodies are shaped like ours, but their beauty is not a thing to be enjoyed – it is a thing to be ensnared by.

I continue with the presentations more gravely. Not even more biscuits can cheer me up.

When no one remains to bow to us, Drystan lifts his chin and eyes me sidelong. 'You don't like it here.' It's clipped, matter of fact – not a question.

This realm is strange to me, disturbing even, but it's his home – one he's stuck in thanks to the unseelie's ancient banishment. From his behaviour, it's clear he's proud of his kingdom, his people. So I temper my response. 'My problem isn't Mordren. It's a magical place – far more so than the surface. I just want to go home.'

He wrinkles his nose. 'Why are you so desperate to return to that little hut and your treacherous family?'

'My father had no choice,' I blurt. 'He would've died if he hadn't . . .' I swallow and take a breath. If I can only make him see, maybe I can find some speck of pity in his cold heart. 'I need to get back to my brother. He's stayed at home, putting his life on hold for me. I need to tell him he can leave – *live*.'

The king sighs. 'I asked, and yet I find that I just don't care.'

First my mouth drops open – humans would at least pretend to give a damn – then irritation prickles over me, and I chew my tongue before it spits out something the fae would consider *most* impolite.

'Family is the first lie we're taught to believe.' His gaze drifts over the revelling fae. 'You should thank me for disabusing you of such a foolish notion.'

How can one man be so wrong? 'They love me,' I grit out.

He scoffs, all detached amusement and utter certainty.

My gods, I want to throttle him. 'Why am I not surprised that's a concept you don't understand?'

'The one who lacks understanding here is you. No understanding of the way either of our worlds work. And as you whine about wanting to go home, you do it with no understanding of how your mere existence has caused me more suffering than you can ever know.'

I can't reply. Did he just say all that so casually, so cruelly, without even looking at me? How can I have caused him suffering? I've barely been here a day.

My mind is still stumbling over the words when he sniffs and finally turns, spearing me with the full force of his intense gaze. 'Luckily for you and your terrible judgement, you're stuck here. You, a little nothing human, will be my queen and my bride. Whether you or I like it or not.'

9

THE NIGHT AFTER my presentation, the king appears in my
room without a sound. One minute I'm humming while I brush
my hair, then I look up and he's there like some prince of darkness,
arms crossed, leaning against the door frame.

I almost fall out of my chair. The hairbrush thuds to the floor.
'Bloody hells. Where did you come from?'

He raises one shoulder, and his expression doesn't change, but I
swear he's amused. 'Around. You looked so focused, I didn't want
to interrupt you.'

I fight the urge to glance towards the gilded mirror hanging
above the fireplace. Just as well he didn't walk in when I was tucking my notebook in the recessed back of the frame. If he'd walked
in half an hour ago, he'd have caught me. And if he'd walked in
ten minutes before that, he'd have found me writing up everything
I've seen and learned about the Underworld and the unseelie.
Something in there will help me escape. I'm sure of it.

Trying to sound more irritated than worried, I narrow my eyes
at him. 'You could've knocked.'

'I could've. Come. You should learn the layout of Rigor Gard.'

I pause in my retrieval of the hairbrush and peer up. 'You mean I'm not confined to my room?'

'Do you want to be?'

This room is almost the same size as our entire cottage, so it's not like my world would become much smaller if I was forced to stay in here. 'I assumed I was only allowed out when . . . required.'

'Like a hunting hound?' He cocks his head, eyes narrowed in this way that makes me intensely uncomfortable. 'Do you want to be treated like a hunting hound? I could put a little collar on you, if you like. Others do that with their humans. If it's what you want . . .'

'That won't be necessary.' My knees are stiff as I rise, but I plaster a smile over the pain. 'So you're going to give me the full tour? And then I'll be allowed to go wherever I want?'

'Within the fortress. And within reason.'

'And the gardens?' I glance out the window, where braziers battle the night.

He holds the door open, mouth twisting like he's making a decision. 'If you're accompanied. I'll have some warm clothing brought to you.'

I'll take it. Cold as it is here, my chest yearns for fresh air. At home, I work in the garden every day I can, as weather and sickness allow.

A pair of the Twylth wait outside and trail us at a distance as we set off.

His suite is near mine. He shows me the doors but doesn't open them. I suspect it's considerably larger, but how does a King of Death decorate his space? So far, I've been disappointed by the lack of skull decor and taxidermy, so maybe he keeps all that in his rooms.

Technically the fortress is all his, but surely his rooms are his private sanctuary. Somewhere he can be himself rather than *His*

Majesty the King. Then again, that would require him to have a personality, and I'm not sure insufferable counts as one.

He explains that the Vost is the steward, responsible for Rigor Gard's staff and upkeep. They do an excellent job, as I don't see a speck of dust or a curtain pleat out of place as we tour a library, various lounges and an armoury that I'm not allowed to enter. That's the limit of 'within reason.' It's not like I can wield any of the weapons in there, but the idea I could possibly be a danger is charming.

My favourite, though, is the heated glasshouse where they grow spindly crops and a fountain trickles into a wide pool. Between the more practical plants a few flowers bloom, and I catch the occasional hum of bees drifting among them.

I look up from a marigold whose colour is a somewhat ridiculous contrast with the king's monochrome appearance. 'Are these *all* your crops?'

His expression doesn't change, but his whole body stiffens. 'Aside from the fields of wheat you see outside.' He gestures with an overdramatic flourish then spears me with a look that says I asked a stupid question.

I bite back a retort and give him an ironic smile instead. 'Where next?' I'll come back to the glasshouse when I have better company. Or *no* company – that would be better than his.

He shows me a grand dining hall that looks large enough to fit all the fae from my presentation. A single long table stretches along its length. As I wander between it and the glazed doors leading on to a snowy terrace, I wonder how much the plethora of gilded candelabra are worth, how old they are, who made them. A close look reveals the slender filigree isn't just a pleasing but slightly unsettling arrangement of organic abstract shapes, but actually tiny bones – femurs and tibias bundled around spines form the main uprights, pelvises join the arms arching out and each candle is held in an inverted skull.

I'm smirking to myself, thinking this is much more the kind of decor I'd expect from the King of Death when Drystan speaks. 'Do you have magic?'

I blink up from the candlesticks, his voice still echoing through the room. 'No.'

He nods once with a soft sound of acknowledgement. The casualness of the gesture is belied by his eyes narrowing as they stay on me for several beats before he turns to the door. 'Come.'

I hurry to catch up. 'Now you've asked me a question, do I get to ask you one?'

'You just have.'

'A real one. It sounds like this kind of exchange is how your world works.' I resist the urge to add 'right?' at the end of the sentence – no doubt he'd count that as a question too. 'Can you tell me exactly what was stated in the bargain our parents made?'

He gives me a sidelong look. 'Searching for a loophole? Trust me, I've tried.'

Fine, so I wasn't subtle about it. 'I'd still like to know.'

'They agreed I would take you away to become my bride. I keep bargains made in my name, however inconvenient.'

'I thought unseelie were meant to be polite,' I mutter.

He pretends not to hear, but his nostrils twitch. We go on in silence for several minutes as I turn over the phrasing in my mind.

I'm summoned from my thoughts by a low, sceptical hum coming from his throat. 'Did your parents really keep you locked in that house without ever telling you about the bargain?' His frown tells me how unlikely it seems.

I can't blame him for thinking it. Staying within an iron-bound wall because I was trying not to become known to the fae would make perfect sense. But if I didn't know they were after me – well, why the hells would I stay at home?

'Mm.' I shrug, conscious of his attention and the need to keep my secret. 'I wasn't locked in. I just don't go out much.'

His gaze sticks to me even as I look away and I search for a way to change the subject. We pass the corridor leading to the great hall, the sounds of revelry drifting down it, carried on rippling shadows.

Pausing, I seize the opportunity. 'So I noticed the shadows here seem different from back home. They aren't just an absence of light, they . . . It's like they have minds of their own, but they're not logical,' I add as shadows tumble into each other, spilling across the floor. 'It's all instinct.'

He stands at my side, arms folded as he joins me watching the dark shapes swarm and spread before dissipating under the wall sconces' light. 'You're observant. Sometimes they whisper, too.'

That makes me swallow. What might they whisper in his ear? Things they've seen? Hundreds . . . thousands of little spies for the unseelie king. Is this place making me paranoid? Am I right to be?

'Some think they're mine to control, but they've always been here and they certainly aren't mine. Not at all.' The cadence of his voice slows and I wonder if he realizes he's thinking out loud. 'The original inhabitants of this place, perhaps . . . or all that's left of the dead who linger too long.'

I frown as a pool of darkness reaches us having somehow dodged all the light to get here. It spills from his feet to mine as if sampling us. After a few seconds, it splits, both parts gathering closer as though drawn to the living flesh contained within our shoes. I back away, afraid it's going to crawl into my slippers.

Still, I can't help feeling sorry for the shadows, if they are what he says, and I find myself murmuring, 'Shades of what they were, whipped into frenzies by feeling.'

'Such a poetic way to think of something so sad.'

'There's usually some other way to look at even the saddest things. When you live your life locked in your home, pitied as someone else's "sad thing", you learn to use a different lens – to see differently. The life in the rot. The beauty in death.'

Now I'm the one who realizes I'm thinking out loud. And the way the king looks at me, all thoughtful and curious, I instantly regret it. I've strayed too close to the truth.

Swallowing, I motion ahead. 'Shall we continue?'

In silence, he leads the way and a short while later he gestures down a corridor. 'The kitchens are down there.'

'Is that where they make the biscuits?' My steps lag.

One side of his mouth quirks as he pauses, studying me. 'It is. You enjoyed those, didn't you?'

'You tried them too – you can't deny how good they are.'

He exhales what's almost a laugh and bows his head. 'I cannot. Perhaps you'll also enjoy this.' With that, he turns and leads the way along a corridor we haven't taken yet.

So many corridors. How do people live in such a massive building? Annem and Pa's bedroom goes straight off the living room at home, and there's only a small landing at the top of the staircase with my room and Lowen's leading off. It's unfathomable to me that people keep track of all these doors and hallways.

But Drystan never hesitates as he leads me through them until we reach a spiral staircase. My thighs groan in anticipation, but I give him a bright smile when he glances back and dismisses the guards before starting his ascent.

At first, it isn't too bad. Then I'm reminded of how little I move around nowadays as my heart drums harder and harder and my lungs drag in sharper breaths. I lean on the wall, grimacing as my thighs make good on their earlier promise of pain. Still going, I lose sight of Drystan's well-tailored back.

When I reach the top, clammy and gasping for air, there's no sign of him, just a door. As soon as I step through, the wind blasts me, chilling my sweaty skin and whipping hair into my eyes, but I see enough to understand I'm at the top of a tower. Curious, I approach the crenellated wall and try to tame my hair so I can take in the view beyond the white-clad rooftops of the buildings huddled within the fortress walls.

A moment later, the wind stops and I can catch my breath without it being stolen by the icy air.

'This is Mordren,' Drystan says from behind me, blocking the wind.

I push the hair from my eyes and take in my first glimpse of the world beyond the fortress walls.

To left and right, chasms drop away into an unfathomable darkness I can't see through. I wonder if even fae eyes, able to see at night, are able to penetrate it. Behind us, sheer rock rises into a forbidding mountain range. No escape in that direction.

And ahead, snow shrouds everything, from the walls, down the narrow stone causeway leading from the gates to the plain lying beyond. It coats the dark tree trunks, and clumps at the edge of an icy-blue ribbon that carves through the land – a frozen river.

There isn't a single spot of green. The Underworld must be in the depths of winter. I bite back a sigh.

I don't necessarily have a problem with the land, it's more the cold. Already my wrists are achy and experience tells me my knees will soon follow. At least if there were signs of spring below, I'd have the reassurance that this weather won't last.

Not that I plan to stay here long enough for it to matter. I have to keep reminding myself of that. The king might think this is all set in stone, but I'm less sure about the bargain. If there's one thing I've learned from the old stories it's that there are always loopholes. Always.

Something moves on the plains. Deer, weathering the cold? I squint and lean over the battlements.

Drystan's presence at my back shifts. 'The River Arawn,' he says in my ear, breath shockingly hot compared to the chill air. 'It once cut us off from the plains where the dead roam. Now we have only our walls.'

My mouth drops open. Not deer. Too upright. And his words –
is he trying to reassure me? 'You mean . . . they're the dead?'

'What did you expect from the Underworld?' He sounds
amused, then his hand closes on my shoulder, while the other points
ahead and his face appears alongside mine. 'They pass through here
on their journey to the Next Place. You see their paths?'

The figures move slowly, dark shapes against the snow, but they
make steady progress in the same direction. Light grey tracks cut
through the white landscape. 'I see them.'

He lowers his hands and we watch for a while. I have to admit,
it's kind of beautiful in an unearthly way. This world has a bright,
silvery moon not unlike our own, though when I look up at it, my
stomach drops in surprise. This moon's craters form patterns I'm
not used to. Similar, but not the same, casting this chilly world in
ethereal light.

I find my gaze tracing the paths of the dead, counting the figures
I spot. Ten. Eleven. Twelve. A constant stream of death. One day
I'll just be another one passing by. Unremarkable and unmarked.

How bloody gloomy.

I grit my teeth, not only because of the cold, and square my
shoulders. I won't be unmarked. I will be home with the people
who love me, and that's enough.

I squint to the left, where the paths disappear into the distance.
'How do they get here?'

'By . . . dying?'

'But I mean . . . are their bodies here? They must be solid to
leave prints in the snow. But people don't disappear when they die.
Unless they—'

'Their souls come here, where they become solid.'

'Hm.'

'Some get lost or linger, wanting to stay. Sometimes they become
dangerous. Sometimes they're just . . . sad.'

I frown out at a knot of figures gathered together. 'I suppose they have left behind everyone they know.'

This time he makes the thoughtful sound but gives no sardonic response.

He's different from last night. I put it down to the fact we're alone, so he isn't playing the part of the king.

As I scan further and further into the distance, I realize I was wrong earlier. Snow doesn't cover *everything* – a strip of grey lies beyond it . . . and a smear of green, too. 'What's over there?' I point out the blurring horizon, where there seems to be a building. 'Is that another fortress?'

I don't realize how close he's been standing, the warmth that's been leaching across from him to me, until now when it fades. I feel him stiffening – a subtle shift in the air like the heaviness before a storm.

'That's my brother's realm.'

That cuts short our tour and seems to cut out his tongue, because he says nothing more as he escorts me to my room, with one of the Twylth stationed outside the door. Another person to watch me. That will be a problem for my inevitable escape attempt.

But I'm kind of glad there's to be no more walking tonight, because my thighs and backside are sore from climbing the stairs, and the cold has ground my bones to dust – at least that's how it feels.

Yet I can't help wondering why his kingdom is frozen and stark while his brother's has been spared this deep, dark winter.

10

FASCINATING AS THE tour is, I'm not staying in the Underworld. So I update my notebook with everything I can remember
about the fortress's layout and doze in my room until sunrise when
the place quietens. I pack up the food that was brought to me for
dinner, securing it in jars I've cleaned out from the bathroom.
There are no large bags, so I use a pillowcase to carry a blanket,
the food and a bottle of water.

The clothing is a little more difficult. It's not exactly practical
and the warm clothes the king mentioned haven't arrived yet.
But digging through the drawers, I manage to find a stash of see-
through shirts that I layer and fine woollen leggings that look
suspiciously like the ones I've seen back home, and a pair of leather trousers. Hopefully it's enough to keep out the cold. Sturdy
leather boots fit over doubled-up socks. For good measure, I set
out a fitted coat and a pale-grey cloak that might blend with the
snowy landscape, but don't put them on. Not yet.

I throw a dressing robe over my outfit and hold my breath when

I reach the door. If it's locked, my plan could be over before I've even started. Admittedly, it's a fairly basic plan.

But when I turn the door handle, it opens.

There's still one more obstacle, though. In the form of Astrid standing guard in the corridor. I bite back a sigh of relief when I see it's her – I get the impression she's most likely to be sympathetic.

It's the middle of the night for her yet her attention snaps to me at once. 'My lady?'

I tug on my robe and bow my head as if embarrassed. 'I – uh . . . I'm not sure if fae have this, but human women . . . bleed?' Not me. I haven't in years. But she doesn't know that.

'You . . . Oh! Once a month?' When I nod, she goes on. 'I've heard of that. Seems inconvenient.'

I huff a laugh. 'You have no idea. It's just . . . usually we have rags or sea sponge to . . .' I gesture vaguely, glancing up to find her looking at me with curiosity.

'Oh, right. Inconvenient *and* messy.' She nods thoughtfully.

Not getting the hint. 'Could you . . . get me some?'

She glances along the quiet corridor as if weighing up the risk to my safety. There's a pang of guilt in my stomach, like a phantom cramp for the bleed I don't have. I was so focused on escape, I didn't consider my success could get her into trouble.

But I have to get back to my family and especially to Lowen. I should've told him the moment I understood why he stayed. The guilt of keeping him at home, even if it's in the hope I return, will be a much worse pain to bear than any cramp.

So I give Astrid a rueful smile and when she nods, I hold my excitement in.

'I think I know where I can get some sponge for you and rags – whatever you need. I'll be right back.'

As she disappears down the corridor, I wave and retreat into my room. The dressing robe comes off. The coat and cloak go on.

With the pillowcase-cum-sack over my shoulder, I slip into the empty corridor.

Step one, complete.

I pass through the fortress, thinking back to my arrival and the king's tour. I've gone over my notes enough times that I don't need to consult the notebook in my pocket. Not a single soul passes me – not a corporeal one, anyway. Shadows slip by and around corners, and I hurry my pace. I'm not taking any chances in case they're spying for the king – if they whisper in his ear and bring him back here, I'll be long gone.

After hitting a dead end in my search for an exit, I eventually reach the door to the kitchens. We didn't enter them on my tour, but I'm counting on the layout being the same as on the surface. Annem used to work in the kitchens of a grand house when I was a little girl. She would borrow books from the library for me, and a few times, I even went with her. The first time I collapsed from one of my episodes, she stopped so she could stay home with me.

But that bustling kitchen is still fresh in my mind. As is the separate entrance it had to allow for all the comings and goings of staff and deliveries.

Inside, warmth still radiates from the huge ovens. The familiar scent of herbs and recent cooking eases my shoulders.

I can do this.

No sooner have I nodded to myself, than my breath catches.

Movement. Someone's here.

If those shadows have told Drystan . . .

Then my eyes adjust to the dim glow from the ovens and I see it's not the king, but a girl, curled up in a low bed. She hugs a lumpy green toy closely – I can't work out what it's meant to be. A frog, perhaps?

Frozen, I hold my breath.

She smacks her lips and nestles into the cuddly frog.

Sound asleep.

One hand braced on the counter top that dominates the centre of the kitchen, I creep by. Because ahead there's a hefty, bolted door, and I'm willing to bet my remaining supply of tablets it leads outside.

There's a jar of the ginger biscuits on a shelf and I can't help pocketing a handful before I pause at the door. With a glance back, I reassure myself the girl is still asleep and no one has followed me. Dark shapes gather at the oven doors as though curious about the orange glow within. But they aren't sauntering off to tell the king about my nighttime jaunt and there's no one else here.

Shoulders squared, I ease the bolt from its keep and open the door.

The ice snatches my breath and pulls on my hair, forcing me to rush outside and push the door shut before the blast of wind wakes the girl.

I stand there, leaning against it, squinting while my eyes adjust to the bright daylight.

Step two – I've escaped the fortress.

Now to tackle the Underworld itself.

The light here is strange and cold, carving harsh lines in the snow-clad landscape. A snowbank heaps against the inside of the fortress walls. Someone's cleared a path from the kitchen door. It seems logical this would lead to a gate . . . but what if it's guarded?

This is where my plan could fall apart.

I'm no fighter. The cold is already making my limbs stiff, and I can *feel* the clumsiness setting in – sneaking isn't much of an option. Besides, fae are known for their keen senses. I doubt the most dextrous human could sneak past them.

But I have to try. And who knows? Maybe there will be no guards at the gate. After all, who would dare attack the King of Death in his own fortress?

I grimace and push into the brisk wind. At least the cleared path won't reveal my footprints. And at least it isn't snowing.

I cling on to those small mercies as I work my way through the frozen gardens. There's a flicker of something overhead and out the corner of my eye, I think I see one of the ravens that accompany the king everywhere. But when I turn, there's no sign of life, save for the bare-branched trees. Huddled against the building are shrubs not covered in snow, but with leaves and pink petals encased in ice. I peer closer. Double flowers and waxy dark green leaves. Camellias.

But camellias flower in spring – their blooms should've fallen months before winter closed in.

Still, I don't have time to linger on that puzzle, however intriguing. I forge onward along the path and after a few turns I'm rewarded.

The fortress gates.

And the gods smile upon me because there isn't a single guard.

I could crow with delight.

Biting back a grin, I throw a triumphant glance over my shoulder.

I'm already taking a step towards the gate as I register the terror flooding me, colder than the snow just starting to fall.

I blink at the gate. At freedom. But my mind trips over what I thought I saw over my shoulder. What I pray was just the product of an overactive imagination and shapes in the snow.

Slowly, slowly, I turn back.

In hazy silhouette, there's a rider. I stare, piecing together features as they drift in and out of focus, blocked by falling snowflakes one moment, clear the next. A spiked helm. His mount's great, branching antlers.

The wind gusts, clearing the flurry, and the grey mass behind him emerges. A dozen more riders. Horses and stags, skeletal with impossible breaths somehow steaming in the cold.

I can't see his eyes. I can't see any of their eyes.

But I know they see me.

It's a shriek in my bones, telling me both to run and that it's pointless.

Because I will never escape. Because this is the Wild Hunt.

I haven't even finished the thought when my legs burst into movement and I'm running.

I haven't done this in years. There's a surreal kind of joy that my body remembers how, but the clamour of my heart throbs through my entire being.

Run. Run. Run.

I obey. My breaths burn. My muscles groan. I won't be able to keep this up for long.

Somehow, over the rushing, thundering sounds of my own body, I hear it.

Haunting howls breaking the day's cold quiet. White hounds emerge from the snow, eyes glowing with feral fire as they lock on me.

Undead and untiring, the Wild Hunt come each month. We shut up the doors and windows and close the curtains – anyone they catch sight of becomes their quarry. And they will chase a soul to the ends of the earth.

Every child knows it. We have nursery rhymes that warn us about the new moon. But here they are in the Underworld's cold daylight, chasing *me*.

Just as I try to push harder, my steps grow clumsier and exhaustion sets in, heavier than the burst of energy trying to flood me. My heartbeats blur together, choking, drowning, a terrified buzz that shakes my entire body.

Still, I try to run.

Please – *please*. I beg my body.

Ahead, the gate looms. Eyes fixed on it, I run. Jog. Stumble. Try to bite back whimpers.

The hooves of their mounts thunder through the ground, closer, louder.

They ride me down without effort. One grabs the back of my cloak, bony fingers biting through my clothes, and suddenly I'm running in midair.

I don't have the breath to shout, 'No.' It's just a gasping plea before I'm slung over a saddle and every hope in me dies.

11

SNOW RUSHES BY, thrown up by churning hooves. I'm too exhausted to lift my head to see where we're going. Since the Wild Hunt have hold of me, I'm not sure it matters. They take the souls. I never thought to ask where.

A nagging reminder snakes through the aching cold and prods me. You can't give up, Rhiannon. You can't die here.

I groan because that bloody survival instinct is right. I swore to myself that when I die, it will be at home with the people I care about. Not alone. Not like this.

I try to wriggle off the saddle, but the rider's bony hand presses into my back. After running, my body has no strength to resist.

There has to be a way to escape. Has to be. I haven't struggled all this time, held on, searched for a cure, just to die alone in the Underworld.

Maybe, if I slump and pretend to be compliant, they'll loosen their grip and the short rest will let me gather my energy.

But before I have a chance, they draw to a halt. With an iron grip, I'm pulled from the saddle and dropped to my feet. The sudden weight makes my knees crumple.

I'm not sure what I expected of the Wild Hunt, but it definitely wasn't delivering me to the fortress's towering main entrance.

And certainly not to the awaiting glower of the king.

Arms folded, flanked by Threnn and Astrid, he stands at the top of the stairs. The look he gives me could crack bone. The look Astrid gives me could crack my heart.

A harsh croak saws through the air, and I spot his three ravens perched on the high arches of the fortress windows. I could swear they sound amused. That flash of something I saw out the corner of my eye – it was one of them, wasn't it? And they told the king. To think I was worried about the shadows – his ravens are the real spies.

From behind me, a rasping voice speaks in a language that makes my nerves itch. I can't make out a single word, and I don't think I could replicate half the sounds they make. I glance over my shoulder to confirm it, just in case someone else has appeared, but yes, the Wild Hunt can speak. And apparently, they can deliver me to Drystan, too. The stories make them sound like mindless hunters, only capable of chasing down their prey.

The king nods as the rider who carried me finishes and bows in the saddle.

'Your service is appreciated, as always.' He takes his time descending the steps, a cold curve to his lips. 'I will handle things from here. I'm sure my future wife must be suffering from some sort of *confusion*.' That last word is gritted out as he stops before me.

'Why didn't you—?'

He silences me with a look. 'Leave us.'

The Twylth disappear inside and there's the creak and crunch of snow as the Wild Hunt turn and ride away. The king holds out his hand. I consider rising without his help, but my thighs have started cramping and I'm struggling to take full breaths.

So I take his hand, let him jerk me to my feet without effort and hobble along at his side as he silently leads me into the fortress. His grip on my arm is like iron.

When we reach my room, the look he gives me is harder, colder than that forbidden metal. 'What were you thinking? That you could run home?'

I'm so exhausted, I just want to crawl into bed, damp clothes and all. Instead, I settle for flopping into an armchair, letting its sides cradle me upright. 'The dead have to get here somehow, don't they? I was going to follow their trail back and . . .' I hate how weak it sounds now I say it out loud. It makes me leave out the part where I was counting on whatever magic guards the door between worlds knowing that I'm not a banished unseelie and letting me pass. 'I belong on the surface. I'm still alive.'

Just, my mind adds. But, no, I have years yet. As long as my heart holds out.

He strides closer, and I think he's going to shout, but instead he looms over me, fingers pressed to his chest. 'And you think I'm not?'

'You don't act like it.' I don't mean to blurt it, but I'm clearly too tired to be sensible.

It's not like I'm wrong. He might as well be made of ice. His people are so lively, laughing and dancing, even if they're cruel. Yet he has a life and doesn't seem interested in living it.

He glares at me a long while before he finally works his jaw from side to side. 'What was the first rule I told you?'

'Your word is law?'

'And you will obey it as such. You will *not* question me. I don't give a damn if you agree or not, but you will not ever question me, especially in front of others.'

So he's more concerned with appearances than the fact I don't want to be here or, in his words, nearly got myself killed? Jaw tight, I glare back at him.

'Have I made myself clear?'

'Abundantly.'

Huffing, he shakes his head and turns away, muttering, 'There are worse things in this world than the Wild Hunt.' He pauses at the door, holding the handle, and pierces me with a look over his shoulder. 'They saved your damn life. Didn't you wonder why we have such high walls?'

'Perhaps if you'd explained—'

But he's gone before I can even finish my sentence. It's all I can do to stagger to bed, crawl under the covers and groan into the mattress as my head rings hollowly.

Following my escape attempt, I'm kept locked in my room with one of the Twylth stationed at the door – never Astrid. It's clearly meant to be a punishment, but it's a relief. I'm fucking exhausted. Bone deep. Bone heavy. Bone weary in a way I haven't experienced for years.

I sleep most of the next day and night, and use what little energy I have to pore over my notebook, which has mercifully remained hidden. I'll come up with another plan – something that plays to my strengths, unlike running away.

For some reason, even though her services as the royal sartor aren't required, Min comes to my room the next two evenings. The king must've sent her to keep an eye on me. Perhaps he hopes I'll believe she's a friend and confide any future plans for escape. Between the ravens, the shadows and Min, he has spies everywhere, while I only have a notebook.

On the second night, she runs me a bath and helps me into it before setting a plate of those thin ginger biscuits down on a table next to me, followed by an object that makes my breath catch.

My medicine bottle.

There's a crease between her eyebrows as she tilts her head. 'This exhaustion isn't just down to your escape attempt or missing your family, is it? Something's wrong.'

I curl around my knees, staring at the bubbles like they might pop and reveal a convincing lie. I'm not sure there is one, but I have to try. 'I'm fine. I just tired myself out running, and I'm not exactly thrilled about being locked up. And they're just to stop me getting pregnant.'

She barks a laugh. 'Don't insult my intelligence. Who are you fucking to need to worry about pregnancy? No one comes here but me and the king, and you don't smell of him.'

'Back home. I—'

'They're nothing to do with pregnancy. No, I've seen how you look beneath the makeup and clothes. I saw how you nearly cried when you saw yourself in the mirror. You're *ill*.'

Shit.

No lie is going to work here. I press my lips together.

Long moments pass.

'Tell me the truth,' she says so gently, my gaze darts to her, 'and no one will hear it from me.' There's a softness in her eyes I haven't seen before. It tugs on me.

Fae can't lie. Deceit yes, but no direct lies. 'You promise?'

'By ash and blood, I promise I won't breathe a word.'

I exhale, blowing a little frothy cloud off the bubbly top of the bath.

'I *am* ill,' I murmur. It's been a long time since I've had to tell anyone that. Annem, Pa, Lowen, everyone in the village – they've known for years. Saying it feels strange, like explaining to someone that the sky is blue. 'It can't be fixed, but the tablets help.'

'Shit.' That's all she says and the quiet that follows is maddening. It might last an hour or only seconds.

Or maybe it's the question in my mind that's truly maddening. 'That's the kind of weakness that's dangerous here, isn't it?'

She makes a soft sound, thoughtful, confirming.

Squeezing my knees until my fingers leave white marks, I finally look up.

Her lips twist, and I hang on that tension. She exhales, and it's like an apology. 'Annon. What you need to understand is that this place is not just dangerous physically, but socially. If you're weak, you can't protect yourself in the games of court, in the bids for power. It is despised.'

How she must despise me.

'And imperfection is an outer marker of weakness. Just as despised.' She traces the crescent scar on her cheek. 'Through the king and those in favour who are allowed to use my services, I dictate what is in fashion, what the highest of his court wear. My taste determines what is considered beautiful. I've even had other kingdoms try to tempt me to join them. But I am . . . outside. Thanks to this.' She taps the scar now, and I understand – part of it, at least.

'An imperfection.'

'A weakness.' Her mouth curves slowly into a smile that only makes her look sadder. The skin around her scar crinkles.

Such a small thing. A silvery-pink arc of smooth skin. That's all it is.

'So you see' – she inclines her head – 'I have all the reason in the world to keep your secret.'

The relief breaks over me, and I lie back. Finally, the bath's warmth seeps into me.

I may not have a friend here, but she's an ally in this, at least.

The bright thought stays with me as I spend the night pondering another escape. Something smarter that doesn't involve running.

The king isn't going to send me back. He may not like the idea of a human wife, but he seems set on going through with it – living by the word of the bargain that was made, following the rules set out by his mother.

The rules . . .

And that's how a new plan starts to form.

12

MAYBE THE KING senses I'm hatching something, because Threnn appears at my door later that night with a message from His Majesty. 'Wear this.' He pushes a box into my hands, a stern look on his face like he takes his king's orders very seriously. 'Be ready to leave in ten minutes.'

'Ready to leave? For—?'

Before I can finish the question, he's returned to his post guarding my room.

My stomach flutters at the word 'leave,' though. As in – to go home? Almost certainly not, yet I can't help hoping.

The contents of the box give no hints. A set of warm clothes and fur-lined boots, which I change into quickly, one eye on the time.

The instant the clock ticks to ten minutes later, the king himself arrives. He's wearing black – shocking. Though he isn't dressed nearly as warmly as I am, with just a shirt beneath the same long, fitted coat he wore the night he took me. A pale sliver of flesh peeks out where the top buttons are undone. I suppose he must be used to his kingdom's temperature – it's as cold as he is.

He casts a judgemental glance over me and makes a faint sound of acknowledgement before turning on his heel with the clipped order to 'come'.

He joked about me being a hunting dog before. Maybe he means to treat me like one.

I grit my teeth and follow. This isn't for long. I'll do my best not to murder him. Although . . . If I do, that would surely mean I'm no longer obliged to stay here and marry him. Something to consider, if all else fails.

'What are you smirking about?' He peers at me out of the corner of his eye.

'Oh, nothing.' I smile back brightly, even though I know killing a fae is no easy feat – and considering this one is a demi-god, running from the Wild Hunt would probably be easier. Still, a woman needs her fantasies.

He guards his expression well, but I'm sure I catch the slightest thinning of his lips, and that keeps my smile in place all the way outside. Waiting for us at the same doors where the Wild Hunt delivered me mere days ago, are two horses.

At least I think they are. Since we ride sabrecats in Albion, I've only ever seen them illustrated in books – aside from the Wild Hunt's skeletal steeds. One looks a lot like the drawings, though its white fur with brown flecks has a metallic sheen that seems . . . unnatural. I've never seen an animal or a pelt like that before.

And the other horse?

That's what really gives me pause. A mare as pale as the king, her violet eyes glow with unearthly light. She paws the ground, and at first I think she's just kicking up snow, but as she prances with impatience, I realize it's vapour hazing around her bone-white hooves.

'In case you're tempted to try another performance like the other day, I've decided to take your education into my own hands.' The king approaches the mare, who settles. 'You will see why we have these walls and why you should be grateful for them.' He mounts in an instant, elegant, efficient, then jerks his chin towards the other horse.

I stare. He expects me to ride it. I've never even ridden a sabre-cat before. I'm not sure where to start. What if it runs away while I'm trying to get on its back?

This harsh sound comes from the king, irritation clear in its serrated edges. 'You can't ride.' His voice is flat. 'Of course you can't.'

I don't see him give any signal, but his horse walks towards me and before I can back away, the king grabs the scruff of my coat and hauls me on to the saddle before him.

At least he doesn't throw me over it like the Wild Hunt did. I'm sitting upright across the saddle, one leg dangling awkwardly, the other one even more awkwardly caught on his thigh. 'Uh.' Trying to rectify that, I shift, slip on the smooth leather saddle, yelp and am caught by an unsmiling king all in one graceless movement. How did he make it look so damn easy?

'Put your leg over the horse,' he bites out, right in my ear.

Grimacing as I discover muscles that still ache from my attempt to run away, I obey and swing my leg up and forward over the horse's neck. Thankfully, the creature lowers her head, so I avoid kicking her – barely.

Again, I don't catch the signal, but the horse sets off, apparently unbothered by the extra passenger, and we leave the other mount behind.

I slip again as we follow the path around a bend, and with a *tut* the king fastens his arm around my waist, clamping me to him. I try not to find relief in the way that, despite his demeanour, he is warm against my back.

His body hums with tension – the same irritation I heard in his voice – which also travels through his unyielding grip.

Reaching the fortress gates is a welcome distraction. I haven't left the walls since my arrival. I'm sure he intends for this to be a punishment – no doubt I'll see something horrible in the kingdom beyond – but I can't help my curiosity. What creatures live down here? Will we see some of those wandering dead I spotted from the tower? Are there pockets of life and growing plants among the snow, too small to detect from a distance?

First, we face the cold, dark shadow of the wall. It's thicker than I realized – fifteen feet at least – and by the time we emerge into the moonlight, I'm chilled to the bone.

Ahead, a narrow causeway leads from the gates, its dark surface cleared of snow. By the time we reach the ground, I'm getting used to the sway as the horse walks, working out how to absorb that with my hips, and that's when we *go*.

The horse surges forward. Wind whistles in my ears. That swaying is but a distant memory as my bones are jolted almost out of their sockets. I cling to the first thing I find – the poor horse's icy mane. The king's hold around my waist tightens, merciless. His fingers bite into my hip.

I can't tell what's my heartbeat and what's the pounding of hooves eating up the ground as we hurtle across the plain. My eyes water so much I can't make out much of our surroundings, and my focus is on trying to slow my breaths in a desperate attempt to stop my heart speeding any further.

'You're not going to fall,' he mutters in my ear. 'Stop fighting and lean into me.'

That's when I realize I'm bouncing with every stride, knees drawn up and halfway into a ball.

I count to six on my inhale, forcing it slower, steadier, but the next bump blasts out my exhale. It's unnatural to try to relax while moving at such speed, but I'll try anything to make this less miserable for all involved. Much as I don't care about Drystan's misery, I'm sure carrying a jolting, panicked human isn't fun for the horse.

Gradually, I manage to loosen my taut muscles. My thighs lower, finding his right behind them. I sit a little more upright, back pressing into his chest. He curls around me, a framework, and as I lean into him, I feel the way he moves with the horse's gait – something akin to the earlier movement of my hips, but more rolling. I don't find the rhythm perfectly, but I'm certainly being jolted around less and can control my breathing.

I even dare to look up.

What I thought was a flat plain is actually gentle hills, so low they disappear from the tower's height.

Snow smothers everything. The trees show no sign of life. I don't see a single living thing. Not even a paw print.

The mare slows, and I think I catch a slight shift in his hand on the reins this time.

'There.' He gestures and turns us.

Not to see a living thing. No. Not in the Underworld.

Just ahead, the dead walk.

'We're glamoured,' the king murmurs in my ear, hot in this icy air. 'They can't see us. They can hear though, so keep quiet.'

Swallowing, I nod.

Some amble along, lips moving like they're muttering or maybe even singing to themselves – a chant to keep going. Their gestures are normal. Their faces like mine or every other person I've met upon the surface. They glance at their surroundings, but it's like they see straight through us as their eyes sweep right past.

Most walk onward, hollow gazes fixed ahead.

Then there are those who pause and peer at us in faint interest as though they sense the glamour, even if they can't see through it. Others narrow their eyes and start in our direction.

We don't stop for long, riding on as soon as they approach.

What he told me on the tower is right, though: they don't look anything like the corporeal dead he raised to attack our home. These just look like normal people, albeit with half the colour leached out.

His grip around my waist has loosened, though I don't realize until his chest presses into my back as though he's drawn in a quick breath. 'Quiet,' he breathes in my ear as he draws the mare to a halt.

His voice tickles, but it's his tone that makes me shiver.

He holds utterly still behind me, mouth at my ear, every muscle held in perfect focus.

I hold my breath. Even the mare is frozen, attention straining ahead.

There stands something monstrous. Shambling. Scraping at the snow. Its body is flat, stretched between six limbs that look more like tentacles than human legs. At the front, its form peaks into a domed head with flat, grey eyes at the centre of an otherwise featureless face. Below spreads another pair of limbs, these two flattened like fins. As it digs, long claws glint in the moonlight.

With a subtle nudge of the reins upon the mare's neck, he signals for her to back away several strides. 'It searches for life,' the king murmurs once we're further from the creature. 'It only knows the cold of death, but it has a terrible yearning. For warmth. For life. For the shadows of what it once knew.'

The sight of the thing has the cold of death eating into me. I try not to shiver, but it's a doomed battle. 'What is it?'

'Now? An abomination with no name. You'd be better asking what it once was. One of the dead, seeking the path through, just like those we've already seen. But one of my kin, like me and not, chanced upon it, a lost soul, and whispered in its ear that it was found. That it had been *chosen*.'

A tiny trickle of warmth runs through me at those words. *Found. Chosen.* Such powerful calls.

'It whispered words like *we* and *us* and promised the soul it would end its loneliness if only it would accept the unseelie's gift.'

I swallow, throat tight with the horrible familiarity of the lost soul's fears. *Don't leave me alone here.* Although I hate the king, I would beg him – *beg* – not to be left to that fate. I nod with grim certainty. 'It accepted.'

'It was a fool. It let the unseelie creature smother it, consume it, suck on its soul and memories. In doing that, the fae grew in strength yet lost itself. Now they walk the Underworld as an aberration, a mindless shambler with a yearning that cannot be satisfied.'

And I thought a lonely death was the worst that could happen. This is a fate far more bleak.

'If you had escaped the fortress walls, it would have found you and made the same offer. Would you have been able to say no to the promise of eternal companionship?'

I knew the answer before he asked the question. So did he.

The flaps between the creature's limbs undulate, slapping into the snow. It looks so pitiful. And yet it's so dangerous. To me, at least.

'It would be drawn to you. To your life. The only reason it hasn't turned already is because it's upwind. If I'd taken us an inch closer, it would have felt you.' His fingers squeeze my hips, the movement so slight, I'm not sure he intends it. 'You are a beacon out here. Do you want to be a beacon, Annon?'

My mouth is too dry to form words. I shake my head.

'Then you will not run again.' It isn't a question.

Wordlessly, he turns us on the spot and we ride back to the fortress.

Waking, sleeping, the shambler haunts me.

13

DESPITE THE KING'S attempts to drive into me the dangers of his realm, the next night, a little buzz of energy flows through me as I get ready.

'You're keen.' Laughter laces Min's voice as she arrives and finds me rifling through the armoire.

'I've decided I've been too miserable since I arrived. I'm going to enjoy my time here and really play the part.'

'His Majesty will be pleased.' But her eyes narrow like she doesn't quite believe it.

I can't blame her.

Still, I channel every scrap of cheer I have, and it isn't entirely faked. Tonight I will make Drystan take me home, because keeping me here will be even worse.

As she's coiling my hair and trying to explain the importance of distance in fae society – how far you stand from someone signifies the nature of your relationship – there's a rap at the door, which is a new experience for me. Annem normally just enters without warning.

I glance at Min in question and she gives a nod that prompts me to call out, 'Yes?'

Drystan pauses in the doorway, giving me a long look that makes me shift in my seat. My heart speeds, anticipating my plan for the evening. He is going to be *so* furious.

For now, he says nothing. A ripple of something cold runs through me, smothering my excitement. Min promised to keep my secret, but has she found a loophole in that way fae do?

She also remains silent, careful hands smoothing and twisting my hair, so I'm the one who has to raise my eyebrows at the king. 'Is something wrong?' *Please say no.*

He draws a quick breath and moistens his lips. 'No. I've come to collect you.' He enters together with his ravens, easing the door shut behind him. His gaze remains on us as though he's fascinated by the process of dressing my hair. The white raven lands on top of the mirror, its claws tapping gently. 'After all, we wouldn't want you to take a wrong turn and end up running through the gardens, now, would we?'

'Gods forbid.' I widen my eyes and flash him a grin. This excitement has me as giddy as belladonna, and it's a strange kind of triumph to see his gaze skip to my mouth. He adjusts his cuffs.

'My apologies, Your Majesty,' Min murmurs, hands leaving my hair. 'I can finish this later, if you wish to have a private moment with Lady Rhiannon.'

'Don't stop on my account. A future queen must look the part.' He gestures for her to continue as he takes a seat by the fireplace. 'I can wait.'

In the mirror, I catch the tiniest flash of surprise on Min's face before she resumes braiding a string of dusky purple pearls into my hair.

A shaft of light from the setting sun slants in through the window, warming my face. Despite this place's sun being dark, it does carry *some* warmth. I close my eyes and soak it up.

Gods, I've missed that sensation. Gentler than a fire. More penetrating, more powerful than curling up in a blanket. It soaks into
me, soothing my stiff joints.

Sometimes I wonder if I'm more plant than human. The books
say they draw strength from sunlight. I've certainly noticed everything in the garden springs into growth as soon as we get a few
bright days.

I feel the same.

Through my eyelids, the light dims as a cloud passes over. When
I open my eyes, I find Drystan watching me, unblinking. It's the
kind of watching that feels like it should be written with a capital *W*, setting my nerves on edge, mingling with the anticipation
already zinging through me. All I can do is stare back.

Surely he doesn't know my plan. Min has made a few cryptic
comments about the king's power being tied to the land, but I can't
imagine he knows everything that goes on in it, thoughts included.
That would be enough to drive anyone insane.

When Min passes between us, I huff out a breath, shoulders
easing. She presses something cold into my hand, the blue bottle of
belladonna, and continues fussing with the tendrils of hair fram-
ing my face. She's blocking Drystan's view, I realize, giving me the
chance to slip the bottle into a hidden pocket she's sewn into the
bodice of this gown. One of the ravens *caws*.

'There we are. All done.' She steps to one side, giving me a lop-
sided smile that avoids the scar on her cheek.

I squeeze her hand. 'Thank you.' Tonight is all about breaking the rules, and I *do* owe Min, so I don't mind being beholden
to her.

Still, her eyebrows shoot up, and she gives Drystan a sidelong
glance.

He wears this thoughtful look as he stares at my fingers
wrapped around Min's. As though feeling my attention on him,
he flows to his feet and inclines his head to Min. 'Yes, your work is

appreciated. Go and get yourself ready for the night's celebrations. In your room, you'll find some clothing options fit for the royal sartor.'

She opens and closes her mouth as though she can't decide how to reply.

I can't blame her. So far, she's always melted away when I've reached the great hall, and although her clothes are elegant, I've never seen her in anything as formal as the fae wear to their events. Her status isn't enough to earn her space in the court gatherings . . . at least not normally.

Drystan might not be saying thank you, but he's showing his gratitude all the same. I squeeze her hand again and nod for her to go.

Once she disappears, I take up the necklace I chose earlier and fiddle with the fastening.

'Here.' His voice right *there* makes me jolt, but he catches the necklace as it falls from my grasp. The violet sapphires glisten as he takes a moment to examine the piece, before inclining his head in what might be approval.

With the lightest touch, he brushes a loose curl from the nape of my neck. There is a practicality to it, yes, and yet it's nothing like the firm, functional touch of Annem bathing me or my brother helping me up the stairs. This is something entirely different. Hidden by the sheer sleeves of my gown, goosebumps lift the delicate hairs.

In the mirror, I note his gaze lingering on the nape of my neck. Those hairs must be betraying my reaction to his touch. Little bastards.

I draw a long, slow breath as he loops the gold chain around my neck. 'You like her, don't you?' He nods towards the door Min disappeared through.

'So far she's the only person here who's been kind to me. And . . . I feel like we understand each other.'

He frowns, and I'm not sure if it's at my reply or the clasp. With a soft click, it closes, and he pauses before taking half a step back. 'Haven't *I* been kind to you?'

I blink, barely holding in a laugh. 'You do remember you're keeping me here against my will, right?'

He opens his mouth to argue, then shuts it, exhaling through his nose. 'You said you'd *come* willingly, not that you'd stay willingly. Of *course*.' He offers his hand and pulls me to my feet, but instead of stepping away, he keeps my fingers caught in his. 'That is . . . a bargain I had no say in.'

'You had a say in locking me in my room.'

'Yes, and I could have done *much* worse.'

This time I do laugh, and the odd look from earlier returns to his face. I raise an eyebrow at him. 'You . . . really believe you've been kind, don't you?'

He frowns, and for a moment I feel bad, because he looks confused, maybe even hurt. But the look is smoothed away in an instant, leaving me doubting what I read on his face. 'Perhaps the idea of kindness is different between your world and mine. Come.' He turns away and offers his arm.

14

ENTERING THE HALL with Drystan is nothing like entering
it with Min or traversing it alone. The curious looks don't feel
so menacing. The smiles are still sharp, but less opportunistic,
more . . . curious. Even the shadows lurking in the corners seem
more serene, idling like smoke on a windless day. They're soon
joined by the three ravens, the black pair disappearing, while the
white one stands out, perched on the rafters, watching.

A pair of Twylth guards I hadn't noticed in the corridors trail us
in and break off, stationing themselves by the doors.

That's when I spot Min. Also near the doors, but less like she's
deliberately stationed and more like she's caught on the periphery
looking in. Alone. I may not trust her, but her isolation makes my
heart clench.

But I can't dawdle – the king leads me in a circuit, showing
everyone we're here, and he's his usual indifferent self. For a
moment in my room, he'd almost seemed human. Silly me.

I occupy myself with looking for chances to put my plan into
action. Coming up with a scheme is one thing, but actually enacting

it? That's something else entirely. Something I have little practice in, especially in social settings.

Before I realize what's happening, Drystan leads me into the chaos of the dancers who spin and press together, couples breaking apart to pair off with other fae, their hungry gazes following me as they pass. The ravens swoop down from the shadows.

'What are we—?'

'Dancing,' he states before I can even finish my question. With a flick of his wrist, he tugs on my hand and brings me around to face him. 'It's expected of us. Though I assume you don't have much experience of it. Just follow me.' I'm still staring up at him as he places my hand on his shoulder, takes hold of my waist and steps into my space.

Only an inch separates us and his grip is iron as he guides me back, giving a faint nod as I take a step.

It's been a long time since I danced. And this step-step-spin with bodies close together is nothing like the raucous jigs we did at the pub in my teenage years.

Hells, it's been a long time since I did anything that used my body for fun. It's always work or looking after myself so I can function the next day.

This controlled whirl blurs the rest of the world, leaving only him in focus. It gives me the uncomfortable sensation that he's the only thing that's real in this whole place.

But in this absence of all else, my body comes alive. Not with aches or stiffness, or the lurch of my heart doing something worrying, but with the simple pleasure of movement. Of taking the right steps. Of the loose locks of hair ticking my bare neck. Of the brush of our thighs as he leads.

He gives another nod as though pleased.

Pleasing him isn't my plan for tonight, but perhaps I can enjoy this single dance before I set to work destroying his entire evening.

'So . . .' He arches an eyebrow. 'What is it you do in that little hut of yours?'

I bite back my irritation at him referring to my home in that way. Though, I suppose, compared to this fortress, it *is* a 'little hut'. My half shrug shifts my hold on him, and I have to admit his shoulders *are* broad and firm and . . . fine, they're another thing I can enjoy, just for this short while.

'Reading. Repairing my father's fishing nets.' My fingers are more slender than Pa's, and although I lack Lowen's strength, I'm nimble. Still, Drystan looks like he's waiting for more from my answer. 'Gardening.'

'Gardening?' He makes a thoughtful sound. 'I noticed the abundance of plants. So they're all yours.' His eyes narrow the barest touch as though I'm a particularly tricky passage in some obscure text. 'Things grow easily for you, don't they?'

It's my turn to arch an eyebrow. 'In my world, where it isn't perpetually winter – yes.'

'I don't mean on the surface in general. I mean in *your* garden. The plants there are more alive, more vibrant, while those outside your walled garden are scrubby, straggly things. *You* made them grow better.'

I almost miss my step, only moving because his thigh presses into mine. I don't know what to say in reply. Or what to make of the look he gives me – intent enough to be a physical presence, the echo of his earlier touch on the nape of my neck.

It's a long moment before he speaks again. 'I do enjoy surprising you. Your eyes go all wide like that. It shows off the colour.'

I scoff, grateful for the excuse to blink and look away. 'They're just dull old brown.'

He jolts to a stop, holding me in place as I try to continue dancing. There's a crease between his eyebrows – I've never seen so much as a line on his face before now.

My heart skips like I've just taken belladonna. Shit. What did I do wrong?

'Brown is not dull,' he bites out. His chest rises and falls on a long breath, and his unyielding grip softens as though he's just blown out all his irritation. 'Black is dull. Grey is dull. *White* is dull. Brown is wood and bark and soil, with all their wondrous potential.'

For a moment, I'm foolish enough to think he's talking about me. It's a nice dream – to be seen like that.

But only for a moment. Of course a man who lives in a realm of snow and death would find those colours dull and anything related to life and growth 'wondrous'.

Although our dance has stopped, my head spins. There are so many things about this place that are different from home. It's dizzying, yes, but also fascinating. I'm almost sad that I won't get to learn more – to *understand* the people here and what makes them tick.

But my family calls to me. I can't leave Lowen wondering, waiting – he deserves an explanation and an apology. I can feel the tether in my bones, as though the stones of our home are a physical part of myself that I've left behind.

I open my mouth to tell him that my desire to leave is nothing personal, but the song finishes, and suddenly the space is quiet, no longer blurred but full of many pairs of eyes on us.

Drystan releases me, inclines his head and backs away. When I blink, he's gone.

My head is still spinning when I weave my way off the dance floor, and my heart . . .

Slow.

There's a table full of drinks just a dozen steps away . . . or is it further? My vision swims so much, I can't be sure. A pair of feet stick out from under the tablecloth, and a dozen empty glasses sit around them, one knocked over. I focus on that fallen glass, willing the world to hold still for just a moment.

'Lady Rhiannon,' someone says at my elbow.

Manners dictate that I should turn and talk to them. But I don't have time. And, no matter the brief enjoyment of dancing with Drystan, I'm not here to follow the rules – not tonight.

I reach the table, try to subtly lean on it, fish out the little blue bottle. The nearest glass bulges and twists as I reach for it. I can't tell if it's the Underworld fucking with me or just my own brain panicking from the lack of blood as my heart beats so sluggishly.

As I grope, my fingertips find cold glass, and I drag it across the tablecloth. I drop a scoop of belladonna into the deep purple-red liquid and give it a swirl. It isn't tea, but it's better than collapsing and revealing to all the Underworld that I'm sick. *Remember*, an echo of Drystan's voice sounds in my head, *weakness is death*.

I gulp it down in one. Sweet and sharp, the elderberry wine fights my bitter medicine.

'*Lady Rhiannon.*' The voice at my elbow is definitely pissed off.

I drag in a breath, eyelids fluttering as my heart leaps and the darkness at the edges of my vision recedes. Nerves crackling, face tingling, I snap back into the world. Bright. Fast. Everything. The dancers. The glasses. The fae under the table. The one pissed off at me.

My jittery body yells at me that *all* of this is important. I leap into the words that come all too easily: 'I'm s—'

I almost apologize, but catch myself before the word is complete.

Just as well, because when I spin, almost stumbling into the table, I find it's Phaedra giving me a narrow smile. It might be my plan to break the rules tonight, but she is not someone I want to be beholden to.

'Lady Phaedra. I was so desperate to get a drink, I had eyes only for the wine.' I tilt my glass, showing off the dregs. A few drops spill on to her icy-blue gown.

'Desperate.' She jerks her chin up as if this close to rolling her eyes at the silly little human. 'Of course. And how is the *future queen* of my dear country faring? We haven't seen you for a few days, though I *thought* I spotted you out the window *playing* in the snow.' Her narrow smile isn't sweet or warm, and the look she gives me is sharp. It says she knows I wasn't playing at all.

'Snow is such *fun*.'

The silence that follows suggests she doesn't agree in the slightest. I watch the dancers, who are rowdy now their king isn't among them. There must be some way I can involve Phaedra in my plan for the evening. The question is, how?

'I have a gift for you,' she says suddenly. 'A way to honour our *future queen*.' She keeps emphasizing it like that – like she can't believe I am really going to sit on a throne at Drystan's side with a crown upon my head.

Not sure I blame her. If I have anything to do with it, I won't be perching on extravagant furniture nor wearing excessively jewelled headgear.

And lucky me, she's just served up a way to break the rules.

'Such a kind gesture.' Clutching my chest, I smile broadly like I'm overjoyed.

Her lips part and almost imperceptibly, she leans closer, pupils blowing so wide there's only a thin ring of blue left around them. 'Yes, I *am* kind, aren't I?' The corner of her lip curls absently as she holds out her hand and in it appears a black velvet jewellery box. 'Your future Majesty.'

I take it, though I can't quite bring myself to thank her. I plan to be out of here soon, but what if owing her follows me back home? Breaking the rules is one thing, but being indebted to someone like her feels much more risky. Instead, I incline my head.

The lid of the box flips up, revealing a choker that glimmers in iridescent purples and blues banded with grey and near-black. It's unlike anything I've ever seen – the only metal is at the catch, while the rest is made from slivers of . . . 'Are they seashells?'

'Gathered from Darkshore itself.' She tosses her head, nose in the air.

Darkshore must be somewhere important, its shells sought after. Unseelie etiquette probably dictates that I should say how honoured I am to receive such a special gift.

So, I sniff and lift my chin, looking down my nose at it, mimicking her. 'I suppose it will do.'

Her nostrils flare for an instant before she smothers the response. 'Such discerning taste already.' She speaks like each word is sour. 'You simply *must* tell me what you have from the human realm that could outshine this piece.'

'Perhaps another night.' But I want to make sure Drystan discovers I've accepted a gift, so I pull out the necklace. The shells' edges glint, razor thin, and I gasp as one of the shards slices into my fingertip.

'*Do* be careful. Darkshore jewellery is known to cut the unwary . . . and the unworthy.'

I grit my teeth as I smile back brightly, like my finger isn't stinging. 'Then I hope your hands aren't too injured from putting it in the box.' I shove the box at her, so she's forced to take it. Breath held, I set the necklace at my collarbone and fasten it in place with the sapphire necklace hanging lower, between my breasts. Staying still like this, the shell choker doesn't cut. As long as I move slowly, I can carry this off.

Smirking, I flash my eyebrows up at the look of surprise on Phaedra's face and turn away.

'The king's favour is fleeting,' she calls after me. 'He doesn't even kiss his lovers, you know. He doesn't *care* about you.'

With a bright smile, I glance back. 'I'm counting on it.' I catch her confused frown before I turn away, a whisper of pain telling me the necklace has nicked my skin again. Worth it.

Paying attention to every movement, I circle the hall and search for any opportunity to upset fae and break those rules Drystan so loves.

I join one group, including Lord Mastelle, a fae so old that although his face doesn't appear any older than forty, grey streaks his hair at the temples. I remember he's important, and pissing off someone important is a surefire way of this getting back to Drystan.

Wincing inside, I tap my lip. 'Lord . . . Lord . . . what was your name, again?' Eyebrows twitch upward. Looks are exchanged. But he obliges and after a few murmurs, he asks how I met the king.

Following Min's advice, the best course would be to dodge the question with a metaphorical answer – I met him in a dream – or to reply with another question. The less information the better.

But what if I give *more* information? Actually answer the question, perhaps even with an answer that slightly undermines Drystan. 'His mother arranged our betrothal, Lord Mustal,' I reply, deliberately mispronouncing his name.

I hate myself for it. Utterly.

As someone who's just lost what she thought was her name, I can confidently say, they are precious. It feels like I've just stomped on Lord Mastelle's.

His ochre-brown face turns ashen, and the others stare at me. His attention darts towards the dais holding Drystan's throne. There's no sign of the king.

'How . . . interesting.' Lord Mastelle gives a stiff nod and an even stiffer smile.

But there's this ripple that flows out from us. Murmurs. Glances. It's as though my mispronunciation has broken something and little fractures spread across the room. Even the musicians hit a discordant note that clangs in my bones with its wrongness.

Names hold power.

The woman next to me clears her throat. 'If you'll excuse me, I need to . . .' The end of the sentence is lost as she disappears into the crowd. Moments later, two more of the fae excuse themselves, leaving just me and Lord Mastelle.

The quiet between us drags on and I fight the urge to fiddle with Phaedra's necklace. One shell sits right in the hollow of my throat and the wrong move will slice my skin again.

But if my plan is going to work, I need to cause more upset, much as that sits wrong in my gut. I haven't mastered the nuances of distance despite Min's attempts to explain, but I take a step closer to him. This *has* to be inappropriately close for our complete lack of relationship.

'Lady Rhiannon.' He inclines his head, gaze everywhere but on me. 'I believe I need to be elsewhere. You will excuse me, I'm sure.' He shoots me a quick, cold glare before turning his back to me and walking away.

I've pissed him off, which should feel like a win. But it leaves me standing here alone in the great hall, with a chill whispering down my back. In the Underworld, just as on the surface, isolation is a weakness.

It doesn't matter. I'll be home soon. I square my shoulders and lift my chin.

The shell snicks my throat, a short, sharp pain that has me gasping.

Unwary and unworthy. Phaedra would be pleased.

As I turn and search for somewhere to go and sow more discord, my stomach sinks. Because there are eyes on me. All the fae nearby watch. Their conversations have fallen quiet. One cocks his head, a dangerous light in his eyes as they flick to my throat.

Another licks her lips, scaled cheeks flushing iridescent blue and purple as she comes closer.

Shadows creep around their feet, stirring like waves in a rising wind.

Swallowing, I back away. Although my pulse isn't slow, I'm suddenly very aware of it as it tolls harder. Something is wrong. Something I didn't account for.

I bump into someone, turn and mutter an apology without even thinking. I catch a glimpse of a cruel smile before I'm jostled again. Someone grabs me – I don't see who, but when I turn I find I'm at the edge of the dance floor.

The nearest dancers spin and cackle, turning in their partners' arms so they can watch me as they pass. One woman with rich red lips and the palest skin I've ever seen scents the air, eyes half closing as she falls back in her partner's hold as if swooning. Eyes on me, he bends and kisses her throat at exactly the spot where Phaedra's necklace has cut me. A widening smile reveals his sharp teeth.

Shrieks merge with the cackling, harsh in my ears, and as I back off, I find the way blocked. The crowd quickens, louder, faster, hotter. My breaths get sharper as the air crackles with wild energy and shadows grab at my legs. Kicking doesn't get rid of them. I can't get enough air in my lungs. My chest's too tight, ribs crushing.

The dancers loop closer, red tongues on show as their mouths loll open like they can taste the air and find something particularly exquisite there.

One grabs for me. I barely dodge, pressing into whoever's behind me. An elbow jabs my back and I stumble on to the dance floor, right in the path of the pale woman, whose wild smile says she's most pleased about it.

Every hair on my body stands on end. Why did I think this was a good idea? Why did I think I could stand alone in the unseelie court? Or anywhere? I need people. I need to rely on them. I need my family. I need—

The air snaps. That's the only way I can describe it.

Just as I suck in a breath that isn't tainted with peril, a grip closes on my arm.

I'm whipped around and find the king standing over me. He says nothing, but his lips are pressed together so hard they're white and the dark lines etched between his eyebrows tell me exactly the question on his mind: 'What the hells have you done?'

15

A FRIGID SMILE on his lips, the king drags me towards the great hall's doors. The crowd melts out of our raven-flanked path, calm again as though they weren't churning themselves into a frenzy moments ago. This time I notice the pair of Twylth guards dropping in behind us.

Only when we reach an empty lounge and the door slams shut with the guards outside does the king stop and whip me around so quickly, my head snaps to one side. 'What in all the seven hells were you doing?'

The ravens croak, just as indignant as him. The largest cocks its head, a beady eye on me.

Now the air around me has calmed, I can think clearly and look up at the king, all innocence. 'What do you mean?'

'Your blood. It smells of life – of the surface. You thought that wouldn't excite them?' He looms over me, nostrils flaring with each breath. 'It's . . . it's intoxicating.'

Have the unseelie been here so long that even a hint of my world is so irresistible? Interesting. And something they have in common with that creature he showed me beyond the fortress walls.

'This whole evening you've disobeyed me. You've been rude. You've ignored high-ranking members of my court and stood *much* too close to others. Threnn told me you spilled a drink on Lady Phaedra.' He blasts out a breath, brows lowering.

Oh, gods, he's angry. So there *is* some feeling in the cold-as-ice King of Death.

'*Then* I hear you've asked Lord Mastelle for his name and yet *still* mispronounced it. I told you names hold power. What do you think saying one incorrectly does?'

That takes the wind out of my sails. I intended to cause a bit of offence and ruffle the king's feathers enough that he would think it better to send me home than keep me here. I didn't mean to cause any actual damage.

The ravens lift their beaks and clack and caw, ear-splitting. The middle-sized one hops along the back of a chair, head bobbing as the others quieten.

Drystan sniffs the air. 'Where are you hurt? I thought you just had some blood on a cloth, but . . . this is fresh.'

I swallow and carefully lift my chin. 'It's my new necklace. Do you like it?' Lashes fluttering, I smile up at him as though full of joy. With any luck, his haughtiness will make him believe my human inferiority extends to my intelligence. 'Such a kind gift.'

His golden eyes flare. 'A gift?' It's less a question, more a growl.

If I wasn't trying to piss him off, it would be frightening. But as it is, triumph kindles in me.

'You accepted a gift?'

'Oh no. I wasn't meant to, was I?' I let my mouth fall open to a perfect *O*. 'It just seemed like such a lovely gesture, I didn't even *think* to say no.'

'And that gift has *cut* you.' He doesn't ask permission, he just reaches around to the back of my neck and unclasps the necklace, managing to avoid causing any more damage.

I try to hold back my sigh of relief at no longer feeling like I have a razor blade to my throat. I fail.

Shaking his head, he rubs his thumb over my collarbone as though his touch can soothe the cuts there. My skin hums, and suddenly I'm aware of the weight of the sapphire necklace he clasped in place earlier, the whisper of my gown over my body.

But most of all, I'm aware of the smoothness of the pad of his thumb, the warmth of his fingers curled over my shoulder and the circles he's pressing into my flesh as he smears away my blood.

'Who gave you the necklace?'

Telling him might cause lasting damage. Min told me Phaedra was favourite to become his consort before I came along, and while she's a nasty specimen, it doesn't affect me if she becomes queen of this gods-forsaken place. 'I swore to secrecy.'

'So you made a promise too?' Eyes shut, he exhales. 'Death and darkness, you are . . .' He exhales like he's kept the breath in for too long and it's been weighing him down. The tension in him fades, but his brow gets lower and his eyelids dip like they're heavy as he looks from my throat to my eyes. 'More is at stake than you understand.' He says it like I'm a child.

My kindling triumph grows hot, turning into something else – something that sears. 'Oh, so it's *my* fault for not understanding? I see. Silly me!' I lift my chin, glaring. 'Here I was thinking it was because you explain nothing. Min had to tell me that manners were armour.'

'I told you to mind your manners.'

'You did. But you didn't bother to give me even a hint as to *why* or what the repercussions might be. Like the power of names – you never bothered to tell me more. How was I supposed to know mispronouncing one could cause harm? If you don't explain, how am I meant to understand?'

His frown clenches tighter, and for a long moment there's quiet.

'Look,' I say, voice lowering, 'this clearly isn't working for *either* of us. You've taken me as your bride. You had every intention of marrying me when you took me away. I just happen to be unsuitable . . .' I think back to Phaedra's words, proven true by the necklace's cuts. '*Unworthy*. But the bargain is fulfilled. You can take me home without any backlash.'

He blinks, something dawning in his eyes. 'You did this so I'd send you away.' The corner of his mouth twitches. 'My sweet little human bride isn't as *sweet* as she seems.'

'I'm clearly bad at following rules. This was only one night. I'm sure I'll cause all sorts of chaos if you keep me here.'

His eyes narrow as if weighing up the threat hanging from my words. 'I could just keep you locked in your room.'

'Then I'll try to escape again.'

He holds my gaze for a long while before his shoulders sink. 'You will, won't you?'

'Absolutely.'

'Fine. You want to go home? By the terms of the bargain that was made, I can't just let you go.' He holds up a hand as I open my mouth to argue. 'But you can earn it. We can make our own bargain.'

As a fae, he can't lie, so there must be something about the agreement between my father and The Morrigan that stops him from simply taking me home. But earning it? I could work for that. It's better than nothing, which his tone suggests is the only other option. 'And what will be our terms?'

'I'll give you a chance to leave the Underworld and return to your family. You'll have half a month to earn it. Meanwhile, *you* will play the part of a good fiancée. You want an explanation? Very well.' He looms over me. 'You undermined me tonight. You sowed discord in my court. You may be nothing, but your actions have ripples. And those ripples affect my power and my ability to rule.' His nose wrinkles as though he hates confessing this. 'If I cannot rule, this stronghold will no longer stand. And when those walls crumble, what do you think will protect my people from the creatures outside? From the dead and the chaos?'

His glare is a cold spear running me through.

I thought I was just irritating him. It was practically a game. My throat grows tight and achy. 'I never meant—'

'It doesn't matter what you *meant*. It matters what you *do*. Repair the damage you've caused. We'll have no more of tonight's nonsense. Even if you intend to earn your chance to leave this place, you will *pretend* that you are very happy as my fiancée, that you're *ecstatic* about the prospect of becoming my queen, that you will rule them with the strength and dedication they deserve and that above all, you will keep them safe. Do we have a deal?'

Although it still feels like something is clawing its way up my throat, I swallow and try to marshal my thoughts. 'So, half a month? A calendar month or—?'

'A lunar month.'

That could mean something different in the Underworld. I open my mouth to clarify.

'Twenty-eight days,' he says, clipped. 'Halved to fourteen.'

Not long. But it's better than the alternative.

'Of course, if you don't want—'

I hold out my hand.

He shakes it, once, hard. 'Good. I've found someone to train you in the ways of Fatework as required of a king's consort. You'll begin tomorrow. For now, though, you can get started on earning your chance to go home.' The cruel edge of his smirk quenches any excitement I might feel at the prospect. 'Your very, *very* slim chance.'

Before I can ask what he means, his arms close around me and my being fragments into feathers and darkness.

*

When I am whole and can move, I'm clinging to him, woozy. I hate how solid he is. Add that to my growing list of things I hate about him.

Top of the list: the fact he doesn't give a shit. Closely followed by the way he's so smug about it. *Family is the first lie we're taught to believe.* Like I'm a fool for caring, while he's the epitome of enlightenment.

Pretty sure enlightened beings don't threaten to cut people's tongues out.

A brand-new entry on that list: the blooming realization of quite how solid his chest is under my hands, broad too, and that it makes a tiny knot of want at the centre of my being tighten. Purely physical and utterly mortifying.

I shove away – or *try*. Once again, his arm is an iron band around my waist. 'Get off me.'

His smirk is insufferable. He knows. My body betrayed me. Bastard. 'You may not want me to let go when you see what's behind you.'

I blink past the curtain of his hair, which moves lazily in a light breeze.

Mountains surround us, that same obsidian black as those behind the fortress, and when I look down, I see we're on a small outcrop of rock. If I take a step back, I'll trip over a root from the stunted tree clinging to the mountainside and I'll fall.

I peer down and my stomach lurches. The depths disappear into mist. His ravens circle below us.

I make a small sound of acknowledgement, and now he's satisfied I'm not about to plummet over the edge, he releases me and backs off half a foot. I never knew nods could be smug, but the one he gives me is. He turns from the mountain we're perched on the side of, indicating a path forward.

'Path' is a generous term for it.

A set of stairs winds from the outcrop, descending into mist and the mountains' shadows. It's narrow enough that we couldn't walk it side by side. There is no handrail, only a sheer drop on either side, and lower down, patches of snow clog the way. I feel unsteady just looking at it.

But I've crossed the natural stone bridge from our cottage to the mainland hundreds of times without falling. I can do this.

I shove down the bits of my brain trying to remind me that I haven't crossed in years and that the bridge doesn't have steps.

I *can* do this.

'So I just need to cross the stairs, and then I can go home?'

Something escapes him that's part breath and part laugh. 'Not quite.'

Once again, I want to punch him. Does the Underworld make everyone more violent or just me?

'The staircase leads you to the start of your challenge – your *chance*.' He says that last part like it's a gentler name for it – a kinder one. Like referring to death as 'passing away' or 'going to sleep'.

My challenge? I squint into the shadow cast by the clawing peaks.

'Just wait.'

One of the ravens squawks, and grey sunlight creeps over the mountains, pushing back the darkness below.

At first I think it's natural rock. But only for a fraction of a second, because natural rock doesn't form right angles and perfect squares . . . or doors.

Little channels twist and wind in nonsense shapes, cut from the dark glassy stone of the mountain. They stretch into the distance, rising in tiers until they reach the peak opposite where a gateway stands.

I stare, struggling to make sense of the scale. The columns flanking the gateway are hewn from rock and stretch halfway up the mountain. The gates are huge – *so* huge. They seem fit not for people or even fae but for *concepts*. The sea could pass through there or the sky or night or darkness – or death. They are far, *far* beyond mortal scale.

'What is this?'

'My labyrinth. It is of my kingdom. Of me. Yet it is also . . . wild. Its own. That gate can take you back to the surface world – for *you* it will lead to that little slab of rock you call home. *If* you can reach it.'

I blink. I realize. I bite back a groan.

They aren't channels. They're walls. The spaces between them are paths in his labyrinth. Cross roads. Winding turns. Dead ends.

Even with it all set out before me, I can't see a route to the gateway.

'By day, you will pit yourself against this place and try to get home. By night, you will be my fiancée, perfectly behaved, just as you promised.'

I've been gaping at the unfathomable maze, but now my mouth snaps shut and my head snaps around to him. Dread blooms in my chest, an ugly, choking flower. 'When am I supposed to sleep – to rest? And this cold – I can't survive this in a dress.'

'Your sleep is not my concern. I've fulfilled my side of our bargain and provided you with your chance. It's up to you how you tackle it.' He smirks, wider than I've ever seen it before, as though he's truly enjoying this.

Meanwhile, *I* would truly enjoy slapping that look off his face.

'As for the cold, consider this my one and only act of charity.' He slips his jacket off and sweeps it around my shoulders.

Fists clenched, mind churning, I take a breath and formulate a question, 'How do I get back to the fortress?' I glance in the direction I think it lies in, but it's hard to get my bearings when I'm surrounded by peaks that block my view.

He glances to one side as though he's fighting not to roll his eyes. 'The same way you got here. At sunset, you'll be transported back.'

'And have to start all over again?' That would be classic fae torture – forced back to the beginning each day.

A deep sigh, like I'm the most foolish creature in the Underworld. 'And the next morning, you'll be returned to the same location you left.' The corner of his mouth twitches. 'Not that I'm expecting you'll make it past the first level.'

'Level?' I turn back to the labyrinth stretching out ahead.

'Levels. Tiers. Whatever you want to call them, there are six in total, leading to the gate.'

The nearest is the narrowest, but from this angle it's hard to judge how much larger the others are, no matter how much I squint. One thing that's unmistakable even from this distance: the line between each level is a sheer cliff.

'You'll need to find the gateway from one tier to the next and there' – a dark glint enters his eyes – 'you'll face a trial. Only if you prevail may you proceed.'

'And if I fail?' The question comes out barely above a whisper.

He shrugs. 'Depends. Others who've tried have faced all sorts. Lost time. Terrible agony. Death.'

Nothing new, then. I almost laugh. But a horrible kind of curiosity tugs on me. 'What happens to those who fail to escape?'

'They are still within. Abominations.'

I was wrong. This just might be worse than the alternative.

'But don't worry, my sweet nothing. If *you* fail to escape, you'll merely stay in the Underworld for ever as its queen and my bride.'

That shit-eating smirk is the last thing that disappears as he bursts into his flock of ravens, leaving me alone on the side of the mountain.

I am going to murder him.

That is, if I survive these bloody stairs.

16

I SURVIVE THE staircase. Just.

That's despite the wind tugging on my clothes, the ice on lower levels and the precipitous drop that disappears into eddies of mist that whisper of an ill fate.

Eventually, legs shaking, heart racing, I reach a large door with a pair of brass knockers.

At first, I place my hand on it, about to push, but then I remember the warnings about politeness and instead, I lift a knocker and rap three times.

There's a grinding that vibrates through my feet, like the stone is thinking, then the door swings inward. An invitation.

When I accept and enter the labyrinth, it shuts behind me with a solid, echoing boom. That's it. I'm in. For good or ill.

A corridor stretches left and right, open to the sky above, with turnings leading deeper.

It's dark down here on the lowest level – the snow collected in corners tells me it gets little sunlight. The cold makes my chest tight. I'm unlikely to have an episode where my heart rate slows right now, but I'm at risk of the pains that come with it speeding up, especially if I ever come here under the influence of belladonna. Tucking my hands into the sleeves of the king's jacket, I take mental note to put warm clothes on ready for dawn tomorrow.

For now, though, the smooth hewn walls offer no clues, so I pick a direction and start.

The king has proven himself to be a royal pain in the backside, so I ignore the first turning and the next, aiming towards the next tier and the final gate. If this labyrinth is his, I wouldn't put it past him to make the correct path the one furthest away.

It's not long before I hear skittering and catch glimpses of *something* on the edge of my vision. Small shapes, dark, swift. I spin, trying to get a better look. Rodents, maybe? Or large insects?

Otherwise, it's quiet, and after a while, I welcome the scurrying sounds of creatures unknown – it's company after all. In the quiet moments, the empty corridor stretching on and on makes the nape of my neck prickle with an eerie feeling I don't want to dwell on.

I keep going until the corridor bends right, then further still until I hit another bend. The passage twists and turns so many times, I lose track of what direction I'm facing. I can't see the mountains surrounding the maze, even though it feels like they should be visible over the walls.

When I hit my first dead end, I groan and turn back. By the time I hit the third, I just sigh.

My next route looks more promising, lifting my spirits even as my feet drag and tiredness shoves its way in. I take several turns, choose left over right, straight on, right. The path widens ahead, and I speed up, heart leaping at the change in scenery . . .

. . . And reach the double doors I entered through.

I stare. Huff. Mutter 'bastard' under my breath.

Then I set off again.

When I come back tomorrow, I'll bring something to record my way – chalk or string or even better, my notebook – I can sketch out a map that should help me keep track.

Time coils and stretches, losing all meaning until the sun crests over the labyrinth's high walls, giving me some sort of guidance. Leaning against the featureless wall, I look up from my rest and work out which direction the gate and therefore the next level must be.

I regret not bringing food, but when I turn the next corner, I find a jug of water and a plate with a small pie sitting at its centre. A rich, savoury smell creeps down the corridor.

There are stories of humans trapped in fae realms after eating the food. And this sudden appearance could be a trap. But I've already eaten food in the Underworld, and I can't get much more stuck than this, can I?

Besides, my stomach hollows out, sore from lack, and I sway on my feet. The only alternative is to keep going, and I'm not sure how long I can manage that.

So I take another rest, staring at the pie, and eventually I reach out for it and gingerly take a bite.

The pastry is crisp, the gravy rich and the meat tender. I make short work of it. There are no glasses, so I drink straight from the jug.

Maybe there's some part of the labyrinth that is benevolent. Maybe Drystan just doesn't want me to die. After all, where would be the fun in that? And he may be the King of Death, but I doubt even he could marry a dead woman.

As I'm licking gravy from my fingers, there's a sound.

Not the skittering of those little creatures, something else. Something large and shuffling. I'm slow getting to my feet, but I no longer sway.

Eyes fixed on the direction the sound is coming from, I drain the jug and clutch it, ready to . . . I don't know – throw it?

The shuffling grows louder. My heart follows suit. I back away as a breathy, gravelly snort drifts around the corner.

First comes a shadow, stretching across the ground, large . . . larger.

Then comes a shaggy, lumbering creature. Faintly humanoid but huge and hunched, with matted, streaked hair dangling from its body. A pair of flinty eyes peer out from what looks like a head – it's little more than a hump above hulking shoulders. Between the hair and bent stance I can't tell how many limbs it has, but among the thudding steps, something hard clicks on the stone ground.

Now it's emerged fully, I can see it's twice my height, almost as tall as the walls surrounding us, and as it takes a step, I catch a glimpse of ivory claws, each as long as my hand.

Those glinting eyes turn on me and the monster lets out a shriek or a roar or something that's like both sounds layered over one another a hundred times over.

I drop the jug and run.

The shuffling sound is gone, replaced by the slap of many feet running and the click of sharp claws.

Gripping the wall, I round one corner, then another. Sharp edges scrape my fingers, leaving them bloody.

I'm already breathless, clutching my chest as I go as quickly as I can. I'm no fool – I know I'm not quick enough. No matter how many turns I take, I don't lose the monster. Running won't save me.

My eyes burn as I search for something that might.

A slanting darkness opens up in the wall to my left. I almost miss it, assuming it's merely a shadow. But when I draw level, I catch a glimpse of light beyond.

It's a passageway. A narrow one. And the slanting shadow is a door hidden in the rock, only visible because it's open.

No time to think, I grab the wall and pivot, using my momentum to send me into the narrow passage. The door pulls shut behind me as I take in the small, ceilingless room – more like a cupboard, really.

I try to catch my breath and watch the sky, wishing myself anywhere else.

There's a cry. The echoes play tricks on my ears, making it sound like a word.

'Where?'

'Where?'

'Where?'

Eyes shut, I press into the wall and make myself small, breathing into the little space between my knees, hoping that will muffle the noise.

'How's the first level going?'

My head snaps up.

Above, sitting on the wall, apple in one hand, dagger in the other, peering down at me as though I'm a curiosity in a box, is the king.

'What are you doing here? Thought you'd be getting your beauty sleep,' I hiss.

'I don't need it.' He shrugs like that's self-evident and cuts a slice off the apple. 'I was curious about how you were doing.' A guttural cry comes from beyond my hidden doorway, and he peers over, raising his eyebrows. 'Not well, it seems.' He raises the dagger to his mouth and takes the apple slice from it, widening his eyes at me.

I glare at him, but the effect is broken by a thud outside that has me shrinking into the wall. 'Shh. You're giving me away,' I whisper.

He ignores me, canting his head as he watches the monster ram into the door again. Its churning cries grow more excited, a burble of what sounds like laughter running through. At least the door opens outward, so the monster's hammering won't push it open.

The king shakes his head, attention returning to me as if I'm some poor unfortunate who's brought all this on myself and not the victim of his whims. 'If you can't understand our ways, you'll never survive.'

Ignoring him, I slide my hands over the smooth walls, hoping for another hidden door that will open under my touch or a subtle crevice that will reveal some secret passageway.

'You do know this is a dead end, right?' He pares another slice from the apple.

'So I'm discovering.' I'm stuck here until the creature gets bored and gives up.

It slams into the door again. A crack races across its surface.

I press into the opposite wall and stare, cold spilling over me like I'm already dead. It's going to break through.

'This is the easiest level, you know,' comes the mocking voice from above. 'If you're not up to it, you can give up now – stay in the warmth and safety of my fortress.'

'For ever? No thanks.'

But my voice wavers, and I'm ashamed to say, I'm considering it. I'm not built for this. I'm not strong or fast. I have no stamina. I can't fight a monster.

Another slam. Another crack spreads from the first.

Maybe I should just accept my fate. Even if I can't escape, there has to be some way I can get a message to my brother.

The monster roars in rising excitement, 'Here!'

I blink. Wait . . . that doesn't just *sound like* 'here', the creature really is saying the word. Only there are other voices too.

'Get her.'

'Now!'

'Nearly.'

'Here. *Here.*'

The words layer and blend, some unintelligible, all garbled, like a room full of people shouting over each other.

If you can't understand our ways . . .

I hold my breath and listen to the voices. 'Where is she?'

'We found her, you fool.'

'She's here, ready for us to eat in one.'

'No, we'll teach her a lesson first,' a slithering voice says, its tone acid.

They're all different. Tones and pitches, but also accents. Some rounded and soft, like Annem's. Some blunt and hard, like Pa's.

'Don't hurt her. She doesn't know.' That dissenting voice is quickly drowned out.

The first crack widens. Through it, flinty eyes fix on me. A roar rattles my bones.

But it isn't the roar of a monster – it's the roar of a *crowd*. Many voices, many people, all shouting at once.

If this thing has a voice, then it isn't a monster, but a person of sorts.

The door crumbles, shards of stone as sharp as glass forcing me to my feet. The creature lunges, sharp teeth snapping inches from me. Its breath fans my face as I press into the wall and will myself to melt into it.

If this is a person, then Drystan has already told me how I should behave . . .

Eyes screwed shut, I whisper, 'Good afternoon.' My voice shakes, but I manage to get the words out.

The clacking rocks go quiet. The voices fall silent. There's only the creature's breath.

It isn't eating me, so . . .

'I'm Annon.' I crack open one eye. 'I'm so pleased to meet you.'

Quietly, its voices pick up again, like they're conferring with each other.

'Yes, that's better.'

'Such a polite girl.'

'At last, she acknowledges us,' the slithering voice adds, still with a biting edge.

It lowers its head, watching me. Its bulky mass seems calmer now the voices are in agreement.

My fear eases enough that I manage to swallow, and my voice comes out stronger, 'I confess, I was afraid when I first saw you, and I quite forgot my manners.'

'Afraid, yes.'

'We don't look like the others.'

'Not any more.'

'Not like we once were.'

It ducks its head lower, almost as if ashamed, and I catch a glimpse of another face among the fur, grey and slack.

I bet there are more hidden on its body – perhaps as many as one for every voice. And its hair isn't streaked with dirt, but with several different colours. I piece together its words, and my chest grows sore.

'It sounds like you've suffered.' Gently, I place my hand on its shoulder. 'I'm sorry that you have. Is there anything I can do to help?'

Its head snaps up, and breath lodges in my throat. But it doesn't attack, only looks at me a long, silent while.

'A kind girl,' the dissenting voice says at last.

'She is. Very kind.'

'But kindness doesn't last here.'

'This isn't court,' a deep voice speaks over the slithering one.

'Here, he decides.'

As if reaching a verdict, the creature straightens and nods. 'We are the Collector,' the voices say as one, 'and we are pleased to find you, Annon. We thought we might collect you.'

I fight against a shudder. Collect me. Like I could become part of it.

'But it's been a long while since anyone not of us has spoken to us, let alone honoured us with an introduction. Longer still since anyone touched us without trying to hurt us.'

Wincing, I pull my hand back. 'I didn't ask. I hope you don't mind.'

'No. No.' They press into my touch. 'It's . . . nice.'

A little awkward, I stroke their shoulder, and the voices settle into a contented hubbub. 'So I just needed to be polite.'

'Politeness is the way,' the deep voice says as the Collector shifts, offering a different part of their back to me.

I shudder as my palm connects with something that feels suspiciously like a nose, but I keep stroking and smiling. 'You are . . . unseelie, then?'

'We are – were. So much of this land is unsafe, we must live in close proximity,' the dissenting voice goes on. 'Trapped in this black glass, we became too close. But we remember how it was outside the glass walls. If we don't maintain the veneer of politeness . . .'

'We'll kill each other,' the slithering voice finishes.

A clipped, feminine voice that reminds me of Phaedra adds, 'The king's ability to keep his subjects in check is a marker of his power and strength – his suitability to rule.'

No wonder Drystan was so angry at me. The ripples of last night must've eroded his position. I glance up, but he's gone.

'Is Annon ill?' They cock their head. 'You lean heavily upon that wall.'

'Just tired.' No matter how alien their rules are to me, there *is* reasoning behind them, and the need to hide my illness has never felt so keen. 'Do you know the way up to the next tier?' If they are the first challenge, it must be near by. 'Can you take me?'

'You have walked far today,' the deep voice booms, echoed by a chorus of agreement.

The sun is sinking – I don't have much left of the day before I'm taken back to the fortress. But now the terror is wearing off, my legs have grown shaky. I'm not sure I can take many more steps.

And yet . . . I turn to what I think is the north, where the final gate stands, six levels and countless steps away.

'We know the way,' the dissenting voice pipes up.

The creature bristles, danger a sharp presence in the air, like a scent upon the wind. 'It's dangerous,' a chorus of voices snaps.

'We won't go there. But we can guard her while she sleeps, then show her to the foot of the stairs.'

Sleep. My gods, sleep sounds good right about now. I steady myself against the wall.

After the rumble of dozens of thoughtful sounds, the creature turns to me and the deep voice speaks. 'Very well. We make you this offer. Sleep and we will watch over you. Then we will show you the staircase to the next tier.' They straighten, broaden, filling the corridor. 'But we will not go with you.'

An offer from a fae. I accepted Drystan's when I shouldn't have. And look where it's got me.

After all, wasn't this creature threatening to eat me mere minutes ago?

As if sensing my unease, they add, 'By ash and blood, we promise not to collect you.'

My knees tremble and my whole body is leaden, reminding me of my profound lack of options.

So, trusting that fae rules about lying still apply to the Collector, I let them take me to a hollow that's been scraped out of the stone walls, with a floor lined in many tiny scraps of fur. And, despite the musty smell, I sleep as they stand watch.

17

ON THIS OCCASION, I'm right to trust, because I wake before dusk and I haven't been collected. The Collector shows me to the base of a long, straight staircase, with a stone arch at the top. I catch myself before I thank them, and instead say, 'I appreciate your help.'

They clasp their hands and touch their chest. I suspect it's been a long time since anyone appreciated them, let alone said it.

Then slowly, steadily, I make the climb and try not to think about the fact that if I fall, I'm falling a long fucking way. Down steps with shard-sharp edges.

Nearly at the top, I dare a glance over my shoulder. The Collector waves from the bottom.

I'm thankful for them giving me a safe place to rest. Without it, I wouldn't stand a chance of making it up here.

At last, I crest the staircase, pass through the arch and glimpse the upper tiers as daylight seeps from them. Crystalline and dark, glinting and sharp, they stretch upward, onward, and just beyond is the top of the final gate – the only thing left in the sun.

A moment later, even that light is extinguished and I scatter into feathers and darkness.

After breakfast, I open a fresh page in my notebook and draw fourteen boxes, representing the days I have to beat the labyrinth. It looks like such a short period of time drawn out like that. And even less as I cross one out.

I might be foolish enough to make a deal with a fae king, but I'm not foolish enough to think I'm going to make it up a tier every day.

Quickly, I sketch out the tiers, label them one to six and tick off the first one. If I'm to stand any chance of winning, I need to get to the fourth tier before the end of the first week. No doubt the labyrinth will get harder the further I go, so I'll need more time. I draw a thicker square for day seven.

Then I have time for some more sleep, which my muscles and joints are thankful for. I'm woken perhaps an hour later by Min, who smiles a bit too brightly and suggests we go for fresh air to wake me up before my lesson with the seer Drystan has arranged.

I bite back a groan. I'd forgotten about that.

So we dress warmly, and, trailed by a Twylth guard, Min leads me through the fortress.

I itch to talk about my experience in the labyrinth and the bargain I've foolishly – desperately – made with Drystan. That smile she gave me before leaving my room stills my tongue. Like she's trying to seem nice rather than *be* nice. Or is my judgement of her clouded by my thoughts of her king, His Royal Smuggesty?

Before I can decide, we reach a large courtyard. The icy air is a slap in the face, pushing my tiredness into the distance, bringing the here and now into bitterly sharp focus. The snow has been cleared and salt crunches underfoot. Braziers light the space and the clash of steel fills it. Alloying iron into steel renders it safe and legal on the surface – their weapons confirm the same applies here.

Fae traverse the edges of the courtyard, some wandering for the sake of wandering, like me and Min, others entering through one door and leaving through another, taking shortcuts through the fortress.

In the far corner, the rest of the Twylth spar and—

I blink.

I stop mid-step.

The breath stills in my lungs.

I'm not sure what order those things happen in or whether they occur all at once, but I know they align with the moment I spot Drystan among the redcaps.

He wields a long blade, thin and curved like the crescent moon. His hair is bound in a knot at the back of his head. But that isn't what's made me come over all unnecessary.

Either he's a fool or can't feel the cold, because he's wearing trousers and boots, but no damn shirt.

His pale skin is perfect, and he doesn't seem afraid of it getting nicked by Astrid's axe, as he dodges one arcing blow, then another. He isn't huge like Threnn, who's sparring with another redcap off to one side, his face the picture of scowling focus.

No, Drystan is tall and lean, muscles taut and swift. There's a particularly fascinating stretch of them running down his side, rippling as he twists out of Astrid's reach.

I've read more anatomy books than I care to remember, but right now the exact name for that muscle group escapes me. Yet I have a sudden, newfound appreciation for what they do. They flare out, contrasting with his narrow hips and waist, leading to the broad expanse of his chest, which flexes as he sweeps his blade horizontally.

Astrid tries to dodge, but has to catch the blow on her axe.

The clang of metal upon metal wakes me from my stupor. I snap my mouth shut and draw a perfectly normal breath, fighting the urge to fan my suddenly hot face.

But my fascination isn't done. Because as he moves, so do the two birds inked over his shoulders and chest. Their bodies stretch along the line of his collarbones, and their wings spread, one each over his chest, and one each disappearing behind his back.

And I'm still gaping.

Clearing my throat, I glance at Min to check if she's spotted my entirely unnecessary and inexplicable staring.

I need not have worried. Her wide eyes are fixed on him. Her lips are slightly parted, and she's leaning ever so slightly forward.

Is that what I looked like a few seconds ago? I fidget and cross my arms, faintly sick at the thought.

He left me at the mercy of the Collector. He forced me into his labyrinth, not to mention bringing me to the Underworld in the first place. I refuse to stare at him with that look on my face, no matter how nice the view.

But Min doesn't seem so concerned.

In fact . . . her expression calls to something in me. Something I understand all too well. I feel it whenever I look out to sea with its wide-open promise. Whenever I watch the beach and the village in the bay below. Whenever I see the birds wheeling overhead, free and unfettered by gravity or illness.

It's longing.

I glance back over at the king, surprised I've never noticed her looking at him like that before. And that's when I realize.

It's not him she's watching.

Sweat gleams off Astrid's back, highlighting the ripple of muscles and the subtle ways her shoulder blades shift as she feints and parries Drystan's blows. Her thick braids are knotted at the nape of her neck, but one threatens to fall free, loosening with each move. She wears a vicious grin, like she'd happily cut her own king's throat (an impulse I understand).

And that is who Min is staring at with such exquisite longing, it makes my heart sore.

With a gesture from Drystan, the fight breaks off, and Astrid steps back, inclining her head. As though feeling the attention, she turns our way.

Min chokes on a small sound, and I laugh and swat her arm as though we were deep in conversation and she just said something hilarious and a little naughty.

Cheeks pink, she drags her attention away from Astrid and takes a deep breath. 'Do you think she saw me?'

Yes. Absolutely. One hundred per cent Astrid saw her staring.

But I can't bring myself to add to Min's mortification. 'I'm sure it's—'

'STOP.' The word isn't spoken loudly, but its presence crackles around the courtyard, coming from Drystan.

My ears hurt, and along with everyone else, I *stop*.

'Singer of songs. Teller of tales.' His voice is soft now, a purr that carries. A warning that should be heeded.

Unhurried, he saunters over to a steel-haired fae who's a little taller than him. The closer the king gets, the rounder the grey-haired fae's eyes become, until I fear they're about to drop out of his head.

'Y-Your Majesty.' The fae tilts as though he wants to back off but his feet are frozen to the spot. At his sides, his arms go stiff.

'I heard a *fascinating* story about you.' Drystan's lips curl, but his eyes pierce the taller fae, not even slightly warmed by the smile. Somehow he looks at him without seeming any shorter. 'You've been singing songs again, haven't you?'

'I-I-I didn't mean—'

'HAVEN'T YOU?'

'Y-yes, Your Majesty.'

'And one of those songs was about *me*.' Drystan places a hand over his chest as though touched by the gesture.

No one else speaks, but there's this tangible sense of expectation. It's there in the glances swapped, the wide eyes, the way many of the unseelie lean in, pink tongues flashing as they lick their lips like there's something delicious on the air.

Despite the warm layers I'm wearing, goosebumps creep over my arms.

Without sparing a glance for anyone else, Drystan gives the fae an encouraging nod. 'Kindly share.'

'But I-I—'

'You mean you don't want to share the brand-new song you wrote? Not with your king?'

Mouth clamped shut, the fae shakes his head.

'Then at least tell me what it's about.'

'It was just a s-silly song, Your Majesty. I didn't mean anything by it.'

With a thoughtful nod, Drystan examines the length of his blade, turning it over to check its edge. 'So you didn't *mean* it when you said I was so desperate, my mother had to find me a bride?' His eyes flick from the blade to the fae.

'Oh no,' Min breathes.

'It was just a song. It was meant to be funny.'

'Oh. Funny.' Drystan makes a sound that on paper might be a laugh, but it makes my blood run cold. 'I see. And does this strike you as funny?' He gestures to the silent, staring courtyard.

The fae shakes his head.

'Just like it wasn't funny when I warned you last time you wrote one of your little ditties that mocked me. What was that one called? "The Unsmiling King"?'

'Please, Your Majesty. Give me one more chance. I'll stop writing funny songs. I'll—'

'Oh, my dear songsmith.' Drystan sighs and shakes his head, hand cupping around the back of the fae's neck.

I let out a breath, relief creeping in to see Drystan drawing him closer.

'You've had "one more chance". The only mercy I have left is that I'll let you live.'

It all happens too quickly for me to see exactly, but Drystan's blade flashes, the fae lurches, screeches, then blood sprays his clothes and the king's naked chest and a moment later there's something pink and floppy in his hand.

My stomach rolls like some part of me saw and understood every moment.

The fae holds his mouth, making a low moaning sound, but otherwise he doesn't move.

'There.' The king tosses the pink thing – the fae's tongue – aside. 'Now you won't be singing *any* more songs, will you?' He stands back as though waiting for a response, then gives a cruel chuckle. 'Oh, of course, you can't reply, can you?' He waves over one of the redcaps. 'Get him to the Physic. Order them not to reattach it.'

With that, he turns and strides in this direction.

I'm frozen. Horrified. Breakfast is a seething mass in my stomach.

Crimson streaks the broad expanse of his chest, running in rivulets over the muscles of his stomach, channelling into the V-shaped dips over his hips before soaking into his trousers.

'Ah, look, it's Nothing,' he says with a smile and a nod, like this is merely a pleasant greeting.

Before I can gather myself to speak, he disappears into the fortress and the spell upon the courtyard breaks.

Several fae hurry over to the puddle of blood with the singer's tongue at its centre. They stand over it, as a dozen hissed discussions break out. They seem . . . excited.

My heart beats so quickly, I'm sure it's going to burst.

All this over a song. I can't marry that monster.

18

I TRY TO sleep before my teacher arrives, but I can't stop thinking about the singer and the king's cruel 'justice'. I struggle to eat lunch, and instead wrap some in a napkin and pack it away ready for the labyrinth.

When there's a short rap at the door, I almost leap out of my seat. I'm still catching my breath when the king enters with his three ravens and a fae who's only a little taller than me.

He wears the customary unseelie half-smile, but there's a warmth in his dark eyes that reminds me of Annem. His long hair is bound in fine braids, each capped with silver, which tinkles as he approaches. 'I am Kishel.' His voice is smooth and low, soothing.

But the king has to spoil it by speaking. 'Kishel will be your guide as you learn Fatework.'

Avoiding looking at the king, I fight to keep my face impassive, while inside irritation coils and hisses. He has his hair knotted at the back of his head again and there's something more casual about his clothing than usual, all of which serves to remind me of how he looked earlier . . . shirtless . . . a little sweaty . . . focused . . . agile.

There's even a damp tendril of hair brushing his cheek, like he came here directly from bathing.

I hate him. And I hate him all the more for looking so damn good.

I even hate myself a little for thinking it.

With a tight smile, I force my attention to Kishel, finding some relief in his deep-set eyes. 'It's a pleasure to meet you. I'm looking forward to learning from you – perhaps even more than I'm looking forward to becoming His Majesty's queen.' I flash the king a smirk. After all, I'm not breaking the terms of our bargain – if anything, I'm speaking just like the fae. No lies, but not the whole truth.

The king gives me a narrow smile back, irritation flaring in his eyes. 'I'll leave you two to your lesson.' He turns and stalks to the exit, the two black ravens following. 'Bran,' he calls from the door, glancing back.

Expecting to find the white bird perched by the window, I look over my shoulder. A pair of pale lilac eyes peer back above a thick beak that's inches from my face. Bran cocks her head, looking from me to Drystan, then nestles on to her haunches with a soft croak.

The king's lips purse as he gestures at the open door that the other two have already flown through. When the white raven doesn't move, he sighs. 'Really? Have you forgotten where your loyalties lie?' A pause where the bird simply watches him. 'Very well. Stay.' With that, he sweeps away, leaving the door to clunk shut.

Kishel watches me as he takes a seat opposite. 'I'm sure Drystan has told you Fatework is part of the consort's duties.' He tilts his head to one side, reminding me for a moment of the raven. There's the edge of a smirk on his lips, and it isn't lost on me that he refers to Drystan by name rather than title. I file that detail away for later. 'But knowing Drystan, he probably hasn't told you *why*.' His raised eyebrow is a question.

I bite back a sarcastic reply that probably would go against my bargain with the king and simply shake my head.

'Of course not.' He shares a soft chuckle with me, and my shoulders ease.

I think I like him. At least my lessons will be spent in good company.

'Then I'll start at the beginning.' He sits back, steepling his fingers. 'The kings of the Underworld draw power from the land. They're like most unseelie in that respect – we pull from the magic around us. But as our kings and as the sons of The Morrigan, they are linked to the land more intimately. They can draw from its deepest reserves and their capacity for magic is far greater.'

Their capacity for *ego*, more like. But I smile and nod, showing I'm listening.

'Yet there are depths to the land that aren't accessible to them. Hidden places, hidden streams of magic – underground rivers if you will – that can only be reached by a consort, once they are bound by the wedding rituals.'

My nodding pauses. If I fail to escape, this will be more than just a marriage.

Maybe it was foolish of me, but I had it in my head that it would be a wedding much like a human one. Some pretty words, the symbolic binding of hands, the sharing of honey and a blessing from a druid, then everyone feasts and drinks and dances until they can't any longer.

But this? Rituals and hidden power that *I'll* have access to? Some humans are gifted with magic. Those who are only have it thanks to the fae. Some have fae ancestry, so they carry that gift in their blood – the fae-blooded. The fae-touched, on the other hand, are given the gift, though it's not as potent. The old tales are full of stories of humans who helped an old woman on the road or saved a child from wolves or drowning, only to find the victim was a glamoured fae who then gifted them or their children – or future children – with some form of magic.

I'm not fae-blooded or -gifted. So how would accessing this hidden magic even work? *Would* it work?

And what would the cruel, uncaring king want me to do with it?

'Is everything all right?'

I suck in a breath, jolting from my spiralling thoughts. 'Yes. Fine! I was just . . . I hadn't realized there was a magical element to the marriage.'

None of this matters, anyway. I'll get home through the labyrinth and Drystan will have to find himself another consort. Phaedra seems much more suited to the role. I'm sure she's already powerful – she'll be able to handle these hidden streams of magic.

Kishel gives an understanding nod, but there's a spark to his eyes that belies his kindly demeanour, like his gaze is skewering through my smiles and soft flesh and reaching the very marrow of my bones.

'I suspect it's rather different to the surface, but I have an inkling you're up to the task. Part of the consort's magic is about seeing the kingdom's fate and working to nudge it into a more desirable direction. I get the sense you want to keep others safe and see them prosperous and happy.'

Min instantly comes to mind. I may not really know anyone else here but I'll do my best to master whatever Fatework requires for her. No one deserves to melt away at the edge of court because of something as inconsequential as a scar.

I see her face as she stared at Astrid, the longing that still speaks to my own heart.

'Does Fatework tell you about . . . love? Can you find out how someone feels? Or, uh, *nudge* them into feeling? No, that wouldn't be fair. But finding out how they feel – that would be all right. How does it work?'

'So many questions.' There's a gently teasing undercurrent to his tone, but it isn't cruel and sharp like the king's. 'Perhaps we should start at that beginning I mentioned, rather than jumping ahead.'

My curiosity has run away with me again. My face grows warm, and I barely stop myself apologizing.

'Do you have what I believe humans call a "fae mark"?'

The sign of a human with magic. Some have elongated canines like fae, others have unusual hair or eye colours or an unnaturally shaped birthmark.

Not me.

With an apologetic smile, I shake my head.

'And did you have an awakening?' He raises his eyebrows hopefully.

I hate to disappoint him, but I had no magical outburst in my teens or early twenties that revealed some latent power. 'I'm afraid not. No mark. No awakening. No magic. I'm entirely ordinary.'

He laughs, but not in a way that makes me the butt of his joke – his eyes are too soft for that, inviting me in rather than shutting me out. 'You may not have magic, but that doesn't make you ordinary. See? Bran believes in you.' He indicates something behind me.

The bird is still perched on the back of my chair, a ghostly presence peering over my shoulder.

'Is the king out in the cold tonight and you'd rather be inside with us?' I ask as I smooth the feathers of her chest. She lifts her head as if she wants me to do it again, so I oblige before returning to my lesson.

Kishel gives me an odd look but after a second it's gone and he places a shallow bowl on the table. He fills it from a bottle that's labelled 'Moonwater', then he sits back and invites me to peer into it. 'Tell me what you see.'

I crane over and look into the water rippling under my breath. I see my warped reflection. I see the ceiling decorated in a grey and white gradient. I see . . . nothing else.

When I report my findings to Kishel, he nods, then rummages

in his bag. 'Try this.' He produces a mirror that sits flat on the table. Its frame is much simpler than the one Lowen gave me, with organic swirls and faintly leafy shapes, but its surface reminds me of that mirror.

In it, my reflection is broken, an eye appearing on my cheek, my nose skewed to one side, sliced by the ceiling paint.

Perhaps if I look hard enough, I'll be able to see something among the chaos. I lean forward, brow tight, eyes burning as I resist the urge to blink.

I don't realize I'm bent right over the mirror, reaching out, until my fingertips brush its surface. It's as cold as ice and ripples from my touch, like I've dropped a pebble into a pond's still surface.

My gaze darts across the scattered reflections, searching.

But there are no great secrets, no profound prophecies. Just myself and the ceiling.

With a sigh, I sink back in my chair and shake my head.

To his credit, Kishel's hopeful expression doesn't dissolve. He just nods and rubs his lower lip, turning over his thoughts.

Movement whispers over my scalp, and when I tilt my head and peer out the corner of my eye, I find Bran playing with my hair. It's oddly comforting.

Kishel clearly isn't one to be put off easily, as he takes me outside next, a Twylth guard in tow. He has me search the movement of the strange stars in this inky sky and the flight of a flock of birds he scares from their sleep in the wintry trees. He even goes to fetch a chicken from one of the coops near the kitchens, but I beg him not to cut the bird open so I can read its entrails, and not only because I'm sure it would be a fruitless endeavour.

Because I don't see anything other than stars in constellations I don't recognize, the flapping wings of alarmed birds and the unerring but doomed hope in Kishel's face.

He leads me to the burbling fountain in the glasshouse. The results are the same. But he squeezes my shoulder. 'Patience, my young apprentice. Perhaps we just need to open the way. Let me scry for you.'

He's waiting, eyebrows raised, as though he needs my permission. I'm not sure what he means exactly, but I nod and gesture for him to go ahead.

Craning over the fountain's surface, he takes my hand. His gaze goes distant, darting side to side as though desperate to quickly take in a scene I cannot see. 'You break this block.' His voice has an odd quality to it, distant and echoing, like he's deep inside a cave and I'm at its entrance. 'You see the horse that's to come. You venture far, towards the great gates and the narrow bridge beyond, but you won't like what you find among the yellow flowers.'

The breath catches in my throat. The gates – they must be the exit from the labyrinth, and the narrow bridge . . .

Could that be the stone bridge that leads to our cottage? The yellow flowers – they have to be gorse bushes, right?

So I will beat the labyrinth. I will escape.

My eyes burn with tears of relief. I've held on to determination, and I've kept hope locked in my heart, but to hear him say I will succeed feels like the universe has confirmed it.

I just need to keep going, and I *will* get home.

'Try not to worry.' He pats my hand, mistaking my unshed tears for frustration at my failure to scry anything but my own reflection. 'We'll try different methods until we try one that works for you. After all, we have nothing but time.'

19

FOR ONCE IN my life, I'm glad that I have less time than others may think. Kishel expects me to stay here for ever as his king's consort. I know I have less than a fortnight.

The idea puts a spring in my step when the next morning I scatter into shadows and appear in the exact spot where I last stood in the labyrinth. At least the king wasn't deceiving me about that.

I press on, despite the exhaustion nipping at my heels. If I keep pushing, I can stay out of its reach. I just need to hold on long enough to reach the gate.

No sign of the Collector, but I have food wrapped up from earlier and I'm prepared with warmer clothes and a cloak I wrap around myself when I stop and rest. I've also packed my notebook and use that and the sun to aim towards the next tier.

But of course the labyrinth doesn't save *all* its challenges for the gateways between levels. There are dead ends and a sunken plate that's pretty obviously the trigger for a trap just like I've read about in adventure stories, so I edge past it and carry on my way.

And all the while I hatch a plan.

If I can't do Fatework, probably because of my lack of magic, I can at least do something to help Min.

So when I return to Drystan's fortress and wake from a nap to find him knocking at the door, I have my politest smile ready.

'Would you allow Astrid to teach me to ride?' It burns my throat to be nice to him.

His pace towards the settee slows and he narrows his eyes at me. 'I won't deny you need it. But why Astrid, in particular?'

Trying to ignore the insult, I shrug like it doesn't matter when in fact my plan hinges on her being the one to teach me. 'Oh, I'd just feel more comfortable with a woman teaching me. I should imagine it involves touching, right?'

He stares at me throughout my answer, as though he can detect any lie if he just pays close enough attention. I keep my hands busy by brushing my hair, but my pulse strikes a little too heavily.

Eventually, he agrees to arrange it for after lunch, but my luck ends there. He refuses to let me contact my brother, then he takes me to the grand dining hall, where we sit at opposite ends of a ridiculously long table and eat. I manage to pass a message to one of the servants, requesting help with my outfit.

One thought consumes me. I'll leave the Underworld within a fortnight, but at least I can do this one thing to make Min a little less isolated before I go.

The moon is high when Drystan guides me down to the stables, my hand in the crook of his elbow, guards, ravens and shadows in our wake. I'm dressed warmly in a whisper-grey coat trimmed with white velvet and fastened with silver buttons, but I'm still grateful for his warmth at my side. I try not to press into it, reminding myself of the singer's fate.

'You don't need to show me the way,' I say lightly, gesturing along the path.

He takes his time peering down at me out the corner of his eye, one eyebrow arched. 'Trying to get rid of me?'

'No,' I lie as we round a corner into the stable yard. It's better if he goes before Min arrives – he's sure to ask questions if he sees her and then he'll uncover my plan. Knowing how prickly he is, he'll put a stop to it.

He makes a sound that says he's unconvinced.

Luckily, Astrid meets us first, crossing the yard. Even though it's cold, she wears a short-sleeved shirt tucked into fitted trousers. Her boots look warmer, with black fur peeking out the top, and a grey cowl covers her shoulders, ready to pull up if snow starts. It isn't lost on me that it stops short of her arms, leaving the muscles barely contained by the shirt. I'm sure Min will enjoy that fact, and I smile to myself at the thought.

Despite the fearsome origin of her red hair, there's a welcoming warmth to her, helped by the ease of her wide smile, bright against her tanned face. It almost makes me miss the sharp length of her canines. *Almost*. They glint like the newly fallen snow that cakes the rooftops, a deadly reminder of all that she is.

And I was foolish enough to cross her in my escape attempt. Wincing inwardly, I return her smile of greeting.

Before the king can say anything, she inclines her head to him. 'I will take good care of your betrothed, Your Majesty. I take this honour seriously.'

He shoots me a mistrustful look. Perhaps he thinks this is another escape attempt. 'And I take my betrothal seriously.' Before I can release his arm, he grabs my fingers and twirls me around to face him. He pulls me close, the heat of his body such a shocking contrast with the chill air, I can't speak. 'Darling Rhiannon.' With a fingertip, he raises my chin, forcing me to make eye contact.

I haven't held his gaze this close before. The glow of his eyes tends to make me glance away, and usually he's transporting me somewhere and I push away as soon as I'm steady. As it is, my hand braces on his chest, but a smirk flickers on the corner of his lips and his thumb joins his finger, gripping my chin in place.

His breaths fan my mouth, my cheek, the side of my neck as he bends closer. 'Ah, ah, ah,' he makes the soft chiding sound right in my ear. 'Our bargain, remember?'

The soft intimacy of his voice, the heat of his breath, his casual proximity – I hate how they streak through my body, bypassing my brain.

So I take a breath to tell him exactly where he can shove his bargain.

And that's my mistake.

Because I've never noticed his scent before, perhaps because I've been more wrapped up in the business of falling apart into flecks of shadow, but now it's *in me* – primal, ancient, familiar in a way that makes no sense. Moss clinging to standing stones. Smoke threading through a still forest. Frost blooming on a velvety night.

But beneath the cold, there's this warm undertow that curls through me – slow, sensual, lingering . . . like secrets. Like lies. Like something I shouldn't want.

I need to shove him away, regain my senses, but I can feel his smile against my cheek – a silent reminder of our charade.

'Remember your manners and everything we've agreed.'

'It's never far from my mind, *dearest*,' I say on a breath, desperate to drive out the smell – the *taste* of him. 'I promise I'll be a good girl.'

This small, sharp huff of a sound drives from deep in his chest, making me realize I'm arched against him. I tighten, pulling away as much as I can within the cage of his arm.

When he speaks again, his voice is laced with amusement. 'Then you can start by pretending I'm whispering something delicious in your ear, rather than standing there stiff.'

My hand is still braced upon his chest. Exhaling, I soften my fingers.

He gives a hum that says he's unconvinced.

I stop pulling away and let my body go back to what it was doing before, pressing my hips, my belly, my chest into all of him.

'Very good.' His lips brush my ear as he speaks, forcing me to gasp, which in turn forces his scent deeper into my nostrils, my lungs. My being.

This has to be what comes from being a demi-god. Or it's fae intoxication – their ability to charm mortals is legendary. I just never realized it worked through smell.

'Now, kiss my cheek.'

I grit my teeth. Thankfully most of my expression is hidden by the long, straight fall of his hair, otherwise I'd be in breach of our bargain. Astrid would know that when it comes to her king, I'm more interested in murder than marriage.

'It's expected.' His lilting tone is as teasing as his scent. 'You *are* my fiancée after all.' He finally releases my chin so I can comply.

I tiptoe so I can get his cheek rather than his jaw. Another mistake. It rubs my breasts against him, a reminder of what it's like to be touched, wanted, craved, my body worshipped. Unwanted heat sparks in my nerves, stealing my breath, igniting every place we touch like kindling.

For a second. A fraction of a fraction of a second, I soften. Press into him. Let the answering tension of his arm crush me against him. I shouldn't want more, but for a heartbeat I do.

Rhiannon Archer. Remember who he is. What he is. He rips out tongues. He rips families apart. And he *just doesn't care*.

It's enough to bring me back to myself, but that doesn't end the torturous burn of his touch. And I need this to be over.

I brush my lips over his cheek. It's quick, but the impression lingers. Hot skin. Abrading stubble. The hard cut of his cheekbone.

'We can work on that, I suppose.' As he releases me at last, he winks.

Chest heaving horribly, I wonder if I could poke his eye out with my bare hands. That would definitely break our bargain.

Instead, fluttering my lashes, I give him a honey-sweet smile until he turns and leaves.

'Hmm.' When my attention returns to Astrid, she's bouncing a thoughtful look from me to Drystan and back again, hand on hip.

'What?' The heat in my cheeks spreads, like I've been caught misbehaving and what had been pleasant warmth low in my stomach becomes a knot of fear that I'm about to be told off.

'You really don't realize, do you?' She cants her head, curious rather than pissed off, which eases that tension in my belly.

'Realize *what*?'

'Never mind.' She shrugs and shakes her head, though as she turns she mutters something that might include the word 'innocent'.

Glad to be out of sight of Drystan's retreating form, I follow her into the stable block, glancing back in case Min arrives.

'Uh, Astrid?' Now we're alone, I stop and knit my fingers together. 'I'm not sure how you deal with admitting that you harmed someone and regret it when you don't do apologies here.'

She chuckles as she ducks into a stall. 'I think you just did.'

'I used you in my plan and I feel bad for deceiving you. I'm sure I got you in trouble, too.'

'I'm guessing you weren't exactly sold on life in the Underworld when you first arrived.' She appears at the door to the stall and shrugs. 'Can't say I blame you – it's not like we chose this place either. But it has its charms. Looks like you've discovered one of them.' Her eyebrows rise as she casts a meaningful look in the direction of the stable yard and my interaction with the king.

I give a sickly smile as she turns and busies herself with the horse inside the stall. At least I'm forgiven, I suppose.

It's the same white horse with brownish-grey flecks that Drystan had ready the other day. I remember now that the book on steeds said a horse with this flecked pattern of coat was known as a flea-bitten grey. Still, it seems strange to call such a pretty creature 'flea bitten' and even stranger to call a white horse grey.

Astrid fastens a saddle on to the gelding with ease, using her arm to hold the girth in place as she buckles it with her hand before I can offer to help.

Just as she's working on the bridle, Min peers through the door. 'Annon? Is everything all right with your clothing? I got a message asking me to—' Her eyes widen when they land on Astrid's red hair and broad shoulders – she's already moved on to saddling up a bay for herself.

Min's silent, but she gives me a pointed look, eyes wider than I've ever seen them.

'That's right, Min. I asked you to join me for my riding lesson.' I flash my eyebrows up at her and give an encouraging nod. 'You don't mind do you, Astrid?'

One arm slung over the horse's back, Astrid turns. She gives Min an appraising once-over. 'The more the merrier. I'll get one of the boys tacked up for you.'

She does so while Min shifts uncomfortably and shoots me looks she thinks I can't see out the corner of my eye.

The pair of them lead out three horses who amble along at a sedate walk. Compared to my ride with the king, this all looks very manageable. Although Astrid has a vicious-looking sword strapped on one side of her saddle and a bow across the back, so maybe she's expecting trouble of some sort.

In the yard, she gives me a boost on to the flea-bitten grey and shows me how to sit. With Astrid ahead and Min behind me, we file into an adjacent paddock as Bran swoops past and perches on a fence post.

Astrid stands at the centre, watching me, while her horse waits tethered at the gate. Min rides behind, ready to come after me and grab my horse's reins if he runs away with me or whatever else can go wrong with horse riding.

I'm trying not to think about that.

Whenever I've seen people ride, it's looked straightforward, easy, even. After all, the steed is doing all the work. But I soon realize that while the rider isn't the one walking, they're still active – even when they're not clinging to a galloping horse controlled by the King of Death. My hips move to absorb the jiggling caused by the horse's walk, and once I get the hang of stopping by making a low sound, starting by squeezing my legs and turning by touching the reins to the side of the horse's neck, we try trotting.

It's a lot like being shaken around in a dice cup. I cling on, hoping not to be thrown off to see which way up I land.

Astrid calls instructions. Keep my legs loose. Rise as this leg comes forward. Up, down, up, down, up, down.

By the time I get the hang of that, I'm out of breath and my thighs are burning. This was meant to be a nice, calm, easy activity to get Min and Astrid together, not more exercise after a day trudging through the labyrinth.

It's a relief when I can slow my horse to a walk and sink back into the saddle.

'Good work, Annon.' We dropped the 'my lady' somewhere along the lesson. From her spot in the centre of the paddock, Astrid glances behind me to Min.

'What do you reckon? Is she ready for a ride out?'

I can practically feel Min's doubt wafting through the air. 'Well, I don't know. She's only just—'

'Astrid is such a great teacher.' I throw a reassuring smile over my shoulder. 'She'll make sure I don't get hurt, plus I'll have you to keep an eye on me, too, right?'

Min's lips press together as she turns from me to Astrid.

'Lady Min,' Astrid speaks solemnly, hand over her heart, voice low, her easy smile gone, 'you have my word, I won't let anything happen to our future queen. Or to you.'

I get a second-hand flutter in my belly at the way she ever so slightly inclines her head as she holds Min's gaze, like a knight of yore pledging his life to a lady's protection.

I think Astrid might like her back. Is matchmaking really this easy?

The urge to squeal comes from deep inside, but I hold my breath until it passes. I'm sure it would break the moment.

Instead, I smile to myself, heart at once full and aching. This is how it was when I was a girl and had friends down in the village school and we'd tell each other about the boys and girls we liked.

The last time I knew anything like this was before my illness took a turn, when I would go with my father to a market town inland and I started a fling with the baker's eldest daughter. It was only physical, but she could make my belly flutter with just a look, and I'd have taken more if she'd offered it.

'We'll stay this side of the river,' Astrid goes on, 'and I have my sword and bow.'

Min blinks as though coming back from somewhere far away. Sluggish, she turns to Astrid's horse as if seeing it for the first time. At last, she nods. Her cheeks have gone pink since I last looked round at her, and I'm willing to bet good money that has nothing to do with the nip in the air and everything to do with the redcap who's now mounting her bay mare.

As we ride out, I hang back, letting them talk. Well, letting Astrid talk, because Min seems to have forgotten how.

The redcap tells us about the scant trees studding the snow once we're a few hundred yards from the fortress's walls. She tells us how the land seems to have warmed a little, because the dead can no longer cross the river, so there must be running water beneath its frozen surface.

I shiver at the reminder of the dead. 'Astrid?' I can't help inter-rupting for the question burning on my tongue.

'You should call me Asti.' She turns to Min. 'Both of you. I'd prefer it.'

It takes every bit of discipline in my body not to turn to Min with a crow of triumph. Maybe Bran feels it in the air, because as she circles overhead, she gives a low croak.

'*Asti*, then. I was curious . . . You said the dead can't pass over running water, but what about a bridge over the sea? Does that not count because it's salt water? Or is the sea not technically run-ning? Or is it because—?'

Asti raises her hand, laughing. 'Whoa, there. I'll answer your question if you give me a chance.' She gestures for me to come up alongside her – the opposite side from Min, I note.

I almost mutter an apology, a little bashful from bombarding her with questions. 'My curiosity ran away with me.'

'Curiosity is a good thing. Especially since the Underworld is very different from the surface. The only way you're going to find out more is if you ask.' She spreads her arms. 'As for crossing water – it isn't the water that's the factor here. I'm willing to bet this isn't a hypothetical question. You saw the dead cross while you were on the surface world.' She cants her head and the corner of her mouth twitches as though she's fighting a laugh. 'Perhaps when a certain king came to collect you?'

'You would win that bet.'

'The dead you saw – risen – they were just husks. Bodies without souls. They aren't contained by the same rules as spirit-made-flesh, like the dead who rove here. These are still people, still have souls, memories. At least, most of them do. If they linger too long, they lose themselves, even though shreds of their souls remain. It's the spirit aspect that stops them from crossing running water.'

That aligns with what I observed. Some who'd lost themselves, some who remembered. I try not to think about the shambler.

'Have you ever been to the surface?' Min asks softly, eyes down-cast, even though Asti's attention leaps back to her before she finishes the first word.

'I've been on raids, occasionally. But not for a long time.'

'Not since you joined the Twylth?'

'I pledged to guard His Majesty and that doesn't leave room for raids. Even though that would save him the exorbitant costs of buying horse feed from our neighbours.' She glances at me. 'This is one of the few times I've worked away from his side for years now. He wants to take good care of you, if he's letting me leave him.'

'He wants to protect his investment,' I mutter before I even think to keep my mouth shut. Shit.

I'm sure that's the truth. It's been echoing in my mind since Kishel told me about the power a king's consort can access. That's why he wants to marry me.

But my statement isn't exactly fitting from an enthusiastic bride-to-be. And I did promise. The last thing I want is for Drystan to decide I've broken our bargain and remove my opportunity to leave, especially now Kishel has made it clear I'll succeed.

I clear my throat. 'I mean – he's been waiting for me before he could take a bride, right? Imagine if he waited all that time and then I got killed because of some silly Underworld danger.'

Asti's jaw tightens and she scans the snowy plain. 'I wouldn't allow that to happen to you *or* to him.'

My thoughtless comment puts a bit of a dampener on Asti's mood, and I struggle to stoke the conversation, until I get Min started on a style of sleeve she's been developing. I don't entirely follow her explanation – a diagram would help – but I note the close attention Asti pays to her hands moving as she describes the delicate bell shape and the gather over the wrist, and that's enough to get me to stop cursing myself for slipping up.

*

Riding is fun. I think. I'm stiff after but it's easier on my body than walking, and I still feel like I'm getting some exercise. I'm sure I'll get used to this new kind of movement.

I used to love walking along the coast to the beach, but I haven't been able to do that for a long time. From horseback, I get the chance to observe parts of the Underworld that were only a blur when the king rode out with me.

It lets me imagine a version of home where I ride and see the surface world. I'd need company, of course, just in case I had an episode. And I'd carry a waterskin, ready to take a gulp with my belladonna. But it feels possible.

We wouldn't be able to afford to buy a sabrecat, never mind feed one, of course. Maybe I can find a way to borrow one, even if it's just once a month.

But the ride doesn't last. We return to the fortress, and Asti's called away by guards, leaving us to return her horse to the stables. Threnn is there, though, ready to take over guarding me.

As we enter the yard, Min straightens, head cocked at some noise I can't detect. As a stable hand rushes forward to take my horse's reins, she dismounts and helps me down. 'What's happening?'

The hand glances at her colleagues who bustle through the yard and stables. 'Effan is missing. You know him – he works in the kitchens, does all the bread.'

'Effan?' She pulls a sceptical face. 'Are you sure he's not just curled up somewhere cursing himself for drinking too much?'

The stable hand shrugs, mouth twisting. 'Cook's asked us to search the stables. There aren't any horses missing, so he can't have gone far. But you could be right and we'll find him passed out in the hayloft.'

'I'll help look once I've taken Lady Rhiannon up to her rooms.'

The stable hand's eyes bulge as she sucks in a breath. 'My lady, of course.' She sketches a bow. 'I should've realized. I should've bowed at—'

'Don't worry, *please*. You have more important things to be thinking about than bowing to some human you don't know. I hope you find Effan.'

She inclines her head with a look of gratitude, and I can't help wondering if she expected me to lop off her tongue for such a minor infraction.

Only once Min and I are away do I ask about the missing baker.

'It's nothing to worry about. He's the restless sort. Likes to lean on his status as His Majesty's half-brother to get away with not doing much work.' At my wide-eyed look, she adds, 'Not The Morrigan's son – the old king's. Think he's a bit too used to court life over kitchen life, though, so a lot of the baking ends up falling on the pâtissière.' The way she purses her lips tells me exactly how much she disapproves. 'But a few months ago one of the stable boys went missing. There were no footprints outside the walls. Not even the Wild Hunt could track him. No one's seen him since. I just hope this isn't more of the same.'

The king's brother. That explains why he reminded me of Drystan. And his behaviour when we were introduced matches Min's summary. I give my most reassuring smile. 'I'm sure Effan's just snuggled in the hay sleeping off the wine.'

She eyes my hand and opens her mouth to speak, when Threnn's shadow falls over us.

'Perhaps you're right,' Min mutters and we go the rest of the way in silence.

Still, it tears at me to be retreating to my room when I could help search. But my eyelids are heavy and my legs grow heavier with each step. I need to rest if I'm to stand any chance of making progress in the labyrinth tomorrow – or is it later today?

I'll get some sleep and they'll find Effan by the time I wake up. I've seen how impossible it is to run from Drystan's court, and, unlike me, it sounds as though the baker enjoys his life here. He has no reason to run.

20

THE NEXT NIGHT, after a frustrating day in the labyrinth where I got turned around and did *not* find my way to the next tier, I make my way to the glasshouse. There wasn't time during my tour with the king, and I'm curious what plants they have here as well as what methods they're using to grow them. It's only a short walk and I'm hoping the gentle exercise will help unknot my muscles and joints from the riding lesson and trekking through the labyrinth.

The warm, damp air and green smell of growing things hit me as soon as I walk in. It's like my mind's clearer now I'm not with the king and I can absorb it all. The narrow stone paths that wind between the raised beds, their grey surfaces damp and dark. The stakes supporting peas and raspberries at the far end. The stunted fruit trees dotted here and there, buds twisted tight like they don't want to bloom.

Threnn followed me here and now waits at the door, standing to attention. One of the other Twylth guards said it was an honour to guard their future queen, and he seems to take pride in his work, gaze sticking to me as I make my way along one of the vegetable beds.

No doubt he's wondering what the hells I'm doing. I don't think unseelie queens generally take an interest in horticulture.

I keep my back to him and tuck my notebook in the crook of my arm so he can't see it as I catalogue what plants they have. Black kale, leeks, beetroot. A leafy thing that looks similar to cauliflower, but its centre is spiked and purple rather than bobbly and creamy white.

Interesting. They have plants I don't recognize, even from books. What botanical treasures might exist in the Underworld? Since the unseelie came here in long lost ages, I assumed they'd brought all the Underworld's flora and fauna with them from the surface but perhaps that isn't the case. There might be something with undiscovered benefits to humans ... particularly humans with unidentified, apparently incurable illnesses.

It's a nice thought.

For now, I'm on the hunt for belladonna. My jar of the dried stuff is half full, so I'm less worried about that running out than I am my medicine, but it's a contingency. Just in case ...

Wincing, I riffle the edge of my notebook and force myself to finish that thought.

Just in case I don't make it home.

Like my illness, I need to be realistic.

I squeeze the notebook, letting the pages bite into my fingertips. A reminder. Of my brother and how I've failed him. I owe it to Lowen to get back somehow. Whether it's through the labyrinth or some other means. If it takes a week or a year.

Nodding to myself, I bend to a creeping weed I've spotted by some parsnips and tug it up by the roots.

Dizziness rolls over me as I try to straighten, forcing me to spin and plop myself on the stone edge of the raised bed.

A shadow passes over me.

Blinking as I steady myself, I find Threnn's towering form, his brow low. He really does take his job seriously.

I wave him off, the dizziness already abating – not a full episode, thankfully. 'It's all right. I just got up too quickly.'

His hands clench and unclench and his weight shifts as if he's about to come closer.

'It's fine. I don't need any help.' If he lifts me to my feet, he'll uncover the notebook hidden half by my arm and half by the light jacket I'm wearing.

He steps forward in silence. He towers over me. I squeeze the notebook, craning to look up at him with a reassuring smile.

'Lady Rhiannon – just who I was looking for.'

Threnn spins at the sound of Min's voice, and she hurries over, wearing an overly bright smile of her own, like she's thrilled to see me. He glances back at me, holds my gaze for a beat, then nods.

Shit, does he suspect I'm hiding something?

But he resumes his vigil at the doors as Min offers her hand to help me up.

Now the world has stopped spinning, I take it. She knows about my illness already – it doesn't matter if she sees the notebook.

She keeps hold of my hand once I'm upright, and bends in. 'What were you playing at last night?'

I blink at the way she asks in a forceful hiss. 'Last . . .? Oh, you mean the ride?'

'*Yes*, I mean the ride. Were you trying to embarrass me or—?'

'What? No!' I slip my hand out of hers and hug the notebook tight. 'I was trying to help. I saw how you looked at Asti when she was practising and I thought . . . maybe you could use a hand to throw you together.'

Her head jerks back. 'You were trying to . . . *help*?'

It may not be one of the rules I've been told, but everything I've learned so far about this culture suggests that pitying is probably the worst thing you could do to the unseelie. So I use one of Min's own suggestions back on her to avoid mentioning her isolation. 'You do like her, don't you?'

Her jaw works side to side and she glances around. Threnn is the only one here, some distance away at the door. 'Of course I do. Have you seen her?' Cheeks flushing, she swallows. 'But she's one of the Twylth.'

I wait for her to go on, but she stops there as if that's explanation enough.

'Do they . . . take an oath of chastity?' That doesn't seem very fae, but it's possible, I suppose.

Min snorts. 'Is that something they do on the surface? Seven hells, humans are weird. In case you hadn't noticed, the Twylth are . . . Well, everyone either wants them or wants to be one of them. They are some of the highest-ranking folk in the entire kingdom. Whereas I . . .' She sighs, a frown etched between her eyebrows as her gaze lands on one of the dormant fruit trees. 'I am scarred. Weak.'

'But . . . Asti's arm. Isn't that a kind of scar?'

She makes a thoughtful sound, a half smile twisting her mouth. It doesn't suit her. 'Astrid is that rare thing – injured, but in an acceptable way. She's marked by battle, and she's still a warrior – fit, strong, capable of killing pretty much anyone she comes up against. She's a hero of the Underworld. I . . . am not.' Warmth, pride, longing all shine through in her voice, right up until it drops on that last broken sentence. 'I make clothes. Out of sight. Even my parents refuse to acknowledge me.'

The ache in her voice speaks to something in me, tightening my chest. My parents kept the bargain with The Morrigan secret, and I've been trapped by that hurt, unable to separate it from my thoughts of them since I got here. But at least I still have them.

Min on the other hand . . .

I shake my head. 'Lord and Lady Song are your parents, aren't they?'

Her mouth flattens. 'I bet they curse the resemblance. My *imper-fect* face doesn't let them forget.' She turns her glower from the twisted buds to me as if realizing how vulnerable she's been. Shutters in her eyes slam. 'So what were you trying to help me do? Look like a fool? Tell Astrid so she could laugh in my face? Or—'

I stop her with a barked laugh of disbelief. 'And you think humans are weird! Not everyone is out to get you, Min. This wasn't some master plan to trick you or make you look silly.' I pause, wrestling with how to explain something so raw for us both. A breath lets me regain control of my voice so I can lower my tone. 'I wanted to help because I saw how isolated you were in the ballroom and . . . that's something I can relate to.'

She opens her mouth. Closes it. Repeats the motion before asking, 'Is this a human lie?'

'No.'

Her eyes narrow.

'No! I swear it on my brother's life.'

She stays quiet. So do I.

Eventually, I turn and continue working my way along the plants, cataloguing them. I expect her to leave, but a moment later, she's at my shoulder. 'It's . . . uh . . . It's hard to grow crops here.' The fragmented sentence feels like a peace offering.

With the glass roof arching over us, I eye the snow outside. 'Why not just stockpile in the summer months?'

She huffs out a laugh, then her hand shoots to her cheek and she looks away. When she lifts her head, her expression is smoothed out. 'What summer months? This winter has lasted forty years.'

'Huh.' I raise my eyebrows at the frozen world outside.

'There's only so much we can grow in here. We have to supplement it with raids on the surface, when our parties can make the journey.'

Forty years. I wander over and press my hand to the cold glass. Such a strange world. 'It came suddenly.' That explains the camellias captured in full bloom. Seasons here don't obey the laws I'm used to.

I jot it in my notebook. Part of me wonders if I can help. Perhaps that's part of the consort's power Kishel told me about. It would explain why Drystan is so keen to keep hold of me even though he's made his distaste excruciatingly clear.

Not that I want to help him, but it would help Min, Astrid and Kishel, as well as preventing raids to the surface.

That's a big responsibility. And no small feat. I'm better off focusing on something more manageable — like growing belladonna. It normally flowers in the summer, but it likes partial shade at the edges of woodland or hedgerows, so the Underworld's seasons, natural or not, would be a relevant factor in its cultivation.

'Do you get belladonna in the Underworld?'

She frowns, tilting her head. 'Is that a plant?'

'About this tall, purple bell-shaped flowers, purple-black berries. Poisonous — to humans, anyway.'

'Sounds like dwale to me.'

Min bolts upright at the new voice, cheeks immediately flushing pink.

I'm already smiling when I turn and find Asti bowing her head to me, gaze quickly flicking to Min.

'Dwale?' I make a note — she's already seen the notebook. 'So that's what you call it. And does it grow here?'

'Not in the glasshouse, but I've spotted it once or twice outside.' Her cheerful expression flickers for a moment and she adds in a lower voice, 'Not in Mordren, though.'

Right. The perma-winter.

'Could you get hold of some for me? Seeds, preferably.'

'For my future queen? Of course.' She gives Min a conspiratorial look. 'Do you think I need to warn her that it won't poison fae?'

I chuckle. 'Not planning to poison anyone with it. It just has . . . interesting effects for humans in a light enough dose.'

'Since Threnn told me you've been in here for hours, I'm going to guess you know what that dose is, so I have no problem ordering our next raiding party to get some. You should take a look in the library – there's a section on plants. But' – she spreads her arms – 'I didn't come here for pretty flowers. I have something to show you.' With a jerk of her chin, she has us follow.

Since she refuses to tell us more, we head outside, skirt the fortress's central buildings where the living accommodation and Great Hall are and arc around to the stables. I let Asti and Min fall a little behind to give them some privacy and try not to eavesdrop, though the latter remains uncharacteristically quiet.

It turns out the king has had a dozen horses delivered from breeders in another kingdom. 'Although our horses require less feed than those on the surface, it's easier to breed in the other kingdoms where they have pasture and hay, then bring them across the border,' Asti explains, stroking the nose of a pale stallion with a luminous coat as we pass his stall. 'Though it costs His Majesty a pretty penny.'

'So . . . it's not winter in all the kingdoms?' It looks like I was right about the smear of green on the horizon.

I cock my head as we stop at a stall with a slate-grey gelding – if I remember rightly this colouring is called a blue roan. Though I don't think on the surface their flecked fur glints like it's made of steel and silver.

'Not all the time, no.'

Yet more about this strange season. I make mental notes to write up into the notebook currently sitting in my pocket. The gelding pokes his head over the stable door and nudges me. 'No carrots here, I'm afraid.' To soften the bad news, I stroke the flat plane of his cheek, and he leans into me.

'Can I ask how the future queen's Fatework lessons are going?' Asti gives me a sidelong look as she pets the horse in the next stall.

I share a glance with Min. I haven't been told the lessons are a secret exactly, but I get the impression they aren't to be talked about.

She widens her eyes in silent answer, as unsure as me.

Asti grins. 'Kishel is my uncle. He didn't tell me any details, but he said he'd had a chance to spend time with you. I put two and two together.'

My face screws up as I fuss the gelding, who seems to love the attention as he presses his great head into me. 'It's not really going.' That's probably more information than I should give – an admission of failing and thus weakness to the unseelie. But Asti feels safe. She has done from the start. And I have no doubt the king has ordered Kishel to report to him, so it's not as if she can go and give him new information. 'Not yet, anyway,' I add with a hopeful smile. 'Probably because I'm human. I'm sure it's just going to take longer – that's all.'

Thank the gods I can lie.

I'm fairly sure it's a case of no magic, no Fatework.

'I don't think my uncle's taught a human before. He probably needs to try some new methods.' She shrugs and I'm this close to hugging her for her kindness. Before I can, she pulls three pieces of carrot out of her pocket and hands them to me, then gestures to the gelding. 'What do you think of him, then?'

Hand as flat as possible, thumb tucked in, like she showed me on my lesson, I feed the horse before he can knock me over. 'He's very enthusiastic – at least when it comes to scratches and food.'

She chuckles. 'Well, don't worry about that – he's going to be a lot calmer when it comes to riding.'

I nod as he lips the last piece carrot from my palm, his whiskers tickling.

'You do realize he's yours, right? A gift from the king.'

I look up. Blink at her. 'Oh. *Oh.*' A horse of my own. 'So we're allowed to continue our lessons?'

'I'd say His Majesty is *encouraging* it.'

At least that gives me something to look forward to when I'm not working my way through the labyrinth. Asti is good company, and I'm sure I'll be able to invite Min on more of our lessons – for practical, non-matchmaking reasons *of course*.

Just as I'm smiling to myself, a bang shakes through the stables, making the gelding toss his head and whicker.

In the stall opposite, a coppery-red horse rolls its eyes, ears flicking back. Chestnut, I remember they called that colour in the book.

'Pay him no attention.' Asti purses her lips. 'He's been temperamental since he arrived. But he'll settle down soon enough.'

As if to prove her wrong, he kicks the wall again.

'Perhaps we should . . .' Min gestures towards the exit.

'Give him some peace. Right.'

I'm glad to get away from the chestnut gelding. He seems as pissed off about being here as I was when I arrived.

Before we reach the double doors leading to the yard, one of the stalls ahead opens and out steps Phaedra, dressed in midnight-blue riding leathers, sapphire eyes fixing on me at once as she leads a magnificent black stallion. She gives me a smile as sharp and narrow as a razor blade as she passes us and leaves.

I swallow and hang back. 'Shit.'

Min waits with me, gesturing for Asti to continue outside. 'What's wrong?'

'Do you think Phaedra heard me?' This stall is only a couple of doors from the blue roan, and it would explain her smile. I can just hear it in her voice: *Drystan's future queen fails at Fatework.*

Min narrows her eyes after the beautiful fae, mouth pressing to a thin line. 'No, I think you're safe. She wouldn't have been able to resist making some snide comment if she'd overheard.'

I don't know Phaedra well, but that certainly seems like her style.

'Besides . . .' She shrugs and leans in with a tentative smile – not the overly bright thing she usually puts on. 'I have a feeling your

Fatework woes are only temporary.' She lifts her chin, and her mouth widens into a grin.

It's one of the most delightful things I've ever seen, and it makes total sense on her face, making her eyes light up, crinkling around the scar on her cheek.

'And,' she says, hand closing around my shoulder and squeezing, 'I can't wait for you to prove Phaedra Asterlin absolutely, utterly, world-consumingly, ego-crushingly *wrong*.'

21

I BARELY WAKE from my nap in time to get ready for the labyrinth. Warm clothes. Food. A waterskin. Then *poof* I'm back in a familiar glassy corridor.

Onwards, I trudge.

I haven't slept enough, and I find myself yawning at every corner. My feet drag, and I stumble, even though the floor is smooth.

Please, gods, don't make me run today. I know how to deal with the Collector now and that they aren't a monster, but I'm sure there are dangerous beasts in here that can't be soothed by good manners.

No sooner have I begged the gods for leniency, than I hear a sound. Something approaches.

I back off as quietly as I can, heart in my throat.

Before I can duck away, it comes around the corner. Broad, shaggy, lumbering.

The Collector.

'Thank the moon we found you.' Their eyes brighten as they hurry over.

'I thought you were staying on the first tier, where you know.'

They duck their head. 'We realized . . . we could stay and be safe and alone . . . or we could come and escape our longing, find something we'd learned to forget.' Their dark eyes meet mine and I realize they're not black like I thought, but a deep dark swirl of many colours. They look hopeful. 'Maybe for one more level. Maybe for more?'

Longing. I understand that. They've been alone in the labyrinth, with just themselves. For all they might look monstrous, I see something of myself in them. 'You can come with me for as long as you want.' I pat their shoulder – or as high up their arm as I can reach when they're standing at full height.

The way is easier with the Collector. They shoulder my bag and scent the path ahead whenever we reach a branch. Their warmth is also welcome, since clouds choke up the sky, making the day chilly and grey.

As we go, I observe a strange effect in the rocky walls. A flicker that's an absence of reflection. Glossy, normal rock one moment – the next the sheen disappears, deepening the darkness. The organic shape of the formation reminds me of an algae bloom, while the surface remains smooth. It's as though this strange phenomenon is within the glassy depths.

I'm eyeing it when the Collector shuffles from foot to foot and whispers, 'We shouldn't linger here.'

So I follow my guide deeper into the labyrinth, watching the blooms whenever they flicker into view. As we thread through a winding corridor, I note they aren't everywhere, but—

A plinth stands in our path.

'Oh no,' the Collector murmurs, shrinking to one side.

'Don't be a coward,' their hissing voice snaps.

No obvious danger. Cautiously, I approach, body tensed and ready to dart back. 'There's nothing here.'

Then, from the air, materializes a key. A sharp black thing made from the same obsidian as the walls.

'It's a trick, isn't it?' I raise my eyebrows at the Collector. 'Or a trap.'

They rock back, arms wrapped around themselves. 'No. And yes. Not a trap for you. A trial.'

'Then we're close to the next tier.'

Their squat head bobs. 'Someone you care for will be trapped in a cage, but you must choose between freeing them and taking a shortcut to the very end of the labyrinth.'

'The end?' So there's a way to negate all these levels. All these challenges. Dread and excitement war in me, spiky and bright.

They peer ahead, scenting the air. 'To the final gate – the final challenge. But you have to choose – the key can only be used once. Then it is destroyed.'

'We chose,' one of their voices whispers, just on the edge of hearing.

'Collector.' A voice like shards of glass cuts through the corridor. We freeze.

A shadow creeps around the corner, tall, slender, impossibly long-limbed, surrounded by shuddering firelight. The creature itself stays out of view. 'Stop lurking. Your stink taints everything. I can't even smell my mealmeat over your foul stench. *Tch. Abomination.*'

I stare a question at the Collector. Who or *what* is this?

They back away and wring their hands. 'We can't. *We can't.*' With a single shake of their head, they drop my bag, then turn and flee.

A broken-glass laugh chimes through the corridor, discordant and sharp. 'Much better. My nose will clear now. Just in time to meet this new supplicant. Come out, child. Come and face the way forward.'

I glance back the way the Collector has gone. Mouth dry, I try to swallow and have to sip from my waterskin before I can.

I take the key. It's cold and sharp – if I ran my fingers over its edges, they'd slice like a razor.

Bag over my shoulder, key in hand, I set forth to face the next trial.

22

THE FIRELIGHT IS almost cosy.

Almost.

Because the sight it reveals is anything but.

To the right, an obsidian cage glitters. Dark eyes stare out from it, catching the orange light.

'Min?'

Someone you care for. I was expecting Lowen or my parents. It makes sense that it would be a fae from the Underworld, though.

She nods once, a tight line between her eyebrows.

'Are you all right?'

She nods again, throat bobbing. Otherwise, she keeps still.

Opposite her cage is a large door.

The best I can tell, it's merely a door. It isn't in a wall, but a stone archway. I can even see by the narrow shadow spilling from it that there's nothing behind.

I have to choose between Min's life and getting home.

Kishel said I would find my way back but what if he was seeing a version of the future where I chose the shortcut? Is that my only hope? Even if it is, can I leave Min to her fate?

'Here she is. My new succulent – *supplicant*.' From one corner unfolds the bearer of the glass-shard-voice. Bone pale. Tall. Slender. She's almost pretty. Red lips. Green eyes. Pale blond hair that pools around her on the floor. 'It's been ever such a long time since I had a visitor.' She smiles, showing off sharp teeth, and as she moves, coming closer, I see the full strange grace of her – the too-long limbs, the jutting hips, the slender fingers that end in sharpened nails.

As I circle to the left, keeping some distance between us, something cracks underfoot.

Strewn upon the ground are bones. Not animal. I've read enough anatomy books to recognize a femur when I see one. I'd bet these don't belong to humans, but fae.

Suddenly I understand the structure over the fire at the centre of the courtyard. A spit.

I swallow down nausea. This creature will eat Min if I don't choose her.

And yet, my sore legs and aching joints remind me I can't walk all the way through the labyrinth. It's only been four days and I'm already struggling.

I need that shortcut.

But leaving Min to the monster is out of the question.

There has to be a way I can have both.

I scrape my thumbnail over the key. This creature must have a key to the cage, so she can get Min out to . . . eat her. If I can trick her into opening the cage. If I were to offer her another meal, perhaps.

Maybe I can trick her into freeing Min so I don't have to use the key. I'll reveal I'm ill – can't risk catching something – and she won't want to eat me, then I can use the key on the shortcut.

It's a scrappy plan, but it's worth a try.

'Another fae for dinner?' I sigh, shaking my head like that's terribly boring. 'Don't you want to try human meat?'

The creature stills. Her green eyes dart over me, evaluating, curious. She licks her lips – tongue just as red.

'Free Min, and you can have me instead.' My voice wavers, like part of me understands this is a terrible idea and is trying to stop it.

She stalks closer, long legs eating up the ground with surprising speed.

'Hold on.' I raise my hands to ward her off. 'You can't eat me until Min is free.' Only then will I reveal I'm ill to put her off. She'll be pissed off, but Min can run, and I'll escape through the shortcut.

I back away, but her hot breath hits me with the stink of putrid flesh. Nausea roils through me, and I double over, heaving.

By the time I straighten, eyes streaming, she's standing over me, fingers poised to grasp my arms. Her delicate nostrils quiver in excitement.

I can't help staring at the grey piece of meat caught between her teeth. Horrified. Fascinated. Dizzy from my attempts to be sick.

Her smile as she bends closer is almost kind. I wonder if she was, once. If she had another life before the labyrinth or if she has only ever known this place, this life with a spit over a roaring fire.

Such a pretty shade of green, her eyes. So unusual.

They hold me still. I can only breathe. Wait. Surrender.

That's what this is, I realize too late. A fae trick. One that, even though I see it, I can't break free from.

She's going to eat me. Then Min.

I hope I make her sick.

The quiet spell around us snaps as she gasps, recoils, crunches bone under her heel as she stumbles back. 'Bad meat. That foul stuff. *Here.*' Her red lips spread as she gags. 'No bargain,' she chokes out between retches. 'I'll keep my original meal.'

Bad meat? I'm almost offended. But relief wins as I stagger free from her magical hold and catch myself on the stone door frame of the shortcut.

Through this door, then one final challenge, then I'll be home. To Lowen. To Annem and Pa. To our cottage and my garden. To the people who know and love me best. To my safe life where I know that when death comes for me, I won't be alone.

The creature coughs, maybe throws up some of her awful meat.

I take my chance. I pick my way between the bones – this would be the worst time to twist my ankle – and reach Min's cage.

She stares at me like I've lost my mind.

The key clicks into its hole, such a brittle sound, I'm afraid it'll break in the lock.

Breath held, I turn the key, and as the door swings free it crumbles. Tiny fragments of glass dig into my fingertips and fall away like sand, until almost the only sign the key ever existed is the open cage door.

'A poor choice,' the woman rasps between retches. 'I shouldn't expect anything better from a human.' She spits in my direction before retreating into a dark corner of her bone-carpeted den.

Mouth hanging open, brow crumpled, Min stares at me, stricken, like she's the one who might've just lost the chance to ever see her family again.

She doesn't need to feel guilty – this was my decision. So I pull my shoulders back and give her a bright smile as I hold out my hand to help her from the cage.

'Why did you—?'

'It was an easy choice.' I'm still shrugging when she grabs my shoulders and gives me a shake.

'You really are a fool, aren't you?'

'What? Why?' Shit. Have I fallen for a worse fae trick?

'No fae would make the choice you just did. You are . . .' She huffs, shaking her head. 'I owe you.' She steps back, releasing my shoulders. Her eyes glisten, over bright. *'Thank you.'*

Then she fragments into dark dust, like the key. I reach out, but she slips through my fingers. 'No.' I can't lose her *and* the shortcut. That's too cruel, even for the unseelie.

'She's merely returned to the fortress.' The king stands on top of the wall surrounding the courtyard. Arms folded, he leans against a column marking a door leading to the next tier. He jerks his chin towards the exit, and I make my way towards it.

I rub my chest. The world spins. It might be horror or my heart. Either way, a touch of belladonna won't hurt. With my back to him, I slip the bottle from my pocket and take a few crumbs.

By the time I open the door, a wave of warmth is rushing through me and my pulse kicks up a beat.

Ankles crossed, leaning against the opposite wall, the king is waiting on the other side.

As I sag against the door, glad to have something between me and the creature, I glare at him. 'She had better be safe.'

'Of course she is. *Now*, anyway. I should probably thank you for saving me the trouble of finding a new royal sartor.'

Meaning that thing really would've eaten her. Or me.

The labyrinth is not a game. This place kills. And he has no problem with that.

His eyes narrow on me and then he gives a half smile like I'm some strange and puzzling little creature he's found. 'This is the first time I've seen anyone hesitate. I've heard of the weakness of mortal emotions, but I've never seen it written so plainly before. How . . . fascinating.'

'I'm so glad I can be a source of entertainment for you.' I hate that the belladonna makes my voice shake, so I busy myself with trying to scrape the key's remnants off my fingers.

There's a stubborn shard that's worked its way into the pad of my thumb. I try to pull it out, but the jittery energy rushing through me makes my hands tremble.

A shadow passes over me, then Drystan's fingers come around

mine. He cradles the hand that's studded with splinters of black glass and tilts it into the light. 'I'm sure you'll be an endless source of interest but not in the way you think,' he murmurs, voice distant as he inspects my thumb. 'Over the centuries, fae have tried to escape the Underworld. The labyrinth is the only permanent way out.' The dark slashes of his eyebrows squeeze together as he uses his nails to grip the shard that's embedded itself in my thumb. 'This is the first time I've seen anyone choose their loved one over the shortcut. Why did you do that?'

As he pulls the glass out, there's a little pain – closer to discomfort than true pain.

'I . . .' I shake my head. It's impossible to explain such an obvious choice.

'You care for her.' He sets to work on another splinter I hadn't discovered.

'Well, yes. But that isn't why. Or at least isn't the *only* reason. Even if it had been someone I didn't care for, like Lady Phaedra, I would have chosen her.'

His eyebrows squeeze tighter as he works the splinter out. 'You'd have helped her over yourself?'

I can't help wrinkling my nose at the thought. 'It wouldn't so much be about helping Phaedra as . . . another person's life is more important than my wish to go home. It's just that caring for Min made the decision much easier than if it had been someone less . . . pleasant.'

He laughs softly as he checks for any more glass. 'Diplomatically put. You're getting the hang of court life.'

Blood beads on my thumb. In the cool, cloudy light, it glistens like a ruby.

Drystan's amusement fades as he falls still. He stares at the drop of my blood.

'You *are* good, Annon.' His voice comes out rough, like he's swallowed the shards of glass he's pulled from my skin. 'Perhaps too good for this forsaken world. But that doesn't mean I'm willing to give you up.' His gaze skips up to mine and I'm suddenly aware of just how alone we are, of how quiet the labyrinth is and how close he is. 'I am not good and I do not care to be.'

It's a dark promise. One that sends a strange thrill through me.

With aching slowness, he bends down, and for a second my belladonna-fuelled heart thinks he's going to kiss me.

And for some stupid reason, I don't pull away. Even though he's just admitted how terrible a person he is and I saw the blood-spattered evidence of that fact in the training yard with my own damn eyes.

It's not my mouth he bends to. No, of course not – the king doesn't kiss.

Instead, he takes my thumb to his lips and I can't tell if it's a nibble, a lick or a soft suck . . . or some combination of all those things. But it is warm and despite myself, it sends a shiver of sweet sensation through my entire body.

His grip is soft enough that I could pull away. I don't.

When he straightens the blood is gone.

I stand there, frozen, my mouth dry, my heart hammering against my ribs like it's trying to break out and offer itself to him on a bloody platter. There's something intimate about knowing a piece of me, a tiny drop, is inside him, consumed, possessed, tasted.

And I'm not sure I like it.

Yet, to use his word from earlier, I can't help finding it *fascinating*.

He watches me, eyes hooded, pupils so wide there's only a thin ring of gold left around them. I lose myself in their inky blackness for an untold amount of time. His dark promise lingers there.

I am not good and I do not care to be.

What must that be like? To not care. To do as you wish. To live rather than worry about everyone else all the time. To take what you want.

A *caw* cuts through our shared silence.

His chest heaves on a deep inhale as though he'd forgotten to breathe for a long while. Almost imperceptibly he leans closer. 'Good luck in your journey, Annon. Though, a word for the wise – take opportunity when it comes your way. You may not get another.'

He fragments into feathers and snapping beaks, the blast of wings forcing my eyes shut.

Once the ravens disperse, I'm left staring at the staircase leading to the next level. But in my mind is etched the image of the door that would have led me to the labyrinth's end.

23

I'M HALFWAY UP the stairs when the Collector shuffles into the space beside me sheepishly. They hang their head and take my bag. At the top, they offer to keep watch while I rest.

As I lie down, they whisper, 'We were afraid.'

I reach out and pat their clawed foot. 'I know.'

It's only when I wake from my snooze that I wonder: 'How did you get up here? Did you have to face the choice with the key?'

They shake their great head. 'We are of the labyrinth. We may move freely between the levels.'

I sit up. 'So you could just . . . carry me through?'

The hair on their face blows as they huff. 'We would if we could. But you are a supplicant, not *of* the labyrinth. You must face the trials before moving on. And we still face the dangers.' They glance back towards the previous tier and shudder before helping me to my feet.

Once more, we set off.

When I return with the sunset, Min is waiting for me, arms

folded, lips pursed. Before she even opens her mouth, I know I'm in trouble. I wince and wait.

'I told you not to make any bargains, and now I find that you've . . .' She blasts out a sigh and shakes her head.

I curl up on the settee as she delivers her lecture and breakfast appears on a side table. She grabs a pastry, continually talking around each bite.

'And a bargain with the king no less. What were you thinking?'

'That I might get a chance to go home?'

She exhales, shoulders sinking as she puts down the remainder of the pastry. 'Your family. You miss them.'

Lowen's grin comes to mind. It's an ache to not see it in person. Since he was born, there hasn't been a day in my life that I haven't seen his face. Until I came here. The realization makes my eyes burn, but I smile and shrug at Min.

I almost ask, 'Wouldn't you miss yours?' But then I remember. Not all families are the same.

'You are too good for this place, Rhiannon.' She huffs. 'Too good for me.'

'I'm sure that isn't tr—'

'It's true.' She plops into the seat opposite, elbows resting on her knees, head bowed. 'I need to make a confession.'

Why do I feel like I'm not going to like this? I set down my cup of coffee.

'When you arrived, the king ordered me to get close to you. To earn your trust. And then to tell him everything.'

The few mouthfuls I've eaten are lead. My illness. The king knows. He *knows*. 'But you promised—'

'Not that.' Her head shoots up, brow crinkled. 'I kept my promise. I didn't tell him that you were ill.'

I flop back into the chair, relief a physical force tugging on every aching muscle. 'Why not?'

She exhales through her nose, frowning at the low coffee table lying between us. 'I know what it means to be considered weak in this court. And I wouldn't wish that upon anyone. Not even my worst enemy.' She presses her lips together and lifts her gaze to mine. 'And you are far from my enemy, Rhiannon.'

I'm not sure what to make of her, of what I thought might be the start of a friendship.

'I *wanted* to think of you as one at first. But then you were . . . *kind*. And' – her face screws up – 'you didn't treat me differently. And then – *then* you helped me. You made sure the king credited my work and rewarded it. You invited me to spend time with Astrid.' She stares at me, lips parted as she shakes her head, eyes gleaming. 'And today you chose to save my life over going home. The thing you want most in all the world. How am I meant to go on betraying you after that?' She rubs her mouth. 'No, I won't tell the king another thing, and I'll never betray you again. I swear it. You have my loyalty, whether you want it or not.'

I hold her gaze a long time. There's a crack in her. It has split apart the too-bright smile she always gives me. A too-bright smile to win me over, I understand now.

It's no surprise that she spied on me for her king. But it still stings.

Though I'm sure stopping is no trifling matter. 'I can't imagine he'll like it if you tell him there'll be no more reports about his fiancée.'

'Oh, he won't.'

'And if he ever finds out you kept my illness from him?'

She sits back, hands behind her head as she gives the ceiling a sardonic grin. 'He could have my heart delivered on a platter, if he wanted – if he found out. I'm hoping I'm unimportant enough to escape his wrath.'

That's quite the gamble. 'Small fry. That's what my pa would call it.'

'Hmm.' It's almost a laugh, but quickly turns into a heavy sigh. She leans forward, hands clasped, eyebrows pinched. 'Do you think we can start again?'

I turn my coffee cup on its saucer, lining the handle up with the black hellebore design. In this world, what she's doing – what she's done – sounds tantamount to treason. She may have let me down, but she's also risked a lot for me.

We can't jump straight to the friendship I thought was brewing, but starting again? 'I think we can do that.'

Her first penitent act is helping me get ready for bed, and I drop into it.

I wake some hours later, pleasantly surprised to find no one's knocked at the door and woken me. But I know better than to think I can push my luck. There's always some meal or appearance in the Great Hall where the king's bride-to-be is required. So, although I'm still tired, I drag myself out of bed and work on making myself presentable.

'Is that deliberate timing?' I ask when I see Drystan's face behind me in the mirror.

He cocks his head in question.

'You somehow manage to always appear when I'm brushing my hair. I'm starting to wonder if you have a hair fetish.'

His mouth twists as he appraises the freshly brushed lengths. 'If I did, it wouldn't be for *yours*.'

Of course not. It would be for the perfect, shimmering locks of some other fae. Humans are mortal. Frail. Weak. And probably quite ugly to fae. I hadn't considered that.

Before I can acknowledge his retort, his eyebrows shoot up. 'I didn't come here to insult you, actually . . . I have a peace offering.'

I'm pretty sure my eyes bulge at that. 'You have a . . .? I didn't know you knew the meaning of the word.'

He exhales through his nose, expression flattening as if he's holding back another rejoinder. 'Annon. You're testing my resolve to be . . . *nice*.'

'Another word I didn't know was in your vocabulary.' But I flash him a playful grin as I turn from the mirror.

In the King of Death's arms is a grey cat.

I stare. It doesn't disappear, and he doesn't threaten to hand it over to a fae with a spit over a fire.

The cat merely stares back with bright green eyes. The roundness of its cheeks suggests it's a male.

I've never had a pet. Pa always says cats are good for ratting and stealing fish and not much else, and Annem's afraid of dogs – says they make her think of hellhounds, which she's been deathly afraid of since she came to Albion, even though she's never seen one. Now I've seen them, I can understand the terror.

The cat pokes his dark grey nose out like he wants to sniff me. My throat feels suddenly thick, because he's so damn adorable, I want to make unnecessarily high-pitched noises.

I turn wide eyes on Drystan, and he holds out the cat. 'He's . . . for me?'

'Peace offering, like I said. I saw how you'd grown attached to Min so quickly, and it made me wonder if you were lonely, so . . .' He offers the cat again, who starts squirming as if he doesn't like having empty air beneath him.

That's almost thoughtful. And he didn't even say lonely like it was an insult.

I straighten in my seat and let him deposit the cat in my lap. The cat sniffs my hand when I hold it out, then rubs his cheek against it. His thick fur is soft, but there's something odd about the sensation. A strangeness I can't name. It isn't cold or wet but something adjacent to that. Something that's not quite substantial.

'He likes you.' Drystan nods, the corner of his mouth twitching like this is a victory for him.

Sure enough, the creature is purring as he rubs his face all over my hand. 'All right, all right,' I chuckle, and set to work rubbing behind his ears. 'What's his name? Or does the taboo about names apply to animals too?'

'I don't know, and it doesn't. You get to choose.' He pulls over one of the armchairs from the fireplace. He's sticking around for a while then.

I busy myself with stroking my new feline friend, because I'm not entirely sure how I feel about having the king in my space after that odd moment in the labyrinth. There's this squirmy feeling in my belly that I don't want to examine too closely.

'I'll have a think.' I don't look at him. The cat curls up in my lap, apparently satisfied he's found a good spot and that I'll continue stroking him, which I do while he rumbles.

'I'm impressed with how well you're doing in the labyrinth so far.'

My head whips up. 'Impressed? You didn't sound impressed by my choice yesterday. And I could've died if I hadn't worked out how to appease the Collector.'

'Do you think I would've let that happen?'

'I don't know, those teeth were pretty damn close to my jugular.'

He huffs through his nose and waves off my concerns. His expression says, 'They weren't *that* close.'

I scowl at him, hand falling still on the cat's soft fur. He might consider my brief, mortal life as unimportant, but . . . 'Min could've died.'

'Why do you care so much?'

My gods, he is exasperating. Sometimes it's like he isn't a real person, but a mannequin that's been enchanted to move like a person and talk like a person, but is missing something vital. 'Because friends care about each other.' I speak slowly, since this is a concept he seems to have difficulty understanding. 'They want to make each other happy. Keep each other alive.'

I could never admit it to Drystan, but this is why it's easy to get past my parents' deception. I'm happy I could play a part in saving my father's life, albeit in a roundabout way.

With a little sound of annoyance, the cat twists in my lap, exposing his tummy. His little grey toes are so adorable, they ease my frustration at Drystan. Maybe that was part of his plan. The cat is a shield. A very cute one.

Lips pressed together, Drystan reaches forward and rubs the cat's belly. There's more squirming and the purr turns into a deeper rumble. 'Is that why you invited Min on your ride with Astrid – to make her happy?' He doesn't look at me while he asks the question, but I feel his attention, keen like a blade.

I don't want to give away that Min is attracted to Astrid – that isn't my secret to share. So I make a noncommittal sound. 'It isn't fun being cooped up in your fortress, you know – even if you're not trapped here.'

'You alerted the labyrinth to the fact that you care for her. Its tendrils spread through the land. It *knows*.' With creases between his eyebrows, he looks up at me and I still under the full force of his attention, the solemnity of it. The way he's leaning forward to pet the cat puts his face perhaps a foot from mine, making it all the harder to withstand his intensity. 'I *told* you emotions were weakness, and yet you've still shown affection for her.'

I swallow but I can't reply. I didn't mean to endanger Min. And yet I can't feel bad for appreciating her and trying to help her, not when I've seen how it makes her smile.

'The things we care for are always taken away.' The softness of his voice cuts into me.

There's a story behind this warning. Something that's carved its way into his chest, leaving him rough and raw.

The quiet between us stretches on.

His hand has fallen still on the cat's belly, and tentatively, I cover it with mine. 'What did you care for that was taken away?'

He flinches like I've hit him, hand snatching away as the cat bolts. Spine straight, Drystan rises. The intensity of his gaze is still there, but where it was penetrating – a point that connected us – now it's a barred door. 'Thanks to my mother's deal with your incompetent father, I have been denied the only thing I ever wanted. And for what?' He glares down at me. 'All so I can marry some weak, magicless human who doesn't even have a name.'

I grind my teeth, then spit out, 'My father isn't—'

But the king is already gone, leaving only the door clicking shut.

24

ALTHOUGH I KNOW I shouldn't spare a thought for the king, that conversation lingers in my thoughts for the rest of the day, including another round of negotiating the labyrinth, stiff and slow, and, after sunset, a lesson with Kishel. Another *ill-fated* lesson.

I'm sure Fatework isn't supposed to be ill-fated, but I'm also sure magicless humans shouldn't be trying to *do* Fatework, so here we are.

There are two things that stick with me. One, which burns hotter and faster, is the way he insulted my father, who's the best fisherman on the entire coast – not to mention that Drystan wouldn't know a competent fisherman if one caught him in his net.

And the other, which remains after my irritation burns out, is how hurt he seemed. The soft voice. The lashing out. The thing he's been denied.

No wonder he hates me.

Which means I can go on hating him without a shred of guilt.

I haven't seen the Insufferable One all night, and I start to wonder if asking him personal questions is the best way to scare him off.

That's when the summons arrives.

Asti collects me for something called the Withan. Like a kind of council for the king, she explains as we wind through stone corridors. When we reach a large set of doors, she nods me through.

I pause, a trickle of dread in my stomach. 'Aren't you coming?'

'I don't have a seat.' She gives an apologetic smile.

I want to say, 'Neither do I,' but the doors are already opening to reveal a large chamber with an intricately vaulted ceiling. Stone beams radiate from slender columns, like the bones of a bat's wing. At the far end of the room, three tall, arched windows frame the moon perfectly, letting its light spill in and mingle with the yellow fae lights caged in wall sconces.

At the centre stands a long table, surrounded by seven chairs.

Well, five chairs and two thrones. Drystan's sits empty at one end and a matching one opposite. Some of the seats are already occupied, judging by the hum of conversation bouncing off the high ceiling, but the nearer throne cuts off my view.

I keep my chin high as I enter, though I want to shuffle in and retreat to a corner. As far as these people are concerned, I'm their future queen, and any safety and power I have here is contingent on that.

When I round the throne, I almost sag at the sight of Kishel. He offers a subtle smile and nods to the seat next to him. My relief at the sight of a familiar face wars with unease at the choice of seat. The empty throne.

I swallow and ease into it, wearing a faint smile as if to say, 'Why yes, *of course* I sit upon a throne. I *am* soon to be your queen, and I'm absolutely comfortable with that.'

Lord Mastelle is here as is Phaedra. They acknowledge me with cool nods, then go back to their own hushed conversation.

'We're still waiting for a few more to arrive,' Kishel explains.

'Astrid said this was like a council,' I murmur to him, not wanting the others to witness my ignorance. 'Does that mean you can outvote the king?'

Kishel chuckles. 'Not at all. Our roles are more . . . advisory. The only people with true power at this table are the king . . .' He inclines his head towards the throne opposite mine, then turns back to me with a penetrating look. 'And his consort.'

That implies I could challenge his authority if we were actually married. He gains power through marriage, but it's also a risk. No wonder his mother had to force him into it.

Before I can ask Kishel anything more, the doors swing open. I resist the urge to crane round and see who's entered – I doubt it's seemly for a queen. She has the patience to wait for people to come to her – and the confidence to know they will.

A petite fae enters, her blond hair tinged green. I only met her briefly at my first presentation. Lady Gewyne.

A handsome, well-built man follows her, ducking forward to pull out her chair. With an indulgent smile, she caresses his cheek and square shoulder as she takes her seat. She acknowledges us all, while he stands behind her, staring straight ahead with glassy eyes like he's gone away inside.

I shift at the hollowness.

At my side, Kishel purses his lips, disapproval clear. He catches my gaze out the corner of his eye, and murmurs, 'He's her thrall. An old-fashioned practice, but still generally accepted.' At my frown, he goes on, 'His will is weaker, so she can control him and feed off his magic to make herself more powerful.'

My skin crawls, cold, tight. Inside my silk slippers, my toes scrunch up – a hidden reaction to the full horror of the thrall.

This is the danger of weakness.

The fae pouring water for his mistress and leaning in close as he delivers it to her, wearing an expression of desperate need like he would cut his own veins open for the slightest scrap of praise from her plate. No will of his own. No life. Just a shade that follows in her footsteps.

In the Underworld, will is tangible. The strong take power. And they doom the weak to powerlessness.

I hear Drystan's voice: *You are either predator or prey.*

I have no doubt which he wishes to make me.

And I have no intention of obliging him.

At least I have no magic he can draw on, but I'm not foolish enough to think that makes me safe.

Just as I grip the arms of my throne, the king enters, followed by the remaining member of the Withan, Threnn.

There are no niceties, just the taking of seats and the alighting of the three ravens on the high back of his throne. One, the smaller of the two black birds, hops down on to Drystan's shoulder, feathers ruffling as she casts a glinting eye upon Threnn.

'Nos tells me our neighbours have been patrolling the border with renewed intensity.' Absently, he strokes the raven's throat. 'What do you have to report about my fellow kings?'

'Yes, I have been wondering about the other six kingdoms.' Gewyne rounds on Threnn with a thin smile, eyes glittering like cut glass.

'Five,' Lord Mastelle says smoothly.

Her gaze cuts to him. 'What?'

'The other *five* kingdoms, Lady Gewyne.' He chooses that exact moment to loosen the fingers of one glove, and I can't help feeling there's some element of display at that – a layer of insult I don't quite understand. 'It's been a century now, do *try* to keep up.' He strips off that glove and starts on the other, not even sparing the woman a glance.

Her smile turns brittle and she makes a faint sound of acknowledgement.

'Or is your precious attention consumed by your little pet? Perhaps we need to examine where your thoughts truly lie.'

The largest of the ravens croaks, the sound as rough as charred wood.

'Tywel and I do so appreciate your sharp sense of duty, Lord Mastelle,' Drystan speaks up from the opposite end of the table as all eyes turn to him and the raven. 'What is it they say about double-edged swords? Best wielded by those with the right to draw them.'

My gaze bounces between the fae and their subtle duelling. Power runs in undercurrents and reprimands come veiled in civility. Just as I thought I was starting to understand the game, I find myself on a new playing field.

'Now,' he goes on, 'if you'll all allow the Baloran to speak, *I* would like to hear his report.'

The redcap nods to his king and gives an update on the current border situation. It sounds like Mordren shares borders with either three or four of his brothers – I can't keep track of what's a person's name and what's another kingdom. They have limited trade, usually one party taking advantage of something the other lacks, as happened with the horses.

While they're discussing how to get the best prices for ice, Kishel leans over. 'I'm not sure how much His Majesty has explained to you about the other kingdoms.'

I give him a half smile.

His lips quirk. 'Right. Nothing. Of course. His Majesty's brothers – or, rather, half-brothers – rule the remaining kingdoms of the Underworld. Long ago, The Morrigan had a son with each of the old unseelie kings, ensuring her blood would rule over this place of finalities. Thus were made the six Kings of Death. The Enderkings.'

There's a faint and horrible familiarity to that name. Something I can't quite place, like a story from a dream.

'They all have their own domains,' Kishel goes on, 'however His Majesty is *the* King of Death.'

'Hence the ravens,' I mutter.

His mouth twitches again.

Despite lacking what I'm sure is many centuries, maybe even millennia, of context, I understand enough from Threnn's report to piece together that while the kingdoms aren't at war, relations aren't exactly *easy*, either.

Drystan nods thoughtfully when Threnn finishes his report. 'Anything else?'

Threnn's customary scowl deepens. 'Your Majesty's brothers haven't responded to our intelligence-sharing requests.'

Phaedra scoffs, raising an eyebrow. 'Would you, if your brother claimed a consort and disappeared the only other person eligible to take his throne?'

Drystan goes very still, then slowly, a smile creeps over his lips – and his lips alone. 'Lady Phaedra, I can't decide if I should be flattered that you think me capable of erasing the only other claimant to the throne so neatly . . . or insulted that you believe I need to.' The slash of his eyebrow rises more sharply than Phaedra's. 'Perhaps the greater threat lies not beyond our borders but within them.'

The pretty pink of her cheeks pales. 'I didn't mean—'

'It certainly *sounded* like you meant Effan could gain support should I prove an unsatisfactory king.' He shoots me the briefest, sharpest look, and my stomach drops.

He said my rebellion against his rules undermined his leadership. This has to be what he meant.

'Remind me,' he goes on, 'what banner is it he stands for that you'd be gathering behind?' He makes a show of frowning and cocking his head as he taps his lower lip. 'Ah yes, grapes and yeast, and the capering of a drunken fool.'

I have to admit, I enjoy the way Phaedra looks away, the delicate dip of her throat as she swallows. It's a delicious and entirely petty victory.

'Your Majesty misunderstands me.' She looks up through her lashes. 'I merely meant how it would look to *others*, particularly those beyond our border – those with no loyalty to you.'

'Ah, of course, you were looking out for me. Such uncharacteristic kindness – I didn't recognize it from you, Phaedra.'

'I admit I only have a passing acquaintance with the concept.' One side of her mouth rises in this smirk that feels so horribly private it makes my stomach burn.

Although Asti dodged the question, I'm positive now that they were – or still are – lovers. She's welcome to him. They suit each other. Cruelty and spite. Beautiful and bitter. How perfect for one another they are.

While the other members of the Withan discuss Effan's disappearance, Kishel again leans over. 'Effan is the son of King Arawn, King Drystan's father.'

'But not The Morrigan's child, right? Not a demi-god?' That explains why Drystan is on the throne instead of him and why, despite being a baker, Effan enjoys an elevated position where he can get away with drinking more than baking.

'Exactly. He's—'

'You don't know who Effan is?' The sharp peak of Phaedra's arched eyebrow is back, her sapphire eyes on me. 'And yet you're sitting in his chair.'

I grip the arms in order to force myself not to shift in a seat that suddenly feels overcrowded.

'As my heir, Effan held that seat.' Drystan dips his chin in acknowledgement. 'But as my betrothed, Lady Rhiannon has now taken it.'

'And just as he's disappeared,' Lord Mastelle mutters. 'How convenient that should happen at precisely the moment some may question whether they backed the right brother.'

A sudden, cold quiet sucks the air from the room.

Did Lord Mastelle just imply *he* is the one wondering if he should have supported Effan's claim to the throne rather than Drystan's? Is this all because I broke a few rules? Shit. Shit, shit, shit. I had no idea of the extent of the ripples I would send across his kingdom.

Despite the chilled displeasure radiating through the chamber, Kishel gives Lord Mastelle a flat look. 'It's not as if he ever took the seat himself.'

'If I have enemies willing to strike down my own blood, it only proves I've been right to remain vigilant . . .' Drystan's gaze sweeps the table. 'And to reward those who stand beside me.' His attention shifts to Kishel and something unspoken passes between them.

In silence, Threnn, Phaedra and Lady Gewyne lean in, like the king has just placed a particularly tasty morsel on the table.

I can't help marvelling. He's just deflected the accusations on to mysterious 'enemies' – his brother-kings, perhaps – *and* turned this into an opportunity for the Withan members to climb over each other for his favour. Loyalty, it seems, is rewarded by the King of Death.

Then he delivers the killing blow.

Straightening, he interlaces his fingers on the table and fixes Lord Mastelle with a pleasant smile. 'As for the recent disturbance at court' – Phaedra looks right at me – 'you'll be glad to hear my fiancée is in the process of being re-educated in the labyrinth.'

Five pairs of eyes turn to me. Even the ravens join them. I hold still, but I want to shrink in my seat.

Drystan's smile widens, growing cooler as he turns it to me. 'I'm sure she'll have plenty of time there to think about her actions . . . and to learn some gratitude for the position she finds herself in. One many others would, I'm sure, *kill* for.'

Phaedra shifts in her seat. I'm suddenly glad the table isn't set for a meal – no sharp objects in sight.

Lady Gewyne eyes me like I'm something she found on the ground. 'You gave her the chance to escape?'

Drystan gives an amused huff. 'Do you really think a human could get anywhere in the labyrinth?'

Aside from Kishel, the fae laugh. At me. At the poor little human.

But, I also notice, Lord Mastelle is laughing *with* Drystan – they all are.

I've been made an example of to smooth over the king's position with the most powerful members of his court. And he's manipulated them all with a half-truth.

I thought the danger lay in his looks or his whispering spies.

But I missed his true power.

It isn't seen or heard.

It's felt. Just barely.

Like the sea inching against the cliffs, slow and patient – only noticed once it's already too late.

And by then, you've already given him exactly what he wants.

25

THE MEETING LEAVES me unsettled the rest of the night. I try
to distract myself by emptying out my tablets and checking how
many are left. It doesn't take long to count.

Four and a half.

It's sobering, but I still feel jittery, so I take a bath to soothe my
aching joints. Afterwards, I don a dressing robe and play with the
cat, who doesn't have a name yet, when there's a knock at the door
and the king himself enters at my invitation. His timing's off – I'm
not brushing my hair.

The cat runs to him, rubbing his face into Drystan's legs.

Traitor.

'You're getting fur all over my trousers.' He sighs yet still bends
down and scratches the cat behind the ears. Fussing the cat, his
gaze skims to the silky dressing robe I'm wearing. 'I've come to
collect you for dinner.' He pauses, mouth open as though a thought
has struck him. 'That is, if you care to accompany me.' It's *almost*
a question, but I'm not sure the king is practised at questions or
requests.

I dangle a string for the cat, who swipes at it, claws out. 'Then I suppose I should get dressed, since I'm such a devoted fiancée.' With a sardonic smile, I throw a ball and the cat streaks after it while I get up and put away the string. I raise my eyebrows when I meet the king's gaze, because he doesn't seem to have taken my hint – he's still standing there. 'I'm going to get dressed now.'

Realization dawns in the widening of his eyes. '*Oh*. I see.' I catch a smirk as he turns his back to me. 'I forget humans have strange ideas about bodies.'

Yet he doesn't leave. He just . . . waits.

I huff a sigh and pull out a dress. It's shimmering white embroidered with silvery thread and crystals, with flecks of shell sewn into the fine lace. It makes my olive skin look darker, healthier, and I've been waiting for a chance to wear it. Glancing over to check Drystan still has his back turned like he's a gallant knight and not the King of Death, I find his broad back is still towards me, but he's leaning his brow on his forearm against the door frame like he needs it for support.

Is he ill? I wonder for a second and I'm about to ask, but that has to be some sort of insult in unseelie etiquette, implying someone has a weakness and is less than perfect. Suggesting such a thing about the king is probably a tongue-cutting-out offence.

So I slip off my robe and hurry to pull the dress on, aware of every moment my skin is bare in his presence and the same air that's touching him is touching me. I even wriggle on my underwear afterwards, hoiking it up beneath the gown's skirts, so I'm not naked a moment longer than necessary.

The gown covers me from its high neck to long sleeves, and I start fastening the many little buttons running up my spine.

And that's when I realize my error with a soft 'Fuck.'

'What's wrong?' Drystan lifts his head but doesn't turn.

'Nothing. I . . .' I pull a face as I twist my arms back as far as

I can and manage to pop another button through its loop, but I haven't got much further than my waist, and the top half of the dress is already trying to fall down and reveal my chest. I hadn't considered the fastening of these gowns – normally Min helps me. 'Could you . . . Would *Your Majesty* send for Min, please?' Pretty sure I shouldn't be asking the king to run around after me, but I don't have much choice.

'She's busy. What do you need?'

'These buttons – they're . . .' Only then do I realize what he's implying.

Luckily, I'm holding the top half of the gown up over my breasts when he turns and says, 'I'll help.'

It seems the king has been learning all sorts of new words. Fairly sure 'help' isn't usually part of his vocabulary – it doesn't seem like a very unseelie word.

Silently, he stalks closer like I'm a creature he might scare away.

My pulse comes faster, and I have to rifle back through the past ten minutes to check if I took belladonna and forgot, because it certainly feels like it's running through my system. But no . . . I took my medicine earlier and that's all. Maybe half a tablet isn't enough.

Clutching the dress tighter, I turn my back to him, grateful to be freed from the intensity of his stare. But the relief doesn't last long, not when I can *feel* his eyes boring into the bare skin of my back. It's a prickle between my shoulder blades that sets every hair at the nape of my neck on end.

There's a pressure at my waist where the fastened buttons end. 'These?' he asks softly.

The gods did a poor job when they designed humans, because there's somehow not enough space in my ribcage for my pounding heart and for my lungs to draw in air – at least that's how it feels as my chest heaves. I certainly can't manage all that *and* speech, so I simply nod.

He makes a thoughtful sound, then his hands close around my waist and he lifts me so I'm sitting on the back of the settee, feet on the seat. 'Saves me bending over.'

To reach such a puny human being the unspoken end to that sentence.

Before I can make some mocking comment, he sets to work. He doesn't touch me directly, but the pull and press of him buttoning his way up my back spreads over my skin all the same, encircling my ribs, ghosting through the pressure of the fabric over my stomach and breasts.

I should've chosen a different dress. Something that shows more flesh but doesn't include fastenings I can't reach.

'Your hair,' he murmurs before gathering it up and draping it over my shoulder, lighting up a hundred points of sensation – hair tickling my neck, more skin suddenly exposed and the warm brush of his fingertips over my spine. My breath catches. I shiver and curse Min for being busy.

The thrall from earlier comes to mind. I see him so clearly. His eagerness. His hollow stare that only lit up for Lady Gewyne.

I am not attracted to the King of Death.

I am not attracted to the King of Death.

I am *not* attracted to the King of Death.

Fine. So I am. A little.

In my defence, he's fae, and they're known for their beauty, their charm that beguiles us mere humans.

Besides, it's been a long time since my body felt like anything other than a burden. I'm long overdue a little pleasure, a taste of what it might feel like to be desired. He doesn't want me, I'm sure of it, but I can pretend. A little indulgence. Some fantasy before I go back home and settle in to live the rest of my life without pretty dresses or fae kings who stoop to fasten them for me.

So I close my eyes and eat up every single speck of experience.

The slight coolness of the air where it touches my skin. His breaths seem louder than usual – he's so close. They blow over my spine and between my shoulder blades, where I'm still bared.

I catch the edge of his scent. Feel the lack of it in that hint. Crave more of it. The ancient solidity of it. The encompassing richness of it. The smoked warmth.

He makes a soft sound – I don't think it's a word, but I can't be sure, and an instant later I'm distracted by the warmth of his hand on that same spot between my shoulder blades. His fingers flex, pressing into my skin.

My breaths have stopped.

But my pulse seems to be trying to make up for it, hammering even faster than before. I lean in to his touch, every ounce of my attention on its warm sweep as he moves upward. He reaches the nape of my neck, fingertips and thumb first, tracing the column of my spine, and my head drops forward.

I fail to bite back a groan as part of me wants, begs for him to plunge his fingers into my hair, pull my head back and kiss me to within an inch of my life.

He doesn't. Of course.

And I'm mortified to have made such a sound. For *him* of all people.

He catches my hair again – sadly, not a grab – and twists it more tightly. 'Take it.' The roughness of his voice is a shock in the silence and I obey without thinking, grasping the lengths so they're out of his way, our fingertips brushing as I do so.

Even that feels like the heady buzz in the air as a storm gathers – electric, dizzying, a maddening pressure in need of relief.

He isn't gentle as pulls the edges of the dress together, confining me in its fitted shell. The fine lace that forms a V between my breasts tightens – this gown isn't low cut, but it might as well be with sheer fabric the only thing covering my cleavage . . . which I now have, I realize. There must be something about fae food that's helping me put on weight.

I smile to myself, tucking away that small victory among the memories of this moment that I'm etching inside my heart for leaner times.

He fastens a few more buttons, then tugs again, and the silk grazes my nipples.

That tiny movement streaks through me, dragging a gasp down my throat.

My nerves catch fire. My body pulls as taut and ready as a drum. I am a blank page that he's just starting to fill in.

I press my thighs together, unable to help squirming as molten heat gathers low in my belly.

He works his way higher, fingers brushing my neck, my hairline, teasing, promising.

And then he's done.

I sit there a long while, swaying, before I realize and the disappointment sweeps in. It would be pathetic to manufacture more reasons for him to touch me like this, I know, but damn is it tempting. I blame my illness and the isolation it forces upon me. I have needs, after all.

'How readily you respond to a simple touch, even though all that lies between us is hate.' His voice weaves between us, low and rough. 'It would be so easy to make you my mindless little thrall, wouldn't it?'

The twin fires of shame and desire burn my cheeks. I hate that he isn't entirely wrong. The life of a thrall must be so easy. A singular purpose. Simplicity of intent. Quietness of mind. No pesky feelings save the joy of pleasing your master.

I don't want it. And yet for a brief, flickering moment, I understand the appeal.

A shaky breath, then I chuckle. 'You really think I could ever be mindless?'

He laughs, and it deflates the suffocating tension between us.

I manage to straighten, head spinning, mind giddy like it hasn't registered there's nothing more to come.

'Here.' Strong hands fasten around my waist, then I'm in the air, lifted off the back of the settee and set on my feet. His hold lingers a moment, leaving me to gather myself before I go to the dressing table to pin my hair up, since that seems to be the done thing in the Underworld.

'Leave it down.' His voice comes from the doorway.

I assume his instruction is a product of impatience – no doubt the unnecessary number of buttons on my gown has made us late. But when I turn, there's no flare of irritation to his nostrils, and his gaze is boring into me like golden fire, something dark and demanding at the centre.

So I dab a little oil on to my fingers and run them through my loose hair before joining him in the doorway. He nods in approval and offers his arm, then we set off into the corridors of his fortress.

26

IT'S ONLY WHEN we leave our guards at the doors and step into a quiet, enclosed space that I realize we aren't in the cavernous dining hall where we normally take meals with the rest of his court. I blame the daze that's settled over me after, somehow, being dressed by him has become one of the most sensuous experiences of my life.

I blink at an empty sitting room decorated in shades of dark grey. A grey room could seem cold, but the velvet upholstery and scatter cushions are inviting, and the thick rug leading from the entrance chamber softens the black-and-white-checked marble floor. The space gives a sense of refined richness.

I look up at him, my frown a question, but, in silence, he leads me inside. We take a door to the left that leads to a small dining room, much more intimate than the grand dining hall. Its round table is set for four. Black candles with white flames light the space, secured in candelabra on the table and mantelpiece and a chandelier hanging from the ceiling, with crystals refracting the light, casting an array of colours over the grey decor.

Drystan pulls out the chair nearest the fireplace.

When I just look at him, not quite able to straighten all my questions into order, he purses his lips and turns his gaze to the candles. 'Min and Astrid are joining us for dinner.'

My eyebrows leap into my hairline. 'Min and . . .?' But her status among the unseelie. From the way she spoke about it, I'm sure she doesn't usually get personal invitations to join the king for dinner. 'I don't . . .' I shake my head, because whatever he did to me when he fastened this dress, it might have rendered me unable to complete a sentence.

'I noted that you invited Min on your ride with Astrid after seeing the way she looked at the dashing second of the Twylth during training.'

I swallow. Does that mean he saw how I looked at him? Was that the reason for the teasing button-fastening and this intimate dinner invite? Did he think I would be an easy conquest? I mean, he might be right, but still – the assumption grates on me all the more because of it.

'You're trying to . . . *encourage* them.' His raises his eyebrows in question, and I nod. 'Well.' He spreads his hands, indicating the table. 'Our last conversation didn't go as I would've liked. I hope this will make it up to you.'

'You're . . . helping me?'

He gives a lop-sided smile, but before I can really enjoy it, there's a knock at the door.

'Come,' he commands, and something about the tone makes me squirm again. 'Through here.'

Min appears in the doorway, eyes wide as she stares from me to Drystan to the table and back to me. If eyeballs alone could speak, hers would be asking 'What the fuck is going on?'

It's a valid question.

My only reply is a helpless and still slightly confused smile. It seems my husband-to-be was replaced by a changeling and honestly? I prefer the changeling.

'My betrothed and I would be honoured if you would join us for dinner.' With a graceful sweep of his arm, Drystan indicates the table.

Somehow, Min's eyes get even wider. Like her body knows she can't deny her king, she walks in, but her shocked expression suggests her brain hasn't entirely caught up yet. 'I . . . this isn't . . .' She clears her throat. Absently, she runs a hand down the sheer silk blouse she wears tucked into billowing trousers. 'My attire . . . I didn't realize this wasn't a work assignment, Your Majesty. I should get changed. I'm not dressed for dinner. I—'

'It's just the four of us.' I take her hand and lead her to the table. 'You look lovely, very . . .' I think back to the word I once read that seems appropriate for Min. 'You look very chic. Doesn't she?' I look at Drystan with a silent appeal for help to reassure my friend.

He inclines his head with a faint smile as he pulls out a chair for Min. 'My future wife is as correct as she is kind.'

From the doorway, there's an 'Ahem.' Asti stands there, head cocked as she takes in Min. 'You are beautifully dressed as always, Royal Sartor. As befits your nature.'

I think Min might combust with how quickly her cheeks go pink, and she mutters something as she takes her seat, fanning herself with a napkin.

Drystan flashes me a rakish grin that shows off one canine, and I can't help smiling back. Our plan is already going better than I could've hoped.

And it continues to go well as we take our seats and dinner appears. Trout, greens and early minted peas. Potatoes crushed with butter, parsley and spring onions. The flavours fill my heart as well as my stomach – all herbs and vegetables I grow in our garden. They must've been raided from further south where spring wakes the land and its bounty a little sooner.

Min is initially quiet, either because of Asti's presence or her king's, but Asti's easy confidence soon lures her out, and I help where I can. Drystan doesn't speak often, but I don't get the impression he's shy so much as . . . curious. He chimes in with witty comments and confirms aspects of Asti's stories of battles against the Underworld's wild dead and the unseelie creatures that rove the land.

But I often catch him sitting back, observing, and I have to wonder if he's ever eaten with such a small group of people before. The carpet in here doesn't look very worn. I steal a glance at the upholstery of my chair. It looks new, and there isn't a single scratch on the table.

Then it strikes me.

Drystan doesn't have friends.

It's between dinner and dessert when I make that shocking realization, only made more shocking by the fact I feel sorry for him. It renders me silent for long minutes as Asti and Min talk about a forthcoming festival, speculating about whether it will be a good year for 'Moonburn', whatever that is.

Drystan's long fingers glide along mine. I jolt. It buzzes along my nerves, a bright spark. I blink from that point of contact to him.

'It's expected,' he murmurs, and I remember that we're in front of other people, so our agreement to play the part of happy bride-and-groom-to-be is in full force.

'Oh. Of course.' I straighten my fingers, letting his slide in between, and tell myself that it's just part of our bargain and not an excuse to enjoy a little physical affection while I can.

His hand dwarfs mine, but he isn't gentle. No. Gentle isn't the word for it. Seeking. Firm. Eager. Any of those would work. He's playing his part well.

'Are you all right? You've gone very quiet.'

He's definitely been replaced by a changeling. That's the only reason he might possibly care.

I smile in reassurance. 'I'm fine. I was just wondering . . .' I take in the room with Min and Asti still chattering happily, heads bowed together. 'Do you do this often?'

His brow creases as he takes in the same space. 'Well, I've had lovers in here. You must know I've lived a very long time, Annon. You're not my first.'

I'm not his lover at all. And I'm just about to blurt that fact, when I catch myself. The others. Right. 'That wasn't what I was getting at. But so you know, I may not be as old as you, *darling*, but you're not *my* first, either.'

One eyebrow rises and he gives me a long look as if reevaluating his dull human fiancée. 'Oh, really?' A faint smile ghosts over his mouth before it's hidden behind a sip of wine.

'I won't be elaborating.' I give him a sarcastic smirk, then take a drink, our eyes locking over the brims of our iridescent glasses.

'Shame,' he murmurs as we lower our drinks.

'I was trying to ascertain whether you had small, *intimate* groups of friends in here often.'

Yes, I deliberately emphasize the word intimate, because for some reason I enjoy playing along with our act. It's fun to flirt, even if we're only pretending.

And I love watching the smirk that flits over the corner of his mouth as I say it, though it soon turns sardonic as he processes the rest of my comment. 'And who, exactly, would a king be friends with?' He lifts his chin, imperious for a moment.

'I don't know – you don't exactly move in my usual circles, but I'd guess kings are friends with other aristocrats and . . .' I shrug and glance at Asti. 'Their guards. You two spar like you know each other well.'

'We've trained together for many years.'

When he says nothing more, I cant my head. 'But you're not friends?'

'A king doesn't have friends. Especially not those who are guards. That's just . . .' He shakes his head.

'It sounds lonely. Maybe you should've kept the cat.'

'And let it get its fur all over my clothes? I think not.' He huffs into his glass and takes a long draught of wine, gulping like he needs it.

To my credit, I'm only very briefly distracted by the cording of his throat as he swallows.

'Stop looking at me like that,' he snaps when he's done. As if realizing himself, he takes a long breath, expression softening as he squeezes my hand. 'I can't be friends with a guard.'

'Why not?'

He blinks. When that doesn't serve as enough of an explanation, he spreads his free hand as if it's obvious. 'There's an order to things. A hierarchy. We can't all live in chaotic little cottages, waiting to get swept into the ocean.'

However pleasing he might be to the eye, he really is an irritant to the mind. Wearing a false smile, I slide my hand out from under his. I don't want to be touching him when he insults my home or my family.

Lips pressed together, he holds out his glass and the carafe of wine rises and pours itself.

Things remain frosty as he summons dessert, and Min tries to catch my eye a couple of times, but I evade her and ask how Asti learned to ride. I guess right – she has an entertaining story that soon draws Min into its web and has her asking questions, and the focus is off me.

Meanwhile, I turn my attention to dessert. A crumbly biscuit base sits beneath a pale-yellow creamy substance. I can't lie – it looks bloody good.

I take a spoonful. Lemon, smooth and creamy, sweet and yet still tart. Then the base – ginger.

The biscuits. Crushed and bound with melted butter. Good gods. I can't help moaning.

And Drystan can't help noticing, gaze twitching to me.

So I make noise when I eat incredible food. He's just going to have to put up with it, like I have to put up with him being the most confusing fake husband-to-be in existence. Hot one minute, touching me like I'm a thing to be cherished, then the cold king insulting everything I stand for the next.

I ignore him and lose myself in the dessert. When I finish and place the spoon on the plate with a slight sigh, he pushes his untouched dessert in front of me.

I look up. 'Don't you want—?'

'Not as much as you do.' I expect his comment to be accompanied by a mocking smirk, but there is none. Just unbroken eye contact as he urges me to 'Eat.'

I consider rebelling. I've spent too much of my life penned in – by my illness, yes, but also my parents. I hate to admit it, and yet it's true. With all I've been able to do since coming to the Underworld, living without being cosseted, I can see how they've kept me locked away.

Arguably for my own good. But absolutely to keep me hidden from Pa's bargain with The Morrigan.

An ambition that was always doomed. She is the goddess of fate, after all.

'Annon?' Drystan's voice brings me back from heavy thoughts, my lashes fluttering.

I could rebel against being told what to do. But in this instance, the lack of a second dessert would only harm myself.

Still, it wouldn't do to have the King of Death thinking he can order me around at any moment. I'm not his thrall.

I narrow my eyes at him. 'To be clear,' I say, quiet enough for his ears only, 'I'm not eating this because you told me to. I'm eating it because *I* want to.'

The corner of his mouth twitches. 'Noted, Your Future Majesty.'

So I lift up his spoon, the handle warm like he's been holding it this whole time, and I eat my second dessert.

I moan again. It's that good.

And I notice him noticing.

And I notice that it isn't a look of disapproval that he's wearing but one of hunger. The dark eyes. The parted lips. The way he sits forward, watching me like I'm utterly fucking fascinating.

Like he wants to devour me.

I don't know what to do. Because a small part of me wants to be devoured. But the rest of me, sensible and apparently not addled by a *look* of all things, says *absolutely not*.

'That was delicious,' Min says, her spoon clinking on to her plate. 'Your Majesty is too kind to have invited us.'

Asti makes a noise of agreement, moving her chair back as if to leave.

'Ready to go so soon?' Drystan's tone is the imperious king's, but he speaks more quickly than usual, betraying an undercurrent of what sounds almost like panic. 'We still have some hours before sunrise.' His gaze flicks to me, reminding me of what happens when the sun comes up.

I swallow down a groan at the thought of another day trudging through the labyrinth. I've encountered a few more traps, but they've been easy to avoid. And I sing Pa's sea shanties and Annem's songs from her homeland as I go, which staves off boredom and entertains the Collector. But I'm wilting in my chair, and yesterday I could only walk for five minutes at a time before needing to rest.

'That's true.' Asti grins as if Drystan's comment is a challenge. 'What would Your Majesty like to do?'

'The question should be, what would Lady Rhiannon like to do?'

They all turn to me as I bury my tiredness under a bright smile. 'Me? I'm not sure that I—'

But Drystan is watching me intently again, pressing forward in his seat.

And the two glasses of wine I've had are whispering that aside from the brief insult, it's been a fun evening, and if this has been fun, then how much more fun would *more* of it be? I can stay up a little longer, then sleep, ready for the labyrinth.

Besides, Min leans on the arm of her chair, closer to Asti, and I can't deny her a little more time with the object of her affections.

My gaze drifts to the distance through a window as I search for inspiration – something that might entertain unseelie fae. A light fall of snow drifts down, bright against the dark night.

'What about . . .?' I trail off, feeling suddenly foolish, even though there's this little leap of excitement in my heart that urges back my tiredness.

I've heard of snowball fights, but I've never actually taken part in or even *seen* one. Living by the sea all my life, I've rarely wit- nessed snow settle for any length of time before it's melted away by the salt air. When we were younger, Lowen and our broth- ers would sometimes walk inland to find a decent snowfall, but I was never allowed to go on account of my illness. I had to live vicariously through their stories when they returned, talking and laughing about great battles waged on a sea of white, with snow- balls instead of cannon fire and sleds instead of ships.

'What about . . .?' Drystan nods, prompting.

'Go on.' Asti leans over and nudges me. 'I promise not to laugh.'

Drystan shoots her a look that suggests laughing at his future wife would mean death.

I don't want Asti dead by any means but I kind of like that look. It lets me imagine that what I want matters.

Then Min smiles in that way that lights her whole face, and my worries flee under that brightness.

'What about a snowball fight?'

Drystan sits back, eyes wide, and all my foolishness rushes back in.

Of course a king isn't going to engage in a fucking snowball fight. What was I thinking?

'Sorry.' I grimace, head bowed. 'It's a silly idea, I shouldn't have—'

'If my betrothed wants a snowball fight, then a snowball fight is what she'll have.'

27

THERE'S SOME REARRANGING as we don warmer clothing and Drystan ties his hair back in the knot he wore while training the other day. I have to look away because the reminder of him shirtless makes me squirm. If he noticed Min watching Asti, he must've noticed me.

'Your hair,' Min states, coming over. 'It'll get damaged in the cold if we—'

'I'll do it.' Drystan intercepts before she can reach me, and then somehow he's braiding my hair.

I'm not sure what to make of him dressing my hair or the fact that he knows how to braid. Even my Pa, who's clever with knots, never learned how to tie my hair back, even when Annem was heavily pregnant with my brothers and I was too small to do it myself. I just had to learn quickly.

But I suppose with his long hair, Drystan knows how to look after it.

He fastens off two braids, then produces hairpins out of nowhere and uses them to coil the braids around my head.

He gives me a look over, the flicker of a smile, then nods. 'There.'

It's only when I pass a mirror on my way out that I realize he's created a crown atop my head.

We leave through glazed doors coming off his sitting room, leading to a large private terrace, thick with snow. One side leads down into a stretch of the gardens I haven't seen before. It's open, with evergreens encroaching at the edges and a single bare tree at the centre. Its black branches are only visible against the night sky thanks to the snow clinging to them, revealing the jagged shapes.

Asti rolls her shoulders like this is a real battle, and I suddenly worry that the term 'snowball fight' means something different in the Underworld – something that involves actual blood and death rather than just laughter and cold.

Min tucks her gloves into her cuffs.

Drystan eyes the snow, a crease between his eyebrows. He toes it as if unsure what to do with it before looking up at me. 'After you.'

This is it. My first snowball fight. The wine is truly winning now, rushing through me warm and assured, convinced I can do anything.

I square my shoulders, take a handful of snow and throw it at him. It's the least I can do after all he's done to me.

Except what should be a triumphant moment of revenge delivered in the form of an ice-cold projectile just . . . *poofs*. The snow drifts in the air between us, harmless and decidedly un-ball-like.

Min and Asti burst into laughter. Drystan cocks his head, frowning at the last of my ill-fated snowball falling to the ground.

'That's not . . .' Asti shakes her head. 'Have you never thrown a snowball before?'

Cheeks hot, I shake my head.

She and Min exchange looks. The latter covers her mouth like she's still smothering a laugh. 'It's not just a handful of snow. You have to pack it together.'

This time it's Drystan and I exchanging looks, both equally blank.

Min gives my shoulder a reassuring squeeze. 'I'll teach you.'

At Drystan's scowl, Asti pauses. 'And I'll . . . *remind* Your Majesty.'

Diplomatically put. I'm sure it wouldn't go down well to suggest the King of Death doesn't know how to do something as simple as forming a snowball.

Min shows me how to form something that actually holds a shape, though it's probably generous to call it a ball. But it'll do to throw.

I look up to find Asti doing the same with Drystan, except he's all frowny and focused, like he wants to make The Best Snowball That Ever Existed. The Snowball to Which All Others Will Be Compared.

The creases between his eyebrows deepen as he holds up what I have to admit is a pretty perfect snowball. 'And people . . . enjoy this?' He arches one eyebrow at Asti.

'Well, not this part specifically. It's *this* part they like.' A grin is the only warning before she lobs her example ball at Min.

'Uh! I didn't know we were starting yet!' But her shock quickly shifts to a devious little scowl and a moment later snow is exploding from square on Asti's chest.

Then all seven hells break loose.

I almost fall back at the first ball that hits me. More from surprise than force. I blink up, see Min covering her mouth like she's worried she's hurt me. Then I laugh, because I have a ball ready and an instant later it's sailing through the air at Min.

Asti's soon covered in snow – I guess as a guard, she feels like fair game. She can withstand battle: she can definitely take a few snowballs. But she's quick to form her own barrage, packing the snow between her hand and the end of her arm. They're not perfect, but her aim is true, smacking into my shoulder as I try to dodge.

My laughter's breathless as I pat together another snowball, using the dead tree as cover. Somehow this play attack and defence sends me giddy. Such a simple thing and yet it's like I'm a child again.

All that matters is looking up and choosing my next target.

Asti and Min are locked in a duel, with Drystan using the distraction to pelt Asti with another perfectly spherical missile.

There's a problem though.

A major problem.

The king's black clothing and sleek, knotted hair are unmarked by so much as speck of snow. No one has attacked him. They've only thrown a few balls at me, perhaps worried they'll hurt the fragile human. But Drystan?

Oh, he can *definitely* take it.

So, I line up my aim, one eye closed, face screwed up in concentration at my target, who's utterly distracted by the other two. I pull my arm back. And I throw.

The snowball sails through the air.

I hold my breath.

The king turns.

And the snowball lands two feet from him.

He looks from it to me. He blinks as though the unfathomable has just happened. 'Did you just attack me?'

Min and Asti's laughter dies. Somehow Min's on the floor, and now she leans up on one elbow, staring from me to Drystan. Her face has gone as pale as the icy garden.

But this is a snowball fight. If the king didn't want to get attacked, he shouldn't have joined in. So I spread my hands and lift my chin. 'Well, I *tried* to. But I missed.'

He continues to stare at me, so I take my opportunity to scoop up a handful of snow and pack it together quickly while he's still surprised. There's no time to aim: I just throw.

It hits. Snow explodes from the very centre of his chest as he takes a step back and stares at the white splatter across his coat like I've just dealt him a mortal blow.

I've never grinned so widely in my life.

Slowly, he looks up, and it's like something snaps in him. His brow settles low as his eyes narrow, glinting like gold in shadow. A wicked, wicked smirk curves his mouth. 'Oh dear, Nothing. You're going to pay for that.'

My pulse kicks up like a dance spinning faster, and I'm already backing away by the time he bursts forward.

He scoops up snow without pausing.

Oh shit. I'm in trouble.

But his smirk widens as he comes, and there's a light in his eyes that I haven't seen before. A light I recognize from my brothers and from Pa long ago when I was little, long before illness was something we needed to worry about, when he would chase me around the garden.

Still, he's running right at me. I turn and stumble through the snow, barely biting back a giggle at the fact I, a fisherman's daughter, have hit the King of Death with a snowball.

He pelts my back before I make it behind the tree trunk. But when he turns, he's the one Asti and Min are laughing at.

I'm forming my next snowball, which definitely has his name on it, when two dull thuds sound. He's got them both in quick succession. '*That's* for laughing at me.'

Asti wipes snow from her face as she turns and exchanges a look with Min, who's brushing off her stomach. An unspoken agreement passes between them before they turn back to Drystan. 'We humbly beg Your Majesty's pardon,' Min says, shaking her head solemnly as they bow.

Asti looks up with a grin. 'For what we're about to do.'

I don't even see them throw, but *doof-doof*, they strike Drystan square in the chest.

And just like that, the fight becomes a free-for-all.

Snow sails left and right. I stumble through it, ducking and shielding myself with one hand as I wait for the perfect moment to launch my next attack. We work our way into the sparse trees, using them for cover, chasing each other around them. The snow isn't as deep here, so running's easier. My hips groan softly, but the wine's warmth is still pretty convincing.

I can rest later. My cheeks are too busy aching and my eyes tearing from laughter.

Drystan chases Asti, Min and I pelt him while he's distracted and he turns on Min. We work on another distraction, and he switches target. Everyone's breathless, focused, like this is the only thing that exists.

Then he comes for me.

It's only play, but energy surges through me all the same, making me as giddy as belladonna does. I flee, staggering, half-blind from the tears of laughter, barely able to plead for mercy. Half-hearted, I chuck a poorly formed snowball back and miss.

But the others haven't forgotten me. They jump out from behind a tree, firing three times at Drystan. He skids to a stop, staring at them, giving me a chance to catch my breath and arm myself. 'You do remember I'm your—'

'Your Majesty,' I call with a teasing lilt.

He turns.

I throw.

This time my aim is true, and a glorious puff of snow bursts right in his pretty face.

From within the snow, he opens his eyes. With a swipe of his hand, he clears the rest from his face, then spits out a mouthful of the stuff.

He launches at me. He doesn't bother with any snowballs this time, just comes straight at me. Even though I can't win, I run. If I can reach the deep snowdrift I spotted just now, I can make a sudden turn and he might run headlong into it.

Even in the snow, his steps are silent, and it sets me on edge not knowing how close he is, making nervy laughter bubble through my gasping breaths.

I dare a glance back.

He's right there. *Here*.

Then he slams into me, arms around my waist, and we fly into the snowdrift. It's cold, creaking, but I land on something soft and warm, and I'm consumed by this sound I've never heard before.

Drystan's laughter.

It breaks through the freezing air. It heaves beneath me, where he's twisted us so he'd land first. And it's broken the cold ice of his face into . . . into . . .

Oh shit. He has dimples.

If I thought he was beautiful before, now I *know* he's the most gorgeous person I've ever seen. Head thrown back, face creased with mirth – he looks less like a perfect mask and more like someone who's lived. Melting snow glistens in his dark lashes and runs into his hair. His body is taut beneath me, consumed by laughter.

When he took me from my home, I thought his laughter was a cruel sound with nothing happy about it. But this? It's happy. It's warm. It's unshielded and free.

And it's bloody contagious.

Because I threw a snowball in the King of Death's face and he laughed. And if this isn't the most absurd thing that's happened in my life, I don't know what is.

I collapse on to his chest, adding my laughter to his.

When I finally look up, wiping the tears from my eyes, and his laughter subsides to soft chuckles, we find we have an audience.

Asti and Min stare at us – well, at Drystan really. Their eyes are perfectly round, their mouths in matching Os, and I know at once why.

They've never seen their king laugh before.

28

I PAY FOR it the next day.

The wine lied.

I can't have fun *and* function. Every step is misery. I don't even have it in me to be cheerful about Min giving me a large ball of red string to help track my path, after I mentioned neither chalk nor charcoal are able to mark the labyrinth's stone and the Collector seems less sure of direction the deeper we go.

The string unravels behind me as I trudge forward, using the wall for support. I avoid the flickering bloom in the stone. There's more of it here, oozing a matte, black substance. I should probably look more closely at it, but if I stop, I'm not sure I'll be able to start up again.

We've hit three dead ends already today, and the string has saved us having to remember which direction we came from. The Collector constantly glances at me, worried. I don't have the energy to reassure them.

With every movement, my joints remind me why I have to stay warm. The cracking of my knees sounds alarmingly like twigs breaking.

I want to tell myself the fun was worth it. I want to believe that making the King of Death laugh is an achievement that softens the pain and lightens the lead in my muscles. I even try to convince myself that the scattered hours of sleep I've had since entering the labyrinth are enough.

But my gods, none of it is true.

So I stare ahead, place one foot in front of the other and just try, *try* to keep moving.

I couldn't even bring myself to eat when I got here, thanks to the sickly, acidic feeling in my stomach, so I'm running on nothing but determination. And right now, determination seems fucking stupid.

But this is my sixth day, and I need to get to the fourth tier by tomorrow if I'm going to stay on track.

I need to get back to Lowen. I need to get home.

'I need to.'

'Annon? Didn't you hear me?'

I jump at the sound of Drystan's voice at my shoulder, but I don't have the energy to turn. No sound of the Collector's shuffling gait beside me. They must've fled when he arrived.

'What?'

'You dropped something.' He appears at my side, smirking and holding out . . .

Balled-up string.

Red string.

That's attached to the ball of string in my hand.

I stare at it. I blink. That's that, then.

I press the remaining string into his hands, turn and keep going.

Fuck you. The words chime in my head but I don't have the energy to say them.

I just need to keep going.

'Is that it?' he calls after me.

I just need to keep . . .

'I thought you'd at least call me a prick or perhaps something more imaginative, knowing you.'

I just need . . .

The ground rushes up. Strange. It shouldn't move like that.

Then it disappears.

Something grabs me. The Collector? Or a monster? I don't have it in me to fight.

'Rhiannon?' It shakes me, then Drystan's face appears. '*Annon* ?'

He's got me. Right. That makes more sense. Not a monster. Though his eyebrows peak together in a way I've never seen before and he's surveying me like *I'm* turning into a monster.

I should push him away. I should pull myself upright and press on.

I can't.

'Fucking hells,' he mutters. 'I thought you were dead.'

'Bad luck.' I manage to shake my head, though it makes the world spin. Only his face, crowding over me, remains still – an anchor. 'Just tired. Just need a sit down. Some rest. I'm fine.' I'm trying to smile when everything goes dark.

29

IT TAKES A few blinks before I understand what I see next. A ceiling tilts overhead. It looks familiar.

Ceiling.

Wait. I'm not in the labyrinth. He's taken me to the fortress – to Rigor Gard.

'No.' I fight his hold, frustratingly feeble against his strength. 'No, you can't. Put me down.' The jolt of panic running through me is at least enough to drive my tongue to form full sentences.

'Definitely not.' As he walks, Drystan looks dead ahead, but I have a close view of his jaw from here and the muscle in it twitching. 'You collapsed. I thought you were dead *again*.'

'But our bargain.' I sound pathetic. Childish. I don't care. Daylight is streaming through the windows, so I should be in the labyrinth. This is eating into my time. I didn't take the shortcut – I need every moment possible if I'm to stand any chance. I can't be stuck here for ever. 'I don't have time. Take me back.'

'You need to rest, not wear yourself into the fucking ground.'

'Take me back.' I try to sit up, but my muscles are not on board, and instead I just flop around like a dying fish.

'*Annon*,' he growls, grip tightening like he's trying not to drop me.

'Please.' It's just one syllable, but my voice cracks all the same.

That muscle in his jaw tightens.

'I can't lose a whole day.' I'm begging. Probably not something that's wise in the unseelie realm, but I don't care. 'I need to tell him.'

The shoulder my head is pillowed against sags as he sighs. 'What if today doesn't count? Will you rest then?'

Despite the sluggish condition of the rest of my body, my heart leaps. But . . . 'What's the catch?'

He glances down at me, frowning in question.

'What do you get in return for giving me an extra day?'

'Oh, I don't know? You not killing yourself through sheer fuck-ing exhaustion?' I've never heard him sound quite so impatient.

'So I won't owe you anything else?'

'No,' he snaps. 'Have you never heard the phrase "don't look a gift horse in the mouth"? It's one of the few wise things I've ever heard a human say.'

I hold my tongue against telling him the story from my mother's homeland about an attacking army who used a giant model horse to infiltrate their enemy's apparently impenetrable city. That seems like a pretty good reason to turn down a gift horse, if you ask me.

'I rest today and it doesn't count, so I get an extra day to work through the labyrinth and escape?' It's always best to clarify the terms of any fae bargain.

'Yes.'

'Fine.' I stop struggling and instantly my body tries to drag me down into sleep.

I half fight it, eyelids drooping, flicking open, drooping until they snap open again to find him lowering me into a bed. A mas-sive bed of reddish wood, covered in grey velvet and draped in softly twinkling lights. I must be seeing things because I can't picture him having such a pretty bed. There's something familiar about it, too.

He sits at my side, muttering, 'What the hells has been digging into my chest this whole time?'

I don't think anything of it as he dips a hand in my pocket. It seems like a distant concern as I exhale and sink into the soft mattress, eyelids drifting shut.

'You're ill.'

As I stir, it's the first thing I hear in Drystan's matter-of-fact voice.

It takes me a long moment of blinking up at the lights slowly dimming and brightening overhead before I register the words.

Shit.

Shit.

Gasping, I try to sit up, but he's tucked the blankets so tight I can't fight past them.

He shakes the jar containing the last of my tablets. Their rattle kills off any chances I have of lying my way through this. Why would I need medicine if I'm not ill?

'You're ill,' he says again. 'And yet you've been doing this for almost a week?' He turns wide eyes from the pills to me. *'How?'*

Not a question I was expecting. I open and close my mouth, then shrug, the blankets just about loose enough for me to do that. 'I've had a lot of practice getting through things despite feeling . . . not so good.'

'"Not so good"? You collapsed – *twice*. I was *this close* to sending for the Physic even though it would damage your reputation. I nearly paced a hole in the carpet from trying to work out what to do – how in the world to care for a human who's barely breathing. And you shrug it off and call it "not so good"?'

I manage a sheepish grin. It's oddly amusing to see his reaction to a situation I take for granted. I can't help wondering how he would fare if he felt this bad. I doubt he ever has – from what Min's told me, it sounds like fae rarely get ill, and their Physic is as much an honorary role as a practical one.

'And now she grins at me.' He sighs and looks at the ceiling like he might find support up there, then he sets off pacing, despite his worries for the carpet. The ravens give a rattling chorus as if indignant on his behalf. 'What's wrong with you? It can't be something that's started since you got here, because I know the Apothic hasn't given you any drugs.'

I'm not going to have this conversation lying down – literally. So I battle the blankets until he comes and helps, and I sit up against the pillows as he goes back to pacing. I hate telling people about this. I hate the pity and how hopeless it all sounds even to my own ears. But I've had recent practice with Min. So I pick at the embroidered coverlet depicting ravens and spears and haltingly tell Drystan about my illness.

He listens, asks no questions. He doesn't shoot me a look of pity when I tell him there's no real diagnosis and no cure. He's the perfect audience, really, just pacing up and down with his eyebrows knitted together.

Only when I've fallen quiet and have stayed that way for a long while does he finally speak. 'I can't undo our bargain, Annon, but if I'd known about your illness, I never would have made it.'

My hands fist into the velvet coverlet.

Scratch that 'perfect'. He's a middling audience and growing worse by the second.

'I knew I was ill and it was my choice to make,' I snap, making him stop mid-stride. 'I need to get home. Don't you understand why now? My illness is a weakness here – you and Min have made that quite clear. If I go, you can marry someone who isn't human *or* sick. Surely it will reflect badly upon you to have a wife who's so . . . imperfect.' I sigh, shaking my head. 'And even if none of that was true, I need my family. They care for me. They help me. If not for them, I wouldn't have survived for this long. And one day . . .' I swallow and will the burning of my eyes to calm, blaming my exhaustion. I refuse to cry. 'One day, I will run out of time. I don't want to do that alone.'

'You won't.' He says it so quickly, I wonder if he understands what I mean. But he's the King of Death – of course he knows what I'm referring to. He comes and sits on the bed, look softer than usual but not, thankfully, pitying. I couldn't take that right now. 'You're meant to be resting. I shouldn't have asked you to explain all this while you were still so tired. Here.' He offers a glass of water, bringing it to my lips himself when my hand shakes too much to hold it securely. There's also a platter of food, and I manage to eat a few morsels of meat and vegetables. The radishes are crisp and refreshing, their pepperiness a delightful reminder that I am, in fact, alive.

Then he tucks me in, giving me an opportunity to examine his face more closely. There are slight hollows under his eyes, reminding me that it's daylight and he should be asleep. In this bed. That's his.

But it's damn cosy, and he doesn't tuck the blankets quite so tightly, but I can feel the pressure of him sitting at my side, the way it dips the bed slightly, the warmth radiating from his thigh.

The idea of insisting he takes me back to my room slips from my mind as I slip from consciousness.

30

I WAKE WITH something warm beside me, and oh gods is it glorious to stretch out, pressing the full length of my body against it, snuggling my cheek into it. When I inhale, I hazily realize all at once that I know the scent, that it's Drystan at my side, and that his arm is around me.

My eyes pop open.

Instead of seeing him, though, there's an expanse of grey fur. The cat. His little body moves gently with sleeping breaths, and beneath him, Drystan's chest rises and falls, long and slow. He must've fallen asleep, tired from the late hour.

I move just enough to peer down at the large windows opposite the bed. The sunset streams through them, a black ball at the centre of hot orange, fading to pink and purple. Time for the unseelie's night to start. But I'm enjoying the softness of this bed, the warmth of its owner and the gilded light spilling through the windows. I don't want the day to end.

Drystan's fingers flex against my side, and when I look up, I find him awake, watching me. The dying light catches on his pale skin, warming the tone. It paints his lashes with gold flecks that match the spark of his eyes. I search for any sign of the dimples I saw the other night. There's maybe a whisper of them, a faint line on each cheek, only visible because I'm so, so close.

His gaze surveys me, too, and I wonder what he sees in the golden light. Do I look more like the woman I once was? Does the sun gild my hair, showing off how shiny it's becoming thanks to Min's care? Does it make my olive skin look warm and sun-kissed rather than pale and sallow?

I open my mouth to break the silence, uncomfortable at how long it's lasting and how much I hate not knowing what he sees with that inscrutable gaze. But he lifts his other hand and presses his finger to his lips, then points at the sleeping cat.

The King of Death is worried about waking up a cat.

That's a new one to add to my list of improbable things that are nonetheless true.

Somewhere between keeping quiet and the combined rhythm of Drystan's breath and the cat's, I drift back into darkness.

When I wake up, my arm's draped over his middle and I'm tucked tightly into the space between his arm and side, cheek resting on his chest. The cat's gone. The sun has set.

'You should be asleep.' His murmur rumbles through me.

'I'm sure the King of Death's future bride has responsibilities,' I say around a yawn, stretching and wincing as my body makes its displeasure known. Though, I'm grateful for the excuse to remove my arm from him without having to address how it got there in the first place.

'Not tonight, she doesn't.'

I look up at him, not able to make out much more than the faint gold glow of his eyes. It should probably be disconcerting, but it's actually a relief to not have to take in the full force of his striking features or try to read his expression to work out what he thinks when he looks at me.

Then I remember fae can see in the dark.

And he's probably thinking about what a poor, pitiful creature I am. Mortal *and* sickly.

I pull back, putting a few inches between our bodies, and sit up. But fuck, it's hard, and I end up flopping against the headboard, exhausted from just that slight motion. 'Then I'm sure the King of Death has responsibilities.'

'Only making sure his future wife takes her medication.' The twinkling lights over the bed emerge from the darkness, followed by the gradual brightening of the wall sconces. He holds up the jar for examination before passing it to me.

There's a lot more air inside than medicine.

'How often do you have to take those?' he asks as I fish one out.

'Once a day. Well, *half* of one.'

'But you don't have many left.'

I bite back a sigh. 'I know. Hence the half.' There will be three and a half after this. Seven days.

The thought of running out is a distant terror I'm too tired to fully acknowledge.

He helps me take a sip of water so I can swallow the half tablet. I'll give it to him – he makes a surprisingly gentle nurse. Another thing for that list. King of Death takes good care of his dying humans.

'I can't just go to the surface and retrieve more for you.' He frowns at the jar while I swallow again, the tablet half working its way down my throat, leaving its bitter aftertaste. 'Being able to travel there requires various things to align. Life, death, your moon. But if you give me one of these, I can have the Apothic test them and analyse what they're made of.'

Lose one tablet for the chance of gaining more? The offer feels like a lifeline. Not a guaranteed solution, but a chance.

And I'm nothing if not hopeful.

I agree to his help. He insists I eat and drink a bit more, though all I want is sleep. He's king, so he wins. Or maybe it's because I, begrudgingly, know he's right. Food might help. A little. Then, at last, he lets me lie down.

My mind churns, dizzy and half delirious from exhaustion.

Drystan being kind is worse than all his taunts. More unbalancing. More frightening because it strikes deeper.

Maybe he's realized he can't break me with beauty, so now he's trying tenderness.

Much more dangerous.

Because it almost – *almost* – feels real.

It takes me more than a day to recover.

Each night, as sunrise approaches, we go through the same argument-cum-discussion. I tell him I can't spare the time. He tells me I can't not spare it, especially if I want to get through the tougher challenges on the labyrinth's final levels. When I ask, he won't tell me what they are. But he promises not to count today, if I'll only rest, and that ends the conversation . . . until the next morning looms.

On the day I manage to sit up on my own and eat the entirety of a small meal under his watchful gaze, I catch him frowning at me thoughtfully.

I cock my head with a guarded smile, wondering if he's about to tell me I have food on my cheek. 'What?'

'I'm trying to work you out.'

I sprinkle cinnamon into my coffee, which is a delightful luxury – one of those small pleasures the Underworld provides. 'I'm sure I'm not that complicated. What exactly are you struggling with?'

'You're sick all the time and yet you're still this . . . *happy*.' His brow scrunches like he's sceptical about the whole idea.

'Would you rather I was miserable?'

He flinches, the lines between his brow etching themselves deeper. 'No. Not at all. I just . . . don't understand how.'

I blow on my coffee as I formulate a response. Maybe presenting the options will help. 'Well, I can choose to give in, right? Or I can try and make the best of a shitty situation. There *are* good things, even if my body isn't always one of them.'

'Like what?'

'Like the sun on my face. The feel of earth between my fingers.' I close my eyes and I can feel them both. 'The sound of the sea on the shore. The scent of flowers in spring and summer – oh! And the way the scents change between day and night. My brother's sketches. Min's smile.' I stop myself before I can say anything nice about Drystan. Because, yes, he raised the dead to force me to come here, threatened to tear my father's tongue out and did in fact cut out that singer's tongue, but there are things about him that I enjoy. He just doesn't need his ego stroked by me mentioning them. And I'm not sure I want to voice the positives, because, really, they should all be offset by his casual disregard for the sanctity of people's tongues.

He makes a thoughtful sound when it's clear I've stopped. 'The sun on your face.' He nods. 'Yes, I've caught you basking a few times.'

I nearly spill my coffee. 'Basking?'

'Yes. Like the cat.' He nods over to the windowsill where the cat is lying on the windowsill, even though night has fallen. 'Whenever there's sunlight in a room, somehow you're there, sitting in it. Sometimes with your eyes shut. Ancient fae used to worship the sun. I sometimes wonder if you're one of them. *Or* a cat.' A faint smile curves his lips, pressing a dimple into his cheek. It makes him look less mocking, more . . . genuine. I'm not sure what to make of that.

'Oh. Right.' I busy myself drinking my coffee even though it's still a little hot.

'You forgot something on your list.'

If he says 'me,' I'm going to pour this coffee on him.

'Ginger biscuits.'

I chuckle into my drink, conscious of his attention and the way he's noticed all this. 'Ginger biscuits,' I say with a solemn nod.

My heart feels . . . weird. I add a quarter measure of belladonna to my coffee and stir it in. He knows about my illness: there's no need to be surreptitious any more.

The giddy buzz is subtle from such a small dose, but it leaves me on edge about his close attention, why he might give it and what it might mean.

Clearing my throat, I search for a change of topic. 'How did he get in here anyway?' I glance at the closed door. I'd wager the door to his suite is shut, too. And Drystan may have let the cat sleep on his chest, but I can't picture him opening the door for a small feline.

'How did . . . You mean you haven't noticed?' At my blank look, he whistles for the cat who jumps off the windowsill and runs this way.

He runs *through* the settee at the foot of the bed, then jumps up. *Through*.

Like it's nothing.

He trots across the bed to Drystan and lifts his head as if to say he's ready for stroking now, thank you very much. Of course, Drystan is powerless to resist and pets the cat, giving a half shrug at the same time. 'He's . . . not entirely corporeal.'

'He's a ghost cat.'

'This *is* the Underworld.'

I'm reminded of that fact each morning when I see a black sun in the sky, but the next day dawns, sunny and warm. Drystan opens the windows and comments that it's the warmest day they've had in years.

The icicles over the windows drip all day long.

31

I SPEND A few days recovering in Drystan's suite. Then, when I'm well enough to move around, he insists I stay a little longer and he won't count those days in our bargain. He even brings me a stack of books about plants and medicine from the fortress library, declaring, 'Since you know about your surface plants, I thought you could learn about ours. Besides' – he narrows his eyes – 'I suspect books are the only way to keep you out of trouble.'

'I suspect you're right.' I've only made it to the library twice since I got here, and both times, I ended up asleep face-first in a book.

Still, as I read, I can't help wondering about his willingness to help me. What are his motives?

Despite his teasing about thralls, I have no power he can drain.

He dislikes me and he's unseelie, so pure and simple kindness is out of the question.

Though he does benefit from having a consort: the power. So he doesn't want me to die, hence the books on plant medicine and making sure I don't expire in the labyrinth or because of it.

And he might not be able to bind me to him through magic, but gratitude comes with its own shackles.

Over the first dinner I manage to eat at the table, he admits he's cancelled our public engagements.

I pause with my fork halfway to my mouth. 'How have you made excuses for me? Surely the people are wondering why they haven't seen their future queen in days. You can't have told them a lie but you also can't have revealed my illness.'

Gaze on my plate, he sucks in his cheeks, and I just *know* he's trying desperately not to smirk. Once he's mastered himself, he takes his glass, throat bobbing. 'That's why I've been eating meals in my rooms and making myself scarce. I don't have to say anything at all. Everyone assumes we're enjoying ourselves.'

'That's a clever way of—'

Understanding bursts in me, as sudden and shocking as a snowball to the face. My eyes about pop out of my head. 'Oh.' I make the strangled sound before stuffing food into my mouth.

He raises his glass to me, grinning before he takes a sip.

'You don't need to go tonight, you know.' He stands in the doorway, arms folded, leaning on the door frame.

'From what Asti said, tonight sounds like something important.'

He raises one shoulder. 'Your health is more important.'

For a moment I can't speak. It's like there's something growing in my throat, spreading down into my chest, but it's warm, not choking. For a few beats, I continue brushing my hair and twist back the front section, catching it with a pin he's given me that's shaped like a raven feather made of blue-black steel. 'I'm fine.'

And for a change, I mean it. I'm not saying it to make him feel better or to stop him worrying. These days of enforced rest have left me feeling better than I have in months.

He's still watching me, a dark presence brooding in the doorway.

I look up from the dressing table and nod. '*Really*.'

That seems to satisfy him, because he stops hovering and leaves me to finish getting ready.

After he's gone, I slip from my dressing robe into a gown. Sea-blue satin ripples with every movement, flowing as I walk. I sneak a little spin now he's not here to see and judge. The back is open, with clasps at my waist and neck – no help required this evening – and a high neckline at the front, though it leaves my shoulders bare, and the fabric clings to my breasts and hips.

I have those once more. Rounded under my hands. Small, but enough flesh to squeeze. The back of my throat aches as I probe these new shapes that the mirror tells me are *me* and yet feel alien. But there isn't time to explore this new frontier of myself tonight.

Min made this gown for me specially. I can't work out how I feel so covered and exposed all at once. That seems to be a speciality of her fashion. She's sewn chips of mother of pearl into the bodice and gathered the silk cleverly so it looks like rippling water, with not a single stitch visible on the outside. She even dyed the hem so the silk deepens into the inky blue of a stormy sea. I can't help but wonder if that's a reference to the bargain made between my father and The Morrigan. A bride courtesy of a storm at sea.

Despite the potential reference, I love the gown. It lets me move freely and the way she's sculpted it to my body, I don't feel like the strip of fabric forming the front is going to gape and expose me, even though it has no back.

And I love the books Drystan brought me too, particularly *The Herbal Grimoire*, which sits on the dressing table. It describes a plant that might even help. Skullflowers. Very Underworld, I know.

The illustrations seem a lot like lily of the valley, but a closer look at the little bell flowers reveal they are the same shape as their namesake. The grimoire says they have the effect of slowing and strengthening the heartbeat.

But they're also toxic.

It's darkly amusing how every treatment I find is also harmful.

Then again, that *is* the guiding principle from the first herbalism book I ever read. *The dose makes the poison.* The same words I've inked into the title page of this new notebook.

Drystan told me he knew where some skullflowers grow and has ordered a detachment of the Twylth to ride out and collect some for me. I didn't want to put them in danger on my account, but he shook his head. 'Nonsense. You are to be my queen. If you have a sudden desire for skullflowers, then skullflowers you shall have. The Twylth can handle any monsters they might find on the road.'

'In fact,' he added with a grin, 'I'm sure they're hoping for trouble: if they don't regularly spill blood, they get restless.'

My smile twists as I tuck the book into a drawer and whisper to myself, 'Gratitude. Shackles. Remember that.'

'I have a question,' I say as we reach the large doors leading to the grand dining hall, our Twylth guards hanging back. My mind's been foggy the past few days, so I haven't thought to ask until now. 'Why am I having another presentation? Wasn't that what my first night was for?'

'That was *your* presentation. This is *our* presentation.' At my blank look, he nods, prompting. 'As a couple. I'm sure you'll be devastated to discover you're expected to play the part of my doting fiancée who's desperately in love with me.' His eyes glint with amusement, but it's warm – more laughing in the snow than the haughty, detached amusement of the king who raised the dead to attack my home.

I sigh like the prospect is a huge burden.

And he smiles. The real smile with the dimples.

I swallow and busy myself with adjusting my necklace. 'You should do that more often.'

'What?'

'Smile like you mean it.' I refuse to look up at him, though my pulse presses at my throat a little harder.

'Perhaps I do mean it.'

My heart dips. Not because I need belladonna, but because at moments like this, he sounds so convincing.

Even though I know it's all pretend, it's such a terrible temptation to *believe*.

Thankfully, the doors sweep open, saving me from myself.

The grand dining hall is full. Just about every member of court and the household is here as far as I can tell. A couple of hundred faces turn to watch us enter and a hush falls over the room.

Silver thread stretches between the arms of the chandeliers and over mirror frames, glistening in the firelight. It drapes over chair backs and table legs, like a thousand spiders have been at work, armed with precious metal. Glittering black crystals hang over the massive fireplaces, throwing motes of light on to the marble floor.

Shadows lurk at the corners of the room, but they seem almost tamed by the brightness of the lights and the glistening silver adornments.

As usual, the two massive fires are stoked, but it's grown warmer outside, and the Vost has thought to open the doors leading out to the great terrace. Still, I catch Drystan scowling at the open doors, then glancing at my bare arms. I squeeze his elbow, and give him a smile that's meant to be both reassurance and a reminder that he's meant to look desperately in love with me.

The briefest eye roll is followed by a faint, reserved smile – no dimples this time – as he nods to the Annuncier, who speaks in the unseelie's old tongue, which I've learned is a language generally reserved for ritual purposes.

I have no idea what she says, but the language is lilting, lyrical, and I find myself lulled by her intonation and the ask and answer between her and the gathered fae. It's like being pushed back and forth by the sea, and I find myself swaying with it, thankful for Drystan's arm keeping me steady.

The speech finishes and everyone turns to us. My spine springs straight, body tense with the unmistakable terror that something is expected of me and I don't know what it is.

But Drystan places his hand over mine as he inclines his head. '*Dethau*.' His voice rings through the silence, its low pitch edged with the power I heard him use in the training yard.

I try not to shiver at the memory. I fail.

He gives me an encouraging nod, and whispers, 'You just need to say "*Dethau*." That's all.'

I gather my breath and courage and speak as loudly as I can. '*Dethau*.'

He squeezes my hand in what might be approval, then the gathering breaks into cheering and trilling cries.

Amidst the chaos, we set off on a sedate walk around the three long tables. The only empty spaces I see are at a table for two set upon a low dais at the far end of the room. Inwardly, I groan. Normally, we're seated at opposite ends of the central table, but it seems tonight the 'happy couple' are to be displayed.

As we go, Drystan catches the Vost's eye and something unspoken passes between them. By the time we finish our third circuit of the room – the fae seem to like the number three, I've discovered – and climb the dais, the doors are shut.

Our Twylth guards station themselves at a discreet distance, Thren to our right, and a jovial woman called Essa on the left. Instead of dining chairs, we have a small settee that curves around the table and forces our knees together. I'm suddenly conscious of the slit in this dress and the way it bares my leg now I'm sitting, letting the whole room see.

We receive exquisite little plates of food so carefully arranged they look like precious jewels, while huge platters appear on the long tables and everyone dishes meats and pies and vegetables I've never heard of on to their plates.

The flavours are incredible, but I can't help wondering how many raiding parties were needed to collect this – or perhaps there's no food left in the glasshouse. The taste is also a little marred by the way our every move is observed.

So I smile and lean closer to Drystan, since he's kept up his side of our bargain and even been . . . I hesitate to use the word about him, but he's been *kind* enough to extend the time I have to work through the labyrinth. Though I wonder if that's because he thinks I'll never make it, anyway.

I cant my head at him, eyes soft like I'm speaking sweet nothings. 'Why have you suddenly decided to be *nice* to me?' The question has been lurking in the fog of my exhaustion, it's only now I'm rested that I can grasp it.

'Nice?' He wrinkles his nose like I've insulted him. 'I'm not being *nice*. I'm being cooperative. Since you're to be my wife and you've been good enough to stop your previous' – he glances at our audience – '*misbehaviour*, why not?'

It's an answer. Just not a very satisfying one.

But the next tiny course arrives in a puff of steam, and it turns out slow-cooked beef with carrot and red onion on a spoonful of mashed potato is enough to distract me.

As I eat, I shift in my seat, wincing as my hips and knees complain at staying still for too long, especially as I'm sat awkwardly to avoid my knees resting against his.

His gaze shoots to me and he leans in. 'What's wrong? Are you feeling unwell?'

'It's nothing.'

He raises one eyebrow. 'I know you can lie, Annon.'

'My hips are getting a little stiff at this angle. That's all.' I shrug it off with a reassuring smile. 'It's not really a lie – it *is* nothing in the grand scheme of—'

He scoops my slippered feet up off the floor and places them in his lap. 'Is this better?'

I take a moment and listen to my body. The ache lessens, satisfied by movement. 'Actually, it is.'

'Good.' He smiles and holds my gaze for a long moment before he clears his throat and the smile shifts into a smirk. He indicates his court, where many of his subjects are glancing over and nudging each other, then bowing their heads and whispering. 'Besides, there's nothing wrong with a little affection between the happy couple. It's—'

'*It's expected*,' I mimic his teasing tone. 'I know, since you do so *love* to remind me.'

He grins, lifting his chin like he's pleased with himself. 'Glad to see you're finally learning.'

But I spot his telltale dimples before he remembers himself.

Still, if he wants to pretend he doesn't care about my suffering, I'm not going to ruin his game. 'Of course.'

He continues eating, just using his fork, while his other hand traces my calves, soothing the tight muscles. Gently, he circles my ankles and rubs my knees.

I try to look relaxed, like this is all entirely natural. But my heart is doing unnatural things and I suddenly wish someone would open the doors back up, because is it me or is it airless in here? And hot? Much, much too hot.

I take a sip of wine, eyeing him over its brim. But he seems absorbed in his two tasks: eating and working the ache out of my legs. 'Is this for the show or because of my illness?'

He gives me a sidelong look, the edge of a smile on his mouth. 'Can't it be both? Or neither?' He shrugs. 'Perhaps I like touching you.'

'I thought humans were distasteful.'

'So did I.' He goes back to eating like it's a flippant comment, so I try to treat it as such.

But his behaviour towards me has changed so radically. He must pity me for being ill. And maybe there's a bit of truth to what he's said – after all, he did give me the cat as a peace offering, and that was before he knew I was sick. As far as he's concerned, we're stuck together for the rest of my life, however short that may be. He's sensible enough to at least try to make it less painful for both of us.

Or he's trying that change of tack. Killing me with kindness. Binding me with gratitude.

My brain is quick to remind me: there *is* an alternative answer.

Just like when I read anatomy books and herbal compendia, it seeks out paths and potential. It can always see possibilities and sometimes impossibilities. Maybe that's why I hold on to hope even when others have given up.

However, just because my brain sees a possible alternative, doesn't mean there's any merit to the idea.

And frankly, I'm not in the mood to entertain impossible ideas.

Because there is no way on earth or the Underworld that the King of Death cares about me.

After the meal, we're expected to do a circuit of the room and mingle with the court. I thank my past self for noting down details of everyone I've met so far, as I'm able to remember names and the correct pronunciations.

We make pleasant small talk. Everyone mentions how warm it is, how beautiful the sunset was and that these are all signs it'll be a good Moonburn this year.

That word again. I haven't got around to asking what it means and publicly admitting I don't know feels a lot like it would be classed as a weakness by the unseelie. There's no time to ask Drystan privately, since we're constantly moving along the tables.

But I have to admit, the fae seem to be in a good mood tonight – perhaps they prefer the warmer weather.

I'm pleasantly surprised to find Min and Astrid sitting together in deep conversation – or should that be in deep flirtation? Especially as they're at a spot closer to our dais and therefore more privileged than Min's parents, who sit further back on another table. Is that Drystan's doing or does it fall under the Vost's remit?

But my pleasure quickly sours as we reach the final section of table and Lord Mastelle.

32

HE GREETS US, albeit the nod he gives me is curt.

Gods willing, the one bit of preparation I did for tonight, aside from my appearance, will help smooth things.

I tiptoe to Drystan's ear and ask for the velvet box I had him place in his pocket. He gives it to me and I present its contents to Lord Mastelle.

The shell necklace from Phaedra.

I've since learned that shells from Darkshore are among the most precious adornments in the Underworld, akin to flawless pearls or rubies and sapphires.

She sits a few seats over and is now craning to look over with barely disguised interest.

'This exquisite necklace was given to me by a very thought-ful member of court,' I explain. 'I tried to wear it, but my human frailty means I was cut to ribbons. Clearly, I'm unworthy of such a precious gift.'

Ignoring Phaedra's smug smirk, I incline my head to Lord

Mastelle. He's wearing a look of indifference, yet his gaze keeps skipping to the necklace.

'However, I believe your poise and strength means you would make a much better bearer of such a fine piece. I have no doubt *you* will be a worthy wearer.' It's a good thing I rehearsed this speech, because this is the part where I would say I was sorry, and thus end up far more indebted to Lord Mastelle than I intend. Preparation helped me work out different phrasing instead, and I go on with my head bowed. 'Please accept it as a token of my regret at insulting you before I fully understood your ways.'

Breath held, I offer the necklace in its box.

I talked through my idea at dinner last night, and Min agreed it would be a suitable peace offering without offending Phaedra. Asti suggested I demand a duel instead and she would fight as my champion, but I suspect that wouldn't be considered the most diplomatic solution, even by unseelie standards.

Min explained that Lord Mastelle is well within his rights to decline the gift, which he'd no doubt do in a suitably slick manner, but that it would signal his enmity. Acceptance, however, would put us back at a neutral position.

I'm stuck here for a while longer, and Phaedra has already made it clear I have her undying enmity. I'd rather not live in the Underworld with *two* powerful fae set against me.

Eyelids part lowered like this is all terribly tedious, Lord Mastelle examines the necklace then me.

It's a battle not to fidget, especially as I've foolishly locked my knees and now they're begging me to shift my weight. But fidgeting would be a sign of nerves, desperation, even, and I'm not about to give my unseelie audience the pleasure of witnessing my weakness. Especially not as Phaedra is watching this whole exchange with all the intensity of a hunting hawk. A glass sits in her hand like she's ready to drink a toast to my failure.

Lord Mastelle's silence scrapes down my spine and it doesn't look set to break.

Perhaps I can force the situation. 'Or, I can keep the necklace.' I shrug like I'm not bothered either way. 'I'm sure once I'm queen and have been connected to the land, I'll have the poise to carry it off. Don't you think so, darling?' I smile sweetly up at Drystan, reinforcing the reminder – I may be little more than a human interloper for now, but as far as they all believe, I'll be their queen soon, and that comes with power of its own.

I can be a powerful ally or a powerful enemy.

Your choice, Lord Mastelle.

His eyebrows creep upwards as he nods. 'Well gifted, Lady Rhiannon.' He takes the box, surveying me with eyes narrowed. 'Very well gifted, indeed. It seems you have learned a great deal since last we spoke.'

Ripples spread along the table as news spread that the enmity between Lord Mastelle and the future queen is over.

Phaedra sits back in her chair, face tight. A moment later, I spot her gulping down her entire drink in one go.

I try not to smile too smugly.

This time, I don't mind failing.

Drystan slips his arm from my grip and takes my hand in his. I try not to react to the skin-to-skin contact or the intimacy of his fingers interlacing with mine, since as far as everyone else believes, we've spent the past several days locked in his rooms fucking each other's brains out. But my stomach flips, apparently not in on our deception.

He squeezes my hand and bumps his arm into mine. Is that what passes for his approval?

I haven't drunk much wine, but I still blame it for the way I place my hand over his chest as we chat with Lord Mastelle and the other fae at his table. Drystan *has* been putting me off balance with his gestures all night, it's only fair I return in kind.

He blinks down at me, eyebrows raised.

'What's the matter, Your Majesty?' I give him a teasing grin as I whisper, 'Don't you want your adoring fiancée to be unable to keep her hands off you?'

He goes still, and there's this delicious tension that cords his neck, leaving only the wild leap of his pulse. I watch it a good long while. It's as sustaining as the food.

When I look up, his gaze is absorbed by the sight of my hand on him. I'm not sure he's breathing, though I think I feel his heart thudding against my palm, like I'm holding it. Something I could crush or cherish.

As if he senses my attention, his gaze skims up to meet mine. His pupils are wide. I could fall into that oblivion. Get lost in it, telling myself it's just for a moment, when really it's eternity.

I kind of want to fall.

'Lady Rhiannon?'

I jolt from his depths, blinking away the lie that we're the only people in the room – the world. I lower my hand to Drystan's biceps, which seems a little safer and lets me take it in when Lord Mastelle repeats his question.

We stay to chat a little longer before musicians troop in, pipes trilling and drums pounding, as they whip the unseelie up in their tune.

Chairs are abandoned. Pockets of dancing break out between the tables and in the corners of the room – then *on* the tables. Min's parents eye where she's sitting with frowns. Lord Mastelle half smiles as the Apothic mutters in his ear with an expansive gesture. I do a double take when I spot Min and Asti speaking with Phaedra.

Quickly, it becomes too hot, too loud, and I start wilting.

'Would my bride-to-be care for some fresh air?' Drystan bends closer but still has to half-shout to be heard over the raucous music and the even more raucous fae.

I nod, not even trying to hide my relief, and he dismisses our guards before leading me out to the terrace. This is much larger than the one by his suite and has been cleared of snow. Dim, twinkling lights like the ones over his bed nestle among the bare trees and trace webs between columns and arches that lead out to the main gardens.

'That was an excellent piece of statecraft,' he says into the sudden silence, gaze fixed ahead and thoughtful. 'The gift was perfectly judged. A priceless piece of jewellery, but he doesn't owe you an unfathomable sum because it had already been gifted to you. Plus, the compliment was exemplary – specific to him. I would say you probably didn't need to diminish yourself so much, but in this instance, I think your humility did the trick.'

'Actually, I can't take the credit. Min helped me understand how your society works, the whys behind your etiquette. Asti gave me some advice, too. You shouldn't discount people just because of their position.'

The corner of his mouth twists as he leads us through an archway and down into the darkness of the gardens. 'I should've known you would find a way to shirk my compliment.'

'I'm not going to take it if it doesn't belong to me.' I keep close to him. The moon is dark tonight and I can't see much at all out here. Plus my slippered feet crunch through snow, so I'm in danger of tripping – or losing the silk slippers. 'I think this air is fresh enough. It probably is back on the terrace, in fact.'

'There's too much light up there. We won't get the full effect.'

'Of what?' I ask as he stops us and steps over something.

'You'll see.'

Actually, all I can see is the gold glow of his eyes and the dim light catching on his teeth as he grins.

Then his hands come around my waist and he lifts me over the obstacle, laughing softly at the strangled sound of surprise I make.

'You really should warn a woman before you—'

'Shh. It's starting.' He places my feet on the crisp ground before him and takes up position at my back, an unseen sentinel.

I squint into the darkness. There's nothing. I can't even make out the snowy shapes of shrubs. 'What's starting?'

Warm fingertips graze over my throat, stealing my breath. They trace upwards, gentle enough to tantalize, firm enough to command. 'Look,' he breathes into my ear as his touch catches on my jaw and forces me not to look ahead but *up*.

A blazing, silver ring burns in the black sky. It flares, a black disc at its centre, and there's a faint roaring noise, like a bonfire.

I stare, mouth open. I've never seen anything like this. It reminds me of an illustration I once saw of an eclipse in a book on astronomy, but the caption explained that would happen during the day when the moon passes over the sun, with the corona burning in the sun's customary gold.

This is celestial silver, the precious metal made ethereal.

And just as I'm staring, a thread spins off from it, flaring through a kaleidoscope of colour and light, dizzying, beautiful, utterly captivating.

I follow its course up, unblinking eyes burning as my neck cranes. I tilt back, feet stuck in the snow, and gasp, braced to fall.

But my sentinel's still there, warmth that braces at my back.

'I've got you,' he murmurs as he cups my solar plexus, holding me flush against him. The heat of his hand blazes through me, and my breath hitches as his thumb slides up between my breasts, casual yet claiming. I wonder who this pretence is for.

His other hand is still around my throat. As I swallow, it presses my flesh into his, warmth upon warmth, my pulse in his palm. He has to feel how it speeds, a fluttering bird he cages so carefully and so completely.

He must realize he's still holding me, because slowly he releases my neck and takes my hip instead, bracing me against him.

My chest heaves on a full, heavy breath, and while I have a

million questions about the King of Death and his true motivations, I trust in one thing.

He won't let me fall.

So, with him at my back, I lose myself in the display as another flare arcs overhead. Threads burn from the corona around the dark moon, spreading and bursting in light and colour.

One balloons out, then turns jagged. For a breathless instant, it looks like the outline of my home upon its clifftop, then it shifts and bursts apart, and I fancy the shapes soaring into the darkness are seagulls. I can almost hear their sharp cries.

No, not gulls. One is an owl, great wings spreading, flying straight for me, before it vanishes.

There's a series of seven arches that crumble. A loop that pulls away, making the ring around the moon look like a pendant hanging from a necklace. The outline of a dark horse that paws the ground, eyes glowing, smoke pluming from its hooves and shedding from its body. Or at least that's what I see. The shapes are as random as clouds, and I'm a child looking for sense among them.

It's beautiful. Such a contrast to the Underworld's grey sky and black sun and flat, white snow. I thank the gods for it, even The Morrigan. Part of me is glad to have a chance to see something few, if any, mortals have ever witnessed.

When I shiver, the cold cutting through Drystan's hold, he slips his jacket over my shoulders and steps in closer.

I have no idea how long passes before the last flare fades into the sky and the silver fire around the moon burns low, leaving only a faint ring in the dark sky.

'What was that?' I whisper, breath misting overhead as I still stare up, hoping for just one more spark.

'Moonfire.' The word brushes my ear, making me shiver. 'It only happens when certain celestial bodies are aligned. That's why I chose tonight for our formal presentation as a couple. Moonburn is a meaningful night for my people – one where we're connected to the surface and the skies we once lived beneath. That's what the strands of light are – glimpses of the true stars and planets, rather than our mere echoes. Our stars are more the idea of stars – the memory of them in the minds of all the dead who have passed through. To see moonfire is significant. An auspicious sign for our marriage.'

Symbol is important to the unseelie, just like ritual. But . . . 'Is it really auspicious if you just chose a certain date?'

'The colours aren't guaranteed, even if on paper everything is aligned. The fact they showed so brilliantly tonight – so bright, so full of colour.' His fingers flex against my hip. 'I call that significant.'

Everything about tonight feels significant. Like I'm approaching a fork in the road or a junction in the labyrinth. But I don't know what my choices are or where I'm trying to go.

In the cold dark, I'm suddenly aware of how flimsy my dress is and the way the stiff peaks of my nipples push against its silk, despite Drystan's jacket. I pull it tighter, hoping he hasn't noticed.

'But you still chose the date, didn't you? I have no effect on what happens in the sky. It could be anyone here with you – anyone presented as your future spouse.'

He huffs, hold loosening. 'Are you deliberately contrary or does it just come naturally to you?'

'Me, contrary?' I splutter, turning. 'You're the one who . . . who . . .' But now I'm staring up at him and his grip has reformed on my hips, I struggle to think of anything particularly irritating he's done lately. Which is irritating in itself. 'Well, you've thrown me into your labyrinth, for one thing.'

'You asked me to.'

'No, I asked for a chance to get home.'

'It's the same thing.'

'You didn't warn me that Min would be in danger.'

'You didn't ask.'

'That is the worst excuse I've ever heard.'

His lips thin, outlined by the faint light from the dim ring lingering around the moon. 'Maybe it is. But I couldn't tell you what the labyrinth would throw at you, even if I wanted to.'

'Why?'

'My word. You always have another question, don't you?' His hands skim up my back, and I'm not sure if he wants to throttle me or crush me into his chest.

I'm not sure which I'd prefer.

'Well, apparently it's the only way to get information from you, since *you* never volunteer it.' I punctuate the 'you' with a prod right at the centre of his chest. 'And you just said I didn't ask. Do I ask too many questions or not enough? It can't be both.'

'Stop.' His fingers plunge into my hair with a grip tight enough to tilt my head back.

I let out a whimper that's part shock, part something hot that I'd prefer not to examine too closely.

His heaving breaths fan my face, and my chest rises and falls to match, like we both sprinted to this point. His gaze skims over my face, from one eye to the other, down to my parted lips.

'Just stop,' he hisses, punctuating it with a yank on my hair that pulls every nerve in me tight.

I'm not sure when it happened, but his other arm is banded around my waist, and my hands are planted on his chest.

'I already did,' I murmur.

'No.' He tugs my hair, the motion controlled, pulling me back so I arch against him, chest and belly pressed against his, the silk of my gown tight over my breasts, my hands fisting in his shirt, feet barely on the ground like that might help him keep control. 'See? It's like you can't help yourself.'

He has me so taut, every nerve hums like a high note on a violin, held and held and held.

I reach the fork in the road. One path is sensible. One path is *this*. A solution to the unbearable tension ringing through me. Something physical that doesn't matter. A choice that, if made with my eyes open, carries no risk. I won't be his thrall – magical or physical.

But I will enjoy this one thing before I leave this world.

I trust my weight to the arm banded around my waist and loop my legs around him. It's natural, easy, and it makes his lips part on this heavy exhale like it's the last thing he expected.

'Can't help myself? You're the one clutching me against yourself like a desperate boy.'

The gold in his eyes flares, as bright as moonfire, as devastating as wildfire. It scorches with his tightening grip – each finger a brand upon my skin. I wouldn't be surprised if I discovered he'd burned away my gown. I'm not entirely sure I'd care.

He half smiles, half snarls, entirely vicious, as he walks me back through the snow until my shoulders hit a pillar. Cold, hard, it bites through his jacket into my flesh, a dizzying contrast to the heat of the king crushing me into it.

'You can't help but retort.' He punctuates each word by grinding against me, wringing a needy moan from my lips. '*Always*.' He drives deeper, harder.

And I love that he isn't gentle.

For so long, I've been treated like something that might break. Or even worse – something that's already broken. Now, his roughness is a balm, harsh enough to sing through my body, controlled enough that I'm not afraid.

Satisfied savagery enters his smile, like he knows he's made me slick, like he wants to drink up the sound of my rising pleasure. 'It drives me fucking mad.'

I don't want to prove him right by replying. But I also can't bring myself to keep my damn mouth shut. And part of me wants to earn this delicious punishment he's doling out tonight. 'Would you prefer it if I was a good little wife, bowing and scraping and letting Your Majesty have the last word on all things?' I use the tiny bit of slack he's left in my hair to raise my chin, defiant.

The gold of his eyes wears thin as his pupils blow wide. He goes still, the tension in his body a solid thing whose trembling is only detectible by touch. And we're touching in a lot of places.

'What did you just say?'

'I say a lot of things, apparently, Your Majesty. You'll have to be more specific.'

'What did you just call yourself?' His voice lowers, rumbling into me.

'A good little wife.' I enunciate each word like they're all separate sentences.

He huffs out a breath, not quite laughing. 'You couldn't be a "good little wife" if you tried.'

That stings. Deep. A lance driven through my chest. Then twisted.

Because I had hoped for that once. Back when I thought I could have the normal life I'd been promised.

I was meant to marry that boy I gave myself to on the beach when I was young and naive and more healthy than sick. I was meant to move away and start my own life and have my own children, just like my brothers have. I was meant to have a home that I ran, a husband I loved, a garden that wasn't bound by walls embedded with iron.

For the man that boy grew into, I would have been a good little wife.

But I never got the chance.

And I never will.

A tight tremble seizes my throat. It's all I can do to try and swallow it down and blink away the threat burning at the back of my eyes. I lower my legs and shove on Drystan's chest.

'Let me go.' I hate the way my voice shakes on those three simple words.

Yet he obeys, eyebrows clashing together.

And, barely holding in tears, I run into the night.

33

AFTER SOME STUMBLING around in the dark, I find my way to his private terrace. From there, it isn't much work to enter his suite and gather my belongings, including the ball of red string. Under the watchful gaze of the three ravens, I pause to write a note requesting that he send me back to the labyrinth at dawn, then return to my room. All the fae are still at the presentation celebrations, so I don't see anyone in the corridors that I have to explain myself to, just the cat, who almost trips me up three times as he rubs against my legs.

I sleep fitfully until just before sunrise, when I get ready for the labyrinth, and sit by the window, holding my breath as I wait for the black sun to break the horizon.

The instant it does, I fragment.

I land in a familiar corridor of black glass full of equal parts relief and dread. My limbs don't ache today, but how long can I trudge through here before they do?

The Collector is huddled, humming a little song to themselves. The moment they look up and see me, they fuss over me, touching my shoulders and hair as if reassuring themselves I'm real. 'We thought something had happened to you. Something terrible.'

'The king,' the slithering voice whispers, and they nod as if all their voices are in accord.

'I'm fine. He didn't hurt me. He . . . I don't think he would.' I frown as I retrieve the ball of string from my pocket and realize that's not a reassuring lie. Aside from emotional pain, at least.

The Collector's various voices mutter. Most are afraid of Drystan, which makes me wonder why.

As we make our way through the corridors, I ask about themselves – their life before the labyrinth.

'Before?' They pause, murmuring back and forth between themselves. 'We don't remember a before.'

'Then you've always been here?'

They stop at an intersection and make a chuffing sound as though sniffing the air, though I've never seen any nostrils among their flecked hair.

I follow as they choose the left-hand turn. Although they don't have experience beyond the first tier, there is some aspect of the labyrinth to them. Their senses steer us true more often than not. I'm grateful – this is my sixth day in here, and I need to reach the fourth tier by sunset if I'm to stay on track.

'Yes,' a handful of the voices answer.

'No,' says one. The dissenter, of course.

Their shaggy head cocks as though the other voices are curious.

'Sometimes . . . sometimes we dream of places beyond obsidian walls. Trees. Snow. Hills. A smiling face. A hearth. A cottage garden with jasmine climbing the walls and lavender above the fire. A table set for two. A swollen belly. A blessing.'

The other voices listen in heavy silence. So do I.

I swallow like that can help the squeezing sensation in my chest. But this ache isn't physical – not a symptom.

The Collector – or at least part of them – had a life before this.

Many lives, if each voice was once a separate person, before they were collected. A partner. A child on the way.

I wonder if their memories come in a complete, comprehensible story or if they're just snatches of moments with no connective tissue. I wonder if they understand the life they lost and why this voice remembers when the others don't seem to. If they were the most recently collected, that might explain it.

We walk on in silence for a long while before one of the other voices pipes up. 'Sometimes we dream of horses. The smell of leather and soap. The stink of their shit. The blast of wind in our ears when they race.' They hang their head. 'But we don't even know what a horse looks like.'

'What's the wide blue?' another voice asks. 'We dream of that sometimes. It sighs and crashes when it's angry.'

'The sea?' I offer.

'The sea!' Their head jerks up and turns to me. '*The sea.*'

I fish out Lowen's sketch of the coast and show them.

They gasp, eyes gleaming, wide, as they take in every inch, the fingertips of two hands tracing the lines. '*The sea.*'

Over the rest of the morning, I catch them rolling the words around their mouth several times, like they enjoy the flavour.

We stop to eat and rest, and I share my food with them. In an apologetic tone, they tell me they have no food for me today, but I tell them not to worry. I'm prepared.

Though, I don't feel as tired as I do most days in here. I try not to think about how I should be grateful to Drystan for the enforced rest.

'You know,' I say as we repack my bag, 'you can go back to the first tier. I appreciate you helping me, but it's frightening for you here. You're under no obligation to stay with me.'

They heft the bag over their shoulder and give me a sidelong look, the skin around their eyes crinkling. 'We know.'

And with nothing more, we set off.

*

As the sun passes overhead, there are increasing signs of the bloom I've spotted before. The matte flicker echoes across the stone, oozing more of the viscous slime that turns my stomach. As we pass, though, this stuff *moves*.

The first time I notice it out the corner of my eye, I think I'm tired and imagining things. The second time, I stop in my tracks.

'What *is* that?' I edge closer, checking there is none of the slime on the floor – the last thing I need is to fall over. Plus, I don't trust the stuff not to be poisonous or acidic or something equally delightful.

Tiny black filaments stretch out from the ooze. As I crane to one side to view them from another angle, they follow. Strange.

They remind me of an experiment the teacher at the village school once showed us using a magnet. She had a tray of metal filings, which stood on end when she placed the magnet underneath, like they had a mind of their own. But they were only cold, dead metal. One of the boys got hold of it after the lesson and shoved the magnet in the middle, so they spiked off its end. The teacher never managed to get them all off the magnet.

She always seemed a bit nervous about the experiment and made it clear we weren't to tell our parents. Now I look back, I suspect those filings were iron – forbidden, even back home.

These filaments look a lot like those filings, but with an organic aspect, like the bristly leaves of borage or furry black mould.

'Lady Annon?' The Collector shifts behind me, a rough edge to the deep voice. 'We should keep going. We don't like that stuff. It isn't right. It doesn't belong.'

'It *is* strange.' I rifle through my pockets and pull out my notebook. 'But I don't think it can hurt us – as long as we don't touch it, anyway. Plus, it might help us understand this place.'

They make a low, begrudging noise.

I tear a strip of paper from the back of the notebook, roll it into a long tube and reach towards the filaments. They strain towards it as though hungry. The next instant, they shrink away, like when the teacher turned the magnet the other way around.

'Huh.' I move the tube and moments later, the filaments reach for it again. 'Now, where's the logic in that?'

'Be careful,' the Collector whispers over my shoulder. 'Don't touch it.'

'It's all right. I won't.' I give them a reassuring smile. 'That's what this is for.' I dip the paper tube into the ooze. It remains visible a little way in – the substance isn't opaque black but slightly transparent, like smoked glass.

When I pull away, it clings to the paper, stringy, sticky. I wrinkle my nose when I finally manage to pull clear and see it's left a greasy mark.

'I can see why you don't like this stuff,' I mutter as I discard the paper in the corner, pull out the pencil and open my notebook.

I'm adding a sketch of the black filaments and a description of their movement to my notes when I spot the ooze creeping over the discarded paper tube. It's almost swallowed it up entirely by the time I bend down and peer at it with horrified curiosity. 'It spreads. Is that what it's doing to the labyrinth?' I hold my breath as the stuff closes over the last of the paper.

A shriek splinters the air.

The Collector's head whips around in the direction of the noise. I've never seen their eyes so wide, their shoulders hunched so low. Their breaths come in staccato bursts.

My mouth dries. The hairs at the back of my neck strain to attention like they recognize the cry from some ancient ancestral memory.

'The Devourer,' the Collector whispers, the slithering voice alone. '*Run.*'

34

THE COLLECTOR GRABS my wrist. I drop my pencil as they take off running and yank me after them. Somehow, I keep hold of my notebook.

My boots slap on the stone, a loud signal of where we are compared to the Collector's fae silence as they move. I glance over my shoulder but see nothing. Maybe they're mistaken. 'What are we running from?'

'*The Devourer.*' Like that explains everything.

'And that is?' I pant as we round a corner.

'Not like the creature that wanted to eat your friend.' Their head turns left and right as we stop at a crossroads, giving me a moment to catch my breath. They throw a fearful glance over their shoulder, then drag me left. 'This is a monster. Can't be bargained with. It kills anything it sees. Mindless. Violent.' Only the slithering voice speaks, soft, urgent. The others have kept quiet since we heard the shriek.

That alone puts me on edge.

But there haven't been any more shrieks. Just that one. Maybe it doesn't know we're here and now—

The air tears apart again. Louder. Closer. Harsher in my ears.

The Collector whimpers and speeds up. I can barely keep up, stumbling, breathless, trying to listen for the sound of pursuit, despite my ringing ears. My joints complain, but they're quiet compared to the Devourer's cries.

Left. Right. Another left.

We reach another crossroads and somehow the creature's shriek comes from our right. 'Are there two—?'

The Collector drags me ahead and down the next long corridor; the sky is blocked out.

For a second, I think it's the monster. My stomach drops.

Then I register the glittering black cliff that marks the line between the third tier and the fourth. Looming, higher and higher, consuming the sky. Cracked. Chipped. Sharp and smooth. Unscalable.

And yet close enough I can see all this detail, including the little, scrubby trees that somehow gain purchase on the sheer rock.

The thought gives me a burst of energy, and I keep to the Collector's heels.

Another shriek cuts through the air, just as the corridor opens up to left and right.

We spill into a small square at the cliff's base. There's a clattering sound behind us. Claws? Hooves? A weapon?

'No.' The Collector's shoulders slump as all their voices speak. '*No.*'

Hands on knees, I fight to catch my breath. 'What's wr—?'

I step around them and see exactly what's wrong.

A staircase rises from this little square, hugging the cliff face – an unmistakable route to the next level.

Except, around forty feet up, it drops away.

A dead end.

Higher up, hidden in the shadows – sunlight gleams on the edge of more stairs. Some sideways. Some upside down. Narrow platforms stud the way in between.

There was once a continuous structure here, but it's slumped over time – a cliff face falling, its footing eroded by the sea.

I squint into the shadows, trying to pick out a clear path. 'Maybe there's a way?'

Eyes rolling in fear, the Collector looks back.

There are no other corridors off this square. The clattering comes closer.

Their eyes narrow. 'No way back,' the slithering voice whispers.

'Come on,' the deep one bites out as they grab my wrist.

I'm dragged up the stairs, less than half-running, mostly stumbling.

Sheets and shards of obsidian litter the way. The Collector sweeps much of it out of the way with their stringy hair, but I still have to pick my route.

We reach a flat landing at the top of the stairs and the dead end.

Still very much a dead end. The shadows hide no narrow ridge we can creep along. There's a small outcrop around a dozen feet away, not even big enough for me and the Collector to stand on together, then another sheer drop between it and a half-slumped section of staircase.

The Collector makes a low keening sound that nips at my own fear, sharpening it to terror that claws at my throat and makes my eyes dart.

'There has to be something,' I mutter. '*Something.*' If I die here, Lowen will never know. He'll keep holding on, waiting for me, feeling guilty about that damn mirror. Or is it that *I'll* die guilty if I don't apologize?

That's a puzzle for later. Right now all that matters is not getting devoured.

I look up at the sheer, black rock. 'Please?' I don't know who I'm asking. The universe? The labyrinth? Any god who's listening – or demi-god.

The air shifts. My ears hover on the edge of popping. Every hair on my body rises.

I swallow down the thing trying to climb out of my throat and turn.

Down in the square. The Devourer.

No mistaking it.

In a way, it looks like a stag. Four legs. A wedge-shaped head. Huge, spreading antlers.

But that's where the similarity ends. This is the perverse idea of what a stag might look like, drawn from a nightmare.

White eyes. Black fur that seems to constantly move. Its legs bend in strange ways, not like any creature I've ever seen.

Oh, and it has fangs.

From here, as it hurtles towards the stairs and takes them half a dozen at a time, I can tell it's fucking massive. Big enough that it could get its jaws around my leg with ease.

My heart hammers harder than it does with belladonna. My stomach cramps around the food we ate earlier.

That thing is going to kill us.

The Collector grabs my wrist, muttering, 'It looks different.'

'I don't want a closer look.'

We run. There's nothing at the end of this broken staircase.

Ahead and above, there's another fractured set of stairs. But it's so far. Even the Collector, tall as they are, wouldn't be able to reach.

I look back.

It's so close. My pace falters.

The Collector grabs me.

Then I'm in the air.

I'm falling.

No. Wait.

The fractured stairs come closer. I'm going up. The Collector threw me.

Threw me.

I reach out, arms windmilling, legs kicking like somehow this is going to help. It's too far. I'm not going to make it.

All the air rushes out of me as I land on the bottom steps.

Wheezing, I scramble into the shade of one of the scrubby trees, almost crying to feel solid rock under me.

Behind me, the Collector is still running, eating up the last feet of the platform below.

Too far away, though. They can't jump all this way. Not quite.

I can't catch them – they're too big, too heavy.

They compress. Spring. Reach.

My throat burns, desperation a raw, wordless cry. Time stretches out as I count down the moments before the Collector stops surging up and starts falling.

It starts too soon. Fingers so close to the steps I'm on. I reach out uselessly.

Their grip closes around the bottom step. Eyes wide, they stare up at me.

Arms heaving, they try to pull themselves up, but they only have a fingertip grip, and the rock is so smooth. There's nothing below for their feet to purchase on.

'Can't get . . . up.' All their voices sound as one.

I grab their arm. Heave.

But they weigh many times more than I do.

My eyes burn as I search for anything that might help. There has to be—

My hand closes on something that isn't cold stone. Something warm. Tough but pliable.

A loose root. It isn't much. But . . .

Almost as thick as my wrist. I give it a tug. It holds.

The Devourer clatters across the platform the Collector

leapt from. On one side its antlers gouge the rock with a tooth-splintering screech.

I bend the root towards the Collector's slipping fingers. 'Try this.'

They reach, grab and by some fucking miracle, it holds their weight as hand over hand over hand, they climb up.

For a second, we're a panting pile of relief.

Then the Devourer shrieks once more.

Its hooves pick through the debris, finding a clear path with ease. As surefooted as a goat.

It doesn't even take the same path as us. It leaps to a tiny outcrop no wider than my hand, then leaps again.

I don't see where it lands – we're already running.

The way to the top is a blur of gasping breaths and heaving muscles, the Collector's wiry arms and many hands helping, pushing me ahead, pulling me after, shoving whippy saplings out of the way. Their softly terrified whimpering.

Somehow, we're halfway. My chest squeezes, agonizing.

I don't even know how I keep moving, but I do.

The Devourer nips at our heels and tries to cut us off. We change course, swerve out of reach, feel the thunder of its hooves right behind us and somehow barely miss it a dozen times.

Three quarters of the way.

I run, stumble, run. Up, up, up.

And then there's no more up.

I can see the top.

The ground rumbles. Dirt chokes me. Grit gets in my eyes, burns.

I'm falling.

Really falling this time.

The staircase crumbles beneath my feet.

I'm one, two, three feet from the top and getting further.

The Collector looks back. Their eyes go wide. They reach.

I reach.

Stretch.

Cry out with the agony of my cramping muscles giving in.

Their fingertips brush mine.

The Devourer shrieks, piercing my ears. Too close. Much too close.

Hot breath brushes my ankle. The stink of rotten flesh roils into my lungs, my gut.

Eyes streaming, one blurred, I look back.

The Devourer is an inch away, springing up the falling rocks, its mouth open, blackened teeth bared.

Its fur stretches for me, every part strained and ready for my death. The death I'm falling to.

A strong grip closes on my wrist.

I stop.

The air whooshes out of me.

The Devourer runs out of falling rock. It's a foot away. Two. Three. Further. Falling.

I look up. The Collector has me – one of their hands fastened around my wrist, the other three clinging to the straining trunk of a young tree.

We lie at the top of the broken stairs, catching our breath, taking in the sun and the miracle that we survived. Somehow.

The Collector threw themselves across that gap for me. Their feet were in the air, their entire weight trusted to that sapling, all to save me. They were already at the top. They could've kept going.

As I lie there panting, trying to take all that in, they start to laugh.

It's a wild sound, giddy with relief.

I find myself doing the same, tears streaming down my temples. I'm alive.

For once I don't care how much longer that may be. A month. Six. A year. Ten.

All that matters is for this moment, with this strange, many-personed friend, I am alive.

35

ONCE WE'VE RECOVERED, we pick ourselves up and venture into this new tier of the labyrinth. I'm pleasantly surprised that my heart plays nice. Of course, my joints ache and groan, and my muscles cramp and burn, but my heart soon stops its angry clench and doesn't retaliate with an episode.

I take that as another cause for celebration.

Today, there are plenty. We've reached the fourth tier. I haven't died. And the Collector just might be one of the truest friends I've ever made.

Despite my exhaustion and questions about what's truly driving me, I find myself smiling as we walk and rest away the remaining afternoon.

Seconds before the sun sets, I throw my arms around the Collector and squeeze.

'What's—?'

'Thank you,' I whisper as I fall apart and am swept back to the fortress.

*

My good mood holds when Kishel arrives for another lesson. He mirrors my cheerful expression as he notes how good it is to see me and sets his scrying bowl on the table. There is a tinge of concern to the look he gives me, which makes me wonder if his Fatework has seen the truth of my recent absence. But he doesn't raise it and neither do I.

'Tonight we're going to try something slightly different.' He pours moonwater into the bowl, but this time it sparks with silver motes. 'It's freshly gathered. The water from Moonburn captures some of the night's magic. But that's not the main difference for tonight. This is.' He holds up a small bottle of what looks like ink, then gestures for me to take my seat.

No ravens tonight. I haven't seen them since I left Drystan's suite and they squawked down the hall as if calling me back.

I pull my chair close to the table and peer into the water. The silver motes glint and flare brightly as they collide, but I don't see any great portents of the future. 'I hope that ink is powerful stuff.'

Kishel chuckles as he uncorks it. 'It's just regular ink. I'll be channelling it, though. It might be that you don't have the magic necessary to move the waters to reveal to you the threads of fate. It might just be that your magic is late awakening.'

A tightness around his eyes suggests he doesn't believe that. It's close to pity. Poor, magicless human!

I make my smile brighter. I'm fine.

'Either way,' he goes on with a shrug that nearly spills ink on the table, 'this is a test that negates magic. We're simply going to see if you have the intuition to read the portents.'

'Is that not a magic ability?'

'Interpreting symbols and signs is a different skill from making them appear.' He tilts the bottle, letting three drops of ink fall into the water. 'Interpretation is harder to teach. Let's see if you already know it.' He sits back and gestures to the bowl.

The water ripples. The ink swirls. As it dissipates, I realize it's actually dark red rather than black.

'What am I—?'

'Shh. You'll know when you see it.' He has his eyes shut, but his eyebrows still clash together and he points at the bowl, like he knows I'm peeking.

Attention back on the ink-streaked water, I stare and stare. I don't dare blink in case I miss something portentous, even though a large part of me is sure none of this is going to work anyway.

Then the hazing ink twitches.

I suck in a breath, bending over the bowl. Ink in water doesn't twitch. It drifts, swirls, fades, but it doesn't twitch. I follow the ribbon of ink that moved so unnaturally.

'Let your gaze soften,' Kishel intones. 'You're not trying to push. Just see what's there. Follow your curiosity.'

I massage my brow, trying to ease out the tension, and let my gaze drift into the distance – through the water rather than on it.

Red oval swirls remind me of my pills. That fills me with dread, a cold tightness in my gut that I can't explain.

It's foolish. My medicine keeps me alive. But perhaps my fear is understandable. My tablets are running out. And what if someone discovers I'm ill through Fatework? That would endanger me and perhaps Drystan.

'Can your own fears show?'

'They can influence what you see. Try to calm yourself and sink past them. This isn't about your feelings, it's about possible truths.'

I exhale, shoulders sinking. I'll be leaving the Underworld before that becomes an issue. I remind myself of this over and over, a comforting chant.

A haze of red dances through the water, indistinct in my soft focus. Not dancing. Galloping.

A horse, copper red.

It rears. Its rider falls. Crimson bursts from their head. Colour leaches from the body. It sinks, turns white. A skeleton. Now a skull. It rises, accompanied by more. There's a blackish-green stalk at the centre and leaves in the same colour – the skulls form a spire of flowers nodding in a breeze that chills me. There are hundreds of them. Each one a death. Each one turning to me.

Gasping, I lurch back, arms tight around myself as I throw a wide-eyed look at Kishel. 'What was that?'

He tilts his head. 'What do you think it was? Think through what you saw. What does it mean?'

My tablets. I only saw those because I'm afraid of running out of them and being discovered by the fae.

I set that image aside. 'A red horse. It threw its rider. They died.'

'It *will* throw its rider. They *will* die.'

Soon. My bones whisper.

I don't know how I know it, but I *know*. I'm certain.

I spring to my feet and run out, urgency gripping my throat.

The consort's duty is to help the kingdom through her Fatework. I may be a failure at making visions appear, but I'm sure of what Kishel's shown me.

I sprint down the corridors, slippers flying off as I run.

The cold doesn't matter as I fling from the door. The stables. I need to get to the stables. I burst past Min who spins and calls after me.

I fly into the stable yard where three of the Twylth are gathered, ready for a patrol. None of them ride a copper-coloured horse.

'Stop! Stop!' My feet carry me into the same block where the new horses are kept.

Still yelling, I skid on straw and dodge guards. Horses whicker and kick on their doors, the bangs following me as I make a beeline for the stall belonging to the bad-tempered chestnut.

And there she is. Asti, a saddle slung over her shoulder, her hand on the gelding. 'What's all this racket about? Annon?' When her gaze falls on me, she wears an uncertain half-smile as though at once confused and amused by my appearance, doubled over and panting. 'Are you all right?'

No. I think I'm going to—

I barely turn before I vomit, catching myself against the neighbouring stall as I stumble and nearly fall under the violence of my stomach's spasms.

'I'm sorry,' I croak out once I'm done. 'I had to . . . Stay away from that horse.' I point as it stomps on the straw-covered floor of its stall, sending up a puff of dust. *'Please.'* Every bone in me shrieks for Asti to get away from it. I assumed the crimson was the rider's blood, but what if it stood for her hair, too? Was the vision about her specifically?

She opens her mouth, but I leap in. 'I saw it. I *saw* someone – you, its next rider – I don't know. I just know that no one should ride it tonight. Please. Don't. And make sure everyone else knows.'

She eyes the chestnut and nods. 'All right.' Not turning her back to it, she edges out of the stall and bolts it shut. Once the saddle's deposited over the stable door, she scoops an arm around me. 'Are *you* all right?'

'I ran.' I sag against her. 'I'm not made for running.' Or for being terrified that someone might die because I failed to save them.

'All right. Your work is done. I'll make sure everyone knows. Let's get you back to your room and cleaned up, eh?'

It's only then I realize there's sick on my gown. And feet. And is that some in my hair too? How queenly.

Face hot and sweaty, I nod and let Asti lead me to my rooms, one thought roiling in my mind.

If I hadn't run . . . would she be dead right now?

36

LATER THAT NIGHT, after a good rest and a long bath, I sit by the window braiding my hair and looking up at the moon. It just looks the same as usual, silvery grey, marked with darker blotches. No sign of the magic of Moonburn.

I've recorded my visions in the notebook. And the patrol Asti was meant to ride the chestnut horse on returned with a supply of skullflowers for me. Asti even dug up a few to see if I could transplant them into the glasshouse. The rest are drying near the fireplace. I've made a plan for my experiments with them, starting with a tiny amount made into tea.

The dose makes the poison, after all.

When a knock sounds at the door, I expect it to be Min. She and Asti came to check on me earlier and I got the impression she would be back – she had that look of concern that said she would.

But instead, Drystan strides in, much to the cat's delight as he springs from his spot next to me on the windowsill and rushes to the king. Tension ratchets Drystan's jaw tight, his cheeks hollow, carving deep shadows beneath his cheekbones. Oblivious, the cat threads between his legs, rubbing up against him.

'You're getting fur all over my trousers *again*,' Drystan grumbles, but he ducks and scratches the cat behind the ears. When he straightens, he takes in the room, jaw working side to side.

'And you're getting king all over my room.' I give him a sardonic grin and tie off my braid. The sting of his unwittingly cruel words is still fresh and I don't know how to address it when there are no apologies among the unseelie and he's all regal and imperious. 'Was there something you wanted from me or did you just come to admonish my cat for the crime of . . . being a cat?'

He places his hand over his chest, fingers drumming. 'I have something for you.' Nostrils flared, he lifts his chin and pulls a jar from his inside pocket and only then does he finally look at me.

I'm braced for it. Thankfully. Because he looks fucking furious.

He isn't glowering and his voice is even. No. This is a far more subtle rage. It simmers in his gaze and twitches in his jaw. It's written in the hard lines of his face, the way every muscle is pulled tight. It's in the clipped way he clicks the jar on the dressing table, rattling its contents.

Red tablets. My medicine. He's had more made.

All my curt irritation evaporates on a shaky exhalation. There's enough to last me at least a couple of months. 'Thank you,' I breathe. '*Thank you.*' I don't know how else to convey quite how much it means to me – a literal lifesaver.

The king, looking particularly kingly with his stiff, straight back and squared shoulders, straightens the jars and bottles on the dressing table, lips pressed together in a straight line as he retrieves the old jar with just two tablets left. Once that's done, he stalks to the fireplace and twitches the cushions on the settee straight. Then he rights the tumbling stack of books I've borrowed from his library.

I open my mouth to ask if something's wrong when he finally speaks. 'Your tablets . . . do they cause you any problems?'

'Problems? No. I mean, they taste kind of horrible, but . . .' I shrug. A bad taste is a small price to pay for continuing to live. 'Why? Is something wrong?'

He lifts one shoulder with a thoughtful hum, gaze on the jar. 'I was just wondering. I've never taken medicine, so I was curious what it was like.'

I pad over, barefoot. He seems more distracted than angry now, but he has this twitchy energy like there's something he's struggling to contain. It was my decision to come back to my room, but I miss the closeness that had developed between us in his suite without me even realizing.

His gaze twitches to the window where I was sitting. 'It's still an hour and a half until sunrise. You've got time for a bath before you return to the labyrinth. Astrid mentioned you ran to the stables. I'm sure your joints don't appreciate that.' He gives a stiff smile.

'I'm glad you added the bit about my run. I thought you were just hinting that I smell bad.' I lift my damp braid. 'Bathing challenge already completed.'

'Ah. I see. Good. Well, I'll let you continue your preparations.' Nodding, he backs away, only turning when he reaches the door.

I stare long after it's shut, trying to work out why I'm flooded with disappointment. What was I expecting, exactly?

Things . . . happened at Moonburn, before the argument turned from delicious to hurtful. I'm foolish if I thought he might apologize. And I'm not sure it's reasonable to expect – he can't know the specific, barbed meaning his words would have for me.

With all his care and attention, I'd started to wonder if he felt *something* for me. Physical, at least.

The distasteful little human isn't quite so distasteful after all.

Maybe I'm even starting to feel something for him, despite all that he is.

Or it's just that this life is a change from everything I've known and I've been feeling better since I arrived. I've been whipped up and pulled along by the adventure and novelty, the danger and beauty of this place, the mystery of what exactly has helped me put on weight. I've even searched the kitchens for answers – nothing, no rare ingredients or magical Underworld herbs. And yet, my symptoms have eased . . . along with my feelings for Drystan.

No. I don't care for him. It's hard to disconnect all this from the man responsible for bringing me here. That's all.

And he doesn't feel anything for me.

There's a darker, far more plausible reason for his behaviour. After all, isn't darker more in keeping with the unseelie? Now he's given me a fresh supply of medicine, he doesn't need to be nice – or cooperative, as he put it – and he doesn't need to seduce me.

He has my gratitude. He controls the supply of medicine that keeps me alive.

He holds all the power he'll ever need.

37

ANOTHER DAY PASSES in the labyrinth without seeing Drystan and without getting killed by anything. It's a kind of victory, I suppose.

But the Collector is on my mind. When I return, they haven't slept. They'll only rest if I promise to keep watch. Even then, they thrash in their sleep, whimpering about the Devourer, until I have to wake them gently and hold them while they shudder.

I have no problem giving them that time, even though instinct tells me I should be *doing*. Moving. Pushing. Because there are thoughts circling that I'm not ready to dwell on.

Instead I busy myself with my notebook and remind myself that if I push my body to the brink, I'll lose days, and I'm not foolish enough to think Drystan will extend his mercy a second time.

So, sunset finds me back at the fortress not utterly exhausted, but frustrated and restless – those thoughts catching up with me. Ever since we narrowly evaded the Devourer, a dark corner of my mind won't shut up. Whispering. Wondering. What's really driving me through the labyrinth? Is it for Lowen – or for me? To help him . . . or to ease my own guilt?

Maybe it's better if I never return. Maybe he'll assume I'm dead.

Maybe that will be the thing that finally sets him free.

Thoughts circling, I make an appearance at the Great Hall, since I'm conscious that I've been neglecting my future queenly duties. There's no sign of the king.

I leave my pang of disappointment unexamined.

The fae around me seem agitated, their dancing frenetic, the shadows around their feet stuttering and twitchy. It puts me ill at ease, so after a circuit of the room, I slip away.

But my feet don't take me back to my room. Instead I find myself, of all things, climbing every staircase I come to, until eventually I'm dragging myself on burning thighs up the tower Drystan showed me on his tour.

The air here is cool and clear. There are no creeping shadows and no fae, just me and the cloudy night sky and the Underworld stretching endlessly into the darkness.

It looks different from the last time I was here. The snowy shroud seems thinner, revealing mounds and what might be roads. The trees within the fortress walls look different and it takes me a while to realize why. Buds have formed along their branches, tightly furled for now, but a suggestion that spring is coming. Further out, the river carving through the land glimmers, rather than sheening dully. It's *moving*.

A laugh flies from my lips, snatched by the stiff wind. The river has thawed.

I turn, ready to rush back inside and find Min to tell her.

A massive, dark shape blocks my path, glinting eyes its only feature.

I gasp, but then the moon comes out from behind a cloud and reveals Threnn. My sigh comes out laced with a chuckle as I clutch my chest where my heart limps its way back to a normal pace.

'Gods, Threnn. You made me jump. I don't need guarding up here, but I appreciate your dedication.'

The redcap's expression is even more severe than usual, though. Forbidding, even.

A cold vice grips my heart. Did I misread the ink in the scrying bowl? Did I fail to save Asti? 'What's wrong? Is it Asti?' I can barely speak past the dread freezing inside my chest. 'She rode the chestnut horse, didn't she?'

'Astrid is well.'

My relief is powerful but short-lived.

'The problem is here.'

I cock my head and search the tower's roof for some danger I've missed, but his massive shoulders block much of my view. There's the distant cry of a raven – a warning. At least I have a guard.

'I'm sworn first to protect the king.'

I look out past the tower's battlements. Knowing the Underworld, there are probably monsters that can fly. 'Of course. We should go inside if there's trouble.'

'I should protect him from you.'

Laughing, I turn to him. 'Oh yes, very funny. The tiny human is such a danger to the King of Death.'

Threnn isn't laughing, though. There isn't even a glint of amusement in his eyes. They're dark. Utterly dark. The moonlight makes his light skin appear grey, like one of Drystan's risen dead.

Dread slams back into me in full force. It grips my throat in a fist of ice. Because Threnn blocks my escape. And now I'm sure he isn't joking.

'I'm – I'm not a danger to the king.' I try to lace my words with a chuckle, like that's a ridiculous idea, but it comes out strangled.

Threnn takes a step closer. I take a step back.

'You are. You will be the end of him.' His nose wrinkles, making his next words come out on a snarl. 'Your weakness.' He takes another step, which I match. 'Your mortal frailty.' Another step. 'Your pathetic lack of magic.' Another. 'You are not fit to be our queen. You are not fit to sit at his side.'

I match his next step and the crenellations bite into my back.

Nothing he says is untrue. I *am* weak. I am a lowly mortal.

He looms over me, a solid mass that blocks the way. 'You are weak, fragile, foul, like all humans. You're not worthy of him and the sooner he realizes that, the better.'

I hate that he's right. I wish those things weren't true.

But I would make an awful queen for Drystan, exposing him, especially once my illness is discovered, which it inevitably will be if I stay.

Yet I don't want Threnn to be right. I don't want those things to be true.

I try to smile, but I know it's tremulous. 'Maybe he won't be stuck with me much longer.' Meanwhile, my mind searches for some of those paths it's usually so good at. My pounding pulse fractures my thoughts, chasing them to find a solution.

If he attacks, would leaping over the battlements be survivable? If I landed in a deep enough snowdrift? Could I duck between his legs and slip through the door? Then fall down the stairs. No. Just as deadly as falling from the tower.

He peers down at me like I'm a creature at his feet and not a person. 'Such a fragile thing.' His eyelids twitch and he raises his chin as though he's just had an idea. 'It would be a service to my king to rid him of you.' His gaze skips to the crenellations behind me, and I see the idea forming.

He's going to throw me off.

He might not think as quickly as me, but he's not stupid. It would look like an accident. No one would know it was him. And he would have 'protected' his king from dangerous little me.

I press against the wall, muscles not aching but ready. If he moves, I'll leap to one side, between his legs – wherever a space opens. Then I'll run. I'll take my chances falling down the spiral staircase.

'If you just hold on a few days, I'll be out of your way.'

'Disgusting humans and their lies.' He sneers, crowding the last few inches into my space. 'Is that what His Majesty sees in you? Enjoys playing with a pretty little toy that can lie? He's had his fun. It's time to put the toy away.' He reaches up.

There is no opening.

His bulk blocks everything. He's too big. Too strong. Even if there was a space, he's fae — too fast.

All I can do is dig my fingers into the wall as I stare at him bending closer, at his hand rising towards my throat.

His eyes bulge. There's a terrible squelching sound and something hot sprays me.

At last, a path opens up.

But I'm rooted to the spot.

Because Threnn is collapsed against the battlements, a hand around his throat, fingers embedded *in* his throat.

At his side, smaller yet standing straight, teeth bared, is Drystan. 'What did you say to her?' His voice is the whisper of the north wind on a frozen night. Its cold fury makes me shiver.

Threnn gurgles, chokes. Blood bubbles from his mouth.

If I thought the squelching was bad, the rending of flesh is worse as Drystan pulls his hand away and tears out Threnn's throat.

The huge fae slumps to the ground. His blood slicks the stones, running between them in thick rivulets. He doesn't move.

Chest heaving, Drystan looks at his handful of flesh. I can't help thinking he looks magnificent. His anger is heady. Powerful. And he's unashamed of it. He doesn't hide or even shutter it, like it's something to temper. He let it tear Threnn apart. And he let it inhabit his entire body. He is the embodiment of rage. Embracing it. Becoming it. The power in that makes me dizzy.

'He insulted and threatened you with this tongue. It's only right he present it to you.'

Perched on the battlements, his ravens croak in agreement.

Threnn's body jerks and rises. Its head lolls to one side, the remains of its neck too weak to hold it.

I stare and stare, brain stuttering over what I'm seeing. Because it can't be real.

Yet it continues as Drystan drops the throat, tongue still attached, into its hand. Two steps brings the dead thing before me.

Drystan glowers at the broken thing, mouth set in a flat line. 'Kneel before your queen.'

It drops to its knees, head wobbling as it stares ahead, eyes empty. It gurgles like it's trying to speak or breathe or something else equally impossible. Then, bowing forward, the thing presents its tongue to me. Fleshy and pink. Still dripping blood.

I don't want it. But I can't speak. And I can't scream. I probably should. It seems like the normal, human thing to do when faced with this. But I also don't want to. What has the Underworld done to me?

I manage to shake my head, declining the offering.

'See? Not even your tongue is worthy of her.' Drystan jerks his chin to one side and the dead thing tosses its tongue from the tower.

The ravens take to the air at once, racing after it. I don't look over to see who wins.

Threnn's body slumps once more, and this time it stays still.

Like that signifies it's over, Drystan's shoulders sag. His breaths heave as he tears his gaze from the dead redcap at my feet and trails it up me. The rage has faded now, replaced by something tighter, closer to fear or perhaps desperation.

He opens his mouth, but before he can say a word, the door to the stairwell flings open.

Asti bursts through, followed by the rest of the Twylth. 'Rhiannon?' Her wide eyes turn from me to Threnn's body as she steps over him. Her hands close over my shoulders as she examines me. 'Are you all right?'

I nod like my tongue went over the battlements with Threnn's.

While Asti issues orders to the other guards, I steal a glance at Drystan.

He's still. Lips pressed together. Closed. But he watches me.

He murdered someone. That's not just cutting a singer's tongue out. That's . . . death. A life. Taken with so little regard.

I remind myself of that as Asti hustles me inside. She keeps one arm around me as she takes me back to my room, and there's the whisper of wings as one of the ravens follows – Bran, I think. 'We'll get you cleaned right up. You'll be all right. A good sleep and you'll forget all about that.'

She thinks I'm in shock. And I am, a little. I feel more dazed, like my head is struggling to catch up with everything that's happened.

I have to keep telling myself the important thing is Drystan is a killer. And so cold about it.

That's the kind of thing that should matter.

38

IT TURNS OUT Threnn was unhappy with having a human on the throne. With him gone, Asti is made the new Baloran, though Min tells me how she feels guilty about Threnn's attempted attack, blaming herself for not seeing the warning signs.

'She shouldn't blame herself.' I blow on my too-hot second attempt at skullflower tea.

The first was directly after Threnn's attack. The tiny dose did help make my heartbeat slower and steadier, but tasted vile. This time I've mixed it with lavender and chamomile, adding to the soothing properties and improving the flavour. Plus, the lavender gives the mixture a charming purple colour. It's stored along-side my belladonna in a little green bottle. No danger of mixing them up.

'We can't always know what's in someone's heart,' I go on after a sip, 'what secrets they're keeping.' Isn't that something I understand all too well?

'Exactly. I think she felt better when His Majesty pointed out ...' Min clears her throat and lowers the pitch of her voice,

'"You went straight to Annon and ensured she was safe and well. You've shown you value what's important."'

Her impression of Drystan is funny, but the laughter catches in my throat. 'He . . . he said that? Really?'

She shrugs. 'Well, Asti's impression of him is better than mine, but yes. *Those exact words.*' She gives me a long, hard look that stays on my mind, even as she goes on to tell me about how Drystan questioned the rest of the Twylth personally, confirming there was no wider conspiracy. Since they're fae, they can't directly lie.

It must be nice to be so assured that what someone tells you is the truth.

I can't help thinking about my parents. They never directly said I *wasn't* the subject of a bargain made before I was born, but still . . . They could have told me.

Neither can I stop thinking about what happened on the tower. Even though I didn't have to fight Threnn, I'm left exhausted by the attack for the next couple of days, forced to take the labyrinth slowly and to rest in my rooms rather than attend the Great Hall. As I get past the daze, I register that Drystan killed one of his own guard *for me*. I don't know what it means. But I know how it feels . . .

And I don't know how I feel about that.

Because I should hate him. I should be disgusted. I should remember the moment with terror, be haunted by it in nightmares. And yet . . .

All I can picture is the way Drystan looked at me after. The shade of desperation on his face. The fading fury that left him so raw.

Unfortunately, news of the attempt on my life spreads. Min mutters something about shadows whispering, and I wonder about them and what they're really capable of. However word got out, the result is that I need to be seen. That means I can't spend the next night resting or avoiding Drystan, and have to attend the endless revelry of the Great Hall.

Since all eyes will be on me, Min spends extra time getting me ready. We start as soon as the sun sets, cleaning me from head to toe, scrubbing, drying my hair before the fire and oiling it, clipping and painting my nails, moisturizing, removing body hair, rouging, sprinkling gold flakes on my cheekbones and eyelids, perfuming and, finally, choosing an outfit from the armoire.

I frown as we flick through. 'Where's the green dress? I haven't worn that one yet.'

Min gives me a bemused smile. 'Haven't you noticed?' She jerks her chin at the armoire. 'This is a whole new wardrobe. None of those other dresses fit you any more.'

At my confused blink, she steers me over to the mirror. 'Don't you ever look at yourself, Annon? You've put on weight. Look.' Sure enough, she places her hands on my waist and beneath the silk robe, my hips flare out even more than I'd realized.

'Huh.'

'I suppose this also means you haven't noticed your skin.'

I peer into the mirror, expecting to find a spot. 'What about my skin?'

'Someone give me strength. Look at it. Look at *you*.' She clamps her hands around my head and points it at the mirror. 'Really look, don't just see what you expect.'

I screw my eyes shut. Seeing myself in Drystan's mirror was an unpleasant surprise. And although I looked better after Min's attentions that first night, I haven't been able to get out of my head all the little ways I was no longer the young, healthy woman I'd once been.

So I just didn't look. Oh, I saw what I needed to pin up my hair and keep it out of my face. I saw how beautiful the gowns were, cleverly made by Min. I even admired the jewels I wore.

But I studiously avoided looking at myself.

Now, with Min holding my face, I take a deep breath, open my eyes and try to *see*.

I *have* put on weight. I have breasts again. And hips. That explains why I bumped into a table the other day – they're wider than I'm used to.

My hip bones still jut out and I don't like how weak my wrists seem, but I look much healthier than I have in a long time.

My skin, too, helps with the effect. It's smoother and deeper-toned, like days in the labyrinth under this black sun have reawakened the colour. It's still a little lighter than Annem's, but no longer pallid and sallow. It doesn't sink under my eyes and cheekbones any more, making my eyes look too big.

And the hair I used to be so vain about is shiny and thick once more.

Min's hands ease away. 'See?'

I turn my head side-to-side, making sure this is me, this is real.

The woman in the mirror turns, too.

She isn't as young as she once was. There's a knowing in her eyes that the girl never had. But she is pretty and alive instead of a husk.

I cover my mouth, watering eyes threatening to ruin the makeup Min's applied.

I feel stronger too. Still ill, still achy, still in need of more sleep than most people, but some days I make it through the labyrinth with more walking than resting.

A stray tear escapes as I laugh. The irony isn't lost on me that it's the Underworld, of all places, that's helped push me more towards life than death. The pages in my notebook where I track symptoms and what's changed tell me I haven't had an episode in days. It must be the magic here. I haven't found any other explanation.

'And that's still in your dressing robe. Wait until you have this on.' Min chooses a gown from the armoire and once I'm wearing it, she steers me back to the mirror.

I gape.

I rarely wear black. Brown is a cheaper colour back home. And here, I've tended to wear colours of the sea and sky. But tonight, Min has dressed me in a rich black gown that plunges to my navel, with a slit that shows off my newly rounded-out thigh.

Of course, being Min, she hasn't left it plain, simple black. Lace and tiny crystals adorn the hem and neckline, trailing over the rest of the dress, gleaming in purple-black and blue-black. 'Like a raven.'

She grins. 'Exactly. It's only right for the future queen.'

My hands smooth over the fine lace. This feels right, like it suits me – like this *is* me. The other nights, I felt like I wore a costume. A clumsy scarecrow stuffed into a pretty dress.

But now, as I lift my chin and Min brings out a tiara of black metal studded with shimmering moonstones, I feel less like a clumsy scarecrow and more like a future queen.

I'm strangely nervous as I enter the Great Hall. I try to tell myself it's because the unseelie might view me as weak for needing someone to save me from Threnn.

But my gaze scans the crowd searching for Drystan, hopeful and afraid that I'll find him.

When I finally do, he's deep in conversation with Phaedra and a couple of other influential fae, and so many emotions stir in me at once, I can't track them all.

Warmth is one I'm sure of: it blooms in my chest – gratitude he reached me in time.

Then his gaze skips up to mine and the madness of the hall stills.

The only movement is my pulse clamouring. The only sound, my breath that seems suddenly loud.

My thoughts are louder.

He killed for me.

By the time I exhale, the world turns again and the chaotic revelry heaves once more.

Someone crosses the space between us, freeing me from Drystan's heady attention.

Blinking, I glance around, searching for Min who's disappeared again. She hasn't gone far, though – I find her a short distance away in Asti's arms. They're deep in conversation, the redcap wearing a teasing smile as she watches Min's mouth like each syllable is fascinating.

My matchmaking has been a resounding success.

I allow myself a moment of gloating, but when Asti bends down to kiss Min, I venture on into the crowd. My meddling is done – I'm not adding voyeurism to my repertoire.

Of course, I search for Drystan again. Apparently I'm weak and predictable.

This time he's broken away from Phaedra's group and stalks through the crowd, eyes on me. Without missing a beat, he takes a glass from a passing server.

I try to turn towards him but this side of the hall is still a little wild, while the unseelie at his end are calmer, making space for him to slip between them with ease. I grit my teeth in frustration, though I manage quick, polite smiles and greetings for the fae who bow their heads to me.

By the time I'm done with them, Drystan has stopped to talk to Lord Mastelle.

We go on like this. A kind of cat-and-mouse game where I'm trying to reach him and failing, and I can't tell for sure if he's evading me.

One thing I do know: I have his attention. It bores into me during his every conversation, each time he takes a drink from a server, whenever I lose sight of him and rediscover him in another part of the room.

Huffing, I turn my back on the king. If he wants to speak to me, he knows where I am.

I'm here to be seen alive and well, so I grab a drink and circle to the opposite end of the room. I pause to watch an acrobat balancing and tumbling on the shoulders of a troll who must be eleven feet tall, and a show of shadows, casting shapes upon the wall.

On the edge of my vision, I catch glimpses of smaller fae dogging my steps, following from a distance. Others turn as I pass, gazes snagging on me as their conversations peter out. Min's dress is doing the trick, I tell myself. But there's a hunger in their eyes that makes me grip my glass tighter.

Thankfully, red hair isn't far away: Asti watches from within the crowd, Min on her arm. The redcap gives me a reassuring nod and raises her glass as though inviting me to continue enjoying myself.

So I do.

And I almost fool myself that I've forgotten about Drystan when I hear his voice. 'Rhiannon.' My name curls out from behind a curtain as though it's part sound, part shadow, an undeniable invitation.

My stomach flips and I down the last of my drink before venturing behind the curtain.

It's dim in here, dim enough to see the glow of his eyes clearly. He waits, watching. His mouth curls in a smirk like he knew I wouldn't be able to resist his call.

My pulse throbs in my throat as I ease into the space opposite him, three feet away. A dark window sits at my right, cool air radiating from it, while on my left, the curtain muffles the noise of the revelry, turning the music into an indistinct pounding.

'Your Majesty,' I say because what the fuck else am I meant to say? I feel like my pulse is trying to throttle me, like the air is too thick in here, like I want to throw myself at him.

Because it feels like he cares for me. And somehow I might care for him too. He's cruel, but he's also kind. He looked after me and has kept my secret.

He killed for me. And in some twisted way, that's the most romantic thing anyone's ever done for me.

That boy I gave my virginity to on the beach – my first love – brought flowers when I got more ill. He bought me chocolates. Kind words. But he didn't choose me. I offered him a way out – who knew how ill I might get – and he took it. With both fucking hands. I can't blame him, no. But I can still feel the barb buried in my chest.

My second lover was a secret. He'd show up, singing love songs on a borrowed lute. I'd open my bedroom window for him, let him in night after night. We talked, kissed, fumbled our way to making love. But the instant my Pa rose early for work, he ran. It took me fucking him three times and even more wishful thinking to realize he only wanted me when no one was watching. I found out a week after our first time that he was already betrothed to another girl.

But Drystan? He ripped a man's throat out for me and made him present his own tongue at my feet.

So, when he takes his time pushing away from the wall and saunters closer, my breath catches. He doesn't stop when he reaches my space, and instinct backs me away until I hit the wall with a soft gasp.

His arms bracket me like he thinks I might try to escape.

Truth be told, instinct tells me I should. My heart pounds like it's ready to send me running. This fae is deadly, after all.

But I press into the wall, willing myself to be brave.

'Such a good girl to come when I call,' he croons, gaze trailing down to my parted lips as he eases closer, body pressing into mine. He bends in and I think – hope – he's going to kiss me, but he dips past my face, mouth grazing my throat as he speaks his next words: 'Such a sweet, pretty thing.'

Of course. The king who doesn't kiss.

Still, his hot breath sets my nerves on alert, priming them for every sensation, and I find myself clinging to his shirt once more. This time, I have no intention of getting into a stupid argument, though.

My head drops back against the wall as his lips skim over my jugular, my collarbone. 'Sweet Rhiannon,' he murmurs. 'My darling little human.'

A shiver races over me, but not of pleasure. The way he's talking to me. Something's off. He rarely calls me Rhiannon when we're alone.

He cups my cheek. That feels right, though. And the press of his body against mine is as hard, his chest as broad as when we watched Moonburn.

By the time I realize he's teasing my dress off my shoulder, following it with the feathering touch of his lips, I've forgotten anything was amiss.

I've wanted his touch for longer than I care to admit. And the fact he wants to touch me is intoxicating. The knowledge is powerful.

I discover a benefit of the slit in my gown – it allows me to wrap my leg around him as I let him crush me against the wall, teasing the ache between my legs. My breaths burn.

'So eager.' He chuckles against my collarbone. 'I want you to tell me all about this moment, how you writhe against me, how you want me, when I fuck you later.'

'What?' He said it like it was a foregone conclusion. Like we've done it before.

I stiffen, and Drystan straightens. 'What's wrong, little love? Are you afraid?' He smiles, wide.

Wide enough that there should be dimples.

There are none.

39

'YOU'RE NOT HIM.'

Throwing his head back, he laughs, growing more high-pitched, familiar in a different way as his skin and clothes split into scales. They flick like cards riffled, colours and features shifting.

Until before me stands Phaedra. A changeling.

I push past her and rush from the alcove, her peals of mocking laughter following me.

My face is on fire as I pull the shoulder of my gown back in place. Fucking Phaedra. It was just her, toying with me.

I'm a damn fool. If Drystan wanted me, he would've made his move already. He's had ample opportunity. Who am I to think a king – a fae fucking king – would want me?

Phaedra knows it too. That's why I can still hear her laughter.

Head down, I walk straight into someone. 'Gods. I'm so—' I barely bite off my own apology.

Eyebrows raised, Lord Mastelle stands before me, large hands catching my shoulders. The shell necklace peeks out from behind the high collar of his jacket, almost like it's the collar of his shirt. I have to admit, it suits him. And there isn't so much as a speck of blood on his white shirt. 'Are you all right, Lady Rhiannon?'

'Yes, of course. I just wasn't paying proper attention. But I'm glad I've bumped into you because it means I get to admire how well that necklace suits you. I knew you were the right person to have it.'

His mouth curls into a pleased smirk. 'Well, look who's been studying our compliments. Might I test whether you've practised your dancing as keenly?' He nods towards the dance floor behind me.

Calling it a dance floor suggests a higher degree of organization than the reality – fae happen to be dancing there, much as they're doing in other corners of the hall.

I can't think of any reason to turn him down, and I'm sure it would be a breach of etiquette. I've only just smoothed over the last one. 'Only if you're gentle with me, Lord Mastelle.'

He chuckles darkly and holds out his hand. 'I can't promise that, but I'll do the best an unseelie can.'

'Why do I feel like that's the best offer I'll get in the Underworld?'

He smirks as I take his hand. 'Because it is.'

He leads me into the swirl of dancers, places his other hand on my waist, then we're off, spinning among them.

I keep my eyes locked on his, mind focused on keeping up with his swift steps. The music is a little frenetic here, and he keeps perfect time.

'It's an interesting evening,' he says at last, gaze slipping over my shoulder like this is effortless for him.

'Oh?' It's the best I can manage at this speed. Much faster and I'll be out of breath.

'Our future queen wears black at last. Our king can't take his eyes off her. And earlier I spotted Lady Phaedra speaking to Lord Allsham. And she *hates* him.'

So I wasn't imagining Drystan's attention on me. Unless that was also Phaedra. But I can't imagine her daring to mimic the king publicly. That definitely seems like it would be a throat-ripping-out offence.

I blink, realizing he's giving me an expectant look. 'Truly an interesting evening. You're so observant, Lord Mastelle.' I give him a winning smile, hoping my response is enough to fulfil my social obligations as a dance partner. We've slowed a little now, so maybe I can manage a bit more conversation.

Before I attempt to, his gaze flicks back to a point over my shoulder and he draws us to a halt.

'You'll forgive me for cutting in.' Drystan's deep voice comes from behind me.

All the heat from the alcove rushes back to me, mingling with the humiliation that came after, and I find myself frozen with a rictus smile on my face as Lord Mastelle inclines his head and makes way for the king.

'Lady Rhiannon, I hope we'll have a chance to dance another night.' Somehow Lord Mastelle bows his head without the necklace slitting his throat, then Drystan blocks sight of him.

He grabs my hand and waist. He isn't gentle. But at least the music has calmed, its rhythm steadier and more manageable for my short legs as he leads us back into the circling fae.

His back is straight, his head lifted. Tension rolls off him, spelled out in the cording of his neck, the tightness of his lips, the too tight grip on me.

If he's still annoyed that I walked away at Moonburn because he made a hurtful comment . . .

I shoot him a scowl.

He merely continues to lead us round and round in our spiralling dance. The song ends but he doesn't release me. 'Another,' he orders the musicians, and pulls me out on to the dance floor the instant they obey.

We're a minute into the next tune before his throat bobs like he might speak. He doesn't.

'I saw you,' he says at last, gaze fixed on a point over my head. At my questioning look, he adds, 'Coming out of that alcove looking rather dishevelled.'

I stare up at him, trying to work out what he's getting at.

'Was it Lord Mastelle? Do I need to remove his hands?' There's something hot in his eyes, something that could burn right through me – right through reality itself.

'Oh. *Oh*.' A breath punches out of me. 'You think . . . me and Lord Mastelle.' He's jealous.

His tension ratchets tighter and I can feel he's ready to shut down like he did when I asked what had been taken from him.

'That isn't what happened at all,' I blurt before he can flee. 'I . . .' Oh gods. Just starting to explain has my cheeks on fire again.

Drystan's eyebrows twitch together as he scans my face. 'Then what has you blushing so furiously?'

I drop my gaze. It's impossible to do this while looking at him. 'Someone lured me in there under false pretences, and when I realized, I was embarrassed.' No way could I admit the lure was *him*.

'So you didn't—?'

'*No*.' He doesn't need to know I *nearly* did, believing it was him. 'That would mean breaking our bargain. I'm keeping up my side – pretending to be desperately happy with my future husband.'

A thoughtful hum rumbles from his chest. 'Right. Pretending.' His gaze goes distant for a while before he draws a long breath. 'I didn't mean to hurt your feelings at Moonburn, but I can see I did. Even if I don't understand why.'

I follow him for a few more steps, thighs brushing his. Unseelie don't say sorry, but this feels apology adjacent.

'When I said you couldn't be a good little wife, I didn't mean you weren't "good enough" to be a satisfactory wife. I meant that you're headstrong and determined, intelligent and curious. You'd struggle to obey someone else's rules, shuttered away in a little house full of children instead of books.'

Throughout his little speech, my eyebrows have inched up bit by bit. 'Is that . . .? Did the king just *explain* something?' I give a theatrical gasp.

He returns with a flat look. 'I won't do so again if it's going to be met by mockery.'

'No, no.' I squeeze his hand. 'Don't you withdraw behind your walls again. I just . . . wasn't expecting it. That's quite the picture you paint, though. Headstrong and determined.' I wince.

'I also said you were intelligent and curious.'

'I've never thought of myself as stubborn before. I'm always well behaved.'

He arches one eyebrow.

'Well, I've always obeyed my parents' rules. I've always kept them happy. Then again, I can see why you'd think that based on the behaviour you've seen from me.' I wince harder at the thought of my night of rule-breaking. Is it him or the blank slate of the Underworld that's brought out a rebellious streak?

'What are you calculating in there?' He releases my waist long enough to smooth a lock of hair from my temple, fingertips whispering over my skin.

'I just reached the conclusion that I'm rebelling against being dragged here as part of a bargain I had no say in.'

He scoffs, eyes rolling. 'Of course you are. As long as your rebellion doesn't break the terms of our bargain, rebel away.' He flashes me a grin, before his expression settles to something warmer, more open than the one he wore when this dance began.

It almost feels like I'm with a friend.

Almost. Because generally I'm not so aware of every single touch from a friend or how they look at me or each facial expression and what it might mean. Friends don't normally feel so dangerous.

We dance on for several beats. 'You know,' I say lightly, 'if you help me beat the labyrinth, you can marry Phaedra. She'd make an excellent queen.' It's true, but the words burn my tongue like a lie.

His gaze snaps to mine. Hard. He says, simply, 'I don't want Phaedra.' Not a word more, but the air between us grows weighted with things left unsaid.

I look away, too afraid to examine what they might be. I've offered him the easiest way out he could ask for and yet . . .

Swallowing, I grasp for a change of subject. 'Since I was honest with you about the alcove, will you be honest with me?'

'I can't lie.'

'But you can deceive. Deflect. Misdirect. All those avenues are still open to you.'

He acknowledges my point with a dip of his chin.

I fix my gaze on the third button down on his shirt. It glistens as we move, and it's right in my eye line – and much easier to withstand than his gaze as I gather the courage to go on. 'I don't know where I stand, what we . . . What's happening. Every answer I can think of seems so slippery. I just need something to hold on to.'

He's quiet for a long while. 'Very well. I'll *try*.'

'Why did you kill Threnn? You could've stopped him, had him arrested if you thought it necessary. If you could rip out his throat, you could have subdued him.'

A low, gravelly sound comes from Drystan's chest, and although I refuse to look up at his face, I can tell his jaw's gone solid. 'I couldn't have him talk to you in that way. The things he said about you . . .' His throat bobs, and I find myself examining its column, wondering exactly where his fingers sank into Threnn's flesh. 'He's lucky I didn't make him suffer longer.'

I swallow. I was expecting an answer involving 'my wife to be' or the 'future queen' – something that said what mattered was Threnn insulting something that belonged to him or injuring his pride.

'Annon.'

The urgency of his tone makes me forget my resolution not to meet his gaze. It kindles, the gold brighter than usual – an alluring treasure trove.

'He threatened you, and I know he managed to get you alone and that must have been frightening. But know this. If he had so much as touched you, I would've flayed each finger that dared to encroach upon you, even if it had only touched a hair upon your head, and I'd have made him sew it into a purse. And *then* I'd have made him offer his tongue to you wrapped in that.'

The room spins. I could blame the dance that turns and turns again and again.

But it isn't the dance.

I see him on the tower roof, and I see him here and now. And all I can think about is that it feels like . . .

He chose me.

I swallow, mouth utterly dry. 'That's quite the picture you paint.'

'I mean every stroke of the brush.'

Long seconds open up where only our steps and his eyes exist.

'Can I ask about something else?'

The corner of his mouth quirks, threatening his cheek with the shadow of a dimple. 'Suddenly my wife-to-be is afraid to ask a question.'

'It's one I asked before and you didn't like it.'

His half smile dissipates.

I've overstepped. He's going to shut down again. I should've left it.

'You may ask.'

'What is the thing you cared for that was taken from you?'

His chest rises and falls. It seems to take aeons, like he's gathering strength. 'A long time ago, there was someone I loved. A seelie woman.'

'From the surface?'

His eyes sink shut. 'Please. No questions or I won't be able to get through this.'

'Sorry,' I whisper, and squeeze his shoulder in a silent invitation to continue without further interruption.

'She was . . . unlike anyone else I knew down here. Our love burned fast and bright. It had been a long time since I'd needed to worry about getting anyone pregnant and I'd grown careless with prevention. I'm sure you're aware fae don't reproduce easily.'

I nod. Books have noted that despite their long lives, fae have few children. The hypothesis being their fertility levels are lower than those of humans. That hypothesis also explains the plethora of tales – both fictional and factual – where fae take human lovers or charm and steal human brides. Drystan's just confirmed it.

Perhaps that's why The Morrigan bargained with my father. Somehow the Lady of Fate failed to foresee that I'd be such a sickly daughter.

'I assumed she took the same contraceptive unseelie women do,' Drystan goes on. 'While she assumed I took the same one as seelie men. I do now, but not back then. Pregnancy is so rare among our kind, our misunderstanding shouldn't have mattered, but by some miracle we conceived. We planned for her to join me here, where we'd marry, but . . .'

My throat clenches. His expression changes little, but there's a well of pain in his eyes. Mine sting in response. To lose someone you love *and* the promise of a child in one fell swoop. I can't imagine having the potential of that life, never mind it being taken away.

'Well, clearly she isn't here. I'm sure you can work out why.' He gives a half-hearted smile that turns bitter. 'My mother dripped information into the wrong ear – someone with their own motives – someone who ensured the way would be clear for *her* choice.'

Me.

Oh gods. No wonder he hates me.

Hated.

Because despite what he's just told me, it isn't hate he's looking at me with. And it isn't hate that made him kill Threnn.

But his own mother? She pulled the threads of fate to get his lover killed. That explains his warnings about family. I thought it was just his brothers, but this?

I shake my head, trying to convey a silent apology.

His thumb skims over my knuckles in acknowledgement. 'When her soul passed through the Underworld, we had a chance to say our goodbyes.'

I hold his shoulder a little tighter, bringing our bodies closer, hoping he feels some comfort.

'She was a star in the darkness of my life.' He blinks as though returning from that great distance of years and for a moment it feels like he sees me – only me, all of me, stripping back the gown, the makeup, the blood and flesh, until my soul is bare. 'So, you see why I can't allow that to happen again. Even if the sun itself threatens to shatter the dark horizon.'

Step, step, turn. Step, step, turn. My heart beats out the steps, the moments – the only accompaniment to our full silence.

'I'm sorry.'

'You didn't—'

'I know. And I know I'm not meant to say that word around here, but it's a lifetime's habit. Besides, I *am* sorry for what you lost. It's not something I'd wish on my worst enemy.'

'Am I your worst enemy, then?' His eyes gleam with a playful light.

'I don't exactly have many enemies, but for a while you were top of that short list.'

'I suppose that's fair.'

At this short distance, our chests bump whenever I'm slow to follow his lead. Or at least, my chest bumps into the area just above his stomach.

He shifts the grip on my waist, pulling us flush. Somehow that makes it easier – my thigh flows with his, our steps merge together, we move as one. I'm not sure if the song ends and another starts or if the musicians just keep playing the same tune because their king is dancing and they don't dare interrupt.

I also don't care.

I don't want this to end. In his arms, I feel graceful. Something precious that's on display but protected.

That's the thing I felt on the rooftop with him, covered in blood, with a lifeless body at my feet.

Safe.

Death couldn't come for me there and it can't come for me here because its king has me.

His eyebrows clench together as he searches my gaze. 'Annon?'

'I should share a secret with you now, shouldn't I? That's how your court works, isn't it? Fair exchange.'

'I didn't tell you all that to get a secret out of you.'

'I know. I'm choosing to repay the debt all the same. I already told you about my illness that has no diagnosis and no cure.'

He nods slowly as if unsure where this is going.

'That doesn't stop me hoping for one. For years, I've researched symptoms and medicine, searching for answers. I wrote it all down. I thought if I just read enough books, I would find out what was wrong with me and there would be a cure, printed in black and white.' I shrug and smile. 'But I never found one.'

'So much has been taken from you and yet . . .' He shakes his head. 'You're still so warm. So bright.' His fingers splay across my back, bracing me more tightly against him.

And in this moment, with the way he's holding me, the way he's looking at me, I can believe – truly believe – the King of Death feels something for me.

For a second, I think the world has stopped, but it turns out it's just our dance. I blink and look around. We're a point of stillness in the dizzying chaos of his court.

But I want more than stillness. I want him to myself. My king. My Death. Mine.

One thing I can enjoy before I go back. If the Underworld is responsible for my improved condition, I need to make the most of it.

A comforting excuse for what I really want.

A curtain wafts near by, and I realize it's the same one Phaedra-as-Drystan lured me behind earlier.

I tug on his fingers, then slip from them and, without dropping his gaze, back into the alcove.

40

ONCE THE CURTAIN flutters into place after me, I hold my breath, hoping he'll follow. If I've misread . . .

But the curtain opens.

He's briefly silhouetted – tall, broad-chested, narrow-hipped. Then he stalks past the curtain with easy confidence, leaving us shrouded in dim, crimson-tinged light.

He stands there. Close. Intent. I want to squirm, so I give a tight little laugh. 'You're looking at me like you want to eat me.'

'I'm starving, Annon.'

The laughter dies in my throat.

His gaze skims over the alcove. 'Returning to the scene of the crime?' There's a flash of long canine teeth as he stalks closer. 'How were you lured in here, Annon? Alone. Vulnerable. It must've been something truly tempting.'

Mouth dry, I swallow. I consider deflecting, saying it was a plate of ginger biscuits, but I stop myself. I've been enjoying our open conversation and I want to continue in that vein, even if it feels like a risk. I might look foolish. I could very easily embarrass myself here. But . . .

'I thought it was you,' I mutter before courage deserts me. 'But it was a changeling.'

'Phaedra.' He laughs softly, edged with danger. I wouldn't want to be Phaedra next time he catches up with her. 'Tell me, what did she do that made you so flustered?' He spears me in place with a look.

Lying seems pointless. Like he'd see through it. 'She backed me against the wall.'

'Like this?' He stalks closer, and I back away until I bump into the window.

'Yes.' I nod, grateful for the cold glass.

'Then what?'

'She caged me against the wall like I might escape.'

'Hmm.' He plants one hand above my shoulder, then the other. His gaze trails to my mouth and stays there. 'Tell me what she did once she had you here, Annon.'

'She – uh – I thought she was going to kiss me, but instead she teased my neck.' I have to pause to drag in a deep breath. 'I can't really remember what she said.'

'Good,' he says as he bends closer. 'I want you to remember what *I* say,' he breathes in my ear. 'What *I* do.' These words are hot against my throat, making my nerves catch light. '*All* of it.'

I arch against the window, giving him full access to my neck, to any part of me he wants.

His lips skim over me, lighter than Phaedra's touch, little more than a breath.

A soft sound escapes me, caught between a whimper and a gasp.

'I've barely touched you.' There's a teasing note in his voice.

'Then get on with it.'

'Headstrong, see?' He nips my collarbone, sending a streak of sensation through me. 'You'll have what I choose to give you, *when* I choose to give it.'

The note of command in his voice stills my tongue and sears my veins. I let my eyes sink shut, waiting for him to choose when, praying it will be soon.

'You have driven me to slow insanity, Annon. It's only fair I repay you in kind.'

Then he kisses my throat. Lightly. So lightly, I almost wonder if I'm imagining it, but he makes this quiet, pleased sound right after. Another kiss follows and another. They overlap and blur together, the pressure of his touch building, his breathing growing heavier. He sucks on my speeding pulse and tongues the hollow where my collarbones meet.

It's like he wants to acquaint himself with every inch of my neck and make me burst with need. I swear the only thing stopping me from melting is the chilly glass of the window I'm pressed against.

He straightens, bringing his hips flush against mine, making my eyelids flutter open. Because damn him, but I want to see his face – the jaw you could cut yourself on, the slashes of his eyebrows, the molten glow of his eyes.

And he takes his time surveying me, too, like I'm part of his realm.

'What gave her away in the end?'

A deep breath presses my chest against him, teasing my nipples, making them furl, tight and achy. 'She smiled.'

'And I never smile?' He cocks his head, smirking as if to illustrate that I'm wrong if I think that.

'When you smile and you mean it, you have dimples.'

It's like I've broken him. Only in a small way, but it cracks the arrogant smirk from his face, leaving him somewhere between confusion and surprise.

'Here.' I graze the pad of my middle finger over his cheek for just an instant. 'And here.' This time I'm braver, fingertips holding his jaw as my thumb strokes the telltale line where the other dimple forms.

He's touched me much more thoroughly, but this feels intimate. Holding his face inches from mine. Sharing air with him. My body drinking the warmth from his as he crushes me against cold glass, the pressure increasing each time we make contact.

'And before that,' he says, voice roughened, 'did you want her to kiss you?'

I'm a coward. I lower my head, gaze skipping to one side.

He finally releases the window and places his cold hand around my throat. Sliding it up, he forces me to meet his gaze. His is molten, matching the heat pooled inside me. 'Answer me, Annon. Answer your king.'

It's easy to give in when it's an order. Not my responsibility. No bravery required. Not my answer to feel embarrassed about. 'Yes.' My pulse peaks on that single syllable.

'Of course you did, needy little thing.'

My cheeks burn, but it's worth it because he bends closer, so much closer. I brace, expecting his mouth to claim mine, feeling the promise of it. Right on the edge. The breath before the plunge.

But he doesn't kiss me.

He stops. Squeezes. Tilts my chin higher, so close our mouths share the same air and I taste him — the sweet-sharp of fae wine. Just as intoxicating.

'So responsive. So *eager*.' It's a tease. A taunt. But he says it with this edge of wonder.

His lips ghost over mine — a brush of heat, no contact.

A torment.

I bend, chase, but he only chuckles darkly and leans away. 'No, my desperate little mortal.' His mouth finds my jaw instead, then the sensitive spot beneath my ear. His hot breath chases goosebumps over my skin, and he kisses that same spot again. I feel his smile, like he enjoys watching my reaction.

Another kiss. Another. Down the line of my throat, across my shoulder, up the column of my neck.

If he was a different man, I might call it worship. But the King of Death worships no one, certainly no mortal.

It's more like an intelligence-gathering mission. My strengths. My vulnerabilities. The places that make my pulse leap hardest.

I whimper without meaning to. As needy as he said.

Still, he never touches my lips.

I tip over. Beyond sanity or madness. I have nothing left.

I bring one leg around him, finding the thick muscles of his thigh. I can't get the right angle to hit the exact spot I want, but feeling him between my legs sends pleasure surging through me.

I rub against him, I revel in the feel of his pulse under my palm as my hand skims up his neck.

Every part of him is solid. He is strong where I am weak. He's powerful where I'm magicless. He's a king where I'm nothing.

And yet I hold his pulse in my hand. I make it throb harder. I make his breath shake as I grind against his thigh.

A creature of want, I press into him, chasing the sensation of his broad, hard chest against mine.

There. I find it. Through the thin silk of my gown, the embroidery on his lapels rubs my nipples. Only fleetingly. But I've been denied long enough that it wrings a moan from me.

'And I thought you were such a sweet, innocent creature.' His dark laughter fills the airless space of our alcove as his arm bands around my waist and his hand plunges into my hair. He lifts me so my hips are level with his.

And then I'm lost.

He surges against me, the hard length of him rubbing right where I'm softest, where I'm most desperate, where all my heat and desire and rising pleasure is gathered so tightly.

'Annon,' he gasps against my neck. '*Fuck*, Annon.'

'Are you trying to form a sentence?' My teasing tone is somewhat ruined by my breathlessness. 'Because I can tell you, you're failing.'

'Fuck is a complete sentence. I look forward to teaching you that.'

My mouth goes dry. More words are impossible. I can barely nod.

With a slow, dangerous smile, he slides one hand up my bare leg. 'Would you like that, Annon?'

I nod again.

His thumb approaches the crease at the top of my inner thigh. 'Tell me.'

'I would like you . . .' I have to pause to catch my breath. 'To teach me.'

He gives a lazy half smile, a dimple pressing shallowly into his cheek. 'There. Was that so difficult?' He skims along my edges, making me arch and tremble in anticipation.

He stays there, watching as I stare at him with eyebrows peaked in silent plea.

Fingertips teasing, he kisses just below my jaw and somewhere between the kisses, I pull together enough self control to whisper in his ear. 'Take me somewhere we can be alone.' There's a shiver from him as my lips brush his earlobe.

'We *are* alone.' He edges the tiniest bit closer.

'I mean *more* alone than this. Somewhere we can get comfortable. Somewhere you can *teach* me.'

He pulls back and surveys me. There's the thinnest ring of gold around his pupils. They're blown so wide, I could fall into them and keep on falling.

Another slow smile before his thumb slides over my apex. Pleasure jolts through me just as raven blackness swallows us up.

I fold with him, into him, into the dark spaces between.

4I

TRAVELLING LIKE THIS while his thumb is *there* is much less disorientating. Aware of those places where we're together in the fluttering dark, I don't feel like I'm falling apart. The points of contact between us are anchors, reminders of reality and of my body – of what's real and true.

Things I can hold on to.

We land in his bedroom and he wastes no time crushing me against the wall and grinding me to within an inch of my life. All the while, his thumb circles, tearing at the threads of my sanity, even though his touch is tempered by the sheer silk of my underwear.

He slips a finger under the fabric and into me, stealing my breath. 'You like that, don't you? I can see you do – it's written all over that pretty face.'

I hate him. Hate what he's doing to me. A little. Love it more.

As he adds another finger, I can't think, not even nonsense.

I whimper against his throat, cling to the back of his neck, drive against his hand, a servant of the pleasure building inside.

I bow to it. Break apart on it. Spill over and into the sweet, dark surge of a fathomless ocean, where I drown over and over.

The world's spinning as I return to it and his satisfied smirk.

'I've barely begun touching you.' He laughs, a low rumble against my chest. 'Ah, Annon, you'd be so easy to ruin.'

I barely take in his words and the delicious promise wrapped between them when he walks me to the bed and turns me to face it. There, he takes his time unbuttoning my dress, peeling it away from my back as he does. My skin lights up just as it did when he fastened the high-necked gown before, but this time he's baring me rather than covering me, and I'm conscious of air reaching my shoulders, my back, the tops of my hips.

I don't realize I'm holding up the front of the dress until he pulls my hands away.

I let go.

It spills from my shoulders and pools upon the floor, beads rattling together softly. Only a scrap of silk covers me, tied with ribbons at the hips.

'Look at you. Shy yet eager. Blushing and wanton. Such a delightful contradiction.' He makes short work of the bows, then tosses my underwear to the floor.

Breath held, I wait. I don't dare look back in case that breaks some unwritten rule and he stops.

He doesn't touch me, but I feel the weight of his gaze. Instead of being bowed by it, it makes me stand tall.

'Aren't you exquisite?' His hands alight upon my hips, thumbs circling the dimples above my backside. 'Such a perfect little creature. I should keep you like this all the time. Bare. Thighs slick. Ready to open for me.' His palms plane up and forward over my ribs until he's cupping my breasts. He pulls me close, so I feel the rhythm of his breathing at my back. 'I hope you understand how lovely you are, sweet sunshine.' His words ghost over my neck, sending a shiver of pleasure through me.

It isn't just the sensation. It's the feeling of being held. Of being protected and precious. It's the vulnerability of being utterly naked while the roughness of his jacket on my back tells me he's still fully clothed. It's the fact that, despite that, I feel safe.

Somehow, it doesn't matter nearly as much as it should that he's the one who's tormented me in the labyrinth. That he's a killer. That he's the King of Death.

He's holding me, and I'm exactly where I'm meant to be. For now, at least.

He kneads my breasts, kindling molten fire low in my belly. He toys with my nipples, driving it hotter. I arch, urgency taking over.

Unable to take it any longer, I turn in his embrace, finding him barefoot. Wordlessly, I start on his buttons with trembling hands.

He smirks. Of course he fucking smirks. He's not just King of Death, he's King of the Bloody Infuriating.

But dimples mark his cheeks, so I feel less like something he's playing with and more like something he treasures. Like sweet sunshine.

He nudges my hands out of the way and takes over on the buttons, working much more quickly. I take in each inch of flesh as it's revealed.

His gaze snaps to my lip caught between my teeth. 'That mouth is going to be the death of me.'

I shiver, wanting that – to be the death of him as he has been the death of me. Greedy to feel his strong body, I go to slip my hands under the fabric.

'You'll wait.' His order comes cool and clipped, and I'm before the king once more.

He holds me still with his gaze as he shrugs off his jacket then peels off his shirt.

In the training yard, I hadn't spotted the fine, dark hairs that spread across his chest nor the coarser line of them leading from his navel down to the waistband of his trousers. But now I follow them, enjoying how they emphasize his appearance of supple strength.

The unbuckling of his belt is a fascinating thing. I can't say why, only that I can't look away from his deft fingers pulling, flicking the prong, sliding leather from metal. Maybe it's the way he does it at a tormenting speed.

I ache and have to clench my hands to keep them from reaching out again. The taut lines of his muscles beg to be touched. That trail of hair invites my fingers to walk down it. Even the *V* over his hips points downward, more of it revealed as he unbuttons his trousers.

Trimmed, dark hair. The base of his cock. Then he frees his length. It springs to attention, sending a thrill of anticipation through me. There's also fierce pride, baring its teeth, because I've made him this way. He's hard because of *me*.

Now, perfectly naked, he cups my cheek, and I reach for him.

He catches my wrist. 'I said you would wait.'

I huff out my frustration and try to tiptoe up for a kiss, but he pulls out of reach.

'Annon. You know better than that.'

Blinking up at him, I remember the warning I've known all along. He doesn't kiss, even if I yearn for the taste of him, the pressure of his lips on mine.

I fancy there's something sad in his eyes. But realistically, that's just me seeing my own disappointment in him.

I thought this would be something soft. Something special.

I thought *I* was something special.

He seemed to have thawed and opened up.

The corner of his mouth rises. There are no dimples. If anything, it's apologetic as he ducks and kisses my brow. 'I'll still show you. I'll still make you come until you forget yourself and know only me.'

My body burns for his promise, unquenched by this distance

that's opened between us. It fluctuates, a little closer with the kiss to the brow, a little further as he turns me away from him, closer again as he envelops me in his hold, the heat of his flesh upon mine searing.

It's like there's a leash between us and he keeps pulling, testing its length, then springing back when he finds its bounds. But he's never quite as close as he was when we were dancing and shared our secrets.

My mind snaps back from that moment as he kisses my neck, nibbles, licks, like I'm a delicious morsel he wants to make last. His cock presses into my back as his hands explore my breasts before one rises to take my throat, and the other glides down over my belly, finding its home between my thighs.

Suddenly distance doesn't seem so important any more. And I can understand it. If he lost her, he might not want—

'Oh!' I buck at the finger slipping inside me.

'That's it. That's what I want from you.'

It feels good for my body to not be found wanting. For tension to coil in it without pain or exhaustion. To simply enjoy being a physical creature.

It strikes me that I should be embarrassed by how quickly he has me writhing against his body, his hand, straining at the grip around my throat. But the heat and the pleasure don't care, they only demand more. I ride them higher, higher, bright and sparkling like one of Moonburn's flares about to split off across the sky.

I fly. Cry out, only kept on my feet by his strong arms, kept in this world by the pretty, filthy nonsense he whispers in my ears.

When the aftershocks stop, he lets me wilt on to the bed on hands and knees before the headboard. The mattress dips as he kneels behind me, and I'm grateful for the chance to catch my burning breath. He takes my hips, his hold firm, sure. Strong enough that I can trust myself to it.

His fingers flex on my hips. The blunt tip of him nudges at my entrance. There's a pause that aches.

I hang there, breathless. Afraid. Have I done something wrong? Has he changed his mind?

I wait, the pressure of him its own torment.

Then he growls, low, torn, '*Fuck*,' and the world spins as he flips me on to my back.

All I see is him. Hear is him. Know is him.

A hissed breath in. The blowing wide of his pupils. The clench of his jaw. Like the sight of me beneath him is some exquisite torment.

One hand in a white-knuckled grip on the headboard, he eases between my legs. He looks like a drowning man clinging to flotsam.

'Lift your hips.' The rawness of his voice sounds wholly unlike him, but I obey, and, kneeling, he slides his thighs beneath me, so my hips are raised, my legs parted by his body.

I'm exposed and more than a little helpless, my weight on my shoulders and in his lap. All I can do is lie back as he aligns himself with my entrance, golden gaze fixed there a long while.

'Look at you, lying there, open for me. So eager to take it, aren't you?'

I nod, then remember how he likes to hear an answer. 'Yes. *Please*.' Desperation wrings my voice, a tightness in my throat.

There's a hint of his self-assured smirk as he presses at my entrance, but it vanishes as he slips inside. The stretch is exquisite, a filling sensation I've missed in all these sexless years. The look on his face is even better, though – a clenching of his brows, the fluttering of his eyelids, the dropping open of his mouth on a wordless groan.

His eyes widen once he's fully seated. He swallows and shakes his head, grip on my hip digging in. '*Fuck*.'

With a roll of his hips, he leaves me and bends forward in one motion, hair spilling around us in a curtain. My whimper at the sudden emptiness stirs the black lengths, then he plunges back inside with a whispered curse.

'You're nothing,' he snarls, hand encircling my throat, strangling my cry as his rhythm falters. 'You know that? *Nothing*.'

I don't care what he says, because his hips snap hard into mine again, drawing my whole body taut with the sweet, hot friction of it. He can call me what he wants as long as he doesn't stop treating me like I'm *something*.

He shudders.

'My Nothing,' he breathes an inch from my lips. 'My *Avellan*. My – *fuck*.'

Then he's kissing me.

Like it's that simple. Like I'm just a fisherman's daughter and he isn't an unseelie king I should not, in any logical world, have ever met.

But our lips *do* meet. And he tilts my chin up so he can make that point of connection firmer. So he can claim me. Taste me. Tear me from time and space, so there is only him and me, his cock driving deep inside me, and his commanding grip on my throat.

I tremble, fighting for breath, for sanity, clinging to his shoulders, losing parts of myself.

I've never been kissed like this before. Fucked like this before.

Like I'm his to take. My lips are his to ease apart. My mouth is for him to make this small hum of pleasure into as his tongue meets mine.

Like he's mine to give himself so thoroughly – every inch of his dick and the rest of him, too. The graze of his stubble upon my chin. The sweet taste of him, fruity and tart like fae wine.

I can only cling on, arch into his wild strokes, tighten around him, edging closer to bliss.

With a grunt, he seems to remember himself, tearing his lips from mine. He peels my hands from his shoulders and pins them to the bed, gaze skimming over my face. 'What are you doing to me?' he asks, shaking his head as he rolls his hips, more controlled than a moment ago.

He releases one hand and reaches between us, thumb rubbing my clit as he thrusts into me.

I cry out. I can't keep it in. Not when he's filling me and stroking me and making my body feel like it's going to fall apart into glittering shards. 'Drystan.'

He stops, eyelids heavy as if making love has dazed him. 'That's the first time I've heard you say my name.' His thumb takes up its firm rhythm again as he pulls out of me. 'Say it again.'

'Drystan.'

He drives in on the second syllable, making me shout it. A hazy, dimpled smile drifts over his face as he pushes me closer and closer to the edge. 'That's right. Come apart for me. For only me.'

I do. I say his name as I do it, eyes wringing shut on the word as I sink into the pure pleasure, washed away by it.

When I bring myself back from that place, there's a wild light in his eyes.

'Annon.' He bends to kiss me, his tongue and thumb dipping into my mouth, the taste of me mingling with the taste of him. I'm high on the pleasure, lost in his merciless rhythm, torn apart by the way he worships me.

'Mine,' he whispers on my lips. '*Avellan*. You will be my wife, and I will do this to you every fucking day.' He punctuates those last three words with his thrusts, and part of me thinks being his bride wouldn't be so bad, not if I got to have this whenever I wanted. 'I will have you.' He presses down on my belly, keeping me in place to accept all that he gives. 'Hold you.' His voice runs as ragged as his breaths. 'Break you apart and drink the sound of your breaking from your lips again and again.'

The promise, the feral ferocity of it, the punishing pound of him into me, does break me. My whole body hums with pleasure, with buzzing energy, with the glorious overwhelm of his presence in me, around me, everywhere and everything. And as I cry out, lost, he loses himself with me, fingers interlaced with mine just as his pleasure is.

Avellan. He says that word, breathless, again and again. I haven't heard it before tonight, but it sounds like the old tongue. A nicer word for 'Nothing', I'm sure of it.

Avellan. It feels like it's mine. Ours.

After, we stay in that curtained space, regathering the fractured pieces of ourselves. His gaze roves over me, a hazed softness to it that I haven't seen before. He kisses me once more, softer now. Almost reverent. Fingers still locked with mine.

I smile up at him, body aching sweetly.

There's the shadow of a dimple in his cheek as he straightens. Then his breath catches. His gaze jerks to the side.

I follow it and recoil with a breathless 'Oh!'

Instead of a pillow, my head rests on a bed of flowers.

42

DELICATE PERIWINKLE-BLUE FLOWERS drift on slender stalks, moving with our breaths, and crinkly pale-yellow petals look cheerful and sunny in the dim light. They grow from the pillow and sheets, while above my head cherry blossom branches from the headboard.

'What is . . .?' My eyelids flutter as I turn from the pale-pink blooms to him. 'Is this a King of Death thing?'

'You think . . .?' With a shocked huff of laughter, he touches his chest and pulls from me. Gently, he lowers my hips to the bed. 'Does this look very deathly to you?'

'I-I . . . I suppose not.' A quick brush of my fingertips over the petals confirms they're real. They seem to strain towards me. 'Then . . . what is this? And *how*?'

Mouth open, he tilts his head, staring for a drawn-out moment. 'You mean you don't know?' Slowly, his eyes widen. '*You don't know.*' He slips from the bed, padding across the room in silence. I sit up and enjoy the view of his bare body, absently running my fingers over the delicate blue flowers. 'Come here.'

His words, the looks he's given me – they add up to a sense of unease in my belly. Like my life is a strange object that's about to crack open in some irreversible way. I make my way over, arms crossed over my stomach.

When I join him at the long mirror in one corner of the room, he cups my cheek and shakes his head. 'I thought you knew. Look.' He turns my back to the mirror and gives me a small looking glass. He helps me angle it so I see myself in the doubled reflection.

Tousled hair covers my back, ends brushing the dimples above my backside. The unease is pushed back a little by warmth as I see the shape that's returning, the fact I have *fat* rounding out my hips and bottom. 'Look at what?'

He gathers my hair and pulls it over my shoulder.

Now I see it.

Between my shoulder blades. For a second, I think it's dirt or inky fingerprints. But then I register the shape. The regularity. The perfect placement at the centre of my upper back.

'What's . . .?' I reach up. It doesn't smear off. I edge closer to the mirror.

Finely inked in black and grey, three flowers bloom on my skin.

'A tattoo? But I've never . . .' I stare at the flowers, some logical part of my brain noting they're apple blossoms.

Drystan traces a fingertip down my spine, stopping when he reaches the cluster of flowers. 'Not a tattoo. When I buttoned your gown the other day, they were pale buds. I assumed you'd lied about not having magic, but . . .' His gaze shifts from the mirror to meet mine. 'You didn't know, did you?'

Not a tattoo, then . . . 'A fae mark.'

The strange object cracks open. Falls apart. Spills a truth that seeps into the very fabric of my life.

A fae mark means . . .

Is this why I've been getting better? Or now I'm healthier, my body has been able to access something that's always been there, dormant?

'Then I . . .' I stare at the bed, which looks more like a wild-flower meadow. 'I did that?'

'You did.' Smiling, he pulls me against him and it's only then I realize I'm swaying. He kisses my brow and strokes my back, lingering on the mark. 'You did, my clever *Avellan*.'

I bury my face in his chest, let him carry me to the bathroom to clean up, then to bed. It's a comfort to let him care for me while my brain stutters over its new reality.

I have magic.

43

THE NEXT DAY in the labyrinth is something of a daze. Sometimes I think I hear Drystan or catch a glimpse of him out the corner of my eye, but when I turn, he isn't there.

Last night has clearly imprinted on my mind.

Between the revelation of my magic and the revelation of us, I find myself exhaling a surprised laugh or smiling a secret smile as we walk and rest our way through the morning. The Collector throws me curious glances every so often.

By the time the sun sets, I'm dead on my feet. It turns out staying up most of the night making love to the King of Death is just as tiring as staying up most of the night doing anything else. The stories always make being taken by fae sound dreamlike and magical – the kind of thing that feels effortless and restores energy rather than consuming it.

Lies and fantasy.

When I return to the fortress, I'm intensely grateful for the simple pleasure of a chair.

*

That night, I go about my usual Underworld routine – sleeping, getting ready, going to lunch.

Playing the part of Drystan's fiancée a little too well.

It's just fun, like the baker's daughter. I remind myself of what Drystan said as he first sank into me. *You're nothing.* But I can't help remembering how he kissed me when he *does not kiss*.

Then, there are the carpets.

Or, specifically, the way they grow as I walk over them. Pretty five-petalled flax flowers follow me through the palace, a dusk-blue wake.

Oh, and the furniture.

After lunch, I get up and find my chair has sprouted branches of fragrant yew while I've been eating. Courtiers eye me, then bend their heads together in hushed discussion.

Drystan lifts his head, unruffled, and places a hand at the small of my back, ushering me out. Later, when we're entwined in the heady haze of *after*, I ask what they're saying. He twists his mouth and I'm sure he won't answer, but after a prod, he sighs. 'They think you've been keeping your magic hidden and have finally chosen to share it. That's a source of curiosity. They wonder why you'd do that.'

'I'm trying to keep it under control.' I wince.

'I know.' His hand finds the dip of my waist and he traces a circle over my hip bone. A reassurance.

'At least it's just rugs and chairs.'

He arches an eyebrow at another branch of blossom that's grown from the headboard. 'And my bed.'

I'm dreaming about that moment later, back in my room, when a rap at the door wakes me. Stretching my aching limbs, I drag myself up, wondering if Drystan's come back – hoping – but instead it's Kishel who enters. His knowing smile makes my throat clench. Is it me and Drystan he knows about? Somehow. I remind myself that he *is* a seer, so I probably shouldn't be surprised.

And then I remember Drystan's deception after I collapsed. Everyone thinks we've been making love for weeks anyway.

'I understand my favourite student has a little surprise for me.' Dark eyes glinting with amusement, Kishel gives me a meaningful look. 'Magic so secret, even you didn't know about it.'

'Ah, so the king told you.' I chuckle with more than a little relief. 'I have to admit, I've spent the day wondering if that really happened.' Both my magic and sharing Drystan's bed. 'I'm thirty-three. I've never heard of magic taking that long to awaken. It happens for most people in their teens or early twenties at the latest.'

'Mm.' Kishel steeples his fingers together, nodding. 'It could be something was blocking you before – a belief, perhaps.' He eyes me for a long while as though he sees the doubts I sometimes have about myself. 'Or maybe it's that you've been here for a while now and the Underworld is affecting you.'

'That's what I've been thinking. I feel more . . . healthy since coming here.' I choose my words carefully, treading between cracks that will reveal my illness. Though, it feels like it would be safe to tell Kishel. He hasn't told anyone about my Fatework failings; I don't think he'd tell anyone about my illness.

'Mortals can't help but be affected by their environment. We unseelie are more permanent beings – more fixed in our nature. Your kind are more mutable. Our horses are the same – they've adapted to our world.' From someone else, Phaedra for example, that could sound like an insult, but he says it thoughtfully and adds, 'I rather envy you that.'

My mouth is still hanging open at the idea of a fae envying humans anything when he pulls out his scrying bowl. 'Since we had luck with you reading ink in water last time, let's try this again. But with this newfound power of yours, let's see if you can direct the ink yourself.'

I wince up at him. 'You mean, I'm on my own?'

'Never alone, Rhiannon. I'm still here.'

It is a comfort.

I can never tell how old he is. One minute, I think he must be ages old – that's what I see in his eyes and calm patience. But then he gets this playful look, accompanied by a mischievous grin, and I'm sure he's more in the range of human reckoning, maybe younger than me.

But whatever age he seems, he has this way of speaking that sounds True – the kind of True that must be written with a capital *T*.

So I lean over the bowl, let my gaze drift softly and follow the threads of ink that he drips into the water.

'What do I do to make it move?'

'You don't need to do anything, just relax, remain steady and open and feel the energy flow through you.'

I try to do as he suggests, but I'm not sure what remaining open means. And I have no idea what energy feels like. Last night, I somehow made those plants grow – the cherrywood of the headboard and the cotton and linen of the bedding. But I don't remember how that felt. It was all wrapped up in the feel of Drystan, of his body, but also his words and the quiet, shared space within the curtain of his hair. And the feeling of warmth, of connection within me, like I'd found a place that could be mine.

The ink curls. My fingertips tingle with the constant brush of sensation, like I'm dipping them into dry sand. Warmth spreads in my chest. I'm part of something. Of this place. I feel the trees outside, the sap moving slowly, the buds furled tightly – not dead, just waiting for spring to finally come.

The ink twitches. Splits. Six strands. Six horizons. A horse gallops across each one. The black horse rears and its outline shifts into a shape I recognize – the towering hulk of Rigor Gard.

'Six horses,' I murmur, voice distant. 'One is Drystan. The others . . .'

'Good. What are the others doing?'

Not just horses, I realize as I peer closer. There are riders on their backs. 'Riding hard. Coming closer.'

A droplet breaks off from each horizon, and the horses dissipate. The droplets merge, bulge, form an oval shape like one of my tablets. My commentary for Kishel breaks off. The shape cracks in two, dissolves into a skull, a tear drop, spreads into a long, flat line.

It trembles, then thrusts upwards, forming the unmistakable shape of our home upon its clifftop perch. Like a bird, I dive closer, through the window.

I breathe a laugh of pure joy when I see my brother's face.

But my joy is short-lived.

His hair is a mess. His eyes shadowed. His jaw thick with a beard – I didn't even realize he could grow one that thick.

He's bent over a book. Working on something. Eyes darting, bright. Feverish.

I mirror him, craning over the scrying bowl.

A plate of food sits beside him. Flies crawl over it.

That shirt. I recognize it. Blood on the cuffs. It's the same one he wore the night I was taken.

When is this? The beard. It looks a few weeks old. I've been here almost three.

My pulse grows heavy. My throat tight.

What is he doing? What's wrong? Why hasn't he washed? Changed his clothes? He can't have gone to work like that.

He huffs and sweeps the book off the table, then grabs another from outside of my narrow view.

I gasp at the title.

Forbidden Rituals of the Underworld.

No. He isn't. He can't.

He cracks open the tome, a desperate frown on his brow. 'Annon.'

The word ripples through ink, space, time – a thread connecting us.

I reach for him, my finger into the rippling surface, my heart into the world that lies between us.

It's like surfacing from water. I can breathe. Smell. Hear.

Rotting food. Dried herbs in the rafters. His voice, rougher than usual, pained.

'I'll keep my promise if it's the last thing I do.'

He is. Oh gods, he *is*.

'No,' I try to tell him, but he doesn't look up from the book.

He can't come after me. It's too dangerous.

'Lowen,' I call. 'No.'

I'm standing over spilled water and ink, the scrying bowl on the floor.

'Rhiannon?' Kishel rises, leaning in, concern etched into his brow. 'Are you all right?'

'I'm fine.' I swallow, rubbing my chest.

I've been so wrapped up in pretending to be Drystan's happy fiancée and getting closer to him, I'd forgotten about my obligations on the surface.

My brother. My little brother.

He thinks he's coming to save me.

But if he makes it to the Underworld, he'll be the one who needs saving.

44

I NEED TO speak to Drystan, see if I can contact my brother. I'm sure he only refused before to be difficult, and things between us are different now. But after Kishel leaves, I barely have time to ready myself for the labyrinth before the sun rises.

Even as fragments of feather and shadow, I can't stop thinking about Lowen's face. I land in the obsidian corridors and he's still there.

'I'll keep my promise if it's the last thing I do.'

No. Don't. Stay on the surface where you're safe. I find myself clutching my chest, silently begging him. If it wasn't so awful, it would be funny – just as I start to believe staying away might be better for him, I find out it's worse than ever now I'm gone.

The Collector, ready, waiting, must sense something's wrong, because they keep touching my shoulder and stroking my hair.

But I march. Cut rests short. Ask them how sure they are about their turnings.

We can't afford any backtracking. I need to get to Lowen and stop him from doing something foolish. He put his life on hold for me, and I've been working to reach him . . . to tell him the truth . . . to, I don't know, give him the permission he needs to *stop*. But his life was always there for him to reclaim. He still had a future.

But now? This? If he pours himself into keeping his promise . . . What lengths wouldn't I go to for him? He would go even further for me.

It's day eleven. We're on the fourth tier. I can see the rise to the fifth, but no sign of the gateway between. If we make it up there today . . .

What about Min? And Asti? The cat?

Drystan?

They'll survive without me. Lowen? He'd die trying to reach me.

And what about the surface? If it makes my symptoms worse again?

I have no answer for that.

With a long exhale, I push the thoughts out of my head. Or try to.

What I want, who will live or die and what I must do – they're all academic if I can't find the way to the next level of this place. And to do that, I need to focus on this, now, not possibilities.

The labyrinth is in worse shape here. The blooms of what look like furry black mould are more frequent, oozing that greasy substance. At the centre of the largest clusters, they're thick, rounded. Pulsing. They remind me of boils, and yet . . . They're unlike any living thing I've seen. Like the juddering flicker on the stone's surface, they work in patterns I can't fathom, fracturing into black filaments, writhing, then reforming with a sickening soft squelch.

My stomach turns as I observe them, but I dutifully note all I see and even attempt a sketch. It isn't anywhere near as good as Lowen's work—

And then I spiral right back to the start of the thoughts I was trying to avoid.

His name a chant in my head, I press on.

We walk into the afternoon, and I'm pleased to see these short rests seem to be doing the trick. I'm tired but only normal-level tired – nowhere near exhausted. My muscles only ache dully, and my joints get stiff after a break, but soon loosen up. This might feel like hell to someone not used to being ill, but for me, it's a marked improvement. The awakening of my magic must be giving me energy or fighting my illness somehow. When I get out of here, I'll have time to study it properly and work out what exactly is going on. I'll ask Kishel—

Except when I get out of here, there will be no more Kishel. I'll be on the surface. He'll be down here. Never the twain shall meet.

And Min. Asti. The cat.

Drystan.

'Is that your brother's name you keep saying?' the Collector asks with a light touch on my shoulder.

'Lowen.' I didn't realize I've been keeping his name on my lips as well as in my heart. I nod. 'I'm afraid for him, Collector. He looked . . .' I shake my head, throat tightening too much to finish.

'We know about fear.' They round a corner in this twisting corridor first. 'It's ridden us for a long, long time. Long as we remember.'

My eyes burn. *Ridden by fear* – I understand the feeling. The weight. The sense that it both directs you and drags on you, a careless rider yanking on the reins.

I nudge into the Collector, glad of their company. Glad I'm not alone.

'But we've been braver recently. We've faced things we fear. And we've learned something. The fear is worse than the monster.'

I'm not sure that's the case when the monster is Death. But I smile and nod and squeeze their hand. 'You're braver than you realize.'

'So are you.'

I'm about to argue when we reach a round courtyard with a plinth at the centre. A prickle of anticipation chases through me.

A challenge.

Aside from the corridor we entered through, five doors lead onward. Approaching the plinth, I find its top is dished, containing a shallow pool of water.

'A scrying bowl? Or a makeshift one, anyway.'

The Collector glances at it with a thoughtful sound, but they're focused on the doors. Recessed into the wall, a mechanism runs from next to the handle and up, where it joins a channel connecting all five doors.

I've read a lot of books, but mechanics isn't my strong suit. I squint at the slots and cogs. 'I wonder what it does.'

The Collector mutters to themselves as they follow the mechanism from one door, up and across. Slowly, they nod. 'When one door handle is turned, the others all lock.'

'So, we can only try one door?' I chew my lip. 'What if I jam the mechanism further along the route, so it can't lock the others?'

The slithering voice lets out a high peal of laughter. 'Do you think fae mechanisms are so easily thwarted?'

The Collector shakes their head, and the dissenting voice goes on. 'Not an option. We must choose the right door or this becomes a dead end. And there's no other way to the next tier.'

My eyes widen from the mechanism to them. 'How do you know that?'

'There's only ever one way up.'

One staircase the Collector showed me to. One beyond the creature that wanted to eat Min. Even the broken stairs had no alternative.

With an inward groan, I turn to the plinth and its shallow pool of water. I've only ever been successful once, and that was with Kishel's support. 'I don't suppose you're any good at scrying?'

I'm still grinning at my own half-joke when a familiar screech splits the air.

45

MY ENTIRE BEING freezes. The Collector flinches.

The Devourer?

'I thought it fell.' My voice comes out breathless.

'That doesn't mean it died,' the Collector whispers, darting towards the corridor we entered through. They scent the air, and the way their eyes gleam when they turn, I know they can smell the creature.

I swallow and glance at the doors. A one in five chance isn't great, and getting it wrong means we'll be stuck in this courtyard sitting prey for the Devourer.

No guessing.

Shit.

The Collector seethes in fear at the entrance, hands clasping, hair swinging as it paces.

'All right,' I say brightly. 'I'll just . . . find the right path.' Sounds so easy.

I peer into the water. Slow my breaths. See nothing.

I've only ever managed this with ink before, not with water

alone. 'I need something I can pour in the water. I normally use ink, but . . .' I shrug and search for a suitable liquid.

A blister of black ooze throbs in one corner of the courtyard. Its surface falls apart. Just before it slops to the ground, it folds back in on itself, shard-like filaments flipping upward, where the blister reforms in its original position.

I could use the ooze.

But . . .

I don't trust it. And it's so viscous, it probably wouldn't move in the water.

Only one option left. Nothing else will show. I draw a small, folding knife from my belt and slice it over the back of my hand. Blood wells up along with pain. But it's a shallow kind of pain – one I can breathe through. One I can certainly suffer to get us out of the Devourer's path.

Crimson drips into the bowl. One drop. Two. Three.

They take so long.

Four. My pulse speeds with each drop. Hurry up.

Five.

A thin stream of crimson. Enough to work with.

'What have you—?' Gasping, the Collector rears up over the plinth, eyes wide. '*No*. You've given *him* your blood.'

I don't have the heart to tell them the master of the labyrinth has already tasted my blood – and more. 'Drystan isn't so bad,' I mutter, bending over the bowl.

'I don't mean—'

The Devourer's broken roar rends the air, splitting my ears, making the Collector cower.

My heart bucks. I try to slow my breaths. But my lungs want to work like bellows, suck in, blast out, ready to run, to fight – *ready*.

We are not doing that. *In, two, three, four, five. Out, two, three, four, five.*

The bowl's surface ripples with my breath and the aftermath of the Devourer's cry. My blood hangs there, suspended in the water, dispersing. Not forming any useful shapes.

On the edge of my vision, the Collector paces between the plinth and the corridor, jerky and frantic.

I shut them out.

This is for them. For me. For Lowen.

I need to *see*.

'Which way?' I whisper. '*Which way?*'

My blood coalesces into a thin, thin thread.

Is that the ground trembling? The clack of hooves?

Focus, Annon. Focus.

Slow breaths. Racing heart.

The thread twists back on itself.

Another high, ear-splitting cry. Closer. Much, much closer.

'Which way?' My voice trembles. My eyes burn, but I don't dare blink. I can't miss it.

The thread of blood twists towards the first door. Still clutching the edge of the plinth, I take half a step back, ready to turn and run.

But the thread turns, swims towards the second door. The third. The fourth. The fifth. Testing them? Questioning. Questing.

The Collector backs from the corridor. Cowering. Their whimpers punctuated by the roaring thunder of the Devourer's hooves.

'It's here,' all their voices rise in chorus.

The thread twists at the centre of the bowl as if thinking.

'Which one?' I whisper to the scrying bowl – beg my blood. '*Please.*'

It shoots towards one door. An unmistakable answer.

'Three,' I shout, stumbling backwards as rot enters the courtyard.

The air is thick with it.

I pull my scarf over my face, groping for the wall.

The Devourer rears in the doorway. Flesh hangs off it in strips. I catch glimpses of bone – rib and skull, femur and jaw.

It's deteriorated so much in just four days. There's something profoundly wrong with the creature.

Its eyes lock on me.

It kills anything it sees.

They aren't white, I realize, but clouded over like the eyes of a dead thing.

I trip over my own feet, trying to get away, heart slamming against my ribs, back slamming into the wall as the monster surges forward.

'Go.' The Collector looks up, hunkers down, and, shoulders squaring, they leap.

Right into the Devourer's path.

They're shoved back five feet, claws shrieking against stone. Hands close around antlers. Muscles strain against flesh.

It's the bravest thing I've ever seen.

And the worst.

All their voices rise in a scream. '*Go!*'

All in agreement.

It cuts through my shock.

I blink, take in where I am – right next to the third door – and fling myself against it. The metal handle, cold under my palm, turns.

Thunk. Thu-thunk. Movement chases through the mechanism. The ground shakes as four bolts thunder shut.

'Come on,' I call to the Collector, as I push the door. It doesn't move. Shit. *No.* Is this the wrong one? I set my teeth, dig my toes into any purchase I can find and heave.

Movement. An inch. Two.

It needs my full body weight, but eventually it rumbles open and I stagger through.

Ahead, a path leads upwards. The next tier. The *penultimate* tier. I chose the correct door. This is it. Our way out.

'We did it! Come—'

I turn back to the Collector. It takes a moment to understand the black lines slicing through the scene before me.

Bars.

Blocking my way into the courtyard.

Blocking the Collector's way *out*.

I tug. They don't so much as rattle.

Beyond, the Collector wrestles the Devourer's antlers, battling to keep its ripping teeth inches from their soft belly.

Heart in my throat, I try to lift the bars, twist them, get them to shift just a damn inch. I reach through like, somehow, I can help.

If the Collector kills it, we can work out the bars together.

The Devourer roars and tosses its head. The black stuff crawling over it sheds, revealing bone and shredded muscle, disappearing before it hits the ground as more forms and creeps over its fragmenting body.

With one hand, the Collector grabs its throat, choking out its shrieks. My hands tighten on the bars. *Yes.* 'Come on,' I whisper.

Eyes roll. Teeth gnash. Black filaments squirm over the Collector's hand. Up their wrist. They flinch.

The Devourer breaks free. Rears. Its hoof hits the Collector clean in the chest, dragging a groan from deep inside.

My breath stops as they fall. I throw myself at the bars as hooves slam down.

The snap of bone. The agonized scream of many voices. My ears ring with it.

The Devourer calms like it knows it's over. Head lifting, it regards the Collector.

My friend.

I stare. Frozen. Cracked open. Chest scoured and raw.

The Collector wheezes, blood bubbling on to their lips on the outward breath. 'Thank you.' The only sound in the sudden silence.

For a second, I think they're thanking the monster.

Then they turn their head to me. A distant smile edges their mouth, lighting the glassy pain in their eyes. 'Thank you . . . for being the first one in so long to see us as people. For giving us back our*selves*.'

I slump into the bars, shake my head, try to form words, but there is no voice save for the Collector's as the Devourer opens its maw and bends down.

'Look away, friend.' The Collector's smile solidifies as they give this tiny nod that must be agony and yet is done to reassure me. 'Look away.'

I touch my chest and incline my head in return, hoping that says all the things my tongue can't. Then, throat burning, I turn my back to the bars and slide down them to the hard ground.

The noises from the Devourer are unspeakable. Indelible.

But the Collector, brave to the end, uses the last of their voices, the dissenter, to say one final word. '*Friend*.'

Only then do I shut my eyes and let the hot tears spill for my fallen friend.

46

I DON'T KNOW how long I sit there. Sob there. No Collector to remind me to get up. Get going.

Eventually, when the sounds of the Devourer's eating and then pacing have faded, I pull myself to my feet.

One foot in front of the other. Somehow. Empty.

I stumble on until I drop. No Collector to remind me to rest. To bring me out of myself. To chatter among their own voices.

Their absence is a broad space at my side. Sore in my chest. A splinter of glass in my finger.

The sun lowers, and I'm glad for a moment of oblivion as I flutter away on dark wings.

It gives me a moment to find calm numbness, so once I'm back in my room, I can wash, braid my hair and throw on something unseelie-suitable before setting off to find Drystan.

I've let the Collector down. I can't let my brother down too.

One of the Twylth shadows me, letting me know Drystan was just in the Great Hall.

That's where I find him, on the gallery overlooking the eternal revelry. Standing up there, not realizing I'm observing him, he is arresting. Pale skin. Dark hair. Stillness made flesh.

Despite the day, despite my fears, the moment he sees me and a small, private smile lights his lips is a comfort.

Gripping the yew banister, I climb the sweeping staircase to reach him and pass Asti, standing guard.

Drystan takes in my pale face, probably notes my lack of jewellery. His expression tightens, hand finding the small of my back. 'What's wrong?'

'I need to see my brother. Contact him. Something. *Anything*.' The numbness cracks and tears threaten in my throat. I can't afford them here. Not in front of the entire court.

I push them back, but I fear they're as relentless as the tide.

'It's not possible.'

I go rigid. 'A message. *Something*. You came to get me, didn't you?'

'Annon.' He speaks my name softly, like a prayer for the dying. 'Why do you think we don't send out raiding parties every night? We're subject to the moon's phases – we may only travel with them. And you . . .' He exhales through his nose, lips pressing together. 'Even if you followed the rules I do, it's harder for a human to cross.'

The hollow thing in me cracks. 'When can you go through then? You can take a message to him.'

'Not for over a week. And even then, it's . . . complicated.'

'Complicated?' I laugh, the sound hazed with barely checked anger. 'I don't care if it's complicated.' I don't care if it requires a pile of severed tongues. I bite my lip to keep from blurting that. I suck in a sharp breath, use it to try to smother the embers leaping to life inside me. 'My brother is in danger. He's trying to reach the Underworld – to reach *me*. If he makes it here . . .' I stare up at Drystan, trying to show my desperation without falling to my knees and begging him *in front of the entire court*.

'I can't help tonight. But as soon as I can get to the surface, I'll take him any message you wish.'

I'll be gone by then. I have two days left in the labyrinth. I only hope I get to Lowen before he finds a ritual that works.

'Is that what these are about?' Drystan touches my cheek, thumb grazing the dried tears.

I grit my teeth. I can't cry any more. I can't. Shaking my head, it takes a moment to master myself. 'The Collector.' In stilted sentences, I manage to explain how they've been helping me through the labyrinth.

His eyes widen. 'The Collector has always been unremarkable. Keeping to its territory. A loyal guardian. But it . . . followed you?'

'They – *they* joined me.' My chest grows tighter as I tell him about today. The Devourer. The end.

'The Devourer was on the fourth tier?' His nostrils flare as he almost imperceptibly recoils. 'It's much more dangerous than the Collector, so I bound it to that level. It shouldn't be able to move between them.'

Knuckles white, I grip the gallery's balustrade. 'Well it escaped your binding, Drystan. And it killed the Collector.'

My snapped reply whips up the fae below, turning their dance into an undulating frenzy.

The shadows merge with them, twisting in the spaces between, lapping closer to us, a seeking tide.

Then the balustrade moves. Rolls under my hand. So subtle I question if I felt anything at all. It's only when Drystan and Asti's heads snap up as one, I'm sure.

I stare as it twitches and slithers. 'What's—?'

The fae at the bottom of the stairs go still. From their centre rises a sharp cry.

Someone's tripped, which is enough to make me gasp – fae never trip or bump into things.

As they right themselves, a familiar face looks up, cheeks uncharacteristically flushed, and sapphire eyes meet mine.

They narrow as Phaedra glowers at me.

Perfect lips pursed, she yanks at her foot, and when I follow the motion downwards . . .

I see it.

The balustrade flows down the staircase, the same piece of wood forming the banister, but instead of ending with the stairs, it has formed a tendril snaking across the floor.

Wrapping around Phaedra's ankle.

From the other shouts, she's not alone. And the coiling branch shows no sign of stopping as it disappears into the crowd.

My magic. Leaking, when I'm trying to hold everything in.

'Your Majesty,' she calls, 'your human appears to have *grabbed* me.' She doesn't so much as look at me, but there are razor blades in her gaze and that just might be worse.

There's a beat where Asti stares, pale, and Drystan gathers himself, chin rising. They exchange a look and he gives the barest nod.

'Now, now, *Avellan*,' he says, pitched for others to hear as he squeezes my shoulder with an indulgent look. 'Play nice.'

Like this is something in my control. A strength, not a weakness. I give what I hope is a mischievous grin and let him escort me down the stairs.

'I see you have energy you need to work off.' He slides his hand to the small of my back and guides me towards the exit as Asti hurries in our wake, signalling to nearby guards, who come forward with axes.

More gazes than usual follow us, and the air thickens, heavy like the night I got Lord Mastelle's name wrong.

Once we're free of the Great Hall, I swallow. 'I'm in trouble, aren't I?'

'Not with me.' He gives me a half smile. No dimples. Like he's trying to reassure me but it's a gesture he's unfamiliar with.

'But?'

'But . . . I daresay Phaedra will be even more pissed off with you.'

'I didn't mean to—'

'You didn't. But it's better they think you did.' At my questioning look he goes on, 'Your magic isn't the kind we see here. That alone is enough to draw attention. Add in who you are – a future queen, a human, and that you've only just started to manifest it . . .' He exhales through his nose like he's holding back a sigh and there's a flash of something in his gaze. Pain, perhaps. 'Your actions are under constant scrutiny. As such, you can't get away with mistakes that might go unnoticed elsewhere.'

Mistakes . . . missteps . . . imperfections. All things that are dangerous in his kingdom.

'Mistakes like being unable to control my magic.'

The flattening of his lips is all the answer I need.

47

THE LABYRINTH IS quieter, darker, slower without the Collector. It's hard to rest without their watchful presence – I'm always on alert. And inside, there's this constant clench of my chest, my stomach. They died so I could get through that door.

I'm so plagued by the final image of them and the sounds of the Devourer, I only dully observe how there are fewer signs of corruption on this tier.

When I take a break, I flick restlessly through my notebook. I'm sure this stuff, whatever it is, starts as flickers of non-reflection blooming across the stone. Then comes the ooze, then the sharp little mould-like filaments.

The Devourer's condition deteriorated in the space of mere days. It's like the corruption has infected it.

But how? And what is it?

I don't even know where to start on that problem.

The attempt is a comfort, though. Theorizing. Speculating. Skimming over my notes.

Logic and observation are perfect distractions from . . .

Ah. And now I'm no longer distracted.

The Collector. Lowen. My heart feels like a broken vase, shards crunching around in my chest, a fresh slice with each movement.

Sleep refuses to come, so I drag myself to my feet and set off once more.

The sun is nearing its zenith when I hear a faint noise. I freeze. The Devourer? It got up the broken staircase – I wouldn't be surprised if it found a way past the barred passageway.

Breath held, I cock my head.

Not a screech. Not hoofbeats. It sounds like . . . flowing water?

Cold, hard dread locks around me. Another scrying challenge.

I'm not ready for another trial. Not with this weight in my chest. But tomorrow is my penultimate day and I haven't even reached the last level, never mind the final gate.

Ready or not, I have to face it.

I take a sip of water and rub my chest, wishing I had some memento of the Collector – some little reassurance that they were here and we got so far together.

There is nothing. Just my memories.

Keeping them fresh, close, even though it burns my eyes, I approach the distant sound.

I think I catch the sweet scent of honeysuckle and lavender. But that isn't possible. The smell must be clinging to my clothes.

The air hazes. I slow, caution in my steps, and draw my little knife. Not that it will do much good, but I feel less vulnerable with naked steel.

At the next corner, I angle the polished blade to try and peer round, but what it shows me doesn't make sense.

Green.

There is nothing green in the labyrinth.

I ease around the corner and—

There is absolutely green.

Leafy fruit trees shade a sunny courtyard full of plants I could spend an hour naming. Honeysuckle clambers over an arbour. A young willow tree weeps over a glistening stream that emanates from a fountain in the far wall.

It's beautiful.

And that's what makes me cry.

Because the Collector would've loved this. There's even jasmine, like they mentioned from one of their dream-memories. I turn, taking it in, writing it in my heart alongside my memories of them and find a slash of darkness in the midst of all this light and colour.

Drystan.

He stands there, brows pinched as he takes in my tear-stained cheeks. His arms open and I don't even want to resist.

I fall into them. Into him. Let him catch me and hold me and stroke my hair.

I choke out something unintelligible about the Collector. About my brother. About how it's too much. Too heavy. Too thick in my throat and lungs, in my damn veins, like grief and fear have infected my blood.

He listens, kisses the crown of my head, forms something solid I can lean some of this weight against.

And once I'm talked out, he peels back and asks so gently, it brings fresh tears to my eyes, 'Do you want to forget for a while?'

I'm looking up and nodding before I even think. The weight is unbearable. I need to set it down. He sounds so reasonable. And I'm so tired. '*Please.*'

He gives a small, sad smile and inclines his head. His hand envelops my cheek, thumb smearing my tears. 'Let's both forget a while. What's brought us here. The sacrifices. The hurt and the hate that dogs our tracks.'

Fingers entwined through mine, he guides me to the stream. The water glitters, mesmerizing. 'These waters strip away the heaviest memories – for a time.' His deft fingers work on the buttons of my clothing. 'Each mote is a memory carried by the stream.'

Colour flashes in the glistening particles, and I wonder how many have shed memories into its burbling waters.

'Have you . . .?' I finish the question by raising my eyebrows at him as he strips away my coat and discards it on the bank.

'A few times. After her . . . I came here often.' My shirt is next. 'Sometimes we need respite from the unbearable weight of *being*.'

Perhaps I can use that respite to make better headway this afternoon – unlike this morning's slog.

Soon, I'm naked, sun bathing me, while Drystan peels away his layers.

He's everything this garden is not. White skin, black hair, black tattoos – stark and cold against the teeming life, the bright flowers, the soft breeze.

Yet there is warmth to his skin now, like he's reflecting this place. And much as there is life here in the plants, life also needs death. That's why our garden has a compost heap – a place to gather the trimmings and dead wood. A space for gentle mouldering and rich loam, ready to scatter on next season's crops to ensure a better harvest.

So he might stand out here. But he still belongs. The death in life. The glow in his eyes and warmth in his skin marking the life in death.

'Come.' He steps down into the stream, then turns and offers his hand.

'It's . . . only temporary, right?' To lose the Collector for ever would be a betrayal. And to forget Lowen? Unthinkable.

'A few hours at most. Just don't drink the water.'

A few hours will let me rest and get some good headway towards the final level before it all comes back.

I let him guide me down into the water.

It's chilly, raising goosebumps as soon as my toes enter. The stream seems to burble along gently, but as my thighs enter, it tugs on me, like much faster flowing water. It reaches my chest, and Drystan steadies me, his broad back a barrier breaking the worst of its force. There's this snatching sensation to it, like something in the water has tiny fingers that pinch ever so lightly.

I frown. It isn't working. I still feel like . . . like . . .

A deep, fresh breath fills me. It's like I've never breathed before. Like my lungs have found new capacity. Like they're free.

Blinking, I look up at Drystan. He watches me intently, and I'm struck afresh by his beauty, like I've never seen it before. I know I have, but it's as though I've never truly taken it in. The strength of his jaw and cheekbones. The severe line of his nose and brows. He could be carved from stone, a statue to an uncaring god.

Except for his eyes.

They are not uncaring. Not as they trail over me. Nor his hands. They cradle my back, hold me close, graze up my spine. One cups my cheek, bathing it in the stream's cooling water. 'Are you all right?' His chest rises and falls: long, slow, deep.

Colours flash in the water. So pretty. So bright. Something that was within me feels like it's drifting further away. There are names, but they're buffed out, smoothed into soft sounds. Pa. Annem. Lowen. Collector.

Even as I think them, they get further away, carried into the distance like clouds. Not something I need to worry about.

I nod at Drystan, loop my arms around his waist, enjoy the slip of wet skin upon wet skin, the precision cut of his lithe muscles.

'Good,' he murmurs, thumb tracing a line to my chin. With ease, he lifts me on to the bank, into the warm sunlight, and follows a moment later.

He turns me and I find a soft rug has appeared on the bank, covering the black stone paving that peeks between the grass and creeping thyme. There's a picnic laid out and glasses of something gold and sparkling with condensation running down the side. Cushions and blankets practically invite me to lie down.

We lie. We eat. We drink. The gold stuff is fizzy elderflower, sweet, refreshing, perfect.

Something tugs on my thoughts, but I shake my head and it slips past.

Drystan sits propped on the cushions and talks, almost like he's a normal person. He's softer, calmer, easier than I've ever known. Though when he catches me admiring the way the sunlight gleams on his tattoos and shoulders, he gives me this half smile that's edged with danger.

It buzzes through me. A thrill. A need.

He sets aside his glass and watches me from beneath his dark lashes. 'Come here.'

The buzz licks through me now, a lightning strike along my nerves. I obey. Not because he ordered, but because I *want*.

As soon as they're in reach, he captures my wrists and pulls them around his neck, making me fall against his chest. 'There,' he murmurs against my lips before he captures those too.

The scent of thyme crushed beneath us rises, mingling with refreshing, sweet elderflower.

Everything else wafts further and further away, pushed out by the sensation of his lips on mine, his tongue, his body, his hands skimming down my arms, my shoulders, my spine, over my backside and guiding my legs apart until I'm straddling him, the evidence of his arousal building between us.

He kisses my cheek, my jaw, the sinew of my neck, licking and nibbling and breathing so deeply it's like he's trying to inhale my entire being. 'Your scent, *Avellan*. Fuck, it's . . .' He shudders a breath out and squeezes my backside, pulling me along his hardening length. 'Intoxicating. Maddening. Devastating.'

I whimper at the way he glides along my slick wetness. 'Devastating?' I barely manage the syllables. 'That makes it sound bad.'

'It's terrible. Glorious. Frightening. Perfect.' Languidly, he runs his lips over my throat as he speaks each word, every sound a spike along my nerves. 'It's like you – sweet.' He tongues the hollow between my collarbones. 'Soft.' He kisses the spot two inches lower. 'Alive.' Lower. 'Beautiful.' Lower. 'You smell like your hands when the green clings beneath your nails from the glasshouse.' He cups my breasts and admires them, a lazy smile softening his flushed face. 'Like growth and soil.' Thumbs grazing my nipples, he plunges his tongue between my tits as if I'm something he needs to discover every inch of. 'Like jasmine blooming after dark.' He nips at my aching peaks.

I moan at the soft savagery of his teeth against my tender flesh. I could weep at the way he worships me with words. So much attention he's paid. So many things he's noticed. So many ways he's chosen to *perceive* me.

He says my scent is intoxicating, but his voice drags me under into a delicious drowning, where his words are water, his touches are a rip tide, and I've given up trying to swim to shore.

He sucks and flicks his tongue over me as his hand planes over my backside and between my legs.

'Wait,' I gasp.

He stills, a question in his eyes.

He broke me apart beautifully our first time together – I remember all he did to me, for me. For some reason that feels important. 'I don't want you to think I only take.'

He chuckles, softly, darkly. 'I don't.'

'But I want . . . I want to do something for you . . .' I reach between us, relishing how his breath catches when my fingers wrap around his length. 'Let me . . .' I work my way down him, gaze holding his. It isn't something I've done much with men – the baker's girl taught me how to make her scream with my mouth, but the men I've been with have always been impatient, choking.

Drystan is patient, though. A man. Not barely more than a boy. 'I want to.'

He catches my chin, gentleness in his eyes as he strokes my chin, my lower lip. 'You really do, don't you? My sweet little *Avellan*.' The corner of his mouth lifts, pressing a slight shadow into his cheek. 'Very well. But I won't have you kneel.'

I'm still processing the layers of his words when his hands wrap around me, the world turns and somehow he's switched our places.

Carefully, he lays me upon the cushions, halfway between sitting and lying, hair fanned around me. He pauses there, taking me in. There's a dreamy, wondering tone to his voice when he speaks again: 'Laid out like a feast for a ravenous god. And I am starving.'

I'm exposed. Vulnerable.

Safe.

Still, as he comes and kneels straddling my chest, there's a flutter of panic. I've only done this a handful of times. And my last . . . well, he lost patience because I struggled to keep going for long.

Drystan pauses, kneeling over me, fingers crooking around my jaw, pulling me back from another world, another time. 'What is it, sweet one?' Head canting, he frowns. 'We don't have to do this, you know. You can change your mind.'

'I want to. I just . . .' I swallow, throat tight, mouth dry. 'I'm not very good at this. I've not done it very much. I'm not sure how best to—'

'Shh.' He smooths hair from my face, touch cool, calming. 'You just haven't had the right direction. That's all.'

I bite my lip and he smiles at the gesture, gaze caught on the movement of my mouth.

He bends down, kisses my brow, swipes his thumb over my lips. 'I'll teach you. Yes?'

My eyes shut, breath easing out. His voice is so lulling, so solid, I can't help believing him. I nod.

'Annon.' He shakes his head in gentle reprimand. 'Haven't you learned by now? I need to hear you say it.'

'Please show me.'

His next exhalation is laced with a groan. 'Your mouth is so pretty when you ask for it.'

His thighs burn either side of me. This close, his scent is overwhelming. That ancient familiarity. Something unknowable and yet right here. Knowing me.

He fists his hard length, pumps it once and eases closer. 'If you want to stop, we can at any time. Just tap me here.' He presses my fingers into the precision-cut lines of his stomach.

I'm somewhat distracted by his dick mere inches from my lips. It's thicker and longer than I've had before, and I'm suddenly unsure if I can take it all.

'It's all right. We can just—'

I slip my fingers free and wrap them around him. The skin's so soft – a delightful contrast with his hardness.

Then, holding his gaze, I place an open-mouthed kiss over his tip.

Another groaning breath out as his head falls back. 'Annon.'

Hearing my name from his lips as I wrap mine around his cock is a strange kind of victory, but a victory nonetheless. One I need to taste more of.

'I want you to lie back and let me use that pretty little mouth.' He speaks in a low tone, gaze back on me with an intensity that lights me up.

He threads his fingers through my hair as I open, ready.

For once in my life, I'm not weak, I'm not ill, I'm a woman having this effect on her lover. I'm widening my mouth, letting him slide in over my tongue.

Hips easing forward, he fists my hair slowly as I take him in.

It's a lot. I can barely breathe. I certainly can't take him all the way. Even closing my hand around the base, there's still a couple of inches between my mouth and fingers.

I'm about to lift my head and try to push further when he nods, gaze hooded. 'That's so good, love. Just lie back for me.'

I do, letting the cushions hold me, letting my body soften into them. He's positioned me perfectly, no effort required. I manage to suck in a fuller breath as he pulls halfway out.

'That's it. Patience. This time, flatten your tongue.' It takes a moment for me to work out exactly how to do that, then he eases back in, further, further, until I drop my hand to his thigh. 'Still with me, *Avellan*?'

I bob my head the tiniest amount, savouring the drag of him on my lips, the thickness of him nudging my throat.

He doesn't make it all the way, but his half-shut eyes say he doesn't mind. 'Fuck. Aren't you a picture?' His throat rises and falls on a thick swallow. 'I've dreamed about this. Filling your hot mouth. Your lips wrapped around me. But this is even better than I imagined.'

My thighs tighten at the praise. Relief and pleasure flood me like I've been waiting a lifetime for his reassurance.

'Now, relax your throat. Let me in deeper.'

This part is easy – I have to do it when I take my tablets.

'That's it. So perfect.' He smiles, dimpled, never taking his eyes off me.

For a while, there are no more instructions, just his controlled thrusts into my mouth, my hands resting on his thighs, noting how their muscles ripple with each measured movement.

I don't close my eyes. I can't. He's beautiful. Glorious. The sway of his hair is hypnotic. The way he drinks me up, intoxicating.

The sun passes behind him, making him nothing more than a dark shape with a pair of glowing, golden eyes. It feels like I'm taking in a god. A myth. A being that's more idea than flesh.

'Look at you laid out beneath me, taking it all so fucking well.' His chest heaves as he traces his fingers over my scalp, cradling my head at exactly the angle he needs. 'You were made for this.'

This time, I moan – at the praise, at the throb of him on my tongue. Heat flares in my cheeks at how loud I am.

He answers with a wicked smirk. 'My filthy little queen likes to be told how well she fucks, does she? And even better – she's embarrassed by it.' He gives a slow shake of his head. 'Oh dear, *Avellan*. You never should have let me see you blush. So prettily. So perfectly. You make me want to praise you all the more.'

Oh fuck. I'm lost. Not safe. In danger. The worst of my life.

He's tender and filthy. Pitching between the two, dizzying. He's fucking my mouth, telling me how prettily I take him, and yet . . .

Laid out on the cushions, I feel like something precious sacrificed to a dark god. A willing, eager sacrifice.

He treats me like I'm sacred – kneeling astride me, hips flexing forward, my mouth full of him, hands gripping his thighs in a desperate attempt to cling to the world.

He sets the rhythm with quiet control, one hand in my hair, the other fisted in a cushion by my head. Not harsh. Not rushed. Pure control like this is an act of worship.

'You're doing so well.' His voice is rougher now, the heave of his chest faster. 'This time, when I pull out, I want you to use your tongue.' He withdraws, leaving just the tip in my mouth, allowing me to catch my breath and do as instructed, swirling over the head.

'Fuck. Yes. That's it. Exactly it.' A breathless laugh escapes him. 'Who told you you were no good at this? You're . . .' The sentence dissolving into a groan, his cock twitches on my tongue. Under my hands, this thighs tense as his hips snap into me.

Control slipping. For me. In me. Because of *me*.

My eyes stream with the depth he takes and my need not to blink in case I miss a delicious moment.

'So pretty on your back.' He huffs, stomach taut, voice ragged, the grip in my hair tightening. 'All mine. Doing so well.'

But there's this tension in his abdomen that tells me he's still restraining himself.

And I don't want restraint. I want ruin. I want to feel him come apart on my tongue.

So I work that tongue on every outward stroke, take him as fully as I can, suck on the flared head, give up on breathing for a few wild moments.

And I am rewarded. Gods, am I rewarded.

He bucks into me, my name a moan in his throat, fingers wound into my hair, biting into my scalp.

I'm triumphant. Salt spills over my tongue and down my throat as he twitches in my mouth, hot and urgent and utterly undone.

He stares at me. Hair messy. Lips parted. Eyebrows drawn together as he bows his head – a true devout.

Stroking my cheek, he pulls from me and I'm able to suck in air, almost as greedy for that as I was for him. He catches his breath, sitting on his heels, watching me as I let my head fall back with a satisfied smile.

'Look at that swollen mouth.' He scoffs softly. 'And so pleased with herself, too.' He kisses my tingling lips, slowly, deeply, and I wonder if he catches the taste of himself as his tongue swipes between them.

I'm boneless yet restless. Satisfied yet needy. Taken yet throbbing.

He knows it – either from the leap of my pulse, the moan he captures in his mouth, or the half-hearted arch my body makes into his.

'Patience, little love,' he murmurs against my lips, teasing reprimand in his tone. 'You've taken me so well, but that doesn't mean I'm finished with you.'

A whimpering sigh spells out my relief as I sag into the cushions.

Unvented pleasure simmers beneath my skin, making it too tight, too hot, my muscles fluttery with need. 'Please, Drystan.'

He groans as I say his name, and I can't pretend it wasn't deliberate. Straightening, he looks down at me. 'Asking for it again.' He absently toys with my tits as he shakes his head. 'How can I deny you?'

Tenderly, he places me on my side before him, parts my thighs, hands reverent, my splayed position profane.

With his arm beneath my head, the clear sky above reminds me that we're in the open. I'm exposed, spread for him. Yet the sun feels good upon my skin – almost as good as he feels at my back. The breeze is another caress. And the sweet smell of jasmine blends with his scent, heady and thick.

This place is right. There's no one else. It's ours.

When his hand slides over my belly and down between my legs and he feels how wet I am, he chuckles, hot and dark in my ear. 'Oh, *Avellan*. You did enjoy that, didn't you?'

Fresh heat blooms in my cheeks, even as his finger slips along my entrance and he builds upon that simmering pleasure.

'My perfect little queen.' The arm beneath me snakes around, so he can squeeze my breast as his finger dips into me.

I clench around him, throbbing, desperate, and my body arches as much as it can in his hold, making him laugh again.

'Such a sweet little creature who loves to give and loves to take and both loves and hates to be told just how special she is.' I'm not sure if it's meant to be reward or punishment as he adds a second finger to the first, palm rubbing my apex, pushing me towards somewhere high and holy.

My eyelids flutter. It's all I can do to remember how to breathe, albeit staccato and frayed.

Then he pulls from me and I'm about to huff out my disappointment, more than a little petulant, when he runs his length along my slick entrance instead. 'See? I told you to be patient, didn't I?'

Whimpering, I tilt my hips, trying to rub against him harder, but he maintains only the pressure he wishes to give. A tiny corner of my mind is still sane and surprised he's hard again so soon. I've heard stories about fae lovers – their stamina, their drive, the way they wreck humans. Turns out, they weren't exaggerating.

'Didn't I, *Avellan*? Remember to use your words – how much I love to hear your sweet voice.'

'You did,' I babble, on the edge of madness. 'You told me to be patient. And I have – I *have*. But I need . . .'

He glides along me at that same pressure that's not *quite* enough. 'What is it you need?'

'I need you to fuck me. Please. Now. *Please*.'

He gives a low, ragged hum of pleasure. 'You even beg perfectly. That's all I wanted.' He pulls back, angles my thigh a touch higher and places himself at my entrance.

With infinite, insanity-inducing patience, he enters. I can't quite breathe. I can't keep my eyes from rolling back in my head. I can't do anything but cling to the arm that's under me.

Just that one thrust has me wrung out. Hovering on the edge of somewhere else. Eyes tearing with how damn close I am.

I'm entirely at his mercy. Entirely filled by him. Entirely his to do with as he wishes.

And yet I still taste the salt of his come on my tongue. I still feel the twitch of the muscles – in his arm this time, not his thighs. I have some small power over him.

'So warm, so wet. How am I supposed to be gentle with you?' His voice is no longer teasing but raw. His chest heaves against my back as though he's wrestling himself from the brink. I *feel* as he masters himself, and he goes on more softly, a low reverence to it: 'You take me like you were made for me.'

Only then does he hook my leg over his and return his fingers to my clit.

I shudder, whimper. Too full to manage the pressure his assured touch drives in me. Close to shattering.

Controlled once more, he doesn't thrust, just stays locked in me as the pads of his fingers work me. 'I want to feel you come on my cock, *Avellan*. Every second of it. Every inch, every clench of that pretty little cunt.' There's a gravelly edge to his voice that speaks of brutal determination and on that final word, he pushes harder, deeper into me, seizing what little breath I have. 'I will not miss a moment of it.'

I'm close. Gods. I'm so close to giving him exactly what he wants.

Tears spill from my eyes. Desperation. Ruination. Terrible, glorious want as my body winds tighter and tighter and—

I cry out. Wordless. Senseless. Lost.

48

HE MAKES ME come apart twice more before he joins me, frayed and raw, forgetting to tell me how well I take it or how perfect my cunt is.

For a long while, we catch our breath, entwined, the breeze cooling our sweat.

It takes time before we can speak in the quiet, aching sweetness of *after*. He rubs between my shoulder blades and tells me how my fae mark has spread. I've never heard of that happening to fae-touched humans. Then again, it isn't my area of expertise.

We eat a little as he asks me about the plants around us. I tell him their names, point out the identifiers. 'Where did they all come from? Plants don't seem to grow so easily here, especially not flowers.'

He makes a thoughtful sound as he places his chin on my shoulder and traces nonsense lines down my arm. 'I found this place a long while ago. It always struck me as strange. Beautiful. A rarity. It's still the greenest place I've ever seen in the Underworld.'

'A long while ago . . .' I tilt my head and peer at him out the corner of my eye. 'Just how old *are* you?'

'Centuries.'

'What?' I twist in his hold so I can widen my eyes at him. 'Centuries? *Plural?* How many?'

He shrugs. 'Once you get to that point, the numbers matter less.'

I can't imagine being so careless about years, when I've spent so much time wondering how few I have left.

'"Long is the day and long is the night,"' he says, intonation low, heavy with the combined years of all those who've said it before.

I stiffen in recognition and continue the saying: '"And long is the waiting of the King of Death." I heard my father say that once . . . right before my mother gave him a pointed look and muttered to "hush or you'll call him here".' I frown up at the noon sun, feeling the sea air, smelling the salt and the smoke from the fireplace, hearing my mother's voice so clearly. 'At the time, I thought she meant it would mean my death . . . not that it would bring a *King* of Death.'

His laugh is low, dark. As it fades, he meets my gaze and I forget about clifftop cottages. There is only him, me, under this high sun.

'It was hard to remain patient for you, *Avellan*.' Lightly, his fingertips trace me from chin to jaw. 'It feels like I've been wanting you for an age.'

'You speak like you're still waiting. You've had me now.'

'Some aches don't fade so easily.'

I don't know what to say to that. What to think. So I kiss him. Softly. Sweetly.

And yet it devastates me.

This was only meant to be physical. Temporary. Something to enjoy before I go home.

But the King of Death has worked under my skin. A thorn I can't push out.

And perhaps I've got under his too.

Because he holds me tenderly and swipes his mouth over my brow before tucking my head beneath his chin, like he's a shelter and I'm something precious he intends to keep safe.

'But I thought . . . Didn't you hate me until, I don't know, the night you killed Threnn? What happened?'

'Annon,' he says softly, massaging my scalp, lulling my eyes shut. 'It was those damn biscuits.'

Next time I open my eyes, the sun is high in the sky. Noon.

It was noon when I arrived.

The sky flickers – the sun suddenly lower for a blink-and-you'd-miss-it instant.

I frown up at it.

Wait. Why am I lying here, in Drystan's arms? Under a blanket?

Wrestling myself free, I sit up and rub my eyes.

'What is it?'

My stomach pulls tight. There's a terrible burn at the back of my throat, scorching, scouring. A punishment for lying here, enjoying myself when Lowen could be performing some dark ritual to reach me.

'What did you do?' I round on Drystan. 'Luring me here. Washing away my memories. Fucking me senseless. When I should be . . .' The guilt is a shard in my throat cutting the sentence short.

Lowen knows nothing of the Underworld's dangers. He has no Twylth to protect him. No position as a future queen to keep him safe.

The worst thing is – if something happens to him, it won't even be Drystan's fault.

It will be *mine*.

'It's just an illusion.'

Oh gods. Wrapping the blanket around myself, I search the sky for any sign of that flicker. 'How long have I been here?'

Drystan takes a deep breath and rises after me. 'Longer than you think.'

I exhale a laugh of disbelief, eyes stinging as I circle and take in this pretty illusion. 'You glamoured the sky.'

At the garden entrance, movement catches my eye. The corruption has crept in while we've been asleep, blooming, pulsing.

'And you sent your rot after me, too. What is it meant to do — scare me into giving up? If I stay still too long, will it grow over me like it did the Devourer?'

He frowns, head canting.

'Just show me the truth, Drystan. How long do I have left?'

His eyes shutter as he stands tall — more king than lover. 'Very well.'

The sky shatters. A thousand shards fall to earth in silence.

A plaintive moan falls from my lips.

The sun is low. So low. Long shadows creep from the fruit trees and the labyrinth walls. In the west, the sky hasn't yet turned honey-warm, but the opposite horizon already deepens to violet-blue.

We're perhaps a couple of hours from sunset.

He's kept me in his illusion all afternoon. I've lost so much time.

Choking on shock, I search for my clothes, strewn by the stream, caught up with his. 'Is any part of this even real? The plants? The picnic?' He's shown me the sky as it really is, but I don't trust what's left.

He crosses his arms. 'Annon, is going home really what's best for you? If your parents have been keeping this dark secret all this time, are they really who you think?'

I spin and toss his trousers at his feet. 'While *you* have been so honest — so *honourable*.'

There's something in the depths of his eyes that holds me there a beat longer than I can spare. I can't quite place it. Regret? I don't think him capable. Sadness? Perhaps.

At the fact he'll lose something he considers his.

'That's it, isn't it?' I tug on my trousers. 'That's why you brought me here, made me bathe in the waters – you wanted to distract me, so I'd waste time and end up stuck here for ever *with you.*'

His eyebrow twitches. 'Would it be so bad?' He yanks on his trousers. 'Isn't your life here better? Isn't what you have here better? Why are you still so desperate to get back to your family? After everything.'

His questions chip too close to bone. 'My brother—'

'Yes, yes, I know. You're afraid for him. But he hasn't reached the Underworld. Leave him be. He'll give up in time.'

I snort and scoop up my shirt. 'He hasn't given up on me in sixteen years. He isn't about to start now. Just because your mother bargained you away to a human bride and your brothers are your rivals, you—'

'And your family's perfect, is it?' He bares his teeth in a vicious grin. 'The same family who has lied to you and manipulated you all your life. That's what *care* looks like, is it?'

I have to stop. Anger simmers in me, making my limbs tremble. I don't trust what I'll do if I let go of this stillness.

The willow tree sways. Its hanging branches snake across the grass. The creeping thyme twists and snares, writhing around Drystan's feet. From among the shrubs, brambles with thick thorns tangle, scrambling over each other to get closer to him, like they feel me unravelling.

Why hold back? It's a soft, purring voice in the back of my skull.

I'm afraid. I'll hurt him. Scare him away. Scare everyone away. I can't be alone.

My chest heaves as I try to squash my anger and hurt down to a manageable size – a convenient little box I can pack away.

After a drawn-out moment, I swallow. 'You don't know what you're talking about.'

He holds my gaze, just as still as I am. 'I know more than you can imagine.'

Brambles cross the ground between us. He jerks back as if he's only just seen the unnatural way the plants are moving as untamed magic leaks out of me.

'What's the matter, Drystan?' I flash him a bitter smile. 'I thought this was "just an illusion" – illusions can't hurt anyone.'

There's this tightness around his mouth that makes me regret mocking him. It's sad. Sadder than I ever expected him to let me see. 'They can if you believe in them.'

More brambles snake in. The willow's branches are nearly at his ankles.

I grab my jacket and straighten, gesturing towards the agitated plants forming a wall between us. 'Leave me alone, Drystan.'

I turn my back on him and walk away, chest cracked wide open.

I swore I'd save my brother.

Yet somehow, so near the end, I let myself be lulled. I closed my eyes to enjoy an afternoon in the sun, and time slipped away.

And I don't know who I'm more angry at.

Him.

Or myself.

49

DRYSTAN'S INTERFERENCE SPURS me on. He wouldn't go to all this effort to distract and derail me if he wasn't worried. And he wouldn't be worried unless I was getting close to the final gate.

I push on towards nightfall, something in my chest telling me which turnings to take. Instinct, the Collector's spirit whispering in my ear, or just plain hope, I have no idea, but I make good progress.

That night, I refuse to go to Drystan. I refuse to attend his court. Instead, I take meals in my room with the cat, and Min and Asti join me for lunch, but otherwise I rest and ready myself.

Tomorrow is my penultimate day in the labyrinth, and I don't intend to get distracted again. When I close my eyes, the mountain gates are close enough that I can see the napped facets of their columns, the razor edges where they open.

I'm close. I'm so close.

It takes two cups of vervain tea before I drift towards sleep. Thankfully, they grow it in the glasshouse. I can imagine sleeplessness is the kind of complaint the unseelie wouldn't see as a weakness but as a sign of strength and vigour.

I wake before dawn, get dressed and pack my bag. I'm standing at the window, shoulders squared, taking in the first rays of the sun, when I'm transported to the labyrinth.

I land, already walking. I follow the pull in my chest at each turn. It steers me true, even though my heart aches for the empty space at my side, and the further I go, the thicker the mouldering, pulsing corruption grows.

The final gate takes up my entire view, blocking out the sky. I could toss a pebble and hit it from here. There must only be a few corridors between me and it. Must be.

I'm going to make it.

I'm going to fucking make it.

Especially as there's a stone arch ahead, and beyond it, a long uphill path. The gateway to the last tier.

I pause at the threshold, searching for any monster or puzzle. It's more like a causeway, stretching upwards, punctuated by more arches, a sheer drop to either side. Not only a sheer drop, but nothing beneath, as though this was all one single piece of rock and the winding way has been hewn from it. Below, there's only darkness.

It's uncomfortable to look at – disobeying some fundamental law of the universe.

Perhaps it's going to fall as I cross. Nothing marks the way – symbols or stones in specific shapes, suggesting I need to work out the correct order or avoid touching the wrong letters or spell out some word in the unseelie's ancient tongue.

I could run. But not that far. Or I can tread carefully. That plays much more to my strengths.

Lightly, I step through the first arch.

Breath held, I listen for the crack or grind of breaking rock. The causeway stands solid.

I nod. Take another step. Wait.

It seems this isn't that kind of challenge.

I keep my head down and forge ahead, avoiding the tendrils of corruption winding their way along the causeway. Five minutes. Ten. Fifteen. I should be nearing the next archway.

Except, when I look up, it doesn't seem any closer than when I set off.

Frowning, I cock my head. It must be a perspective trick – something to do with where I'm standing. A short rest gives my thighs and hips the chance to recover from the light ache before I set off again.

This time, I keep my head up, gaze locked on the arch.

I walk. And walk. And walk. And walk.

And it gets no closer.

What the hells?

Looking back, the entrance is far, far away, and the causeway seems narrower than I realized. If I stumbled, I could easily fall off the edge.

What if I have an episode? Consulting my notebook, I count back. It's been days. I'm due one. Before I left home, I was having to take belladonna every couple of days. If that happens in here and I don't realize in time . . .

My pace slows.

I'm alone. With Drystan's taunts, Min's appearance, and the Collector's strange but sweet company, I hadn't felt it before now.

If I fell and hurt myself . . .

I could hit my head. Smash it on the cold, hard stone. No one would know. Sure, Drystan shows up sometimes, but after I told him to leave me alone, I don't expect to see him until I reach the final gate.

If I reach it.

'I *will*,' I mutter. And when my heart slows, it gives me enough warning to sit safely rather than falling. I can take belladonna. Haven't I been looking after my medication and managing my heart for years?

My strides lengthen. The way eases.

Lightheaded, I look up and find myself at the stone arch. The sense of connection in my chest snares into a knot as I pass under it.

No walls, just a chasm. Just oblivion. Only a few feet of slippery black stone stands between me and it.

Besides, I don't need to fall to fail. My body already fails me every day. I'm weak. Damaged.

Why worry about falling when I'm dying anyway?

I swallow, throat tight and thick with the threat of tears. Everything spins as I rub my head, and my knees shake with each step. 'I can do this,' I wheeze.

Alone, what chance do you stand? A small voice in the back of my skull.

None at all.

I might as well give in.

I might as well throw myself on the ground and cry. It's not like I'm going to succeed anyway.

It feels like an age before I reach the next arch. I stagger as I pass under its shadow.

See how slowly you go? How hopeless this is? Why bother? You'll never succeed.

It's right. *I'm* right.

But my brother. I can't let him come here. I need to stop him – to save him.

My legs steady. Teeth gritted, I push on – and every step truly is a push, like there's an invisible weight on each thigh.

Of course you're right. You poor thing. You were never meant to succeed.

I ignore the thought. Try to. But it's persuasive, especially as a truth I've always known threads through it.

I wasn't made for this.

Oh, child. It isn't you. He didn't even tell you, did he?

'Tell me?'

No one has ever made it through the labyrinth. And every other sup-plicant was fae. As a human, what chance do you stand?

I stop. 'No one?'

No one.

I let out a broken laugh, half-hysterical. What a fool. To think I could win. Such pride. Such foolish, foolish pride.

My knees hit solid stone.

I'm trapped here. For ever.

Vision blurring, I stare at the next gate.

It's miles away. Or might as well be.

I crawl, the weight of despair full upon me. With each shuffle of my knees over rock, the sun gets lower.

Somehow, I make it to the next arch. Its bleak black rock towers over me. Passing through it feels impossible.

Arms shaking, heart heavy, I crawl beneath its shadow.

I'm dying. Does it matter how it happens? Or when or where?

Why am I bothering with this?

With anything?

I should just lie here and let it come.

So I do.

The cold ground bites into my cheek, my chest, my thighs. I stare across the endless chasm.

The sun dips out of view, casting darkness upon me. I can't bring myself to care. I barely shiver at the creeping cold of the closing dusk.

Overhead, a raven's caw splits the air.

I don't turn to check which one it is. I just watch the sun setting upon the labyrinth and upon me.

I have these few minutes and then just one day left.

It would be impossible, even if I had a year.

50

I LAND ON my bed in the fortress. My tears soak into its sheets as I stare into the inevitability of my own failure.

Now I'm out of the labyrinth, though, I can pick myself up. Everything was too heavy to manage that before. I curl up, back to the headboard, and hug myself for a good, long while, before I drag myself to the bathroom. Half-heartedly, I bathe and dress.

A summons arrives. Breakfast with the king. In the dining hall.

I go. I find him sat alone at one end of the table, another place setting at his side. Remembering politeness, I smile. It's tremulous.

Nothing feels as bad as it did in the labyrinth, but I still can't shake the feeling that this whole endeavour is doomed.

Drystan pulls out my chair before resuming his seat, and food appears not long after. I pick at it, trying to persuade myself that eating isn't pointless.

The feeling has to be a challenge. I've never felt so hopeless in my life as I did passing through those gates, and with each one it grew worse.

But even if it's *only* a feeling and not even a real one at that, it brought me to my knees. How can I overcome that?

'I know you're annoyed at me about my little . . . distraction, but are you going to give me silence for ever?'

'What?' I blink up from the potato I've been pushing around my plate for untold minutes. 'Oh. No.' I shrug.

'I need you to understand. My brothers are not . . . well, our relationship isn't the same as the one you share with your brother. None of them would try to cross between worlds to save me, for one thing. And if one of them were to get killed by one of our monstrous kin, that would be a cause for celebration. I've tried to use the mirror to stop your brother, but he's too set on reaching you. I cannot control the actions of mortals – not when their will is this strong.'

I dimly register that he's explaining himself to me without prompting. Maybe another night that would feel like a victory. But not tonight.

'Look. Annon. *Avellan*. I don't want you to leave. I told you I wasn't a good man and I don't care to be – I will do whatever's required to keep you here. Because I – I genuinely believe your life will be better.'

Nodding, I spear the potato and rub it into some congealed butter. 'Right.'

'What?' He chuckles. 'No witty retort?' He leans in, nudging me with his elbow. 'No cheerful reassurance that you're going to escape despite my best efforts?'

My fork clangs into my plate. Because I'm tired. I'm so fucking tired. Of smiling when I don't mean it. Of reassuring others. Of being on and ready at every damn moment. My head snaps around and I finally meet his gaze. 'What if I don't feel cheerful, Drystan? What then? Am I no longer valuable? No longer useful?'

He flinches. 'What?' He reaches across the table, hand stopping short of mine. 'That's not what I . . . I don't . . .'

'What if I just pretend to be cheerful all the time for everyone else's sake? Does that make me less interesting to you? Do you not want to take me back to your bed or have me as your wife if I'm not a cheery little beam of sunshine?' My voice wavers, though I try to keep it together. 'Does it make you feel bad that I feel like shit? That my wrists and knees hurt, that my legs ache, that my chest feels tight and I'm always waiting for my heartbeat to tick-tick-tick slower? Is it better for you if I smile and pretend none of that is true?'

He sits back, eyebrows peaking. 'You've reached the Gauntlet of Despair. Of course.' He presses his lips together, a contrite look on his face as he examines his hand spread on the table. 'You wanted to give up today, didn't you? That's what the gauntlet is designed to do. To make you give in. It's just the gauntlet making you feel this way.'

I slump back in my seat, part of me horrified at what I've spilled out, the rest of me too tired to care. 'Is it?'

'Perhaps not all of it.'

Silence yawns between us. I'm not sure what was me and what was the gauntlet. And I'm not sure if any of it was inaccurate.

'Is it true?' I ask after a long while. 'Has no one ever made it through the labyrinth?'

He sighs, gaze sinking to the table. 'It's true. None have ever succeeded, even after taking the shortcut to the final challenge.'

My gods. What is the final challenge? Something that's beaten every single fae who's tried. What chance do I have?

An aching heaviness drags on my chest, like I've brought part of the Gauntlet of Despair back with me.

After a thoughtful nod, Drystan stands. 'Right. Come on.'

It's only when he pauses at the doorway that I drag myself after him.

Asti and another of the Twylth step from their stations and go to follow us, but Drystan stills them with a look. 'This is for us alone.'

As he leads me through Rigor Gard's corridors, he mutters, 'It must be bad if you're not asking where we're going.'

We reach the stables where he waves off help from anyone else and saddles my horse. Asti told me that after Threnn, Drystan had instructed her to let no one else fasten my saddle when she took me out riding, in case they didn't tighten the girth enough. His attentiveness is almost touching, but I'm curling in over my crossed arms, thoughts knotting because I've shared too much, and worse still, I've complained.

He lifts me on to the horse, readies his own steed and we ride out in silence.

I'm faintly surprised when instead of staying within the fortress walls, he takes us out the main gate and along the causeway, down to the featureless plains of Mordren. But the deepening night quickly distracts me with the knowledge that only one day remains in the labyrinth.

One day left to reach Lowen.

Since my vision, I keep having the same nightmare. I'm at the frozen river. Standing on it. Ice creaking. Beneath, the dead scratch and writhe, desperately trying to break through. They all have Lowen's face. The ice cracks, and I fall through, waking sweaty and tangled in the blankets.

It's not real and yet it feels like a threat of what's to come.

As I ride with Drystan, I glance back to the fortress. This is the furthest I've been since he took me to see the dangers of the Underworld. On the walls, small figures keep watch, lit only by the moon and stars.

I spend the rest of the ride staring into the snowy distance as everything inside me churns, only looking up when he announces, 'We're here.'

Tucked against a rocky outcrop is a semi-ruined cottage. The roof and walls are mostly intact, but the door looks ready to fall off its hinges and its windows are cracked and empty, save for tattered curtains.

The back of my nose stings. It reminds me of home. A similar size, though it looks older, and this place is only one storey. But it *feels* like our cottage. There's the crumbled remains of a wall encircling it, and we walk over fractured stones that were once a path to its entrance. Icicles hang from what were once vigorous plants, including something that climbs over the windows and would've made this a pretty home.

Drystan pushes the door open with an almighty creak, but somehow it stays on its hinges. Old furniture and cobwebs greet us, as well as dried herbs nestling in the roof and a table set for two. A tall cupboard stands empty, its door hanging open. There's the scent of life here, too – old perfume, the smoke from a fireplace that was once well used, dead flowers in a sky-blue vase. I even fancy I catch the familiar warming smell of bread baked long ago, trapped in the oven.

'What is this place?'

'It used to be someone's home. Now . . .' He spreads his hands. 'You see what it is now. When it became clear winter wasn't ending anytime soon, most of my people sought refuge in Rigor Gard. Not the woman who lived here, though. She refused to leave, sure she could make it through the cold.'

'Let me guess. Her stubbornness killed her, and you've brought me here to teach me that lesson?'

'No, actually.' He turns with a half-smile, but it's more apologetic than mocking. 'When the river froze and the dead ventured across, growing wilder and more dangerous, some consumed by unseelie creatures, that's when she left. She escaped with her life, but not her belongings.' With his fingertips, he caresses a plate left on the table like it's ready for dinner to come from the oven. 'But I didn't bring you here for any reason to do with her. I brought you here so we could be alone, and so you could do something other than being cheerful – or beating yourself up for not faking it.'

I screw my face up at him, not really sure how to do what he's asking. 'I'm sure I've snapped at you enough times already.'

'Hmm, but it's usually playful – more entertaining than hurtful. It still feels like a veneer over what you're really feeling. And I think the odd moments you've told me how much of a dick I'm being don't really outweigh everything else. Show another emotion. You wear cheer for everyone else. What's beneath that? What does Annon feel?'

I swallow, only realizing I've backed away when my hip bumps a threadbare armchair by the fireplace. He asks his questions softly, but there's a threat in them. 'I don't . . .' I shake my head.

'Of course you don't.' He sighs, giving me a sad smile like I'm a hopeless case. 'I'll show you.' With a sweep of his hand, he indicates one of the dining chairs. 'Threnn. I'm still so fucking furious he frightened you.' His fist crashes down on to the back of the chair, sending splinters flying. 'He got you alone. That never should have happened.' Another smash and the chair is no longer a chair but bits of wood clattering to the floor. He takes one of the broken legs. 'See? Name something you're hurt or angry about, then . . .' He makes a hammering motion with the chair leg before handing it to me. 'Now it's your turn.'

I eye the chair leg. 'This feels a bit ridiculous. What's it going to fix?'

'Nothing.' He shrugs. 'The point of it is to turn your feelings outward so they're not all inside, hurting you.'

He seems convinced. I suppose I can play along. Maybe it's to ease his guilt over distracting me in his garden for so long.

'I'm pissed off that you tricked me with your garden.' I bring the chair leg down on the table.

A plate smashes. Cutlery spins away, landing in the corner. It's surprisingly satisfying.

'I hate that you're trying to keep me here against my will.' Another smash, another plate becomes shards. This time, a fork pings up, hitting the ceiling before crashing down into the shattered crockery. I smile. Not a forced smile for someone else. Real. For my own satisfaction.

He nods at the ruined table and clears his throat. 'Just so you know . . . they don't all have to be things related to me. It just so happened my most recent examples revolved around you.'

The hot thing inside me stirs beneath the ashes where I've kept it buried. 'I could probably trash an entire table just for you, Drystan.' I flash him what feels like a dangerous smile. I don't think I've ever worn one of those before. It feels strange. Strong. Something that's done to please me instead of someone else.

I name another half dozen things he's done to irritate me and destroy everything sitting upon the table. 'Maybe an entire cottage.' My gaze snaps to him before I turn my attention to another chair – my chair leg is looking a bit splintered by this point and I'm sure it's going to disintegrate in a few more strikes.

I close my fingers around the chair back, its elegant lines reminding me of – 'Phaedra. I'm annoyed at how unrelentingly cruel she is.' I bring the chair down on the stone floor. It smashes into pieces. 'And the village girl who pushed me over and I cut my hand so badly, they thought I might lose it.' I toss the chair's back against the wall where its dried-out husk explodes.

Now my hand's empty, the scar stands out pale against my olive skin. From palm to wrist – that's the original cut. But a twisted line comes off it where the village doctor had to cut out an infection.

Annem stood over my bed, wringing her hands as the cold compresses failed to bring down my temperature. 'I told you. You've wished her away. Our little girl will be taken by the Dark Lady.'

At the time, I was half feverish and not quite sure what was real, so I never thought too deeply about my mother's words. But now . . .

I snatch myself away from the memory and find Drystan scowling at the scar. It isn't a pitying look he wears, thank gods, but one of simmering anger, like he wants to smash another chair.

But I'm not done.

Because although I shy away from thinking too closely about my mother's words or the bargain my father made, I have more to be angry about.

'Being tired.' I go to push over the table. 'No, wait. Being tired *all the fucking time.*' The table goes. 'I bore myself with it. The pain in my joints.' I kick over a chair, laughing wildly at the irony of my hips hurting as I do so. 'The way my heart betrays me.' The final chair shatters and I search for the next thing to break, pulse thrumming with exertion.

The vase. It sits on the side board. Sky-blue ceramic painted with daisies. Such a pretty thing.

I pick it up, its delicacy visceral in my palms.

'Being ill.'

I bring it down with a roar. The crash mingles with my shout. Pieces fly everywhere. And it finally feels like the world understands something of what's in my heart – the suffering and fear I keep locked inside.

It's the first time I've said any of this out loud. In this cottage, I don't have to worry about hurting anyone.

'It taking my freedom. My friends. My life.'

The hot thing inside me breaks free of the cold ash. I let it burn me. I let it take me.

The air cracks with the sounds of destruction, filled with shards and splinters, the tear of curtains, the smash of windows. My throat tears from raging. My body complains, but I don't listen.

'No diagnosis. No cure. And I tried and tried all these years to find something . . . and they burned my work anyway.'

The hot thing takes over completely and I become a savage ball of destruction, body barely able to keep up with all the things I want to break.

And I want to break it all.

I rage. I scream. I grab and tear and claw at anything I can get my hands on. I forget myself and find myself all at once.

And when there's nothing left to break I stand there, breathless, hoarse.

Sure there's nothing else, I'm left staring at the fireplace with its pretty floral plaque above the mantelpiece. Lavender, I think. Like in our garden. The hearth is empty. Not even ash remains, but I see the charred remains of my notebook – it's seared in my mind. 'They burned it all anyway.'

My knees crumple at the same moment my face does. He catches me. Of course he catches me. 'They burned it all.' I bury my face in his arm, clinging to it, and I weep.

I don't just weep, I sob. It's deep. It's ugly. It hurts. But it's a release. And for once I don't try to dam it and I don't care that someone else can see.

He has me. He holds me. He lets me lay bare all the broken things inside.

I don't know how long we stay there, tangled together. I just know that my sobs fade and I come to realize I'm sitting across his lap, clinging to his arm like it's going to save me from a flood.

My breaths ease from shuddering to calm as he strokes my back, though I still give the occasional hiccough. Eventually, I lift my face from his arm and grimace at the wet patches I've left. 'Sorry about your shirt,' I whisper with a watery grin.

'Don't do that.' Before I can ask what, he smooths away the hair stuck to my wet cheeks. 'Deflect. Pretend all that didn't happen. Go right back to cheerfully denying all your feelings. We don't have to talk about them, but don't pretend.'

I take a breath to say sorry.

'And don't apologize.'

I laugh, which becomes more tears, and he cradles me against him. It's easy to let go when he holds me like this. Like I don't have to worry about anything, not even sitting upright.

'I have you, *Avellan*,' he murmurs against the crown of my head.

When my tears settle once more, I don't lift my head and look at him. That might make it easier to stay in this state of speaking rather than locking up or deflecting.

I'm angry at my mystery sickness, yes, no surprise there, but my parents? That feeling is a strange, hot coal in my chest. One I turn over and over.

Life at home has been suffocating for some years now. Annem is always there, keeping an eye on me. But does she need to be? I've survived in Drystan's fortress without someone always on watch in case I drop dead.

Asti and Drystan have both protected me in the Underworld and Min takes care of me, but I've never felt suffocated in the same way.

Of course, my parents have spent my life protecting me from The Morrigan and her bargain. But they've also been keeping me from what little life I could have.

The labyrinth has been tough, but it's shown I have more strength than I realized. I could walk from our cottage to the woods and enjoy their shade in the height of summer. I could walk down to the village and beg a ride back from one of Lowen's friends. I'm not too proud for that. I might not be able to do all I once could, but I can see a bit of the world beyond our garden walls.

I can live rather than sitting atop my cliff, longing.

And yet . . .

'At least with my family, I know there will be someone there. They care about me. Love me.'

Although, things in the Underworld aren't the same as when I made my deal with Drystan. I'm not alone.

He hums a soft acknowledgement and I think that nudge is him nodding against my crown. 'Of course they do. Who could fail to love you?'

It's a pregnant question, even if it's only hypothetical.

But there's still a cold knot inside me. 'Drystan?' He answers by stroking my back, and I press into him. 'I'm afraid.' It's a whispered confession I barely dare to voice.

He says nothing, just keeps this quiet space safe.

'My illness . . . I know it's coming for me, even if I feel a bit better for now. I'm still . . .' My eyes burn as I try to breathe past the terror that saying this out loud will make it come true. 'I'm afraid I'll die alone.'

His hold tightens, strengthens, like his arms are fortress walls and I'm the precious thing they're keeping safe. '*Avellan*,' he sighs.

I nod, waiting for him to admonish me for fearing him or tell me that death is natural and must come for all. Even little nothing humans, however pretty the nickname may sound in their old tongue.

'Do you think Death would let that happen to you?'

I frown in his hold. 'But he—'

'*I*.'

A single word. A single letter.

A tear through the fabric of everything I thought I knew about him. About life. About Death.

Through the tear, the remaining lines of the rhyme find me.

Death upon the water.

Death upon the land.

When your Death comes calling

The Raven King will take your hand.

I always thought it meant Death would come for me, not . . .

'I am the god of death, *Avellan*. And I wouldn't let you die alone. Not ever.' His voice rumbles through me, in my flesh, my bones, a promise that doesn't vanquish my fear entirely, but leaves a crack in it – makes it conquerable, so I can take this moment of peace.

Death holds me tight, and I find myself not wanting to escape.

We sit there a while longer. Me and Death. I have no concept of time, I only know it's dark outside and something sweet dusts the air.

Eyes sore, I lift my head, blinking at the white blur at the window. It resolves into clusters of star-shaped flowers. 'I didn't notice the jasmine was flowering when we arrived.'

'It wasn't.' He sits back and follows my gaze. 'It blooms for you.'

Sure enough, as I watch, it grows through the window, buds forming, unfurling, spreading their heady scent.

I enjoy it until my eyelids droop.

'Come on.' Somehow, he manages to stand and lift me, all the while keeping me clear of the debris on the floor. 'Let's get you home.'

Home. Not the cottage. The fortress. Yet somehow thinking of that cold place feels as warm as his arms coming around me.

As he carries me from the cottage, my thoughts drift, aimless in their exhaustion. I can't help thinking how he's acted against me, but only in the labyrinth. We seem to have reached a strange kind of alliance outside of it, where he guards the secret of my illness and runs me baths that smell as sweet as this night. Maybe he isn't so different from my parents – they were trying to keep me home, and he's trying to keep me here.

Yet as he places me on his horse and mounts behind me, I register something. He didn't need to help me tonight – that does nothing to prevent me escaping.

There's a far simpler explanation. Old as he is. Old as all the tales I was read as a child.

He has feelings for me. I'm not delusional enough to call it love. But something on the way to it.

And I have feelings for him too, even if I shouldn't.

This is messy, isn't it?

Especially as, if I can get past the Gauntlet of Despair, and somehow beat the final challenge, I'll be watching tomorrow's sunset over the sea, back on the surface where I belong.

The perfect kind of bittersweet ending to one of those old tales.

For tonight, though, I'm here. And in his arms, I know one thing.

I feel more at peace than I ever have before.

51

BACK AT THE fortress, I sleep in Drystan's bed, in his arms, for a good long while. It isn't the kind of sleep that locks me in because I'm so exhausted, it's something gentler than that. When I wake, he runs me a bath and joins me in it, making love to me in the slippery suds.

But he's the king and has business to attend to, marked by a message from Lord Mastelle. Whatever is in the note makes Drystan scowl and leave with heavy feet like he doesn't want to go anywhere.

His suite isn't the same without him, and the clock strikes five, reminding me that I have one more day in the labyrinth to get ready for, so I head back to my room. The longer I'm without company, the more the image of that walkway under those heavy arches weighs on my mind.

I need to find a way to get through them or all this will have been for nothing. Risking my life. Risking Min's.

I'm frowning as I enter my room and find her waiting for me. 'There you are! I was worried I'd missed you.' Her warm embrace is welcome. 'I'm going to visit Asti, and I was hoping you'd give me a second opinion.' She gives me a twirl, skirts flowing, hair swinging.

Despite the echoes of despair chiming in my heart, I can't help smiling. 'The fact you want a second opinion on your appearance when you're the royal sartor is adorable. You look gorgeous and you know it. Besides, even if you don't, Asti knows it.' I wink and bump my shoulder to hers.

'It's just . . . I think I . . .' She takes a long breath, rubbing her chest. Her cheeks flush. 'I'm going to tell her tonight how I feel and . . . What if she doesn't—?'

'She does. I've seen how she looks at you. It's the same way you look at her.'

Her eyebrows peak and she throws her arms around me. 'Thank you. I'm not sure how I earned such a kind friend, but I'm grateful I have.' She holds me at arm's length and a frown spoils the look of joy she wore moments ago. 'Are you ready?'

There's no doubting what she means. My last day in the labyrinth.

I go to say yes. To reassure her that everything's fine. But the image of the ruined cottage flares in my mind, reminding me of how good it felt to let myself express something other than cheer.

'No.' I sigh, head hanging. 'Not at all.'

'That sounds like you need to tell me all about it.' She glances at the window. 'We have time.'

We sit by the fire and eat supper while I explain the trial by despair that brought me to my knees. She listens with crinkled brow and hand on her chest.

'That sounds . . . like a hardship I wouldn't wish on my worst enemy. But giving up? Losing hope? That isn't the kind of person you are. It has to be some powerful magic to make you falter.'

'They were things I've thought before, all of them.' I frown at the fire, nibbling on a handful of almonds. And yet . . . 'You're right. I don't feel that way now I'm away from those arches. Nothing seems quite as bleak.'

'Good. Because it isn't.' She slips from her armchair and kneels at my feet, taking my hands in hers. 'You are kind. You are clever. And you have strengths I don't think even you realize. You *will* get through this. You *will* get home.'

My sore eyes water all over again, but I don't want to cry any more. Enough. 'Thank you. You should get to Asti.'

'Not yet. I'll help you get ready.' She rises, chin wavering. 'It's your last time after all.'

In silence, we pack my bag and pull out practical clothing. She helps me change and braids my hair, then stands back, hands on my shoulders, looking me over like I'm one of her creations about to go out into the world and be worn for the first time. 'You look ready and that's half the battle. Rhiannon Archer. My friend who would've been the future queen. And a damn good one at that.'

I narrow my eyes at the points of her ears. 'Are these fake? I thought fae couldn't lie.'

'It's no lie. We need a little kindness. Some life and colour. A person willing to bend old rules if not break them outright. And most of all, we need hope. You are all those things, and that's why, if anyone can get through the labyrinth and get out of here, it's you.' Lip wobbling, she pulls me into another hug – this one squeezes the air from my lungs. 'I'm going to miss you, Annon.'

That's when it hits me.

I'm not just going home, I'm losing all this. Her, Asti, Drystan, the cat. Even Kishel's lessons, his playful coaxing. I've been so focused on escape, I've missed what I have here.

My throat tightens. 'And I'll miss you. Becoming your friend has been an honour.'

She pulls back, her face tear-streaked, though she wears a tremulous smile. She tucks my hair behind my ear, giving a small, determined nod. 'The honour is all mine. It's been a privilege and a pleasure to know you, Rhiannon Archer. And though I selfishly want to keep you here, I also want to see you happy. Show that labyrinth who you are. You've gone through worse than its whispers. *You'll* be the one to break *it*.'

Swallowing, she turns and strides from the room.

As I watch the door click shut, fighting yet more tears, I catch the sweet scent of jasmine. In the mirror, I spot Min's last gift to me.

Tucked behind my ear is a single jasmine flower. White and blooming.

I wonder how she snuck it there, but the world fragments and I spill through it, thoughts scattering on the wind.

52

THE INSTANT I land in the labyrinth, despair smothers me, a heaviness upon my skin. A thickness in my lungs, like hot, damp air.

I brace for it, but I still waver on my feet.

Nodding, I remind myself. I'm strong.

You are weak. It's a whisper in my own voice. It speaks with the same certainty I have when I say I'm dying. It knows.

It's the labyrinth. It doesn't know the truth. It only knows my fears.

I plant one foot in front of the other. And again.

I can do this.

You can't.

Each step is a battle. Each movement makes my muscles ache like I'm pushing a boulder up a hill and not my body a single step forward.

I just need to keep going. That one simple thing.

Simple. And yet impossible. I hear the smile in that voice that is mine and yet not. I have never sounded so cruel.

He confirmed it. It turns singsong, mocking. *No one has made it through the labyrinth. No one.*

Then I'll be the first.

The only reply is laughter.

I don't know how long I've been here. It feels like years. Time seems strange, like a current I'm battling against rather than the normal ticking of seconds.

Sweat beads on my lip and gathers beneath my shirt, but I don't dare expend the energy to lift the waterskin hanging at my waist. Dimly, I notice that there's less corruption here, as though it's climbing up the gauntlet slowly.

The sky above and the chasm below spin. I try to keep to the centre of the walkway but walking is effort enough. My heart tolls, heavy and slow – an episode or just the strange effect of time here?

Another archway looms ahead.

Not much further. I can make it through.

And what then? Seven archways for seven brothers. Seven depths for you to fall into, little human. Seven hells and seven deaths.

The words echo through me, a horrible truth ringing through them – one I don't understand but *believe.*

I whimper. Stumble. Reach for something to steady me, but there's nothing and no one left.

You will fall. You will fail. And when you do, I will be right here to crush your bones to dust.

I have to keep going.

Do you? This time the voice isn't cruel, just curious. *Wouldn't it be easier, kinder to just . . . not?*

I try to take another step. I can't. It's too much. This weight is too heavy on my shoulders. My muscles groan, my joints ache.

Why not lie down in my sweet earth, child?

Why not?

I only want you to lie down. To rest. To leave striving to the strong.

Its lulling words slide over each other, hissing in my ears. *You'll only hurt yourself. Break yourself more.*

My head dips. My pulse pounds in rhythm with the voice. My body resonates with its words.

'It's so hard,' I say, plaintive.

It is. So, so hard. You can't do it. Come rest in my sweet earth.

I try to take a step and stumble. On my knees, I blink at the walkway ahead. Between the rock is soil, rich and dark. I want to press my fingers into it, feel its softness, give up on hard things. I can't do them anyway.

Happiness isn't meant for you. Only struggle. You're bound to The Morrigan, girl. What happiness has the Lady of War and Death ever brought anyone? Better you look for strife.

The archway is still so far away, and I can see there's another beyond it. It's impossible. I can't.

Some part of me cries out that I must, but its voice is very small and so far away.

I manage half a crawling pace forward. The hewn obsidian cuts my knee. A dull throb. Slick warmth. It doesn't matter.

Give in.

It sounds easy. Simple. A final answer to a question I've been asking for too long.

I lie down. There's cool, soft earth under my cheek and stone for my bed.

How silly I've been. Thinking I could do this where no fae has ever made it through. Me, a human.

Thinking hope would be enough.

I drag in a deep breath, not caring if it's my last.

It's sweet. Heady. *If anyone can get through the last challenges of the labyrinth and get out of here, it's you.* Min's voice. Her fierce kindness is a small spark of warmth, bright against the frigid black rock.

Show that labyrinth who you are. You've gone through worse than its whispers.

I remember her hug, the strength of it, the belief in it.

Another breath, floral and redolent of Drystan's arms around me as we sit in the wreckage of that cottage, my fears closing in. *I wouldn't let that happen to you. Not ever.* The ferocity of his voice says I'm safe. Cherished.

Maybe even loved.

I fancy I can feel them both, bright threads buried in my chest that not even despair can sever.

I inhale again, eyelids fluttering closed at the familiar scent. Bathing with Drystan, his touch upon me, within me, his whispered prayers against my skin. Riding with Asti and Min, noting the trees budding, laughing as Asti tells a filthy joke. Sitting in the sun, my hands in the earth as I sow peas in our cottage garden. Teasing Lowen as I cut his hair, asking who he wants to make himself pretty for.

Little happy moments kindle in my chest, each one another thread to another person. Thoughtful, patient Kishel who never gave up on me. The Collector who died for me to get here.

A tear trickles across the bridge of my nose and plops into the soil.

They're my moments. My people. Happiness that *is* meant for me.

I feel it. I know it.

The air thins as though the thickness can't compete with the sweet scent surrounding me. Another breath, and I can sit up, though it's hard, like the Underworld is trying to keep hold of me.

A flash of green catches my eye, utterly out of place in the labyrinth's obsidian.

The jasmine flower Min tucked behind my ear. It's crushed into the patch of soil that formed my pillow.

From its green stalk, a tiny sprout grows.

Warmth surges in my chest. An answer. If this plant can grow here in nothing, then I can go on.

No. You can't.

But I barely hear the voice – I'm too busy watching the seedling. It isn't done. Tendrils spread in all directions, one questing towards my hand. Green threads along the edges of the obsidian paving, and when its cool, damp touch reaches me, it is everything.

Flesh to flesh. Sap to blood. It has a beat, a flow of its own. Not quite a pulse, but close.

A little miracle.

There are no miracles.

Shaking, I push myself to my knees.

Leaves unfurl. Buds form. Branches twist towards the next arch and around my thighs.

Its growth is swift, streaking across the ground. It spreads.

I spread.

And when we reach the arch, I spread my fingers, spread my branches.

You can't.

But I can.

I have to save my brother from my silence, from himself.

Stone cracks. Shrieks. Shards break off, pushed apart by the inching, soft growth of a simple plant.

Obsidian's sharp edges slice into us, our delicate flesh, but we grow back, two new stalks taking the place of one that breaks. We find the nooks, the cracks, the little points of weakness barely the breadth of a hair. And we press with the endless patience of things that grow.

The arch splinters, and I stand.

The moment I reach my feet, white flowers open, little stars that smell like summer and hope, like the sun on my face and a garden by the sea. Their blooming path races along each tendril, eclipsing the black rock.

As I take a step, the vines around my legs loosen, letting me move, their cool touch just a reminder, a connection. A held hand in the midst of an oppressive crowd.

Cracks race over the walkway. It shakes, threatening to crumble underfoot.

I encircle it, branches rambling, binding, able to walk on as more shoot ahead.

You will not overcome. You will not pass.

The voice gets louder the closer I get to the arch.

But I am life and this place is death. And although death might win one day, this is not that day.

The jasmine and I move as one. Onward. More powerful together than we could ever be alone. We crush the next arch with barely a thought. Vines triumph over stone.

With the setting sun on my back, the final arch splinters, leaving only a dark doorway before me.

53

THROUGH THE DOORWAY is a huge square, sized for something much larger than mortals. Overhead looms the final gate. I can barely see its top. Carved in obsidian, it looks like shadows made solid.

And I'm standing at its foot.

Through dangers, death and despair, I have fought my way here.

The Collector should be at my side. What would they have wanted to do? Could they have come to the surface with me?

I swallow and rub my chest, the threads of connection still bright inside.

'We did it,' I whisper and hope, somewhere in the Underworld or the Next Place, they can hear me. 'Thank you.'

I stare at the gate so long it's burned into my eyes. Statues flank it – a huge obsidian dragon on one side, a rearing horse its match on the other. At a smaller scale, in a pair of alcoves, stand two human-oid statues, one in armour, the other in a robe, their arms crossed.

'Congratulations,' a familiar voice sounds behind me.

I draw a breath and brace for an argument before turning.

Drystan stands tall and sombre, his black hair and outfit at one with the labyrinth. Somehow, he looks paler than usual. The corners of his mouth rise, but the rest of his face remains utterly still. 'You've come so far, but I can't—'

Stone grinds.

I spin on my heel.

The robed statue steps down from its alcove. 'Your Majesty,' he says in a deep, scraping voice as he approaches.

Drystan stands there, regal and expectant. 'Strife.'

Within the statue's shadowy cowl, late-afternoon sunlight catches on a handsome, cruel face – hard lines, chiselled lips, a cleft chin. The name Strife suits him. He bows with the sound of rock chips pouring down a mountainside. 'You are here about the presence within the labyrinth. His influence has not yet reached this tier.' He inclines his head. 'I fear it is but a matter of time.'

I drag in a breath as I realize. 'The presence? You mean the corruption? What do you know about it?'

Strife eyes me, mouth flat, before cocking his head at Drystan in askance.

'Answer her.' Drystan's jaw ripples.

'As Your Majesty wishes . . . I will answer the *human*.' His nostrils flare as he turns his attention to me. 'A fragment of something arrived here years ago – a seed upon the breeze. But not an entity of life. A maelstrom. He remained dormant, seething in his own wildfire. But when he got your scent – a taste of potential, perhaps, or an outlet for his rage – he rose from his slumber and began to spread.'

Drystan cocks his head. ' "He"?'

'He speaks sometimes. Calls to me and the others who reside within the labyrinth's walls. Calls us to him. I ignore him. Not all do.'

'The Devourer,' I murmur. Their attention snaps to me. 'It was . . . corrupted. Like the thing had infected it.'

'Hmm.' Strife nods slowly.

'And this ... *presence* wishes to harm Annon.' Drystan's lips flatten. 'The first person to attempt the labyrinth in centuries.'

'He appears to have been waiting for some unwary soul to set foot in here.'

'This is a matter I will attend to.' Drystan lifts his chin, the matter dismissed. 'For now, however, she has reached the final challenge.'

'So she has.' Strife speaks slowly, taking me in. 'The first supplicant in centuries. The first human supplicant *ever*.'

'I forbid you from opening the gates for her.'

'What?' I stare at Drystan.

He makes no reaction.

Strife bows his head. 'I am loyal to the end of time, Your Majesty. But you know I cannot end a trial on your whim. You may pass through with her, and I will keep the way open for your return, but that is all.'

Drystan's neck cords, and between us, his hand fists.

Strife turns to me and with a carved hand indicates the giant gates. 'The way lies before you. One gateway, but many paths.' As he speaks, light flickers on their stone surface like shadow and sun on the sea. 'One path leads you home. One to failure. And one to death.'

I see it. Each one.

Our cottage under a cloudy sky. Me, tucked up by the fire. Lowen smiling as he sketches at my side. Annem and Pa repairing nets while we sing one of his sea shanties. It's warm. Familiar. Painful.

Drystan's fortress clad in night. I sit upon the consort's throne, at his side, a crown upon my head. I'm smiling like my heart might burst with happiness. The corner of his mouth curls subtly, pressing a dimple into his cheek. The cat is at my feet. Asti guards us. Min and Kishel stand at my side. It's clear – *so clear*. Unexpected. Aching.

And then oblivion. Me alone. Suffocating in nothingness. Dying. My knees tremble. I can't face that. Anything but that.

'I will open one path for you, but only one.' The images continue to cycle through as Strife explains. 'All you must do is answer but a single, simple question. Surely that's something even a mortal can manage.' His fingertips clink against a ring of keys hanging from his belt.

I swallow back my fear at the image of oblivion and tear my attention from the flickering lights. 'How do I know which path you'll open for me?'

'You don't. I will choose based on your answer to my question.'

'Annon.' Drystan's voice comes out low, torn at the edges. 'No one who's come this far has succeeded. *No one*. Give up and our bargain ends at sunset – you can come home with me.'

Home. That used to be such an easy concept. Now . . .?

Now it's unimportant. I finger Lowen's sketch in my pocket and shake off the thought. 'The others. They ended up trapped here, didn't they?'

'Or dead.' He twirls me to face him, fingers biting into my shoulders like I'm his lifeline. Bending so we're eye to eye, he gives me a slight shake as he speaks slowly. 'I can't save you if he opens the wrong path. You'll die. Alone. That path – it's the one place I can't reach.'

Desperation gleams in his eyes, shadows the creases pinched between his eyebrows.

That look frightens me. Oblivion frightens me. But the idea of staying? That might terrify me more.

But I need to get to Lowen before he does something irreversible. He's risking everything to save me. I owe it to him to do the same.

I swallow, throat thick. Holding Drystan's desperate gaze, I raise my voice: 'Ask your question.'

Shoulders sinking, nostrils flaring, he bows his head and releases me.

Strife strokes his keys, striking discordant metallic notes from them. 'Supplicant, which desire is it that burns brightest in your heart?'

Not a question I expected. But then, I should've learned by now – the unseelie are nothing if not surprising.

Also, this isn't the simple question it once was.

I want a cure. To save my brother. To get back to the safety of my family. To curl up with the cat beside the fire with an interesting book ... with Drystan. To hug Min and Asti. To master Fatework and learn more about my magic.

There are more desires in my heart than there once were. And not all of them compatible.

I turn the wishes over and over, like they're gems and I can find a facet that will tell me which one I want most.

The solution doesn't lie in my answer, though. My desires won't tell me why everyone else has failed this final challenge and therefore how I can succeed.

There must be some way I can work this out. It's a mental puzzle, and compared to all the physical hardships of this place, that's my strong suit.

There has to be something the previous supplicants have all done wrong. *Or* they've each made different mistakes. Not comforting.

It doesn't help that I know little to nothing about them. Only that they failed. None passed the obscure test in Strife's question. That's all I've got.

The first human supplicant.

They were all unseelie.

At my side, Drystan paces, his movements clipped, tight. 'Just ... just come home.'

All fae.

Every single one of them had a limitation that I do not.

Surely it can't be so simple.

My heart thuds in my throat. I open my mouth. Close it.

What if I'm wrong?

Then I'll face the consequences. I've already decided I'm not giving up. The sun is setting. It's this or nothing.

'I have my answer.'

Strife's lips curl, something anticipatory in the gesture. 'Then give it.'

I formulate my lie. The phrasing has to be right to satisfy whatever criteria Strife will measure me against. 'I want to stay in the Underworld for ever. At Drystan's side, as his queen.'

As I say it, my voice catches, because I realize . . .

It's barely a lie.

A few weeks ago, it would've been. But now . . .

The image flickers across the stone gates. In it, look happy. Truly happy.

Drystan has gone stock still.

Strife's head tilts to one side. He hesitates over the ring of keys in his hands.

My pulse is thunder. I squeeze the bottle of dried skullflower in my pocket.

The guardian selects a key and slots it into the final gate. It grinds as he turns it.

A gateway that has never opened to the surface.

The images flickering over the gates slow, casting light over Strife's obsidian eyes. They narrow. He makes a thoughtful sound, a tinge of annoyance serrating it. 'I see. *Clever*.'

Strife. Of course someone with that name isn't going to give people what they want. And yet fae are doomed to answer with the truth.

The huge gates groan open.

Ahead is a view I know, all colour leached out. But otherwise familiar.

I square my shoulders, take a final breath of Underworld air and walk through.

54

SEAGULLS. SALT. SUN.

Along with the sea breeze, they blast me. Things I've only dreamed of for weeks.

Ahead, yellow gorse flowers mark the path to . . .

'Home,' the word comes out on a wavering breath, not quite as warm as I expected.

'Annon.' It's Drystan, behind me. He sounds broken.

His presence tugs on me, and I have to press my palm to my aching chest like that might help.

'It's over. I won.' I can't bring myself to look back at him. The sight might be enough to make me doubt myself. 'You can come and see me to my house, see that I'm safe . . . and we can say good-bye, but . . . this is it. I'm staying here.'

I don't wait for an answer before I cross the stone bridge.

It feels like a dream, my fingertips skimming the gorse's prickles. But, no, I never feel the golden sun quite like this in my dreams.

Ahead, there's apple blossom and a familiar roof. Sunlight flashing off my brother's bedroom window.

Despite my tired legs, I break into a run. It's more of a fast stagger, but . . .

There's a shout from inside the house, then the front door flies open.

'Annon?' Lowen spills out, eyes wide like he's seen the dead rise for the second time in as many months.

'It's me.' I choke on the words and the tears tangling together in my throat. 'I'm home.'

He hurtles through the gate and hugs me. Crushes me. He stinks, unwashed. But he stinks of *him*.

And he's alive. He's safe. Here on the surface where he belongs.

I peel back, grab his hands. 'You have to live. Even if I don't. You don't owe it to me to wait here.'

He stares at me, open mouthed.

'Lowen, you don't owe me your life.'

There. It's out. I can breathe now. I can sob into his shoulder, let him hold me without guilt, because I've been brave enough to speak the truth that I hope will set him free.

'You are a fool, sometimes,' he whispers, voice cracking. His sigh ruffles my hair before he pulls back and cups my cheeks. 'You never held me back, Annon.'

I blink at him.

'I was just afraid to live because I didn't know how to do it without you.'

'I don't—'

Annem and Pa rush from the house, slack-jawed.

Arm around my shoulder, Lowen walks me through the gate. We'll have time to talk. Maybe while I help him pack.

There are more tears as I reach them. During this time apart, I find the anger in me has burned low. They're my parents. Misguided, fallible. Human.

Pa throws his arms wide, eyes brimming. 'My girl. My little girl is home.'

Annem gasps and points at my feet. 'Her gift.'

Or, rather, she points at what's growing around my feet. Seedlings and saplings sprout where I step, trailing behind me in a green wake.

Pa's smile dims. 'You stopped taking your medicine.'

I laugh, shaking my head as I cross the final feet to him, ready to run into his arms like I've done all my life. 'My medicine? I almost ran out, but I didn't—'

Darkness looms over us. 'NO.' Drystan's voice shakes the ground. He grabs Pa's throat and shoves him against the wall.

For a second I stare at my father's face going red against the pale skin of Drystan's hand, at the dark scores in the cottage's stone walls, left there by the dead.

Then my mother's shrieks bring me back to myself. My heart surges.

'Drystan, stop!' As I reach for him, Lowen grabs his arm – or tries to. He's thrown to one side like he's nothing more than a pesky gnat.

'You don't get to hug her and pretend.' Drystan shakes my father until his teeth rattle.

Pa's toes scrabble for purchase, but he's a good few inches off the floor. He grabs at Drystan's wrist, hitting ineffectually. His face goes purple.

'Drystan, please.' My eyes burn. 'Put him down.'

But he doesn't so much as blink. His eyes are fixed on my father, the cold light of fury in them. His whole face creases into a snarl as his knuckles whiten.

I add my weight to Pa's grip, but I don't make the king's arm so much as wobble. 'You're going to kill him.'

He can't be this angry that I'm leaving. And even if he is, it's my choice, not my father's.

Does he think if my family is dead, I'll go back with him?

'Please.' My voice cracks as I drag on his arm, as effective as a teapot made of ice.

'Are you going to tell her the truth?' Somehow he gets the question out between gritted teeth. 'What you've been doing to her all these years. Why she's so exhausted she can barely walk from one end of my fortress to the other?'

I blink from him to my father, grip falling slack as his words hit me. 'What truth? What's he talking about? Pa?'

I glance at Annem, but she's on her knees sobbing the words 'Tell her' over and over. Lowen sits a short distance behind her, cradling his arm, his face a mirror to my own confusion.

Chest heaving, Drystan drops my father, who stumbles against the cottage, clutching his throat. 'Tell her the truth.'

55

'TELL HER.' DRYSTAN'S irresistible command rattles the roof tiles.

Pa's palms flash pale as he raises his weatherworn hands to ward off the King of Death. 'Yes, yes,' he croaks, still catching his breath.

I search Drystan's face, then my father's. Dread unfolds in me, cold and heavy like I'm back in the Gauntlet of Despair. I have to swallow twice before I can whisper, 'Tell her what?'

Pa's shoulders cave in as he rubs his hands over his face as though he's trying to wake from a nightmare.

I feel like I'm at the edge of this cliff. One step will throw me over the edge. So will a good shove.

Only rock and roiling sea wait below.

The past few minutes churn, odd moments coming back over and over.

'What did you mean about my medicine? Why would you think I've stopped taking it? I don't understand.' And not understanding feels dangerous. Knowledge helps. Always. Questions, reading – all these things illuminate, letting me see the way and avoid pitfalls. '*What did you mean?*'

'The plants.' Annem's the one to speak up. 'They grow in your footsteps, at your touch. It's your gift.'

How would she know that? And why doesn't she seem at all surprised by it?

I look at my father in silent question.

He closes his eyes and heaves a sigh so deep it comes from his bones. 'I made that bargain. I want you to know that. *I* did it. It was nothing to do with your mother. And this was my doing too.' Head bowed, he keeps his gaze fixed on the ground and the little creeping plants at my feet.

Meanwhile, it's dread creeping through me.

'We kept you safe, didn't we? In this house. Within these walls. I built them with my own two hands, cut my fingers on the iron wire, made sure it ran under the threshold of the gate, too. I did it to keep you safe.'

Mechanically, I nod. 'To stop The Morrigan and the fae from finding me.' Why does it feel like there's more beneath the surface? A tangled fishing net catching on my heels, ready to drag me down.

Desperation haunts my father's eyes. 'I did it for you. All of it.'

'ENOUGH.' Drystan straightens at my side, anger radiating off him in dark waves. 'Your excuses disgust me. Tell her the truth or I'll throw you into the sea and we'll see if any gods come to save you this time.'

Lips sucked in, tears gathering in his eyes, my father shakes his head.

'COWARD.' Drystan fists his hand in Pa's shirt and snatches him from the ground.

I'm reaching for them, pulse surging with the need to stop one and save the other, when Annem's voice stops everything.

'You aren't ill.'

Silence rings out. Her words buzz in my ears. They don't make sense.

I shake my head, turning to her, though it feels like I move through treacle. 'I don't—'

'You never were.'

An abortive laugh bursts from me as I look at Lowen, thinking he's going to confirm this is a terrible joke. He's too busy staring at Annem, mouth open.

'You kept wanting to go out,' Pa croaks in Drystan's grip.

Nostrils flaring, Drystan drops him to the ground with a look of utter loathing.

'That was fine when you were a girl. But after you started making the flowers grow so well . . .'

Something slithering and awful has hold of my throat. I can't look away from my father's hunched form, but I want to. I want to close my eyes and cover my ears. Whatever he has to say can't be good. Not when he looks so full of shame.

'The second time your vegetables won every prize at the village fair, we realized you were gifted. And if your magic was free, out in the world, then it was only a matter of time before The Lady found you. Human magic comes from the fae, and I'm sure yours is from The Morrigan herself. She would *know*. We tried to keep you in, but you were a teenage girl. Wilful. So sure she wants to dance at the pub and run around the beach with boys.'

A hot flush rushes over my face in sickening contrast with the cold grip tightening on my throat.

'If we couldn't stop you going out, we had to block your magic so they wouldn't be able to sense it.'

My father falls silent.

I tug on my collar, swallow, snatch in a sharp breath. 'How?'

But I think I know the answer.

'Your medicine,' my mother says in this small, broken voice. 'We had a travelling apothecary mix aconite and iron—'

Drystan flinches with a hissing inhale, like the word itself burns him.

Iron.

It poisons fae. Kills them if you use enough.

And aconite. One of the few ways to end an immortal's life.

'Just a little,' Annem goes on with a nervous glance at Drystan. 'Just enough to stop your magic. But it . . . had an effect on you.'

I stare.

It blocks magic. It burns fae. It poisons those with magic in their blood. And I've been taking it for sixteen years.

'You poisoned me.'

'We didn't mean to. It was just—'

'We didn't know.' Pa steps between me and Annem. 'Too much iron will poison anyone – fae, human, with magic or not. We just wanted to make it so they couldn't find you if you left the safety of the walls.'

It makes a horrible kind of sense. No magic, no connection that The Morrigan can follow to find the girl who's been bargained to her son.

My mind is remarkably quiet. Logical. I almost sound normal as I ask, 'And when you found out it was poisoning me?'

Before my father's head bows, I already know the answer. I knew it before I even asked the question.

They didn't stop. They never stopped.

'It was that or keep you locked in the house.'

I round on my mother, pointing at her with a shaking finger. 'And when my body kept me locked in? When I couldn't leave because I was too sick? Did you at least lower the dose? Give me fake pills so I thought I was still taking medicine but my body had a rest? Or did you load me up with iron upon iron upon iron until my body couldn't take it and I could barely walk up the stairs without help?'

Her lips fold. My father steps to the end of my pointing finger, brow clenched.

'You didn't, did you?'

His jaw tightens. 'It was to keep you safe.'

Every word they've spoken is a weight that's been dropped on me. And all the slippery secrets, the words unsaid – they're another weight.

The world reels and I back away. My heart feels like it's going to implode. I stumble backwards until I hit something solid that catches my shoulders and stops me falling.

How could they have done this? All this time? That isn't just a mistake, an accident. It's over half my life.

I can't deal with this. I can't process it. I don't understand it. And I sure as all the seven hells don't want to believe it.

My breaths stutter. I tear the collar of my shirt. I drag in air over and over, but I can't get enough inside my lungs.

'I can't . . . This isn't . . .'

I want to scream as Pa puts his arm around Annem. Lowen rests against the wall, shaking his head over and over.

I want to break down the garden wall with its hidden iron wire again. I want to ruin this cottage that has been my prison for a decade and a half. I want to smash everything that's inside – evidence of a lie I've lived for too long.

I could crack this stack of rock and crumble it to dust.

I could make the earth itself tremble.

The terrible, crushing weight of that feeling terrifies me most of all.

I lock it inside, though the effort makes me tremble.

Tears well up instead of rage, the price for a thousand pinpricks I turn inward.

I thought I was fighting to get home.

But all I've come back to is an illusion.

Heart tangled, every beat of it agony, I turn away and find Drystan waiting.

His face is empty like someone's poured everything out of him.

'Take me home,' I choke out.

For a beat, he stiffens. Then he opens his arms and welcomes me into his darkness.

56

THE JOURNEY'S OBLIVION doesn't bother me, but it helps steady my too-fast breaths. I don't notice where we materialize. I'm locked in my own agony.

I'm only really conscious of anything when he presses a hot cup into my hand and the bitter smell curls into my nostrils. Skull-flower tea.

'Your heart. It's erratic. I've watched you make it before, I know I have the dosage right.'

It's almost funny. He's so careful with the quantity of poisonous tea when my parents have been filling me with iron and aconite for years.

A slow creeping death.

I stare into the fire and drink.

The cup is cold when he takes it from my cradled hands. That's the only concept I have of time.

My mind keeps looping over and over everything they said. It seems like something that isn't real. A passage from a book I keep reading because I can't understand it.

But it burrows under my skin in a way nothing fictional ever has. A barbed thorn that I can't pull out, only work it through to the other side.

I rake my hands through my hair, finding Drystan in the armchair opposite, hand clenched in front of his mouth as he watches me.

'Was that all a lie?'

He blinks, head canting to one side.

'Did you make them say that?' I nod, encouraging, eager to follow this idea, since it's so much better than any other possibility. 'So I'd come back with you.'

'No.' His gaze lowers. 'Though you make me wish I had.'

I spring to my feet. 'It has to be.'

Hands spread, he stands slowly.

'You wanted me to stay here.' I seize on the idea, clinging to it like a lifeline – like my father clinging to The Morrigan's hand in that storm, despite his saviour's bitter cost. 'You tricked me in the labyrinth – I wasted a whole afternoon with you. You did this too. You tricked them . . . controlled them . . . You did it.' Something else tugs on my mind, some other detail aligns with this version of events, but it lies just out of reach.

'*Avellan*, I swear to you on all that I am, I had no part in this, only that I witnessed it.'

He can't lie. Not even a comforting lie. I know it. He knows it.

'No. *Please*. You had to.' My voice breaks and *I* break. 'You had to,' I wheeze between sobs as his arms come around me.

I lose myself there. Try to lose the terrible truth.

But it's a barb working its way through my heart.

I don't know if it's day or night. I just know I'm in Drystan's bed, in his arms. The cat is lying on me purring furiously.

And nothing is the same as the last time I was here.

The conversation in the garden haunts me. Over and over, I replay it. I turn over each word. I try to make it all sink in. It doesn't.

None of it damn well makes sense with the shapes I've already made of my life. None of it fits. It's like being given a boulder and told to make it fit in a wooden puzzle cube.

These things are not the same.

At some point, Drystan gets up. There are soft voices out in the main living area and he returns. I bury myself under the covers and lose track of whether my eyes are open or shut.

Later, he summons me food and drink. I gulp down water, eyes gritty from crying too much. They're so swollen, they barely open. But the water helps my body feel better at least. He tempts me to eat one of the amazing ginger biscuits, but it isn't the same.

Nothing is the same.

The Collector died for a foolish idea I had of home and family. A lie.

The only thing softening the blow is that I got to speak to Lowen. I know they would've wanted that.

It's a pinprick of comfort as I live that whole scene again and again.

I don't know how long it is before I realize the detail that was tugging on my mind. Something Drystan said. The idea solidifying, I curl up against the headboard, hugging the blankets to myself, watching him pour us both coffee.

'How long?'

He stills. My coffee almost brims over. Just in time, he jerks the pot upright. With a long, defeated exhale, he returns it to the bedside table.

'Since the Apothic analysed your medicine.'

I huff out my surprise. 'That long. I expected it to be a secret the labyrinth whispered in your ear or something you heard through the mirror I assume is still in my . . . in the cottage.'

'I have no interest in that place now you're not there.'

'Hm.' I frown at the coffee cups, searching for shapes among the steam. Plumes of it spread and snap, like cut strings on a puppet. I touch my chest, trying not to think about the threads between me and my parents that I thought were so unbreakable. I felt them when I broke the Gauntlet of Despair's arches.

I feel nothing now. Just tired.

'When I discovered the ingredients, I suspected the medicine was blocking your magic, but I didn't realize that was the reason your parents had given it to you. Despite my anger at you being fed poison, I thought – hoped – it was helping your symptoms alongside harming you. After all, you take deadly nightshade for your heart, don't you?'

He gives me this odd look, like I'm unfathomable but if he just looks hard enough, deep enough, he might be able to understand.

'When I saw your father's reaction and heard your mother it confirmed my worst suspicions. They knew about your gift and had fed that stuff to you, *poisoned* you, under the guise of medicine, when really it was their tablets that were making you so ill.' His brow clenches, desperate.

My throat tightens in response. The truth. The awful, awful truth.

'Nothing cuts deeper than kin,' he says softly.

I hug my knees to my chest. 'How did the Apothic make more of the stuff? I thought the dark metal wasn't allowed in the Underworld.'

'It isn't. He . . . didn't. I ordered him to make you tablets that looked the same but contained harmless herbs.'

I thought there wasn't room in me for any more shock. Turns out I was wrong.

'Huh.' I work my tongue around my mouth, searching for a response. 'So you . . . you just changed my medicine without even thinking to involve me in the decision?' I sound remarkably calm. 'What if I'd got worse?'

The bed shifts as he leans towards me, gaze intent, earnest. 'I wouldn't have let that happen.'

'Not all things are in your control!' I'm shocked to hear my voice rise at him, but who I am is broken. I'm just pieces, smaller, less real than when I travel with him as feathers and shards of darkness. Rhiannon is truly no more.

'I was keeping an eye on you. I would've made sure.' His hands clench in his lap and he straightens. 'I knew that "medicine" was making you worse, if not ill in the first place. And I knew you'd get better without it.'

I squeeze my coffee cup. Should I be surprised that a king – a *demi-god* – would be so self-assured that he wouldn't hesitate to play with a mortal's life?

Not surprising. But also not excusable.

'*Avellan.*' He hangs his head, frowning at the dark surface of his drink. 'I should have told you when I found out. But I didn't know how or if you'd even believe me. And when I thought about it, I figured it wouldn't matter, because you would never see them again. You'd be here with me and I would protect you for all time. There would be no more poison. No more harm. You never needed to know what they'd done to you.'

My family was meant to protect me. How could I need protection *from* them?

This time it isn't pieces of me falling away, but pieces of my world. If I can't rely on them, how does the universe even work? Who am I meant to turn to? There has to be more than just me.

'I'm sorry.' He looks up, expression tight as he gives a small, emphatic nod. '*I'm sorry.*'

Death just apologized to me. The man who warned me never to apologize in his unseelie realm for fear of being beholden to the other person. And he's now beholden to me.

But I find my head shaking. The steam from my coffee, the blanket and my knees form a wall around me.

His jaw clenches. 'That's the first time in my centuries that I've apologized, and all you can do is shake your head?'

'This isn't just about not telling me, Drystan.' He flinches when I say his name, like it's a curse. 'It's about making a decision about my medicine – my *body* – without even thinking of getting my consent. You decided and you made it happen, and I was none the wiser.' My chest feels like it's caught in the slowly squeezing jaws of a vice. 'My health. My trust. My body. All of it has been broken. Taken. By people I thought cared about me.'

'But you needed—'

'No. Listen to me. Hear what I'm saying.' I pause, seizing control of myself, making sure he's paying attention. 'It wasn't your decision to make. It was my body. My choice. Not anyone else's, no matter how good or bad their intentions. My choice. *Mine.*'

He frowns at me a long while, thinking, and gradually the expression eases. 'I can't pretend to understand. But I know I'd rather cut my own heart out than hurt you. Yet it's too late, isn't it? I've done it.' His frown tightens like he knows there's something broken between us but he doesn't know how to fix it.

His apology is a start.

It isn't a full acknowledgement of his part – I'm not sure he can do that if he doesn't understand – but it's something. And right now, sitting here with nothing and no one, I will take something.

We remain in silence for a long while, drinking our coffee.

At least if I'm no longer being poisoned, then that means I'm not ill. I don't need a cure, just to stop taking the tablets. I'll get better on my own. Even taking a half dose during my first couple of weeks here, I started putting on weight.

But . . .

'If I haven't been taking poison for over a week and it's cleared my system enough for my magic to awaken, why do I still need belladonna and skullflower?'

He swallows and looks away. I swear he grows even paler than usual.

The hesitance, so unlike him, has me on edge. Eventually, he stands, goes to his bedside table and pulls a book from the drawer. 'I was wondering the same. I couldn't ask the Apothic without revealing your secret, so I consulted this – it's the only book we have on human physiology, but it's advanced. I had it stolen from a dark place.' At my questioning look, he elaborates: 'An ancient surface-dweller who experimented on your kind.'

My gut twists.

'I don't approve of her methods, but her records were thorough and tell us this . . .' He flicks to a bookmarked page and hands it to me, his lips pressing into a flat line.

Smooth, cursive handwriting states:

An excess of iron in the subject causes a variety of ailments. Excision on the living specimen reveals a gathering of the element within the joints, causing stiffness and aches. These symptoms appear to lessen over time, supported by blood-letting. I must admit, it's amusing that such a primitive practice recommended for anything and everything by human so-called doctors actually confers some benefit in this instance. Hypothesis: iron circulates in the blood. This would explain the red colour, not unlike rust. Since our blood is also red, posit we are able to synthesize a small amount of iron, but anything more leads to acute poisoning in our kind, not unlike the chronic poisoning observed in the subject.

Eyes shut, I swallow back nausea. She fed someone iron and then cut them open while they still lived.

And blood-letting – the one treatment that might've actually helped. I thought it was old-fashioned quackery. Dismissed the doctor as a fraud. If I wasn't so wrung out, I'd laugh.

I skim back over the text. My aches have lessened, like her poor subject's. But nothing here explains my continued symptoms. 'Which part, specifically?'

Drystan trails a long finger over the page, stopping at a para-
graph towards the bottom.

Subject is still complaining about heart episodes a year after
the last iron exposure. Recovery appears to have halted. The
experiment has run its course.

Post-mortem Dissection Results

Cessation of excess iron consumption has cleared the element
from the joints — consistent with decreased complaints from the
subject in their final months. However, closer inspection reveals
damage to the muscles of the heart, which normal iron levels
have failed to reverse.

I stare at the final sentence. Blink. Swallow. Read it again and
again until the words look like nonsense scribbles.

'I'm sorry,' Drystan says softly.

My eyelids flutter as stupid tears gather in my gritty eyes and the
full depths of this truth open beneath my feet.

I've felt better since coming to the Underworld. Maybe there's
still poison leaving my system. But the damage is done. My heart
won't recover.

There is no cure.

57

OVER THE FOLLOWING days, the shock abates, leaving me with the pieces of everything that's broken. I gather those and myself and return to my rooms while Drystan is asleep. Though his breathing shifts from its sleeping rhythm, so I suspect he knows what I'm doing, which allays any guilt I might feel.

Min visits almost as soon as the sun sets. I can't bring myself to verbalize all that's happened. But she stays with me. We eat breakfast and sit in silence that's only punctuated by the cat's purrs. He's glued to me, even following me to the bathroom.

Min reads. I watch the fire. I flick through books and my notebook. The quest for a cure seems so foolish now, when the answer all along was to stop taking poison.

Now I'm no longer replaying the conversation with my parents, other moments come back to me. *Bad meat.* That creature wasn't disgusted by my illness, she could smell the iron in my blood: *That foul stuff. Here.* In the Underworld where it's forbidden.

Gradually other little moments slot into place. Not boulders but puzzle pieces.

When Min has to go, Asti appears and takes up vigil at my side. I'm not sure how she knows to come, but she's here and I'm glad of it.

Ginger biscuits appear alongside hearty meals like soup and roasted meats with braised vegetables. Once again, I'm grateful to Min for her care and attention while my mind circles on what to do next.

I've earned the right to return to the surface world. But I can't face my parents and the ugly truth. I will go back. I need to work out the how and where, but not yet.

For now I lose myself in books, reading everything I can about poisons, iron, aconite.

Belladonna is mentioned as a treatment for the symptoms if not the root cause. I chuckle to myself, a mirthless sound almost as hollow as the first laugh I heard from Drystan.

As much as her methods make my skin crawl, I note down what I can remember from the ancient fae's experiments. Anything to help me understand all that's been done to me and the lingering effects that I'll never be without.

There's a kind of peace in ink. In words. In paragraphs. In page upon page of text and diagrams and botanical drawings.

It helps me start to make sense of everything. Slowly. On a surface level, at least.

After almost a week of quiet, I speak to Min. I ask her to bring Asti – I only want to tell this story once.

Asti doesn't know I'm ill, but she's no fool. She understands something's wrong and she's been here every night since I returned. So when she arrives, I explain it all from the start – the truth, this time, not the lie I've been told for half my life. My poisoning, the deal with Drystan, escaping the labyrinth and my return to the place I can no longer bring myself to call home.

Min listens in horrified silence. Asti tugs on her braids, and when I finish, she's the one who asks, 'What will you do?'

'I don't know. I can't go back there. I can't face them.'

She makes a dark sound, dipping her chin.

'But I don't have anyone else up there. And I don't think I can manage on my own.' There's Lowen, of course, but he has a life to live. Now he knows about our parents, I'm sure he'll leave. I can get a message to him soon – one that explains I'm safe and recovering. I rub my chest, heartbeat deceptively solid, even though it's ready to betray me at any moment.

Since reading about the effects of iron, I've been especially cautious with dosing on belladonna. If my heart is damaged, then those giddy, pounding heights could prove too much for it. I'm reminded of the occasions it's felt horribly like my chest was being turned inside out. What if that was the warning of a heart nearing its limit?

Bringing myself back from my thoughts, I find Asti and Min exchanging a meaningful look. They've been here every night since I returned to my room. Without fail. I haven't been left alone for an instant, save for sleep. And even then, I've often woken to find one of them already here, sat by the fireplace.

'You two don't have to supervise me, you know.'

Min shrugs and smiles. 'We know.'

'You could go and . . .' I wave at the door. 'Spend time together.'

'We *are* spending time together.' Asti gathers her thick braids over one shoulder and shares a lingering grin with Min. 'And with our friend.'

Min leans into her, covering her hand. 'I'm just glad we knew you were back.'

'Huh.' I sit up, finding the source of a nagging feeling that's been at the back of my mind for days. 'As far as you two knew, I'd gone h—'

I catch myself. The word 'home' is a thorn.

'You thought I'd gone *back*. How did you know I was here?' I saw no one when I moved between Drystan's suite and my rooms – the whole fortress was asleep.

Min winces, fingertips pressed to her mouth. Eyes wide, she glances a question at Asti.

The warrior sighs and spreads her arms. 'His Majesty told us. He said something was wrong and he couldn't comfort you, but that he didn't want you left alone.'

'He was worried about you,' Min adds. 'Still is, actually.'

'He asks after you each night.' Asti scoffs. 'But he's also ordered me not to betray your confidence.'

'He did . . . what?'

'He didn't want me to tell him anything you'd said, only to give him a general idea of how you were, whether you were eating the food he's had sent here.'

I pause with a biscuit halfway to my lips. 'He's been sending these?'

'Obviously. Who else?'

'I thought . . . you two.'

As one, they shake their heads.

Alongside the barb still working its way through my chest, something warm sprouts.

Because I've been wrong.

I may have lost my family, but I'm not entirely alone. I have friends. I have a cat kneading my thigh.

And I have Drystan.

Who's somehow been comforting me from afar. Who's shown compassion. Who tried to protect me from the pain of my parents' betrayal. Who may have gone about things all wrong, but still managed to end my slow poisoning.

Who has shared his own vulnerabilities with me and who, impossibly, has somehow come to care for me, a weak and imperfect human.

And despite his failings and imperfections, I care for him, too.

There is a solution. Not a perfect one. But it means I don't have to go back to the family who's been poisoning me for a lifetime, and it means I don't have to die alone either.

I turn to Asti and nod. 'I think I know what I need to do.'

58

I STAND OUTSIDE Drystan's study, stomach a tangle of nerves. I straighten my gown for the fifth time and my hair for the tenth. Min helped me get ready, picking out something gorgeous and diaphanous, gilding my cheeks with tiny flecks of glitter, clipping tiny butterflies made of raven feathers in my hair, so I look more faerie creature from legend than frail mortal.

The instant I raise my hand to knock, the door swings open. This is a room I've only ever glimpsed once, all those weeks ago during his tour. It's bigger than I remember. And more him than the rest of the fortress, I now realize. The wall lined with well-worn books. The wingback chair in rich oxblood red velvet, the same style as those in his suite – formal looking but deceptively comfortable.

The dark cherrywood desk he stands behind. Imposing and handsome, but suffused with surprising warmth.

The king himself. Fingers splayed over the desk's black leather surface, sleeves rolled up to his elbows, jacket discarded.

No. Not the king. The man. The one who has to run Mordren.

Keep his people safe – from the world outside as well as from the chaos of unseelie nature. Asti and Min told me he's been visiting the labyrinth, investigating the corrupting presence there. Protecting his kingdom.

He nods, deep in conversation with the Apothic, but his gaze flicks in my direction.

'Much of my equipment has been damaged,' the Apothic goes on, 'so it's hard to tell if anything is missing.'

Eyes locked on me, Drystan keeps nodding.

The Apothic glances over his shoulder, noting my entrance before turning back to Drystan. He shifts his weight awkwardly. 'If Your Majesty wishes it, I can take another inventory, but I'm not sure it will achieve much.'

Drystan pushes his sleeves up, though they haven't slipped down.

The Apothic clears his throat.

'Hmm? What?' Drystan draws a quick breath, straightening as though he's just returned to himself. 'I'm sure that won't be necessary. No doubt it's the work of mischievous kin drawn to the shiny glass.' With a flick of his hand, he dismisses the Apothic, but I catch his mutter as the other fae sweeps past me. 'Or discontented former favourites.'

He rises and circles the desk so it's no longer between us but says nothing more until the door closes behind the Apothic. 'I'm glad to see you're feeling well enough to leave your rooms.'

Hands clasped, I nod, searching for how to say what I came here to say. Ideas are so simple. Execution? That's the tricky part.

I consider turning around.

'I've reached a decision,' I blurt out before cowardice wins.

His eyebrows rise, prompting. 'Oh?' He settles on the edge of his desk, putting his eye line closer to mine.

'I succeeded in beating the labyrinth. And the whole point of that was to return to my family. But I've changed my mind.' I don't have enough bravery to hold his gaze as I get closer to the

nature of my decision – and the point where he can decline – so I
fix mine on his forearm.

I square my shoulders. His grip on the edge of the desk flexes,
making the muscles I'm staring at ripple in the most fascinating way.

'I will marry you.'

The muscles twitch. His knuckles go white. He says nothing.

There's a flutter of panic in my chest. Maybe I misjudged.
Maybe he just wanted a wife – any wife – and now I've earned my
freedom, he's found another candidate.

Oh, gods, he could have set up this whole bargain in order to
work his way out of the one between my father and his mother,
making me feel like it was *my* idea.

'You . . . will?' As soon as he speaks, my traitorous gaze snaps
up to his, so I see how he says it with a smile. A tiny one. But it
presses the shadow of a dimple in his cheek.

'If you'll have me, that is.'

The dimple deepens. 'Of course I will.' He pushes up from the
desk and crosses the space between us like he's going to kiss me.

The panic comes back, overshadowing my relief. 'I don't—'

I throw my hands up, swallow, gather my flitting thoughts and
he pauses just out of arm's reach. 'This doesn't mean I've forgiven
you. What you did is still . . .' I exhale, shaking my head. 'There's
a stipulation – you're never to keep anything like that from me
again. *Never.*'

He nods. Once.

'And you're never to make decisions about my body for me. I
appreciate that you've apologized. I understand the significance
of that for you as unseelie and as the king. I know it wasn't easy.
But . . .'

He holds there, waiting, and I can't help remembering.

*Long is the day and long is the night and long is the waiting of the
King of Death.*

I thought it only meant that he was old, but now I see something else in the way he stands, unmoving, unprompting, simply giving me time to think and speak.

Death is old, yes, but he is also patient. All things come to him, eventually.

I seize on an analogy that I hope he'll understand, even if he doesn't fully grasp the damage he's done to my trust. 'A bandaged wound still bleeds.'

He makes a low, thoughtful sound, then inclines his chin. 'It does. And not all wounds heal, but I hope this one can.'

Relief is a physical force rushing through me, as dizzying as belladonna. It's not the marriage I dreamt of as a girl, but that girl and her dreams are as dead as any shambling spirit in the Underworld.

I will marry Drystan. Not because I have nowhere else to go, but because I have found something here. An odd life with him, Min, Asti and the cat who really needs a name now I'm staying, but a life nonetheless.

There is truth in our feelings for each other, proven all the more by his actions since I returned to the Underworld. I don't know where they will lead us or whether the bandaged wound in our relationship will ever heal, but I know I deserve a chance to find out.

59

THE OFFICIAL WEDDING announcement comes quickly. Maybe Drystan is worried I'll change my mind. We have to stand before the entire court and declare who our attendants will be. The Apothic looks pleased when his name is announced – Drystan repaying him for his work on my medicine. And his silence.

There's some upset when Drystan chooses Asti as his primary attendant rather than someone of higher political ranking, like Lord Mastelle.

Seeing her reaction, though, the surprise and then the dawning pride – it fills my chest. Both for her and because . . . I think Death might be making friends.

Meanwhile, my choices receive a more mixed reaction. Min. Of course. And, *of course*, that raises eyebrows. A scarred royal sartor as *the future queen's* attendant.

'How provincial.' I hear Phaedra say those exact words as Min comes and stands at my side.

Which makes my second choice all the more interesting. *Her.*

It silences her for a long moment as she eyes me as if seeing me

afresh, before approaching the dais and standing the other side
of me.

Covered by the applause, she leans over. 'It's a peace offering,
isn't it?'

I barely incline my head, smiling out over my future subjects.

'A politically shrewd choice,' she concedes. 'I have to respect
that.'

And maybe she does, because in the run up to the wedding,
she's compliant – helpful, even. She works on my pronunciation
of passages I have to recite in the old tongue. I check them with
Drystan – I wouldn't put it past her to teach me the wrong thing
so I make a fool of myself.

But she steers me true.

She even takes charge of decor for the event. I brace myself for
some subtle insult in the choice of colour or motif. That's exactly
the way unseelie would spell out their displeasure.

As promised, Drystan gets a message to Lowen at the next
opportunity, though of course he can't come to the Underworld to
attend. Still, I know he's safe and well, preparing to move out from
the cottage. His employers have even given him a second chance
after he abandoned work to throw himself into his search for me.

It feels like we've barely finished the announcement when the
wedding day arrives, less than a month later.

My stomach is in knots, though Min does all she can to settle me
as we get ready. Even Phaedra tells me I look 'very pretty. For a
human.'

At least it's civil.

The cat snakes around my legs, purring furiously, tangling in
my gown. He only comes out when Min crawls in and grabs him.

Then, she insists on placing me in front of the mirror, which
she's covered with a velvet drape, and, with a suitably dramatic
flourish, sweeps it away.

To show . . . me.

At least, I think it's me.

Because this woman . . . She's *resplendent*. Radiant.

The gown Min's made for me isn't just fit for a queen – it's fit for a *goddess*.

From a distance, at a casual glance, someone might think it was simply white.

But that isn't the whole picture.

Just like a shell that seems white, then catches the light in an iridescent rainbow, the sleeveless gown glistens in the pale whisper of pink, purple, blue, green, yellow. It shows off my olive skin, how rich the colour has become since I stopped taking poison.

It takes me a moment to register exactly how low the neckline slashes – as far as my navel – and I throw Min a questioning look.

But we have a wedding to get to.

Jewellery is placed around my throat. A pearl-studded veil is attached to my hair with a gem-encrusted comb. Min works her magic with some shimmering powder that disappears into my skin until it catches the light in gold, shifting to copper and teal. We almost forget my shoes.

Then, somehow, I'm at the doors to the ceremony hall.

I drank skullflower tea while we were getting ready. It feels like I need more.

Or – gods – no. Did I get it mixed up with my belladonna?

Min squeezes my shoulder and raises her eyebrows meaningfully, while Phaedra fusses with the floor-length veil. 'Everything all right?'

'Yes, just . . .'

'I know.' She smiles, eyes bright. 'If it helps any, you look gorgeous, and we unseelie are a shallow lot – we'll forgive a great many sins if you're only beautiful enough.'

Laughing eases the tension quivering through me, making it easier to breathe.

Phaedra gives me a once-over then nods in what *might* be approval. 'It's time.'

The doors to the ceremony hall open. It's a match to the Great Hall, with a higher ceiling, taller windows and rows of seating. Phaedra and Min leave me, passing sedately down the central walkway, arm-in-arm as though they're the best of friends.

Then it's my turn.

A raven caws. Silence reigns, leaving my breath loud in my ears.

Hundreds of eyes are on me, sharp like they're waiting for me to trip.

My vision swims. The walkway seems as long as the Gauntlet of Despair. Somewhere at the end, Drystan is a tall, black shape. Behind him three arched windows show the clear night sky bright with moon and stars.

I see everything and nothing. The room seems so full. Of people. Of glittering lights. Instead of black, Phaedra has chosen clear-crystal droplets, which hang from the ceiling and windows. As the light hits them, they throw tiny rainbows into the room and on to the faces of all the watching fae.

One thing I've learned since arriving in the Underworld is that they don't have rainbows. Something to do with the light given off by their sun. It's something they remember from the surface – something they miss. So this feels like . . . Well, from Phaedra, it's a compliment. Good things come from the surface – sometimes.

The shimmers hit my gown, merging with the opalescent colours, glistening on the beads and gemstones Min has sewn on.

Once I've taken in the excess, I push my attention towards the front. I focus on Kishel first. He wears that small, encouraging smile. It's like a comforting hand upon my shoulder.

He glances at the tall, dark form to one side and gives a subtle nod.

The king – *my* king – turns. His lips part.

Suddenly, I can take a full breath.

Suddenly, the way to the front doesn't seem so long.

As I get closer, I realize he isn't in black. Not entirely. The fabric of his suit sheens blue and purple like Nos and Tywel's feathers. The dark counterpart to my outfit.

He seems taller than usual. Regal. Unreadable. The only movement is his eyes, following me all the way until I stand before him.

Once I'm close, he gives me a tight smile. As we turn to face Kishel, he tugs at his cuff.

I suppress a frown as Kishel begins his opening speech, welcoming our guests.

At my side, eyes still on Kishel, Drystan turns his head fractionally towards me. 'Has anyone told you that you're breathtaking?'

I duck my head, trying to hide my smile, grateful I'm wearing a veil and have my back to the members of his court. Our court.

'Because if they haven't, I'll have to take all their tongues. You look . . . You aren't just breathtaking – you've got Death himself forgetting what it is to breathe.'

My throat is tight at the compliment, but I find myself reminding him of the precipice we stand upon: 'Last chance. You can still marry a fae, someone easier, someone who—'

'Did it ever cross your mind that I don't want someone else?' he hisses. 'That maybe I *want* a troublesome human who's possibly the strongest *and* most stubborn person I know? Who's not afraid of me and tells me *exactly* what she thinks?' His eyebrows slash upward, cutting off any argument. 'Because I can't think of anyone better to be my queen. Anyone better for my people . . . or for me.'

Words escape me. I blink up at him, nod once, then let out a soft 'Oh.'

Like that settles it, he inclines his head and gives me a faint smile. But I catch how he straightens his perfect cuffs, *again*.

'What's wrong?'

He gives a low sigh. 'I didn't want to worry you. The Consort's Seal is missing.' He glowers at the altar behind Kishel where a black velvet cushion sits, conspicuously empty.

'Not down the back of the settee, I'm guessing?'

The corner of his mouth twitches. 'Unfortunately not. It was in the vault. Only someone with the blood of Arawn's line and the key may enter. I have the key, but . . .'

'Your brother? Effan?'

'He's the only other person who can enter. It would explain his disappearance – theft and fleeing rather than kidnap or murder.' He glares ahead with a look that could incinerate. 'I'll send the Wild Hunt after him and, if that doesn't work, I'll go after the damn fool myself.'

'Does it matter that much?'

'Without it, your position isn't considered symbolically legitimate. It's a missing piece.'

I hear the gaps in the words. 'I need it to access the consort's power.'

He dips his chin infinitesimally.

Kishel finishes his speech on the importance of marriage to the kingdom of Mordren and the people of Rigor Gard, his gaze sliding to us. 'If you two are quite finished?' he murmurs for our ears only before circling behind the altar.

He spreads his arms. The drifting fae lights dim. And the ceremony begins.

'The surface is for the living,' he intones, voice deep and slow as he crumbles rich, dark soil into a huge pestle and mortar. 'This world beneath is for the dead.' From a shallow case, he produces a single small bone.

A finger bone.

It goes into the mortar.

'Yet we are alive. Here. Still burning.' The two thick candles at either end of the altar splutter to life. He nods and Drystan takes my hand, placing it above the mortar. The Apothic takes the obsidian blade from the altar and gives it to Drystan.

My breath catches. I've been so caught up in reading about medicine, I haven't looked that closely at unseelie wedding rituals aside from learning the lines with Phaedra. There was something about a binding, but . . .

Not this.

'With this blade crafted from the Dark Throne, we let the offering of life.'

Drystan takes the blade and holds my gaze with a level look. I need to hold still. Hold steady. Show no fear.

He presses the razor edge of the glassy black stone into my palm, following the line a fortune teller once said meant I would never find love in this world.

He said nothing of the Underworld.

Before I can follow that thought far, a bead of blood wells up. I school myself to stillness, ignoring the sting of my broken skin. He only allows a drop to fall before he licks my skin clean.

I can't suppress the shiver that runs through me at the hot, slick touch of his tongue, the intensity of his gaze, the feeling again that he has consumed some vital part of me.

It's only a drop, and yet the fae in the front rows lean in, eyes wide, breaths heavy, hungry gazes upon me.

I swallow, afraid, excited, unsettled, and carefully cut him in the same spot.

'Take more,' he murmurs as I tilt his hand over the mortar, and I understand. He took only a drop of my blood to avoid stirring his subjects into a frenzy, but the mixture requires more liquid to make it bind.

A thin, crimson rivulet runs off his palm and over the bone, soaking into the soil.

After a few seconds, Kishel nods and indicates for me to return the blade. 'The offering is made. Death. Life. Our king and his chosen queen.' He raises the pestle high above his head and brings it down, thundering.

The sound echoes off the walls. Within the mortar, there's a crack.

He does it again. Again. Then, chanting in the old tongue, he grinds the pestle in circles.

Bone crumbles into soil, binds with blood. Life and death and death and life, all together.

Messy. Transformative.

Inevitable.

Death stands at my side and he is not what I expected at all.

Kishel lifts the mortar above his head. At his direction, Drystan unbuttons his shirt. I freeze. Please don't say we have to fuck on the altar in front of the entire court. I hold my breath, waiting as Asti slides it from his shoulders and folds it. He doesn't remove anything else.

He circles around to my front and lifts my veil, while I face out over the hall. He pauses there for a long moment, surveying my face, chest rising and falling deeply, slowly, before at last he dips his thumb into the mixture.

A steady drum beat reverberates through the space. My pulse falls into time with it.

He smears a line upon my cheek. Surprisingly warm. Smooth. Thoughts of whose bone coats my skin fade away as I enter a different space. One where there is only Drystan and I and blood, earth, bone.

He speaks in the old tongue, but I hear the translation I've memorized.

'In blood and bone, I take thee.'

A line upon the other cheek.

'In ash and earth, I give myself.'

A line down from lips to chin to throat to chest, as low as my navel. Daubs on my shoulders, the insides of my elbows.

'In life, in death, in all the aching moments between, I am thine.'

My skin tingles. The hairs on my arms rise. The thundering drum beat takes over.

It's my turn to plunge my thumb into the mortar, to trace lines upon his cheeks. I'm so consumed by it, I barely remember speaking the words. It's as though I'm not there at all and yet entirely present. My body remembers each stroke of the ritual like it's inked upon my nerves.

My thumb dips into the divot between his collarbones, down over the steady rise and fall of his chest. He doesn't blink, merely lifts his chin as I take the line downward, daring me to continue. The corded muscles of his stomach tense under my touch, and I only stop when I hit the waistband on his trousers.

I pause there. His skin is warm beneath my thumb. The blood smear tacky, slow to dry. A heartbeat later, it does – mine on him. His on mine. A perfect mirror.

Pale, painted in blood and limned in half-light, Drystan looks all the more a dark god. Primal. Sacred. Eternal.

The god inclines his head, eyes bright in this dim light, and speaks one soft word as his gaze skims from my lips down the lines he's marked upon my flesh: 'Flawless.'

I think he means how I look, but Kishel makes a sound of approval before he raises his voice. 'The Rite of Blood is complete. Your queen stands before you wearing the bones of our people, the blood of your king, and she wears it well.'

Drystan takes my hand and lifts it so they can better see where he's daubed my shoulder and the crook of my elbow.

Applause rushes over us. Warm. Overwhelming.

'Flawless,' he says again, low in my ear.

My cheeks flush. I've performed well. Lines correct. Not a wince at being cut. No foolish human recoiling at the smear of bone upon my skin.

As the crowd quietens, I gather myself for the next rite. We're not married until the entire ceremony is complete.

Forward steps Phaedra. She smiles at me as absolute silence descends. Drystan's fingers twitch around mine.

That tiny reaction makes dread twist in my belly.

She sweeps around to address the crowd. 'Our would-be queen certainly looks the part, but a consort must do more than wear blood and bone prettily.' She lifts her chin. 'I invoke the Right of Challenge.'

60

A HUNDRED GASPS suck the air from the room.

I barely stop myself before looking at Drystan in question. Now more than ever, I'm on display. If I give away I don't know what the hells that is, I'll seem weak.

Instead I paint a vague, unconcerned smile upon my lips as she draws level with me and says beneath the chatter that's broken out, 'Your kindness might have beguiled the king, but it doesn't fool me. You are weak and not fit to be our queen. Let's see how your Fatework has progressed since the stables, shall we?'

I bite back a groan. At least it isn't trial by combat, I suppose.

At my side, Drystan has gone preternaturally still, eyes blazing as he takes in the chattering crowd. Their excitement is tangible. For them, things just got *interesting*.

Kishel comes forward and murmurs in my ear, 'The Right of Challenge simply states the prospective consort must overcome a trial by scrying. Usually it's predicting the outcome of something random.'

So I might be able to guess my way to victory. 'Why didn't you tell me about this?' I glance between him and Drystan.

Kishel winces. 'It hasn't been used in millennia. I wonder if—'

'WHAT CHALLENGE DO YOU LAY BEFORE MY QUEEN?'

The hanging crystals shatter under the onslaught of Drystan's voice. Rainbows and quartz rain down, tinkling against the marble floor.

Then silence.

The delicate lines of Phaedra's neck constrict as she swallows. She's a few shades paler than usual. But I will give it to her, she stands tall, composed. 'An important item is conspicuous in its absence today. Your Majesty wouldn't have *misplaced* the Consort's Seal, would he? And on such an auspicious occasion.'

A small muscle in Drystan's jaw tics.

'No matter.' She cocks her head at me. 'I'm sure Lady Rhiannon will find it. *There* is your challenge. After all, if you're meant to be queen, surely you'll be able to find what's rightfully yours.'

I *appear* perfectly calm. At least, I pray I do. Inside, my stomach flip-flops and my heart thuds too heavily, counting down until I fail this test.

I exchange a meaningful look with Kishel. We both know my scrying is patchy at best.

From the Collector's reaction, I understand using blood is considered taboo, dangerous. And Kishel has confessed to me that adding a substance to water is only a training tool. Some consider it cheating. But I've never managed a successful scrying with water alone.

My muscles hum as my mind races. I'm going to fail. And then I'll lose my place in the Underworld – they don't want or need a random human here, no matter what their king thinks of her.

Kishel inclines his head, though tension lines the skin around his eyes. 'Perhaps Your Majesty—'

'*Lady Rhiannon*.' Phaedra looks down her nose at him. 'The ceremony isn't complete. She isn't queen.'

'*Yet*.' Kishel's smile could freeze the ocean. 'Perhaps *Your Majesty* would like to carry out her scrying in the glasshouse pond.'

A lifeline. I think. It certainly feels like one as the entire court decamps to the glasshouse, buzzing with burgeoning gossip.

Drystan holds my hand all the way, thumb stroking my knuckles in a soothing, hypnotic rhythm that reminds me how to breathe steadily.

When we arrive, I understand Kishel's plan.

Lily pads cluster at the pool's edge where there were none days ago. It's a long shot, but my magic might help me. Somehow.

Never mind that I haven't managed to use it deliberately yet. Or that—

'Annon.' Drystan's voice, commanding. 'Stay with me. Stay here. Do this thing and *show her* you were made for me.'

The low urgency of his words cuts through me. I'm back in the labyrinth's garden. Despite his illusion and trickery, I know there were truths spoken that day.

You were made for me.

It's enough to break my spiralling thoughts.

Shoulders set, I approach the pool.

Other times when I've channelled my magic, I've felt the point of connection inside. So I place one hand on my chest, the paint crumbling.

Min. Asti. Drystan. Kishel. Lowen. The Collector. They all believe or believed in me. That the Collector is past tense is an exquisite pinprick of pain in my chest. But it's warm. And there's a thread of connection to their memory.

The lily pads stir. Something moves beneath the water. I settle my breathing and let it all unfold before me.

Buds rise from the depths and break the water's surface.

Low murmurs surround me and I sense the crowding of fae bending in for a closer look.

At the centre of the pool, a single bud, the largest, unfurls, revealing a snow-white bloom.

Moments later, a dozen more follow in rich pink and white with golden yellow at the centre.

The fae's awe is audible. Gasps. Soft sighs. Exclamations at the *colour*.

But I watch the water. It ripples as stems and petals shift, as new leaves grow.

And in the light and shadow, I see a house I recognize.

My voice sounds like it comes from far away. 'We'll need to ride.'

An hour later, we arrive at the half-ruined cottage. Half the fae look intrigued, excited by this unexpected turn of events. The other half seem pissed off that they've had to throw thick cloaks over their rich attire and ride to this inauspicious little house in the middle of nowhere.

All the way here, people rode too close for me to warn Drystan where we were going, but he made a soft sound as we cut between scattered boulders and I guided us left. I think that was when he realized.

He lifts me from my horse, gaze seeking answers in mine.

All I can do is murmur, 'This is what I saw.' I was wondering if he hid the seal here and staged this whole thing so I could find it and lay to rest any questions about my suitability as queen. But that look tells me he knows nothing.

Most of the court hangs back, but Lord Mastelle, Asti, Min, the Apothic and the rest of the Withan follow us inside.

The floor is still strewn with debris.

'What happened here?' Min stares at the destruction.

Drystan says nothing, so I follow in kind.

Asti wrinkles her nose. 'That smell . . .'

Kishel stands at my side. 'What did you see in the water? Sometimes chaotic scenes like this can . . . confuse our vision.'

'Just this place.' Then I see the tall cupboard, door shut where we left it open, and there's a pull in my chest like someone's tied a string around my heart and is tugging on it. The tug continues along my veins. Not pain, but the most hideous sensation I've endured in my life. My stomach rolls. I sway.

Drystan's hand spreads over my back, a subtle support.

My lips dry as I gasp for breath. 'There,' I croak and point.

Asti opens the cupboard.

There's a scrape. A thud.

And at our feet lies a black-haired fae. Face grey and sunken, unmistakably dead, yet still recognizable.

Effan.

61

I'VE BARELY TAKEN it in when there's a cry at the window. 'It's Effan. Dead!' The news spreads outside, while within the cottage, I blink at his corpse.

No obvious marks. Some of the anatomy books I've read describe the body in different phases of decomposition. All I can tell from here is that he's been dead a while. But this cupboard was empty when I came here with Drystan – his body has been moved.

The Apothic hangs back. He's probably used to dealing with medicines but not patients.

Questions and suspicions cross the room in darting glances.

'How did he get here?' Lord Mastelle strides in. 'And how *long* has he been here?' Lips flat, he crouches and peers at the once-handsome features.

'Someone must've brought him here.' Asti nods. 'Look at all this damage. They kept him here. Tortured him most likely.'

I press into Drystan, silently urging him. I don't dare speak the truth if he won't – there must be some reason he's keeping it quiet. Probably something to do with emotion and weakness.

'We can clear this up quickly.' He steps forward, expression set in grim lines.

The body twitches. Its head snaps up. There's a wet sound as it rolls over, thuds on to its front. Eventually it pushes itself to its feet, hollow eyes on Drystan.

I don't know if it's shock that holds me still or if I've seen the dead rise enough times that I no longer react.

This is simply what Drystan does. Who he is.

King of Death. God of it. A simple fact of life.

'BROTHER.' The cottage trembles. Its foundations groan. 'TELL US HOW YOU CAME TO BE HERE, HOW YOU CAME TO DIE.'

Effan's mouth opens. A croak comes from inside, incomprehensible, then he opens wider. Inside is a rust-brown ruin.

Old blood. I clasp my hands together to avoid recoiling.

I am nearly queen. I am not afraid of this poor, murdered creature.

Because no way did he come here and die after Drystan and I were here. And no way did he cut out his own tongue.

Every pair of eyes flicks towards Drystan. Some slide away again. Others stay on him.

He *does* have a reputation for severing tongues.

'It can't speak. How convenient.' Lord Mastelle huffs in irritation. 'Can it write?'

Drystan's mouth flattens. 'The dead can rarely manage such fine movements. Not at this stage.'

'Well it's worth a try.' Lord Mastelle pats his pockets, but it's Min who darts forward and offers the sketchbook I've seen her plan her creations in. She places her pencil in Effan's hand.

Lord Mastelle merely grunts in acknowledgement. 'Who killed you? Write it—'

But the dead heir doesn't write anything.

He lifts his arm and points.

Right at Drystan.

*

That sets the news blazing outside, and more suspicious glances darting inside.

'It . . . *he* mustn't understand.' I step forward. Drystan can't have done this.

No one answers.

Even Asti and Min frown and share a long, questioning look.

'No, look, it's just giving His Majesty something.' Phaedra stalks closer to Effan, peering at the little glint of gold tucked between his fingers.

Eyes narrowing, Drystan approaches his brother. Even though Effan's skin is sunken and blotchy, I see the similarities more starkly than when I met him in life. The proud line of their noses. The cut of their jaws. The same straight, black hair.

Drystan holds out his hand, and Effan drops something into it, sighing out a heavy breath and slumping to the floor.

A gold coin sits at the centre of Drystan's palm.

Such a small thing.

Yet the king's face goes slack. Just for an instant. Enough for me to spot and not an instant longer. Then he masters himself, pressing his lips together.

After a long moment, he closes his hand around the coin and looks up as if returning from far away.

'What is it?' Phaedra cranes to see.

He drops it into his pocket and adjusts his cuff. 'Just a coin.' His gaze skims away, shadowed by the furrowing of his brow. 'Something to remember my brother by.'

We search the body and the cottage, but there's nothing else that seems like a clue, and, as Phaedra's keen to point out, 'No sign of the seal.' She wears a bright smile. 'Fascinating as this little jaunt has been, the king's brother is not the missing item that was named.'

I grit my teeth, but I can't say she's wrong. I've failed the challenge.

Glowering, Asti steps forward. '*Little jaunt?* She found out what happened to a member of our court who's been missing for months.'

Phaedra spreads her hands and shakes her head. 'Alas, she was *meant* to find the Consort's Seal. She merely brought us here. Clearly she isn't—'

'Her *vision* brought her here,' Kishel smoothly interjects, flashing Phaedra the same smile as earlier – chilly, devastating. 'As true Fateworkers know, the threads weave in mysterious patterns, connecting even the things we cannot yet see. *Clearly* Effan's disappearance and murder have something to do with the missing seal. Finding his body must be the first clue to its whereabouts. I say she has passed the test.'

'But—'

'The laws of the land are clear, Lady Phaedra. This matter only requires a majority vote by the Withan. Not a unanimous one.'

Her jaw turns solid as she goes quiet.

The Withan members break into a couple of separate conversations, weighing up Phaedra's words and Kishel's.

Drystan stands before the fire, still, silent.

As I reach him, I graze the back of his fingers.

He sucks in a breath, snatching his hand away like he didn't hear me approach.

I pull back, not wanting to touch where it isn't welcome. 'Are you all right?'

He frowns at the dust on the hearth. 'Some things should stay buried.' His fingers find mine though, and he gives them a comforting squeeze.

Before I can ask what he means, Kishel clears his throat. 'Then we're in agreement.'

Every member of the Withan turns to me.

'Her Majesty completed the Right of Challenge successfully, albeit unconventionally.' He bows his head, teeth flashing as he smiles. 'The wedding may continue.'

62

DEATH IS A different thing in the Underworld. All the way back to the fortress the court chatters and gossips. To them, death is a transition rather than a cause for mourning.

Drystan, though, is silent as the grave. He helped me on to my horse but didn't react to me squeezing his hand in thanks. He didn't seem too concerned about his brother going missing before. I have to wonder if that was a front to pretend he didn't care for him when he really did . . .

Then again, it could be that killing the king's brother is a calculated message, one that strikes too close to the heart of his kingdom.

A chilly ride later, everyone is back in their seats. Someone has swept up the broken crystals, though the hall is duller without them hanging from the vaulted ceiling. Asti slides Drystan's shirt from his shoulders, and the Apothic folds it before returning it to its velvet cushion.

Min unclasps the cloak I wore for the ride. Our paint remains. 'You're to wash it off each other later,' she whispers, winking as she sweeps off the cloak.

Mechanically, Phaedra folds it. She stands to one side, a sickly smile on her mouth as she stares out over the guests, like she refuses to believe this is really happening.

The King of Death is marrying a human.

Kishel's chest rises and falls as he eyes me and then Drystan, before nodding as if deciding we're ready.

He holds aloft an ash-grey cord and the room falls silent. They have to wonder what surprise comes next. None, I hope.

'With this cord, we bind you.' He hands the ends to Min and Asti, who wrap it around us – our waists, criss-crossing our backs, over our shoulders.

The cord tightens, drawing us together. Inevitably. Inextricably.

They don't stop until we're chest-to-chest, mark-to-mark, sharing air. They wind the ends around our wrists and tie knots so intricate, I'm not sure they can ever be undone.

I look up at Drystan, who calmly holds my gaze like he's returned from the preoccupied place he's been in since we found his brother's body. We're bound so tightly that when he breathes in, I must exhale, and only when he breathes out can I take air in.

'By death, by life, you are tied. And by twin fires, you are joined.'

Phaedra and the Apothic take the candles from the altar and light the two ends of the cord.

I tense with a quiet gasp, but Drystan dips his chin in subtle reassurance.

Red flame rushes along the cord with a soft hiss, leaving only ash and not so much as a scorch upon my gown.

The crowd leans in with a low murmur of awe.

Sooty black lines criss-cross our skin, adding to the blood-bone paint.

Kishel spreads his arms and presents us to the court. 'By ash and blood, I declare you married. May your nights be long and your deaths far from this day.'

The audience claps. Cheers come from the back of the hall.

Kishel leans over to Drystan. 'My king.' Then inclines his head to me, the tease of a smile on his face. 'My queen. This is the point where you would traditionally kiss. Might I suggest you make it a good one for your subjects. They've been waiting a long time.'

'Do not presume to tell me how to kiss my wife,' Drystan says, eyes on me as he steps in. He takes my jaw, my breath, angles my face and bends to me.

This isn't hard. Delving. Claiming.

It's a question. An apology written in tongue and teeth. Firm. Honest. Penitent.

Somehow it scrapes over my nerves, rattles my bones, even though the only places we're touching are his mouth on mine, his fingers on my jaw and my hand wrapped around his wrist, like that can anchor me.

When he pulls away, there are tears in my eyes, and I have to take a beat, eyes still shut, before I trust none to fall.

It's chaos. As if powered by the presence of a queen in their court, the unseelie are wilder, louder, more hedonistic than ever before. And all of them seem to want to talk to me. Some remark on the milder weather – whispers that spring is finally coming. Others mention the greater variety of food from the glasshouse – a hopeful sign after decades of scarcity. I find myself wondering if the seasons are finally turning, or if it's just a false dawn.

Drystan accompanies me around the Great Hall, always touching me. A hand on the small of my back. Fingers brushing mine. Twining together. He passes me food and drink. Watches me consume them. When I sway, he pretends he wishes to sit, so I have an excuse to rest.

I don't know how many hours pass, but eventually he turns us from a conversation, muttering, 'Enough.' I expect him to lead us out of the hall and to his rooms – our rooms. But instead we arrive at the dance floor.

'After all that, you want to dance?'

'Seems it's the only way I can get you to myself. We need to show ourselves a little longer before we're permitted to slink away to be alone.' On that last word, his gaze follows the mark still trailing down my throat and chest.

The ceremony is the first time we've kissed since I found out he knew about my medicine. It felt good. Right. Not fixed, but further along the healing process. And now, the way he looks at me scorches.

And does something deeper, more sustaining.

But he's been through so much tonight, and now I've got him talking, I need to know. 'Are you all right? Earlier . . .' I shake my head, unable to find the words to encapsulate all that happened in the midst of our marriage ceremony.

His attention slides to my hand in his. He runs his thumb over my skin. 'My brother is dead.' His eyelids flutter, bringing him back to me. 'But all that matters tonight is that you did beautifully.' The low reverence in his tone reminds me of the labyrinth's garden. The way he praised me. Worshipped me. Laid me out and adored me.

And yet . . . 'Are you sure you're—?'

'*Yes.*' A quick dimple-studded smile.

We dance on in silence, moved by the beat of the music. I let my thoughts spiral with our steps.

I'm married. In the Underworld. Not battling the labyrinth. Yes, unseelie court is dangerous, but I'm queen now. I have a degree of power. I'm certainly less vulnerable. And Drystan, for all his failings, is on my side, keeping my secrets by doing things like pretending he's the one who wants to sit for a while.

This Great Hall, this fortress – it's my new home. With this man – this *demi-god*. With friends. With a ghost cat. I chuckle softly to myself.

'What I wouldn't give to know what elicited that.'

'How about your hand in marriage?' I make a show of noticing the lines of ash around his wrist. '*Oh*. Well, in that case . . .' I take a long breath, gathering my scattered thoughts into a form that might make sense to someone else. 'For the first time in a long while, it feels like I have a future that isn't just about getting by and waiting, wondering when my illness is going to get worse. It's . . . nice.'

'*Nice?*'

'Yes. And all the things that go with that word. Calm. Pleasing. Boring in the best possible way.'

A slow smile dawns on his lips, shadowing in his dimples. 'Good.' His voice rasps. '*Good.*'

That deep, sustaining feeling returns. Warm. Close. A shared breath. A whispered devotion. A tight embrace on a dark night.

Something I cannot name, but it's written on my soul.

Like he sees it, he pulls me closer. He draws breath like he knows the name and is going to speak it.

The doors crash open. The music stops. The crowd parts.

By the time I've registered any of it, Drystan's hand is splayed across my chest, and he's pushed me back, blocked by his squared shoulders. As regally as I can, I peer past him.

In the doorway stand five men. Fae I don't recognize. Tall. Handsome in a devastating way.

They each wear variations on the unseelie amused-disinterested smirk as they survey the room. And one by one, their attentions land on Drystan and me.

One, blond and artfully windswept, pulls off his leather gloves with a dramatic flourish. 'Sorry we're late. Seems our invitations went astray, *brother*.'

63

DRYSTAN'S BROTHERS. BOOTS wet like they've only just arrived through the snow. Eyes sharp, smiles sharper.

The not-quite enemies. Certainly not friends.

The blond one who spoke first steps forward. 'And this must be the brand-new bride we've heard *so much* about.' He circles around Drystan, violet-blue eyes intent on me.

'Ostir.' Drystan's voice is as cold as his domain. 'What a surprise to see you here, in my fortress. In *my* kingdom. I wasn't aware you'd sent us word of your coming – nor sought permission.'

'Oh, Drystan.' The shortest yet most handsome of the brothers approaches, throwing casually devastating smiles at the fae pressing back out of his way. His teeth flash pale against his rich brown skin – such a contrast with Drystan's. I thought his hair was ash blond, but it catches the light with a greenish gleam. 'Who'd have thought you were the youngest of us when you're such an old stickler?' His eyes are so arresting, when they dart to me, I fall still. They're the bright, deep green of the algae that coats rocks on the shore. He bows his head. 'King Malvorn, at your service.'

I stand as tall as I can and give a small, polite nod in return.

Those arresting eyes, still on me, widen and he huffs a soft laugh. 'My, my, my. It's true, gentlemen,' he calls over his shoulder. 'She *is* human.'

The red-haired king blasts out a breath, dark eyebrows clashing together. Lips pressing tight above a dimpled chin, he tosses a tinkling purse at Malvorn.

He snatches it out of the air with a mocking grin. 'There, there, Gatterglan. No need to be aggrieved I won our little bet. I'm as shocked as you are.'

Gradually, they prowl from the doorway, fanning around Drystan and me. He hasn't drawn a weapon, though I spot the Twylth stationed on the edge of the crowd, attention locked on the brothers.

An outright attack doesn't seem like the unseelie style, yet the air in the Great Hall strains with so much tension, it's hard to breathe.

I mirror Drystan, who stands straight, regal. The hand that was splayed on my chest now sits at his side.

'Have you taught her no manners, brother?' Malvorn cocks his head. 'She hasn't even offered her name.'

Shit. One of the first rules I learned. And such a simple one.

I wear a calm smile, but I have to swallow before I can speak. 'I was merely waiting for you to offer. But now I have half of yours, I will give you half of mine. Rhiannon.'

'Rhiannon.' The pale-eyed brother who hasn't yet spoken rolls my name around his mouth. I want to fidget at the way he tastes it, gaze on me all the while. 'Rhiannon,' he purrs with a slow smile.

'That's *Queen* Rhiannon to you, Lithern.' Drystan's voice, soft like distant thunder.

'Stickler,' Malvorn sighs.

'Is it so wrong to wish to congratulate our brother on his wedding night?' Gatterglan lifts his chin, a challenge in his eyes, even though he wears that unseelie half smile. 'What say you, Prindar?'

'Are we fools to expect a warm welcome from our brother when we visit his court?' The last, with ash white hair, watches me with a hungry look. The shadows under his cheekbones are sharper than Drystan's, the blackness of his pupils deeper.

The tension ratchets tighter. Out the corner of my eye, I search for Asti. In my heart, I curse Drystan for not carrying a weapon. Unable to control my magic, I'd be no help.

I've never heard a whole room of people so quiet.

I barely breathe. Waiting. Praying. Please gods, let this break without bloodshed.

Malvorn laughs. It echoes off the vaulted ceiling, sending the shadows scattering. 'You all look so serious. Drystan, you always were the most dour of us – except for maybe Gatterglan. Who can blame us for being curious?' He spreads his hands. 'Especially when you're the first to take a consort.'

The brothers smile, but beneath that veil, there's something sharp about the looks that bore into Drystan. Daggers hidden by velvet.

The consort's power. By marrying first, Drystan gains an advantage over them – for himself and his kingdom.

Perhaps if they think I'm no advantage at all . . . A mere human. Let them see how small and inconsequential I am.

I step forward and take Drystan's arm. He doesn't move. Doesn't speak.

Very well. *I'll* disarm this situation – or try. 'You're quite right.' I share a grin with Malvorn. 'Your curiosity is understandable – admirable, even. It's so kind of you to visit us upon this special night.' I indicate the Great Hall, the shimmering decor that matches the ceremony room, the half-drunk guests. 'Won't you join us – eat, drink, be merry?'

Gatterglan doesn't bother to disguise his snort. Malvorn flinches at the sound before smoothing it over with a charming smile. 'My lady – my *Queen* – you just might be the cleverest one in here.' He looks back at his brothers.

I don't spot their responses, but after a couple of seconds, he bows his head to me. 'We accept your gracious offer, Your Majesty.'

'You heard your queen.' Lithern's voice slithers through the room, lifting the hairs on my arms. 'Play on.'

The music resumes. The crowd stares for a few beats longer, then drinks return to lips alongside gossip and hungry kisses.

Drystan's chest rises and falls twice, long and deep, before he finally moves. We leave the dance floor and circle the room. He speaks. Drinks. Walks at my side. But it's like he's barely there. Phaedra made a better Drystan than the man standing next to me.

Speaking of my favourite saboteur . . . I note more than one of the brothers speaking to her as night deepens. Ostir and Malvorn in particular.

It makes sense. She's of royal lineage, and since Drystan has snubbed her, one of the other kings might expect he can tempt her to his realm with the promise of a crown of her own. It seems unlikely the brothers will allow Drystan to be the only one with a consort for long, even if marriage is a risk to their absolute power.

Despite being a celebration of our wedding, the night grates on me. And the more distant my new husband becomes, the more agitated this feeling in my chest grows. Not my heart playing up, but a restlessness that fills me, like words unspoken.

It becomes too much to bear, and catching Drystan's eye, I retire to his suite. *Our* suite.

Thinking of this space as ours makes it seem strange and new. I pass through the rooms, touching everything with a new sense of permission. His favourite chair by the fireplace. The mantelpiece in the small dining room. A small bird skull on a side table – the King of Death's one obeisance to decorative cliché. I grin to myself as I enter the bedroom.

On the bedside table is a vase of whisper-pale blossom.

My steps still as I realize. Not just any blossom – the branches I grew when we first made love and my magic awakened.

The sight of it, right there where he sees it each night when he wakes, speaks to something in me. It straightens out the tangle behind my ribcage. My heart drums a solid, strong beat, certain in a way I'm not sure I've ever been certain before.

I love him.

'Shit.' I laugh out the word, rubbing my chest.

Somehow.

Some-bloody-how, I, Rhiannon Archer, have fallen in love with Death.

64

NERVY EXCITEMENT MAKES me pace the room, and when I'm too tired for that, I sit on the bed, fidgeting, gaze fixed on the door, ready for him – for my husband who I've fallen in love with by mistake – to come to bed.

Hours pass.

He doesn't come.

My excitement to tell him how I feel twists. 'Where the hells is he?' I mutter at the window and the melting snow. 'All that time in the labyrinth and he'd turn up out of nowhere, now when I want him here, he doesn't appear.'

I frown at the delicate, crinkled petals. It's another sign that he cares. Why keep them if he doesn't?

He's helped keep my illness secret. He gave me the cat so I wouldn't be alone. That night he came to me with new medicine – fake medicine, as I know now – he seemed agitated. I assumed he was pissed off at me for some reason or just being his insufferable, kingly self. But now, knowing the truth, I can't help viewing it differently.

He knew.

He'd found out from the Apothic what my tablets really were, that my parents had been poisoning me, whether deliberately, unwittingly or as a side-effect of treatment. And he was angry for me.

He cares for me. The fact he was willing to apologize when the unseelie *do not apologize* tells me that much.

But does he feel the same way I do?

I scowl at the door, which still doesn't open.

If the king won't come to me on our wedding night, then I will go to him.

I pass through the Great Hall, doing my best to shut out the ongoing revelry. We're close to dawn now and it shows no sign of slowing.

But the crowd parts for their queen. Another thing that's strange and new.

I have to remind myself to stand tall and keep that neutral look of faint amusement on my face, rather than letting my frustration show.

It takes a while, but I eventually find Drystan. He and his brothers, together with a handful of other fae, including Min and Asti, occupy a smaller room off the Great Hall, all lounging in varying states of inebriation. Drystan sits at the far end, legs sprawled wide, golden tumbler in hand, glowering off into the distance.

Asti has Min tucked under her arm but she keeps an eye on her king. I doubt she's as drunk as the brothers.

'And that's when I made him jump.' Ostir thumps the table he's sitting at and the others burst into roaring laughter.

'Oh, lighten up, Drystan,' Malvorn calls across the gap between their tables. 'You make it look like a death sentence rather than a marriage.'

'Same thing.' Gatterglan bares his teeth, raising his drink in Drystan's direction. 'Here's to your death, little brother.'

My husband's scowl deepens.

As I edge past, Ostir pipes up. 'Ah, and Her Majesty blesses us with her presence.'

Drystan's head snaps around. If anything, he looks even paler than usual.

'Don't worry, gentlemen,' I say as smoothly as I can, as if I've been chatting with kings all my life. 'I have no intention of ending your festivities. I've only come to collect my king.' I smile at Drystan, giving him a pointed look.

'Oh dear. Someone's forgotten it's his wedding night.' Lithern smirks from behind his cup.

I stop in front of Drystan, my look becoming even sharper. His brother isn't wrong.

Sighing through his nose, Drystan turns his gaze back to a point in the distance. He takes a gulp of drink. 'You go to bed, *dear wife*. Don't wait for me.'

My hands fist for a second before I remember myself. Not only is this the unseelie court where feelings need to be controlled, but I'm queen now. I need to guard my heart all the more. 'But, *darling*, I need to speak to you.' I lean in and whisper, '*Alone*.'

'Don't think any excuses are going to cut it, Drystan.' I don't see which brother speaks – I'm too busy trying to communicate with my husband through eyeballs alone.

'Rhiannon.' He cuts the air with my name, seizing my wrist before pulling me aside, so I'm tucked against the wall. 'Leave me be. I'm having a few drinks with my brothers. I'll find somewhere else to sleep tonight – I have a whole fortress, after all.'

I flinch, blinking up at him. 'You'll . . .?' This is *not* how I expected our wedding night to go. I lean in, whisper, 'But I thought—'

He huffs like I'm the most exasperating creature in the Underworld. 'Whatever you thought, it was wrong.' He plants one hand over my shoulder and leans in so our eyes are level. 'Whatever faerie tale image you had of our marriage, whatever sweet romance you thought this would be – you are *wrong*. I needed a bride. Now I have one. Faerie tale over.'

A rush of hot shame is chased by a blast of cold. I swallow past the tight knot in my throat. I have to be misunderstanding. This isn't . . .

But perhaps it is. The power. *The Underworld's power.* Marriage is the only way to access that. The consort's connection . . .

'No. The cat. The biscuits. Sending Asti and Min to me when I was upset.' I shake my head. 'If you just wanted a bride, you wouldn't have been *kind* to me.'

I'm right. I have to be right.

Why keep the blossom? Why help me? Why do all those little things, say all those sweet things? The promise that he would never let me die alone . . . I stare up at him, willing him to confirm I'm right, that this is just a horrible joke.

'You just can't stop pushing, can you? Headstrong woman.' Eyes screwed shut, he drags in a breath. Between the twitch of his jaw and the cording of his neck, there's a battle waging inside him.

An instant later, it stills.

With a cool smile that's all Death and not at all Drystan, he tips the rest of his drink down his throat, then straightens until he's looking down his nose at me. 'Poor, foolish human. Let me spell this out so you get it into your thick skull.' He lifts his chin, eyes piercing. 'I tried to make you fall in love with me.' The words run together, blunted by drink. 'And you did. That's the tragedy, isn't it?'

My heart stops. The blood in my veins stills. The world becomes a dull roar.

'What?' The strangled word makes everything skip back into motion, and I realize it was only that a single second seemed to stretch on for horrifying moments.

'I was nice to you so you would fall in love with me and marry me. No more silly little escape attempts.'

Fae can't lie. This is real. And it makes sense.

It's the kind of merciless logic that made the ancient seelie scientist do her horrifying experiments. The kind of logic an immortal would use when dealing with fragile, simple humans whose lives are over in mere moments. In the grand scheme of things, what does their suffering matter?

I try to take a step back, but my heel hits the wall.

For a moment, his jaw works side to side, as though he's going to say more, but a smirk wins out and he drops his arm, freeing me.

'Looks like he's broken the bad news,' one of the brothers hisses, loud enough to carry around the whole room.

'And judging by the look on the little thing's face, I'd bet my kingdom that she believed the illusion.' That's Ostir's voice, seeming to come from far away.

'No, no, no,' Malvorn says with a lilt. 'It's worse than that. Look at her. She *loves* him.'

'Well, isn't this crushing?' Gatterglan rumbles.

Trying to ignore them, I stare up at Drystan. I see the logic, but that doesn't mean I want to believe it. Some balled-up part of me still guards hope. It wills him to say something – anything.

'Drystan,' I whisper, trying to remind him of how he said he loved it when I said his name. '*Please.*'

His eyes flicker. A beat of something that looks like desperation, then they widen and I'm sure – *sure* – he's going to tell me this is a game. A joke. A lie, somehow.

'I tried to warn you. I told you I wasn't good.' He shakes his head, voice rough like he's truly sad. 'I *said* I could make you my thrall.'

There it is. Oh gods. *There it is.*

I'm frozen in place. Locked in this moment where I'm breaking. I've been such a fool. Done the thing I swore I wouldn't do. I won my freedom and threw it away. I practically begged him to marry me.

My mindless little thrall.

He *did* warn me. My face tingles. Numbness creeps over my body. I'm vaguely aware of the brothers' laughter fading.

I'm about to turn and run when Drystan wheezes in a breath. His eyes go wide, desperate like he can't breathe. There's none of his usual grace as he lurches back, grabbing his chest, frowning at me like *I've* betrayed *him*. What little colour is in his cheeks leaches.

The cup drops from his hand. Clangs to the floor. Rolls, echoing through the silence like a warning bell.

Before the final toll, Drystan collapses onto the cold hard marble, still and silent and utterly pale.

Acknowledgements

By the time I finish a book I always owe a ton of thanks, and *King of Ravens* is no different. In particular, thank you . . .

First, to Bibi Lewis for being the most badass agent a very unbadass author could ask for – and a diabolical partner in scheming.

To Alyssa – the best PA and right-hand woman I could ever hope for. My gods, where would I be without you? (Answer: crying in the corner, rocking back and forth over the state of my inbox.)

To Lara Stevenson, Katrina Whone, Catriona Camacho and the incredible team at Wayward TxF, and to Sam Brody, Leah Hultenschmidt, Dana Cuadrado, Carolina Martin, Tareth Mitch and the phenomenal team at Forever – thank you for seeing something in Annon and Drystan, for believing in their story and for helping put this Underworld adventure into readers' hands.

To the amazing team at FairyLoot for championing my work before I even knew you were watching.

To Re Gwaltney for helping me navigate the areas of Annon's illness that aren't part of my own experience and being an all-round wonderful and gracious sensitivity reader.

To my work wives, Carissa Broadbent, Tracie Delaney, and the first-among-wives, Lasairiona McMaster for comforting, commiserating, cheerleading and helping me hatch villainous plans (and encouraging me to go *full evil*).

To Alyssa (again), Andra, Andrew, Clare, Laura, Lizzy, Michelle, Rachel, Shelly and Tina for enduring my early drafts and helping me to dial everything up to eleven.

To all the readers who allow me to do wild job full-time – who squee on socials and recommend to friends, leave reviews visit me at signings and see themselves in my imperfect, overthinking heroines.

And always, always, always to R – my very own Alpha Cinnamon Roll. ;)

About the Author

Clare Sager writes darkly addictive romantasy full of slow-burn steam, gut-wrenching conflict and morally grey *everyone*. Dubbed the Queen of Edging by readers, she takes no responsibility for lost sleep or therapy bills.

When she's not breaking hearts with her *Shadows of the Tenebris Court* series, Clare can usually be found drinking coffee, lifting weights or impulse-buying stationery. She lives in Nottingham, Robin Hood country, so it's no surprise she writes about characters who don't always play by the rules.

Find out about the latest news, events and how to keep in touch at www.claresager.com or follow her on Instagram @claresager!